U0084631

序 言

　　欲取得理想的托福成績，首先必須加強字彙的能力。「托福字彙進階」(*Advanced Vocabulary For iBT TOEFL*) 擺脫一般字彙書籍按照字母排列的窠臼，將 1500 個重要常考單字分三十個單元介紹，您可以認識各種單字，不必永遠在 A、B、C 這些字母為首的字上打轉。除此之外，它還有如下的特色，可助您在考場上克敵制勝：

★ **同義字多** —— 每個單字均補充同義字，一方面幫助您了解字義，同時讓您的字彙能力倍增。

★ **字源分析** —— 針對難背的單字，我們提供圖解的字源分析，讓您對造字的法則一目了然，提高背單字的效率。

　　例：**prohibitive**〔 proˈhɪbɪtɪv 〕*adj.* 禁止的；嚇阻的

pro + hibit + ive	—— intended to prevent the use
| 　| 　|	or misuse of something
before + *have* + *adj.*	

★ **密集練習** —— 每單元均附填充式的 Exercise，供您在背完單字後，自我評量。TEST 為字義測驗單元，與托福命題方式接近，是評估實力的好方法。

　　本公司本著出版好書與服務讀者的宗旨，投入大量的時間與心力，編輯一系列的托福參考書，誠盼您能不斷地給予批評與指正，以求盡善盡美。

編者　謹識

什麼是TOEFL-iBT？

托福測驗（Test of English as a Foreign Language, TOEFL®）由美國教育測驗服務社（Educational Testing Service, ETS®）在全世界舉辦。托福測驗是測試母語非英語者之英語能力，此項測驗是計畫申請美加地區大學或研究所的學子，所必須參加的測驗。台灣地區的托福測驗自西元2006年4月起，由電腦測驗（CBT）改為網路化測驗（Internet-Based Testing, iBT），透過網際網路，即時連線至ETS。

TOEFL-iBT考些什麼？

TOEFL-iBT分為閱讀（Reading）、聽力（Listening）、口說（Speaking）以及寫作（Writing）四個部分。閱讀與聽力約2小時，中場休息10分鐘後，再考口說與寫作。

閱　讀	1. 題數：36～70題 2. 內容：3～5篇學術性文章 　　　　新增2個特殊功能：① Glossary — 簡單的單字解說 　　　　　　　　　　　　　② Review — 快速地檢視已填寫的答案 3. 測驗時間：60-100分鐘 4. 題型：選擇題（包含完成表格、將句子插入文章中適當的位置、同義字、代名詞、看圖選項…等的單選題或複選題）
聽　力	1. 題數：34～51題 2. 內容：2～3段對話，包含兩個或兩個以上的對話者 　　　　4～6篇演說，學術性演講或學生在課堂中討論的對話 3. 測驗時間：60-90分鐘 4. 題型：選擇題（含單選及複選題）
口　說	1. 題數：6大題 2. 內容：看完或聽完題目後，有一段準備時間，然後再回答問題。準備時間與作答時間皆有限制。 3. 測驗時間：20分鐘 4. 題型：2種題型—— ① 聽一段對話或演說後作答 　　　　　　　　　　 ② 先看一篇文章再聽一段說明或對話後，再作答
寫　作	1. 題數：2題 2. 測驗時間：50分鐘 3. 內容：應試者根據電腦所指定的題目，於電腦上打字作答。 4. 題型：2種題型—— ① 看一篇文章，再聽一段說明或對話後，寫一篇相關的文章。測驗時間20分鐘。 　　　　　　　　　　 ② 就一個題目寫一篇文章，測驗時間30分鐘。

TOEFL-iBT 的計分方式

TOEFL-iBT 分數等級	
測　驗　項　目	分　數　等　級
1. 閱　讀	0～30
2. 聽　力	0～30
3. 口　說	0～30
4. 寫　作	0～30
總　　分	0～120
總分：1＋2＋3＋4	

TOEFL-iBT 與 TOEFL-CBT 的比較

	TOEFL-iBT	TOEFL-CBT
閱　讀	0～30	0～30
聽　力	0～30	0～30
口　說	0～30	
寫　作	0～30	
文法／寫作		0～30
總　　分	0～120	0～300

TOEFL-iBT 和 TOEFL-CBT 的總分對照表

iBT	CBT	iBT	CBT	iBT	CBT
120	300	71	197	30-31	93
120	297	69-70	193	29	90
119	293	68	190	28	87
118	290	66-67	187	26-27	83
117	287	65	183	25	80
116	283	64	180	24	77
114-115	280	62-63	177	23	73
113	277	61	173	22	70
111-112	273	59-60	170	21	67
110	270	58	167	19-20	63
109	267	57	163	18	60
106-108	263	56	160	17	57
105	260	54-55	157	16	53
103-104	257	53	153	15	50
101-102	253	52	150	14	47
100	250	51	147	13	43
98-99	247	49-50	143	12	40
96-97	243	48	140	11	37
94-95	240	47	137	9	33
92-93	237	45-46	133	8	30
90-91	233	44	130	7	27
88-89	230	43	127	6	23
86-87	227	41-42	123	5	20
84-85	223	40	120	4	17
83	220	39	117	3	13
81-82	217	38	113	2	10
79-80	213	36-37	110	1	7
77-78	210	35	107	0	3
76	207	34	103	0	0
74-75	203	33	100		
72-73	200	32	97		

📝 **LIST ▶ 1**

＊**abandon**〔əˋbændən〕v. 放棄【最常考】
　　——同 desert, abdicate, relinquish, quit, forsake
The bad weather forced the campers to *abandon* their tent on the mountain.
惡劣的天氣迫使露營者放棄在山上的帳篷。

＊**addicted**〔əˋdɪktɪd〕adj. 上癮的【最常考】　——同 habituated
Helen drinks ten cups of coffee every day; I think she is *addicted* to it.　海倫每天要喝十杯咖啡，我想她是上癮了。

＊**allure**〔əˋlɪur, -ˋlur〕v. 吸引；引誘【常考】
　　——同 seduce, coax, tempt, lure, attract
The beauty of the sea *allured* the young man, who immediately decided to become a sailor.
大海的美麗吸引這位年輕人，決定馬上去當水手。

＊**approximately**〔əˋprɑksəmɪtlɪ〕adv. 大約【常考】
　　——同 roughly, about, around, close to
Janet said she would arrive for the party at *approximately* eight o'clock.　珍娜說她大約八點會到達舞會。

baffle〔ˋbæfḷ〕v. 使困惑
　　——同 confuse, perplex, bewilder, puzzle, confound
The police were *baffled* by the false clues left by the clever thief.　聰明的小偷留下假線索，讓警方十分困惑。

caliber〔ˋkæləbɚ〕n. ①能力 ②直徑；口徑
　　——同 1. ability, capability, quality 2. breadth, diameter
The enemy was armed only with low *caliber* guns.
敵人只配備了短口徑的槍。

clot 〔 klɑt 〕 *n.* 凝塊　——同 mass , lump , coagulation , cluster , clump

The pipe under the bathroom sink was blocked by a huge *clot* of hair. 浴室洗手台下的水管被一大團頭髮所阻塞。

* **compromise** 〔'kɑmprə,maɪz 〕 *v.* 協調【常考】

——同 mediate , negotiate , bargain , reconcile , arbitrate

Jane and Alex *compromised* and went to see a movie they both liked. 珍和亞歷士達成協議，去看一部他們都喜歡的電影。

* **contemporary** 〔 kən'tɛmpə,rɛrɪ 〕 *adj.* 當代的；同時代的【常考】

——同 current , modern , present-day

Ethan enjoys reading *contemporary* British literature.
伊森喜歡閱讀當代的英國文學。

dam 〔 dæm 〕 *v.* 築堤；以水壩攔阻

——同 block , confine , restrict , hold back

The beaver *dammed* the stream with mud, branches and leaves.
海獺用泥土、樹枝和樹葉在河裡築水壩。

* **depict** 〔 dɪ'pɪkt 〕 *v.* 描述【常考】　——同 portray , picture , describe

This story *depicts* people who live in poverty as hardworking and wanting to improve their lives.
這篇故事描述窮人努力地工作，想改善他們的生活。

disclose 〔 dɪs'kloz 〕 *v.* 洩露

——同 expose , unveil , divulge , uncover , reveal

The government refused to *disclose* the names of the informers. 政府拒絕透露告密者的姓名。

* **eccentric** 〔 ɪk'sɛntrɪk 〕 *adj.* 古怪的【常考】

——同 odd , queer , strange

Mr. Wang is an *eccentric* old man, who likes to collect tea pots. 王先生是個古怪的老人，他喜歡收集茶壺。

endowment〔ɪnˈdaʊmənt〕*n.* ①天份 ②捐贈

——同 1. talent , faculty , attribute 2. donation , bestowal

Alice's beautiful painting shows her artistic *endowment*.

愛麗絲美麗的畫作顯露她的藝術天份。

estate〔əˈstet〕*n.* 地產；財產

——同 domain , demesne , manor , property

The Jones' *estate* was very large, and it included rolling green hills and a large fish pond.

瓊斯家的地產非常龐大，包括了起伏的綠色山丘以及一個大魚池。

* **fabric**〔ˈfæbrɪk〕*n.* ①質地 ②結構【常考】

——同 1. textile , material 2. framework , structure

Many people believe that corruption is destroying the *fabric* of our society. 許多人認為貪污正在破壞我們社會的結構。

Exercise *Fill in the blanks.*

1. After many years of smoking cigarettes, she has become _____ to them.

2. Doctors were _____ by the new virus and struggled to find a cure.

3. Roger likes _____ music, but his father enjoys classical music.

4. Superman knew that _____ his true identity to the woman was risky.

5. My mother's sister is an _____ woman, but she is very friendly.

【解答】1. addicted   2. baffled   3. contemporary   4. disclosing   5. eccentric

* **famine** (ˈfæmɪn) *n.* 飢荒【常考】　——同 hunger

There was great fear that people would die of hunger if the *famine* continued. 如果飢荒持續下去，人們恐有餓死之虞。

* **fusion** (ˈfjuʒən) *n.* 結合【常考】

——同 merger , coalescence , union

The musician's *fusion* of modern music and traditional Chinese music was very popular.

這位音樂家將現代音樂與傳統的中國音樂結合，十分受歡迎。

haggard (ˈhægəd) *adj.* 憔悴的

——同 gaunt , careworn , fatigued , wan , emaciated

The soldiers looked *haggard* after their ten-hour march.

這些士兵在行軍十小時之後，看來非常憔悴。

illiterate (ɪˈlɪt(ə)rɪt) *adj.* 不識字的

——同 unlettered , uncultured , uneducated , ignorant

The university set up a center where *illiterate* adults could learn to read. 該大學成立一中心，可供不識字的成年人學習閱讀。

inadvertent (ˌɪnədˈvɝtənt) *adj.* 不注意的

——同 accidental , fortuitous , unintentional , incidental

The auditor determined that it was merely an *inadvertent* mistake made by a junior accountant.

查帳員認為，這只是年輕會計師的無心之過。　＊auditor (ˈɔdɪtə) *n.* 查帳員

innermost (ˈɪnəˌmost) *adj.* 最深處的　——同 deepest , private

Tom and Joe were best friends and shared their *innermost* secrets with each other. 湯姆和喬是好朋友，彼此分享內心的秘密。

** **jeopardy** (ˈdʒɛpədɪ) *n.* 危險【最常考】　——同 risk , peril , hazard

This building is in *jeopardy* of collapsing if there is a major earthquake. 若發生大地震，這棟建築物將有倒塌的危險。

lace〔les〕*v.* ①繫（帶子）②穿（帶子）
——同 1. tie , fasten 2. pass through
The little child's mother had to help him *lace* up his shoes.
這小孩的母親必須幫他繫鞋帶。

lull〔lʌl〕*v.* 使平靜；使入睡 ——同 calm , pacify , quiet
The father sang a song to his daughter to *lull* her to sleep.
那位父親唱了一首歌哄女兒入睡。

* **magnificence**〔mæg'nıfəsn̩s〕*n.* 壯麗【常考】
——同 brilliance , grandeur , majesty , resplendence
We were all impressed with the *magnificence* of Russia's
Winter Palace. 我們對俄國冬宮的壯麗，都留下深刻的印象。

* **mercurial**〔mɝ'kjurıəl〕*adj.* ①多變的 ②水銀的【常考】
——同 1. changeable , erratic , mobile , capricious , inconstant
Few people can stand Michael's *mercurial* personality, so he
does not have many friends.
很少有人能忍受麥克多變的性格，所以他的朋友不多。

nasty〔'næstı〕*adj.* ①污穢的 ②令人不快的
——同 1. filthy , foul 2. disagreeable , unpleasant
What is that *nasty* smell coming from behind the house?
房子後面傳來的令人作噁的味道，到底是什麼？

* **obituary**〔ə'bıtʃu‚ɛrı〕*n.* 訃聞【常考】 ——同 death notice , necrology
Martin was very shocked to see his best friend's *obituary* in
the newspaper. 馬丁在報上看見好友的訃聞，感到非常震驚。

* **ornamentation**〔‚ɔrnəmɛn'teʃən〕*n.* 裝飾品【最常考】
——同 adornment , decoration , embellishment , elaboration
The *ornamentation* Vincent used to decorate his house at
Christmas was very tasteful.
聖誕節期間，文森家裡使用的裝飾品非常有品味。

pacesetter 〔'pes,sɛtə 〕 *n.* 定跑速的人；引導者　──同 leader

Harry was the fastest runner, and was the *pacesetter* for the entire marathon.

哈瑞是所有跑者中最快的，而且也是整個馬拉松比賽的引導者。

＊＊pernicious 〔 pə'nɪʃəs 〕 *adj.* 有害的；惡性的【最常考】

　　──同 harmful , deleterious , venomous , noxious , poisonous

William's *pernicious* accusation that the company produced inferior products hurt the company's business.

威廉惡意指控該公司生產劣質品，使公司的生意受到影響。

plot 〔 plat 〕 *v.* ; *n.* 密謀；計畫

　　──同 (*n.*) intrigue , scheme ; (*v.*) conspire , intrigue , scheme

The three thieves *plotted* how they were going to steal the painting of Mona Lisa.

這三名小偷密謀要偷取蒙娜麗莎的畫像。

Exercise　*Fill in the blanks.*

1. Because of her hard life, the old woman's face had grown _____.

2. The man made the _____ mistake of taking the wrong subway line and got lost.

3. The mission to rescue the hikers in _____ was canceled due to snow.

4. The artist's painting managed to capture the _____ of Japan's Mt. Fuji.

5. Their marriage was destroyed by _____ gossip.

【解答】1. haggard　2. inadvertent　3. jeopardy　4. magnificence　5. pernicious

* **prey** 〔 pre 〕 *n.* 獵物【最常考】　——同 game , quarry , victim

Cats often like to play with their ***prey*** before they actually kill it.

貓在殺害獵物之前，常喜歡玩弄牠們。

quarantine 〔'kwɔrən‚tin〕 *n.* 隔離　——同 isolation

My pet dog had to be kept in ***quarantine*** for six weeks when I moved to England.

當我移居英國時，我的愛犬必須被隔離六個星期。

* **radiance** 〔'redɪəns〕 *n.* 發光；閃爍【常考】

　——同 light , gleam , luminosity

People like to lie on the beach and enjoy the ***radiance*** of the sun.　人們喜歡躺在沙灘上，享受陽光。

* **relevant** 〔'rɛləvənt〕 *adj.* 有關的【常考】

　——同 related , pertinent , fitting , proper

The lawyer presented information to the judge that she thought was ***relevant*** to the case.

律師將她認為與案件有關的資料，呈交給法官。

* **retaliate** 〔 rɪ'tælɪ‚et 〕 *v.* 報復【常考】

　——同 revenge , reciprocate , get even with , exact retribution

The poor peasants ***retaliated*** against the king because of his unfairness and cruelty.

由於國王既不公平又殘忍，所以貧苦的農民對他施予報復。

* **sagacious** 〔 sə'geʃəs 〕 *adj.* 睿智的【最常考】

　——同 wise , intelligent

Whenever Saul was confused about what to do, he would always go to his ***sagacious*** grandfather for advice.

每當索爾覺得困惑、無所適從時，總會向他睿智的祖父尋求意見。

* **sentimental** 〔͵sɛntəˈmɛntḷ〕*adj.* 情感上的【常考】
——同 emotional
Albert has kept his grandmother's favorite record for
sentimental reasons.
艾伯特保留他祖母最喜愛的唱片，是因為情感上的理由。

slither 〔ˈslɪðɚ〕*v.* 滑行 ——同 glide , slide , skitter
Tonya screamed when she saw a snake *slither* across the
yard. 唐雅看見有條蛇爬過院子，高聲尖叫了起來。

splice 〔splaɪs〕*v.* 接合
——同 join together , connect , interweave , unite
Film editors used to *splice* reels of film together to make a
whole movie. 以前的電影剪輯人員是將幾捲影片接合成一部電影。

streamline 〔ˈstrim͵laɪn〕*v.* 使有效率 ——同 smooth , simplify
The only way our office can *streamline* its operations is by
using computers.
唯一能使本辦公室提高效率的方法，就是使用電腦。

* **surly** 〔ˈsɝlɪ〕*adj.* 粗暴的【常考】 ——同 sullen , uncivil , brusque
Frank's *surly* manner always makes everyone around him
feel grumpy. 法蘭克粗暴的行為總令他身邊的人覺得生氣。
* grumpy 〔ˈgrʌmpɪ〕*adj.* 脾氣暴躁的

taboo 〔təˈbu〕*n.* 禁忌 ——同 ban , prohibition , proscription
In Western countries, there is a *taboo* against burping at the
table. 在西方國家，在用餐時打嗝是一種禁忌。 * burp 〔bɝp〕*v.* 打嗝

thwart 〔θwɔrt〕*v.* 阻撓 ——同 prevent , obstruct , balk
The police *thwarted* the robbers' plans by finding their
hideout and arresting them.
警方阻撓了搶匪的計畫，找到其藏匿的地點，將他們逮捕。

ultimate 〔'ʌltəmɪt 〕 *adj.* 最終的   ——同 final , terminal , eventual
"Our ***ultimate*** goal is to find a cure for AIDS," said the scientist.
「我們最終的目標，就是找出治療愛滋病的方法」，那位科學家說道。

* **vacant** 〔'vekənt 〕 *adj.* 空的【常考】   *n.* vacuum
——同 empty , available , disengaged , unoccupied
Children in the neighborhood liked to play in a nearby ***vacant***
lot. 鄰近地區的小孩喜歡在附近的空地上玩耍。

****waive** 〔 wev 〕 *v.* 放棄【最常考】
——同 give up , relinquish , renounce , abandon
Our school ***waives*** its strict dress code once a week and allows
us to wear what we want on that day.
本校一星期有一天解除嚴格的服裝限制，並且在那一天允許我們穿便服。

Xerox 〔'zirɑks 〕 *v.* 影印（Xerox 為一影印機的廠牌）   ——同 copy
Ms. Harris asked her secretary to ***Xerox*** seven copies of the
contract. 哈里斯女士要求她的秘書，將這份合約影印七份。

Exercise ⟩ *Fill in the blanks.*

1. The townspeople _____ against the soldiers who had
   attacked their homes.

2. You shouldn't be so _____ about an old pair of smelly
   sneakers.

3. The broken bridge _____ their effort to cross the river.

4. Winning an Olympic gold medal was the skater's
   _____ goal.

5. The building next to my house had been _____ for
   several months.

【解答】1. retaliated   2. sentimental   3. thwarted   4. ultimate   5. vacant

·List 1· 難字分析

compromise (ˈkɑmprəˌmaɪz) *v.* 協調

com	+	pro	+	mise
together	+	forth	+	send

— to reach a settlement by mutual concession

contemporary (kənˈtɛmpəˌrɛrɪ) *adj.* 當代的；同時代的

con	+	tempor	+	ary
together	+	time	+	adj.

— modern; of or belonging to the same time

eccentric (ɪkˈsɛntrɪk) *adj.* 古怪的

ec	+	centr	+	ic
ex				
out	+	center	+	adj.

— deviating from the norm

illiterate (ɪˈlɪt(ə)rɪt) *adj.* 不識字的

il	+	liter	+	ate
in				
not	+	letter	+	adj.

— unable to read and write

inadvertent (ˌɪnədˈvɝtnt) *adj.* 不注意的

in	+	ad	+	vert	+	ent
not	+	to	+	turn	+	adj.

— without paying attention or by accident

magnificence〔mæg'nɪfəsn̩s〕 *n.* 壯麗

magni + fic + ence
great + make + n.

—— stately or imposing beauty

obituary〔ə'bɪtʃu,ɛrɪ〕 *n.* 訃聞

ob + it + uary
near + go + n.

—— a notice of someone's death

relevant〔'rɛləvənt〕 *adj.* 有關的

re + lev + ant
again + raise + adj.

—— connected with what is
happening

sentimental〔,sɛntə'mɛntl̩〕 *adj.* 情感上的

senti + ment + al
feel + n. + adj.

—— having to do with the feelings

ultimate〔'ʌltəmɪt〕 *adj.* 最終的

ultim + ate
last + adj.

—— last　　.

📖 LIST ▸ 2

**abash 〔 ə'bæʃ 〕 v. 使困窘；使侷促不安【最常考】
　　—— 同 embarrass , shame
Ellen was **abashed** at the enthusiastic applause of the audience.
對於觀衆熱情的掌聲愛倫感到很困窘。

* adequate 〔'ædəkwɪt 〕 adj. 足夠的；適當的【常考】
　　—— 同 sufficient , ample , suitable , enough
Mother decided that we had **adequate** rice for the week, so she
didn't buy any at the store.
媽媽認爲我們的米這禮拜還夠，所以沒向那家店買。

aloof 〔 ə'luf 〕 ① adj. 漠不關心的 ② adv. 遠離地
　　—— 同 1. indifferent , detached 2. apart , at a distance
The principal kept himself **aloof** from the arguments between
the teachers.　校長置身事外，不想捲入老師間的紛爭。

* aptitude 〔'æptə‚tjud 〕 n. 能力；資質【常考】　—— 同 flair , gift , knack
Dean's **aptitude** for math helped him to become a successful
engineer.　狄恩在數學方面的才能，使他成爲成功的工程師。

ban 〔 bæn 〕 n. ; v. 禁止　—— 同 (v.) forbid , prohibit ; (n.) restriction
The country **banned** the sale of ivory in an effort to stop the
poaching of elephants.
該國禁止買賣象牙，以遏止非法獵殺大象。　* poach 〔 potʃ 〕 v. 偷獵

calm 〔 kɑm 〕 ① adj. 平靜的 ② v. 使安靜
　　—— 同 1. mild , gentle , serene , pacific , tranquil 2. still , pacify
Richard seemed very **calm** when he answered his wife, even
though he was really very nervous.
理查回答他太太時似乎十分冷靜，然而事實上他非常緊張。

chapel 〔 ˈtʃæpḷ 〕 *n.* 小教堂   ──同 oratory

On our tour of the castle, we saw the private ***chapel*** where the king prayed. 在城堡之旅中，我們看到了國王禱告用的私人小教堂。

compulsory 〔 kəmˈpʌlsərɪ 〕 *adj.* 強迫的；義務的

──同 obligatory , required , requisite , mandatory

Elementary education is ***compulsory*** in almost every country in the world. 幾乎在全世界所有的國家中，小學教育都是義務的。

＊＊**contemptuous** 〔 kənˈtɛmptʃʊəs 〕 *adj.* 輕蔑的   *v.* contempt

──同 scornful , sneering , disdainful 　　　　　　　　【最常考】

Samuel made some ***contemptuous*** remarks about how no one in the office worked hard.

山米爾用輕蔑的語氣指出，辦公室裡沒有人認真工作。

＊**dank** 〔 dæŋk 〕 *adj.* 潮濕的【常考】

──同 damp , moist , wet , soggy

The basement in our house is dark and ***dank***, so it is full of mold. 我們家的地下室又暗又潮濕，所以裡面長滿了霉。

depose 〔 dɪˈpoz 〕 *v.* 廢除（王位）；罷黜   ──同 dethrone , oust

The angry citizens wanted the king to be ***deposed***.

憤怒的人民想要廢除國王。

discord 〔 ˈdɪskɔrd 〕 *n.* 意見不合

──同 disharmony , dispute , conflict , quarrel

We should try to talk with each other about our feelings, so there will be no ***discord*** among us.

我們應該談談彼此的感想，如此才不會意見不合。

educe 〔 ɪˈdjus 〕 *v.* 引出   ──同 bring out , draw forth , elicit

The teacher was unable to ***educe*** an answer from her pupils.

老師無法從學生口中得到任何的答案。

‡**endorse**〔ɪn'dɔrs〕 *v.* 贊同；背書【最常考】

——同 approve , support , sanction , advocate

The political party *endorsed* Mark Wang as their candidate for governor. 該政黨同意王馬克成爲該黨的州長候選人。

esteem〔ə'stim〕 *n.* 尊敬 ——同 respect , honor , reverence

I have the highest *esteem* for my colleague, Mark Wang.
我對我的同事王馬克極爲尊敬。

facet〔'fæsɪt〕 *n.*（事物的）一面 ——同 aspect , face , side , part

Being a well-paid businesswoman is only one *facet* of her life.
身爲高薪階級的職業婦女，只是她生活的一部分。

‡**fluctuate**〔'flʌktʃʊ,et〕 *v.* 波動；變動【最常考】

——同 alternate , wave

Some investors panic when stock prices *fluctuate* wildly.
當股票價格波動屬害時，有些投資者便開始恐慌。

Exercise ▷ *Fill in the blanks.*

1. I didn't have _____ time to finish the book before class.

2. If the United States _____ the import of Taiwanese products, our economy will suffer.

3. All students at university had to pass a _____ swimming test.

4. _____ between the two political parties lessened slightly after the elections.

5. The low _____ they felt for him was obvious when they ignored his every word.

【解答】1. adequate   2. bans   3. compulsory   4. Discord   5. esteem

gainsay 〔 gen'se , 'gen͵se 〕 *v.* 否認　——同 deny , disagree

There was no ***gainsaying*** the astronomer's knowledge about planets. 這位天文學家對於行星的知識是無庸置疑的。

　＊astronomer 〔 ə'strɑnəmɚ 〕 *n.* 天文學家

hybrid 〔'haɪbrɪd 〕 *n.* 混種；混血兒　——同 half-breed , mixture

Scientists have developed a ***hybrid*** of rice that is more resistant to diseases and insects.

科學家已發展出一混種米，它對疾病與蟲害更具抵抗力。

＊**idiom** 〔'ɪdɪəm 〕 *n.* 成語；慣用語【常考】

　——同 expression , phrase

When studying a foreign language, ***idioms*** are often the most difficult thing to learn.

學習外語時，成語常是最難學的一部分。

inappropriate 〔͵ɪnə'proprɪɪt 〕 *adj.* 不適合的

　——同 unsuitable , improper , unfit , incongruous

This movie is very violent and is ***inappropriate*** for children to watch. 這部電影十分暴力，不適合兒童觀賞。

＊＊**innocuous** 〔 ɪ'nɑkjʊəs 〕 *adj.* 無害的【最常考】

　——同 harmless , inoffensive , vapid , insipid , innocent

I don't understand how such an ***innocuous*** children's book could cause such an uproar.

我不明白何以這本對兒童無害的書，會引起如此的騷動。

　＊uproar 〔'ʌp͵ror 〕 *n.* 騷動

jerk 〔 dʒɝk 〕 *n.* 拉扯　——同 twitch , pull , yank

I felt a ***jerk*** on my sleeve, but then realized it was just a tree branch.

我覺得有人拉我的袖子，但是後來發現只是樹枝而已。

**laconic〔ləˈkɑnɪk〕*adj.* 簡潔的【最常考】

——同 concise , compact , pithy , short , succinct

Henry's date was very ***laconic***, saying only two sentences the entire evening.　亨利的約會十分簡潔，他整晚只說了兩句話。

* lumber〔ˈlʌmbɚ〕*n.* 木材【常考】　——同 wood , timber , logs

A lot of ***lumber*** was needed to build the Smith's new house.

建造史密斯的新家時，需要許多的木材。

* magnify〔ˈmægnəˌfaɪ〕*v.* 放大【常考】

——同 enlarge , expand , amplify , augment

Danny used a lens to ***magnify*** the tiny insect.

丹尼利用鏡片來放大那隻微小的昆蟲。　　*lens〔lɛnz〕*n.* 鏡片

* maritime〔ˈmærəˌtaɪm〕*adj.* 海洋的【常考】

——同 marine , oceanic , nautical , seafaring

The city is building a ***maritime*** museum near the harbor.

該市正在港口附近建造一座海洋博物館。

merge〔mɝdʒ〕*v.* 合併　——同 combine , blend , amalgamate

The two mountain streams ***merged*** to form a single stream.

這兩條山裡的溪流匯合成一條。

* obsequious〔əbˈsikwɪəs〕*adj.* 逢迎的；諂媚的【常考】

——同 abject , servile , fawning , cringing

The manager's ***obsequious*** assistant annoyed the other employees in the department.

諂媚的經理助手惹惱了部門內的其他職員。

* ornate〔ɔrˈnet〕*adj.* 裝飾的；華麗的【常考】

——同 beautiful , ornamented , elaborate

For my birthday, my father gave me a pair of ***ornate*** silver earrings.　父親送給我一對華麗的銀耳環，作為我的生日禮物。

pact 〔 pækt 〕 *n.* 協定；條約

—— 同 agreement , treaty , compact , contract

The two countries signed a ***pact*** to end their fighting.

這兩國簽署了一項協定要終止戰爭。

perpendicular 〔 ˌpɝpənˈdɪkjələ 〕 *adj.* 垂直的

—— 同 at a right angle , steep , upright

Main Street runs ***perpendicular*** to Pine Street, and they meet at the city library.

梅因街與松樹街垂直交會，路口就是市立圖書館。

plume 〔 plʌm 〕 *n.* 羽毛   —— 同 feather , plumage

The ***plumes*** of the peacock are beautiful and brightly colored.

孔雀的羽毛十分華麗而且顏色鮮豔。

| **Exercise** 〉 *Fill in the blanks.* |

1. It is _____ to wear a T-shirt and jeans to a wedding ceremony.

2. The teacher's _____ explanation answered all our questions.

3. The cell was _____ ten times under the lens of the microscope.

4. These two banks have _____ to form the largest bank in the country.

5. The trade _____ was the most important agreement ever signed between the two countries.

【解答】1. inappropriate   2. laconic   3. magnified   4. merged   5. pact

prickly 〔'prɪklɪ 〕 *adj.* 麻煩的;棘手的
—— 同 complicated , troublesome , intricate , trying
She doesn't know how to deal with the *prickly* problem of having to invite her ex-boyfriend to her wedding.
必須邀請前任男友參加婚禮的這種棘手的問題,她不知道該如何處理。

querulous 〔'kwɛrələs 〕 *adj.* 愛抱怨的;發牢騷的【最常考】
—— 同 complaining , discontented , fretful
The child's *querulous* questions were driving me crazy.
那小孩所抱怨的問題,快令我發瘋了。

radical 〔'rædɪkl̩ 〕 *adj.* ①基本的 ②偏激的【最常考】
—— 同 1. basic , fundamental 2. extreme , rash , drastic
There was a *radical* difference between the two professors' theories. 這兩位教授的理論基本上就不相同。

relinquish 〔 rɪ'lɪŋkwɪʃ 〕 *v.* 放棄;撤退
—— 同 give up , forgo , disclaim , renounce
Nora was not willing to *relinquish* her high paying job for more free time.
諾拉不願意為了擁有更多的空閒時間,而放棄高薪的工作。

retard 〔 rɪ'tɑrd 〕 *v.* 阻礙 —— 同 delay , hold up , stunt , impede
Lack of sunlight will *retard* the growth of most plants.
缺乏陽光會妨礙大多數植物的生長。

saline 〔'selaɪn 〕 *adj.* 鹹的 —— 同 salty
Ocean water is so *saline* that you cannot drink it.
海水太鹹而不能飲用。

sequel 〔'sikwəl 〕 *n.* 續集 —— 同 consequence , continuation
"Scarlett" is the immensely popular *sequel* to "Gone with the Wind." 「Scarlett」是「Gone with the Wind」極受歡迎的續集。

slogan 〔'slogən 〕 n. 標語；口號　 ── 同 motto , catch-phrase

The advertising company had to come up with a good ***slogan***
for the new brand of soda.

廣告公司必須爲這新廠牌的汽水，想一個很好的標語。

* **spontaneous** 〔 spɑn'tenɪəs 〕 adj. 自然的【常考】

── 同 natural , impulsive , ingenuous , instinctive

The group of children on the bus began a ***spontaneous*** singing
of songs.　公車上的那群小孩很自然地唱起歌來。

strenuous 〔'strɛnjʊəs 〕 adj. 費力的；奮鬥的

── 同 energetic , ardent , arduous , vigorous

Ralph was not used to ***strenuous*** exercise, and hiking up the hill
exhausted him.　拉爾夫不習慣費力的運動，所以上山健行使他筋疲力盡。

surmise 〔 sɚ'maɪz 〕 v. 臆測

── 同 guess , presume , conjecture , suppose

We ***surmised*** by the clothes she was wearing that she was a
chef.　我們由她的穿著推斷她是個主廚。

* **tactic** 〔'tæktɪk 〕 n. 策略【常考】　 ── 同 maneuver , strategy

Harry often cleans his room as a ***tactic*** to avoid doing his
homework.　哈瑞常以打掃房間作爲策略，來逃避做功課。

tier 〔 tɪr 〕 n. 層　 ── 同 layer , stratum

The newly-married couple had a three-***tiered*** wedding cake at
the banquet.　這對新婚夫婦在喜宴上擺了一個三層的蛋糕。

　* banquet 〔'bæŋkwɪt 〕 n. 宴會

ultimatum 〔ˌʌltə'metəm 〕 n. 最後通牒；哀的美敦書

── 同 demand , exaction , requirement

The kidnapper's ***ultimatum*** was two million dollars by
midnight, or the man would be killed.

綁匪發出最後通牒，在半夜以前須備妥兩百萬元，否則那名男子將遭殺害。

vagabond 〔'vægə,bɑnd 〕 *n.* 流浪漢
——同 wanderer , vagrant , hobo

In the past, many *vagabonds* would gather at the back of this restaurant to beg for food.

從前，有許多流浪漢聚集在這家餐廳的後面乞討食物。

walkout 〔'wɔk,aʊt 〕 *n.* 罷工　——同 protest , strike , stoppage

Factory workers staged a *walkout* to protest the poor working conditions.

工廠的工人發動罷工，抗議惡劣的工作環境。

yearn 〔 jɜn 〕 *v.* 渴望　——同 desire , long for , covet , hunger

Elsa *yearns* for the day she can return to her native country.

艾爾莎渴望有朝一日能回到自己的祖國。

Exercise ＞ *Fill in the blanks.*

1. Lack of money will definitely _____ our project's progress.

2. Thomas suddenly stood on the restaurant table and broke into _____ song.

3. Nora has developed many _____ to avoid running into her boss in the hallways of the office.

4. The _____ found a bench in the park to sleep on for the night.

5. He was _____ to return to his home once more and see his family.

【解答】1. retard　2. spontaneous　3. tactics　4. vagabond　5. yearning

·List 2· 難字分析

aptitude 〔'æptə,tjud 〕 *n.* 能力；資質

| apt + itude |
| fit + *n.* |

—— a natural ability or talent

compulsory 〔 kəm'pʌlsərɪ 〕 *adj.* 強迫的；義務的

| com + puls + ory |
| with + drive + *adj.* |

—— put into force by the law, orders, etc.

fluctuate 〔'flʌktʃʊ,et 〕 *v.* 波動；變動

| fluct + uate |
| flow + *v.* |

—— rise and fall; to change from one state to the opposite

inappropriate 〔,ɪnə'proprɪɪt 〕 *adj.* 不適合的

| in + ap + propri + ate |
| ad |
| *not* + *to* + *proper* + *adj.* |

—— not proper

innocuous 〔 ɪ'nɑkjʊəs 〕 *adj.* 無害的

| in + noc + uous |
| *not* + *injure* + *adj.* |

—— not causing injury or harm

obsequious 〔 əb'sikwɪəs 〕 adj. 逢迎的；諂媚的

ob + sequ + ious
near + follow + adj.

— too eager to obey or serve; overly submissive

perpendicular 〔 ˌpɝpən'dɪkjələ 〕 adj. 垂直的

per + pend + ic + ular
through + hang + adj. + adj.

— exactly upright, not leaning to one side or the other

relinquish 〔 rɪ'lɪŋkwɪʃ 〕 v. 放棄；撤退

re + linqu + ish
again + leave + adj.

— to give up; yield

strenuous 〔 'strɛnjuəs 〕 adj. 費力的；奮鬥的

stren + uous
firm + adj.

— requiring or characterized by great effort or energy

surmise 〔 sɚ'maɪz 〕 v. 臆測

sur + mise
over + throw

— to imagine or infer without conclusive evidence

vagabond 〔 'væɡəˌbɑnd 〕 n. 流浪漢

vaga + bond
wander + husband

— a person who wanders from place to place, having no fixed abode

 **TEST ▸ 1**

請由 (A)～(D) 中選出和畫線部分意義最相近的字。

1. Our company's workers are all of very high <u>caliber</u>.
   (A) number
   (B) value
   (C) ability
   (D) normality

2. The farmers <u>dammed</u> the stream to divert the water into their fields.
   (A) blocked
   (B) enlarged
   (C) restricted
   (D) encased

3. The complicated <u>fabric</u> of our society is made up of many parts.
   (A) expansion
   (B) framework
   (C) solidity
   (D) appearance

4. We were expecting <u>approximately</u> twenty people to come to the party that night.
   (A) over
   (B) around
   (C) exactly
   (D) perfectly

5. All the office staff was wary of the boss' <u>mercurial</u> moods.
   (A) stable
   (B) gregarious
   (C) erratic
   (D) depressed

6. The artist's <u>fusion</u> of visual and musical arts made for an interesting display.
   (A) explosion
   (B) decision
   (C) enhancement
   (D) merger

7. We were very shocked to see Mrs. Jones' <u>obituary</u> in the newspaper yesterday.
   (A) death notice
   (B) wedding announcement
   (C) promotion report
   (D) engagement notice

8. Mother's words of comfort <u>lulled</u> any fears she had about the dark.
   (A) renewed
   (B) soothed
   (C) encouraged
   (D) destroyed

9. The prime minister was forced to <u>relinquish</u> his office.

  (A) give up

  (B) improve

  (C) elect

  (D) take

10. Wesley always listened to the <u>sagacious</u> advice of his grandmother.

  (A) interesting

  (B) animated

  (C) fanciful

  (D) wise

11. The regular entrance fee to the National Museum is <u>waived</u> on Sun Yat-sen's birthday.

  (A) doubled

  (B) enforced

  (C) forgone

  (D) reduced

12. Some social <u>taboos</u>, such as kissing in public, are slowly being changed in Japan.

  (A) prohibitions

  (B) practices

  (C) customs

  (D) structures

13. Janet has quite an <u>aptitude</u> for theater production.

  (A) deficiency

  (B) interest

  (C) knack

  (D) responsibility

14. The fact that the earth is not flat cannot be <u>gainsaid</u>.

  (A) proved

  (B) spoken

  (C) denied

  (D) realized

15. Mr. Jackson had only <u>contemptuous</u> things to say to his employees.

  (A) scornful

  (B) flattering

  (C) ambiguous

  (D) uncertain

16. Margaret will be <u>abashed</u> to hear that everyone was making fun of the dress she wore.

  (A) elated

  (B) impressed

  (C) confused

  (D) embarrassed

17. The queen was <u>deposed</u> and replaced by a distant cousin.

  (A) mortified

  (B) ousted

  (C) crowned

  (D) incompetent

18. The psychiatrist was able to educe the patient's suppressed memory with hypnotism.

   (A) bring out
   (B) cave in
   (C) lessen
   (D) return to

19. In math class we learned about the properties of lines that are perpendicular to one another.

   (A) on the same plane
   (B) opposite
   (C) side by side
   (D) at right angles

20. My querulous next-door neighbor never has anything good to say to anyone.

   (A) silent
   (B) fascinating
   (C) complaining
   (D) introverted

21. Public transportation workers staged a walkout, causing terrible problems for the city.

   (A) production
   (B) event
   (C) strike
   (D) employment

22. Alice does not know how to handle the prickly problem of negotiating with her landlord.

   (A) overdue
   (B) troublesome
   (C) alleged
   (D) trite

23. The travelers were suspected of carrying a deadly virus so they were put in quarantine.

   (A) surveillance
   (B) repression
   (C) isolation
   (D) hospital

24. Because construction work is so strenuous, it is often well paid.

   (A) complicated
   (B) straight-forward
   (C) desirable
   (D) arduous

25. His words seemed innocuous when he said them, but now I suspect they had a hidden meaning.

   (A) suspicious
   (B) articulate
   (C) harmless
   (D) informative

【解答】

1. C	2. A	3. B	4. B	5. C	6. D	7. A	8. B	9. A	10. D
11. C	12. A	13. C	14. C	15. A	16. D	17. B	18. A	19. D	20. C
21. C	22. B	23. C	24. D	25. C					

LIST ▸ 3

abate 〔 ə'bet 〕 *v.* 減弱

——同 diminish , lessen , subside , reduce , curtail

The rain did not ***abate*** the crowd's enthusiasm for the baseball game.　下雨並沒有使觀眾看棒球比賽的熱情稍減。

adhere 〔 əd'hɪr 〕 *v.* 黏附；附著

——同 stick , cling , cleave , attach , cohere

If the surface is wet, the tape will not ***adhere*** to it.
如果表面是濕的，膠帶就黏不住。

* **alternate** 〔'ɔltə‚net 〕 *v.* 交替；輪流【常考】

——同 rotate , reciprocate , interchange , take turns

Dan and Mike ***alternated*** washing the dishes every night.
丹和麥克每天晚上輪流洗碗。

‡ **aptly** 〔'æptlɪ 〕 *adv.* 適當地【最常考】

——同 appropriately , properly , suitably , fittingly

The breathtaking green valley below was ***aptly*** named Beautiful Valley.
下面那令人讚嘆的翠綠山谷名字取得很貼切，叫美麗的山谷。

‡ **banal** 〔'benḷ , bə'næl 〕 *adj.* 陳腐的【最常考】

——同 common , trite , stereotyped , stale , hackneyed , clichéd

Chris' ***banal*** advice was no help to us in solving our problem.
克里斯陳腐的勸告，對於解決我們的問題，完全沒有幫助。

* **campaign** 〔 kæm'pen 〕 *n.* 活動；戰役【常考】

——同 operation , movement , battle , fight , combat

The ***campaign*** to end poverty in the country is far from over.
該國想要終止貧窮的行動，絕不會結束。

* **cluster**〔'klʌstɚ〕*n.* 聚集【常考】 ——同 clump , bunch , batch
The tree had ***clusters*** of white flowers at the end of each
branch. 那棵樹在每根樹枝末端，都長著一叢白花。

compute〔kəm'pjut〕*v.* 計算
——同 count , estimate , calculate , measure , reckon , figure
Darla had to ***compute*** exactly how many chairs and tables
would be needed for all the dinner guests.
達拉必須準確計算出全部晚餐賓客所需的桌椅數目。

* **contention**〔kən'tɛnʃən〕*n.* 爭論；爭鬥【常考】
——同 competition , struggle , argument , conflict
There was much ***contention*** about the proposed city subway
system. 關於提議的市區地下鐵系統，有許多爭論。

* **dawn**〔dɔn〕*n.* 黎明【常考】 ——同 sunrise , daybreak
Jane awoke at ***dawn***, while everyone else in the house was
still sleeping. 珍天亮就醒了，而屋子裡的其他人都仍在睡夢中。

** **deplore**〔dɪ'plor〕*v.* 感到遺憾【最常考】
——同 mourn , grieve , sorrow
Ms. Adams ***deplored*** the lack of money in education and made
a large donation to her local school.
亞當斯女士對缺乏教育經費感到很遺憾，因此捐了一大筆錢給當地的學校。

** **discreet**〔dɪ'skrit〕*adj.* 謹慎的【最常考】
——同 prudent , cautious , judicious , careful , wary
Pauline was ***discreet*** about handing me a note in English class.
上英文課時，寶琳很謹慎地遞給我一張紙條。

* **eerie**〔'ɪrɪ , 'irɪ〕*adj.* 陰森的；可怕的【常考】
——同 weird , awesome , fearful , ghastly , spooky
That night we heard an ***eerie*** sound as we were playing cards.
我們在玩牌的那晚，聽見了奇怪的聲音。

＊egotistic 〔͵igəˈtɪstɪk〕 *adj.* 自負的【最常考】

──同 self-centered , egocentric , narcissistic , self-important

As he began to earn more and more money, his personality became more and more *egotistic*.

當他錢越賺越多時，他的個性也變得越來越自負。

endure 〔 ɪnˈdjʊr 〕 *v.* 忍耐；持久　　*n.* endurance

──同 bear , abide , tolerate , stand

I cannot *endure* the noise and dirt from the construction site next to my house.　我無法忍受從我家隔壁工地傳來的噪音和塵土。

facile 〔ˈfæsḷ〕 *adj.* 輕易的；靈巧的

──同 easy , skillful , adroit , effortless , simple

Her *facile* reply to the problem with the computer was to turn it off.　對於電腦發生的問題，她的簡單回應就是關機。

Exercise ▷ *Fill in the blanks.*

1. We compromised and ＿＿＿＿＿＿ between watching the drama series Joe liked and my favorite sports show.

2. A ＿＿＿＿＿＿ to end corruption in the government has just begun.

3. The large classes are a cause of ＿＿＿＿＿＿ in the teachers' contract negotiations.

4. After all they had ＿＿＿＿＿＿ during the war, anything seemed possible to them.

5. The ＿＿＿＿＿＿ movement of her hands over the keyboard showed her years of practice on the piano.

【解答】1. alternated　2. campaign　3. contention　4. endured　5. facile

flush 〔 flʌʃ 〕 *v.* ①臉紅 ②逐出
——同 1. blush , redden 2. eject , expel
When she smiled at him, his face ***flushed*** bright red.
當她對他微笑時，他的臉漲得通紅。

gallant 〔'gælənt 〕 *adj.* 勇敢的　——同 brave , daring , courageous
A ***gallant*** man jumped into the river to save the drowning
child.　一位勇敢的男子跳進河裡，搭救那個溺水的小孩。

* **halt** 〔 hɔlt 〕 *v.* 停止【常考】　——同 pull up , stop , pause
The soldiers at the border ***halted*** the travelers to check their
passports.　把守邊界的士兵把遊客攔下來，檢查他們的護照。

idolize 〔'aɪdḷ͵aɪz 〕 *v.* 崇拜　——同 admire , worship , adore
Jackie ***idolizes*** her math teacher and wants to be just like her.
賈姬崇拜她的數學老師，想成爲和她一樣的人。

* **incessant** 〔 ɪn'sɛsṇt 〕 *adj.* 不斷的【常考】
——同 continuous , constant , ceaseless , continual , everlasting
The ***incessant*** barking of my neighbor's dog keeps me awake
at night.　鄰居的狗不停地叫，使我整夜無法入睡。

inordinate 〔 ɪn'ɔrdṇɪt 〕 *adj.* 不節制的；過度的【最常考】
——同 excessive , immoderate , intemperate , exorbitant
Doctors have reported an ***inordinate*** number of patients with
the flu this winter.
醫生的報告指出，今年冬天有非常多人罹患流行性感冒。

jettison 〔'dʒɛtəsṇ , -zṇ 〕 *v.* 丟棄；放棄【最常考】
——同 cast , throw , hurl , abandon , give up
The ship's captain ordered that all extra cargo be ***jettisoned***
to prevent the ship from sinking.
船長下令把所有多餘的貨物都丟棄，以免船隻沉沒。

* **lament** 〔 lə'mɛnt 〕 *v.* 哀悼【常考】　——同 deplore , bemoan , bewail
Everyone in the neighborhood *lamented* the death of my uncle
Robert. 鄰近的每個人都爲羅勃叔叔的死哀悼。

* **luminous** 〔'lumənəs 〕 *adj.* 發光的【最常考】
——同 bright , radiant , shining
We looked up in the night sky and saw something *luminous*,
which we thought was a UFO.
我們仰望夜空,看見一個發光體,我們認爲那是幽浮。

* **magnitude** 〔'mægnə,tjud 〕 *n.* 強度【常考】
——同 extent , immensity , great size , enormity
The *magnitude* of the budget deficit is growing every day.
預算赤字的情形日益惡化。　* deficit 〔'dɛfəsɪt 〕 *n.* 赤字

merit 〔'mɛrɪt 〕 ① *n.* 優點;價值　② *v.* 應得
——同 1. credit , virtue , worth　2. deserve , be entitled to
The city government's efforts to improve traffic safety deserve
merit. 市政府在改善交通安全上所做的努力,值得嘉許。

navigate 〔'nævə,get 〕 *v.* 駕駛;航行　——同 sail , cruise , steer
We *navigated* the ship across the channel to return home.
我們駕船穿越海峽回家。

* **oblique** 〔 ə'blik , ə'blaɪk 〕 *adj.* ①歪斜的　②閃爍其詞的【常考】
——同 1. slanting , inclined , sloping , tilted　2. evasive , roundabout
James planted his flower garden with *oblique* rows of tulips.
詹姆士在花園裡種了斜斜的幾排鬱金香。

* **ostracize** 〔'ɑstrə,saɪz , 'ɔs- 〕 *v.* 排斥;放逐【最常考】
——同 shun , banish , expel , exile , expatriate
After telling the teacher about their plans to cheat on the test,
Billy was *ostracized* from the group.
比利把他們打算考試作弊的計畫告訴老師後,便受到同組人的排斥。

palatable 〔'pælətəbḷ 〕 *adj.* 美味的；合口味的

—— 同 delicious , savory , tasty , dainty

This cake Albert baked is quite ***palatable***.

亞伯特烤的這個蛋糕相當美味。

* perpetrate 〔'pɝpə,tret 〕 *v.* 犯（罪）；作（惡）【常考】

—— 同 commit , perform , execute , inflict

The police have not been able to find out who ***perpetrated***
the crime. 警方還無法找出犯罪的嫌犯。

plunder 〔'plʌndə 〕 *v.* 掠奪

—— 同 rob , pillage , ravage , harry , sack , loot

After the battle, the victorious soldiers ***plundered*** the
villagers' houses.

戰鬥結束後，勝方的軍士們大肆掠奪村民的財物。

Exercise ⟩ *Fill in the blanks.*

1. His _____ effort to save the drowning child led to his
own death.

2. All the people _____ the death of their president.

3. Walter responded to my question with an _____
answer which only confused me more.

4. When traveling abroad, we always worry how _____
the local cuisine will be.

5. During the riot, many nearby stores were broken into and
_____.

【解答】 1. gallant　2. lamented　3. oblique　4. palatable　5. plundered

prorogue〔proˈrog〕*v.* 休會　——同 adjourn, postpone
The legislature moved to ***prorogue*** the present session.
國會提議停止目前的會期。

* **quest**〔kwɛst〕*n.* 探求【常考】　——同 search, expedition, pursuit
Many explorers' ***quests*** to find the source of the Mekong River were unsuccessful.
許多探險家想探尋湄公河的源頭，但都沒有成功。

raid〔red〕*n.* 襲擊
——同 attack, invasion, assault, inroad, incursion
The general led a ***raid*** on the enemy's camp.
將軍領軍襲擊敵營。

relish〔ˈrɛlɪʃ〕① *v.* 喜歡；享受　② *n.* 美味；喜愛
——同 1. enjoy, appreciate　2. taste, flavor, gusto, savor
Paul and Wanda ***relished*** the time they had off from work.
保羅跟汪妲喜歡休假不用上班的日子。

retort〔rɪˈtɔrt〕*v.* 反駁　——同 respond, reply, answer, retaliate
Amy ***retorted*** that she was not the one who left the dirty dishes in the sink.　艾美反駁說，把髒盤子留在水槽裡的不是她。

salutary〔ˈsæljəˌtɛrɪ〕*adj.* 有益健康的；有益的
——同 wholesome, helpful, salubrious, healthful
Tina's losing the long distance race was actually ***salutary*** because it made her practice harder.
蒂娜輸掉這場長途比賽也有好處，因為那會使她更加努力練習。

* **serene**〔səˈrin〕*adj.* 寧靜的【常考】
——同 calm, peaceful, composed, tranquil, pacific
David finds the sound of ocean waves very ***serene***.
大衛覺得海浪的聲音非常寧靜。

sluggish 〔ˈslʌgɪʃ〕 *adj.* 遲緩的；怠惰的

—— 同 idle , indolent , lazy , inactive , lethargic

The medicine Gary took for his cold made him feel *sluggish*.

蓋瑞吃了感冒藥，使他有點遲鈍。

✻sporadic 〔spoˈrædɪk〕 *adj.* 零星的【最常考】

—— 同 occasional , irregular

Sporadic loss of memory is common in old age.

人老後偶爾忘東忘西是常有的事。

strident 〔ˈstraɪdn̩t〕 *adj.* 粗糙的；尖銳的

—— 同 harsh , shrill , rough , sharp

Larry's *strident* voice was difficult to listen to for more than five minutes. 賴瑞粗啞的聲音讓人聽了五分鐘就受不了。

✻surmount 〔səˈmaʊnt〕 *v.* 克服；超越【常考】

—— 同 exceed , overcome , conquer , vanquish , surpass

Ada was able to *surmount* her fear of heights by learning to rock climb. 藉著學會攀岩，艾達終於能克服她的懼高症。

tally 〔ˈtælɪ〕 ① *n.* 計算 ② *v.* 符合

—— 同 1. count , reckoning , score 2. accord , match , conform

The final *tally* in the soccer match was 7-3.

足球比賽的最後比數是 7：3。

✻tilt 〔tɪlt〕 *v.* 傾斜【常考】   —— 同 incline , lean , slant , cant

Don't put your glass of tea on that table; it *tilts* to the left and your drink might spill.

別把你的茶放在那張桌子上，那張桌子往左傾，你的茶可能會溢出來。

unanimous 〔juˈnænəməs〕 *adj.* 全體一致的

—— 同 harmonious , united , accordant , agreeing

It was our office's *unanimous* decision to take the day off.

我們辦公室裡一致決定那一天要休假。

vague 〔veg〕 *adj.* 模糊的；曖昧的

——同 dim , obscure , ambiguous , indistinct , unclear

Janet's answer to my question was ***vague*** and did not help me understand my problem any better.

珍娜給我的回答曖昧不清，無法幫助我更加了解我的問題。

wallow 〔'wɑlo〕 *v.* 打滾 ——同 toss , tumble , roll , flounder

Because the weather was so hot, the pigs were ***wallowing*** in the mud trying to cool off.

因為天氣太熱了，豬都跑到泥沼裡打滾，試著能涼爽一點。

* **yield** 〔jild〕 *v.* ①讓步；屈服 ②生產【常考】

——同 1. succumb , give in , submit , surrender 2. produce , bear

Carl finally ***yielded*** to his son's demands for a new toy.

卡爾終於讓步，答應讓他兒子買新的玩具。

Exercise ⟩ *Fill in the blanks.*

1. Mark is _____ his deserved long vacation from the office.

2. The magazine article I just read tells of the _____ effects of regular exercise for older women.

3. The pain in her arm was _____; it always seemed to disappear when she went to the doctor.

4. Gary and Amy are _____ the results of the class elections.

5. Sergeant Ames was a cruel man who would not _____ to the civilians' pleas for mercy.

【解答】1. relishing 2. salutary 3. sporadic 4. tallying 5. yield

· List 3 · 難字分析

alternate (ˈɔltɚ,net) *v.* 交替;輪流

altern + ate
other + make

—— to do or use by turns

contention (kənˈtɛnʃən) *n.* 爭論;爭鬥

con + ten + tion
together + stretch + n.

—— the act of disputing, quarrelling, etc.

egotistic (,igəˈtɪstɪk) *adj.* 自負的

ego + tist + ic
self + person + adj.

—— self-important

incessant (ɪnˈsɛsn̩t) *adj.* 不斷的

in + cess + ant
not + cease + adj.

—— continuing or being repeated without stopping

inordinate (ɪnˈɔrdn̩ɪt) *adj.* 不節制的;過度的

in + ordin + ate
not + order + adj.

—— lacking restraint or moderation

navigate 〔'nævə,get 〕 v. 駕駛;航行

nav + ig + ate
ship + drive + v.

— to steer or direct a ship or aircraft

oblique 〔 ə'blik , ə'blaɪk 〕 adj. ①歪斜的 ②閃爍其詞的

ob + lique
towards + bent

— having a slanting position or direction; not straight to the point

prorogue 〔 pro'rog 〕 v. 休會

pro + rogue
publicly + ask

— to discontinue or end a session of a legislative assembly

salutary 〔'sæljə,tɛrɪ 〕 adj. 有益健康的;有益的

salut + ary
health + adj.

— promoting or conducive to health or some good purpose

unanimous 〔 jʊ'nænəməs 〕 adj. 全體一致的

un + anim + ous
one + mind + adj.

— united in opinion

📋 **LIST ▸ 4**

abbreviate〔 ə'brivɪˌet 〕 v. 縮減
—— 同 shorten , reduce , condense , abridge
Scott *abbreviated* his speech, so he would not bore anyone.
史考特將他的演講濃縮，不致讓人感到無聊。

adjacent〔 ə'dʒesn̩t 〕 adj. 鄰接的
—— 同 adjoining , bordering , neighboring , contiguous
Nick's house is *adjacent* to a large park. 尼可的家與大公園毗鄰。

alternative〔 ɔl'tɝnətɪv 〕 n. 選擇
—— 同 choice , option , selection , substitute
Fred felt he had very few *alternatives* in choosing a career.
弗瑞德覺得他在謀職上的選擇機會很少。

⁑arbitrary〔 'arbəˌtrɛrɪ 〕 adj. ①武斷的；專制的 ②隨意的
—— 同 1. dictatorial , subjective , domineering　　　　【最常考】
　　　 2. random , capricious
The boss's *arbitrary* demands of his staff were unbearable.
這位老板對於職員專制的要求令人無法忍受。

avocation〔 ˌævə'keʃən 〕 n. 副業；嗜好
—— 同 diversion , hobby , occupation , pastime
Louis' *avocation* as a ski instructor gradually became his
full-time employment.
滑雪教練一職已從路易斯的副業，逐漸變成全職了。

candidate〔 'kændəˌdet 〕 n. 候選人
—— 同 nominee , office-seeker , applicant , aspirant
Teresa has decided to become a *candidate* for mayor of our
town. 泰瑞莎已決定成為本鎮鎮長的候選人。

* **coagulate** 〔 ko'ægjə,let 〕 *v.* 凝結【常考】

—同 solidify , jell , congeal , clot , curdle

The blood around the wound began to ***coagulate***, slowing the bleeding. 傷口周圍的血開始凝結，減緩了流血的情況。

conceal 〔 kən'sil 〕 *v.* 隱藏 —同 hide , cover , secrete , stow

The brothers tried to ***conceal*** the puppy from their parents, but it was soon discovered.

這幾個兄弟試著把小狗藏起來不讓父母看到，但不久就被發現了。

contiguity 〔,kɑntə'gjuətɪ 〕 *n.* 鄰接

—同 juxtaposition , abutment , union , meeting

Our apartment building's ***contiguity*** to a supermarket is very convenient. 我們的公寓和超級市場相鄰，相當地方便。

daze 〔 dez 〕 *v.* 使暈眩；使困惑 —同 dazzle , confuse , stun

The difficult math problem ***dazed*** all of the students in the class. 這題數學難倒了全班學生。

* **deprive** 〔 dɪ'praɪv 〕 *v.* 剝奪【常考】

—同 strip , dispossess , divest , bereave , denude

The prisoners were ***deprived*** of any communication with the outside world. 這些囚犯被剝奪與外界溝通的自由。

discrepancy 〔 dɪ'skrɛpənsɪ 〕 *n.* 差異；不符

—同 inconsistency , disagreement , divergence , discordance

The manager found a ***discrepancy*** between the company's records and what was actually sold.

經理發現公司的紀錄與實際售出的不符合。

* **efface** 〔 ɪ'fes 〕 *v.* 削除【常考】

—同 erase , eradicate , expunge , delete

The wind had ***effaced*** the deer's hoofprints from the snow.

風吹散了雪地上鹿的足跡。 * hoofprint 〔'huf,prɪnt 〕 *n.* 蹄印

engross〔ɪnˈgros〕*v.* 使全神貫注

—— 同 absorb , preoccupy , engage

Richard is *engrossed* in the study of marine biology.
理察全神貫注在研究海洋生物學。

ethnic〔ˈɛθnɪk〕*adj.* 種族的；人種的

—— 同 racial , national , native

Our school has students from many different *ethnic*
backgrounds. 本校的學生來自許多不同的種族背景。

facilitate〔fəˈsɪləˌtet〕*v.* 使容易；促進

—— 同 smooth , ease , promote , speed up

Melissa's help *facilitated* our work to clean up the garage.
梅麗莎的幫忙使我們打掃車庫的工作加快了。

Exercise > *Fill in the blanks.*

1. Eating more grains is a healthy _____ to eating a lot
   of meat.

2. Three of the presidential _____ participated in the
   televised debate.

3. Jenny was _____ by the breathtaking scenery of the
   waterfall.

4. Diane was _____ in reading a book when I entered
   the room.

5. The fax machine has _____ communication between
   offices and homes considerably.

【解答】 1. alternative 2. candidates 3. dazed 4. engrossed 5. facilitated

foamy 〔'fomɪ 〕*adj.* 起泡沫的　——同 bubbling , sparkling

The storm had made the ocean waves hitting the shore rough and *foamy*. 暴風雨使得海浪大力沖擊岸邊，激起泡沫。

garment 〔'garmənt 〕*n.* 衣服

——同 clothing , robe , costume , attire , dress

Charles decided to have several *garments* made by a local tailor. 查爾斯決定讓地方上的裁縫師作幾件衣服。

handicap 〔'hændɪ͵kæp 〕*v.* 妨礙

——同 penalize , hamper , encumber

A sore right arm *handicapped* Laura's tennis playing.
右臂酸痛妨礙了蘿拉打網球。

* **ignite** 〔 ɪg'naɪt 〕*v.* ①點燃　②煽動【常考】

——同 1. kindle , catch fire　2. agitate , stir , excite

A carelessly thrown, lit cigarette *ignited* the house fire.
一根隨意丟棄未熄的煙蒂，讓這個房子起火燃燒。

* **ingenuous** 〔 ɪn'dʒɛnjuəs 〕*adj.* 率直的【常考】

——同 frank , trustful , plain , innocent

It was his *ingenuous* smile that won Deborah's heart.
是他率直的笑容贏得了黛博拉的芳心。

inquiry 〔 ɪn'kwaɪrɪ , 'ɪnkwərɪ 〕*n.* 查詢；調查

——同 search , research , quest , investigation , inspection

The police led an *inquiry* to try to find the stolen paintings.
警方展開調查，試圖找出被竊的畫。

jocular 〔'dʒakjələ˙ 〕*adj.* 滑稽的；詼諧的

——同 joking , funny , jocose , humorous , jesting

William's *jocular* personality makes him a very popular person. 威廉風趣的個性使他成為廣受歡迎的人。

landscape 〔 'læn(d)skep 〕 *n.* 風景　——同 vista , view

Bernard's art class took a trip to the country to learn how to paint *landscapes*.

伯納的美術課到鄉下去，學習如何畫風景。

lure 〔 lur 〕 *v.* 誘惑　——同 entice , tempt , coax

Patricia was *lured* by the glamour of Hollywood and decided to become an actress.　＊glamour 〔 'glæmɚ 〕 *n.* 魅力

派翠西亞被好萊塢的魅力所誘惑，決定要成為女演員。

martyr 〔 'mɑrtɚ 〕 *n.* 犧牲者　——同 victim , sacrifice

When the police shot the young student, she became a *martyr* for the democracy movement.

警察射殺這名年輕學生，使她成了民主運動的犧牲者。

＊meticulous 〔 mə'tɪkjələs 〕 *adj.* 小心翼翼的【最常考】
　　——同 careful

We were *meticulous* in cleaning the car, washing and polishing every inch of it.

我們小心翼翼地清理車子，將每一吋都沖洗和打蠟。

nebulous 〔 'nɛbjələs 〕 *adj.* 模糊的
　　——同 ambiguous , hazy

The company had only a *nebulous* idea of the next model of car they would manufacture.

該公司對他們下次要製造的車，只有模糊的概念。

＊oblivious 〔 ə'blɪvɪəs 〕 *adj.* 忘記的；不注意的【最常考】
　　——同 forgetful , unaware of

Warren was *oblivious* to the yelling and fighting in the apartment next door, and continued reading his book.

華倫對公寓內鄰居的叫喊與吵鬧渾然不覺，繼續讀他的書。

ostensible 〔αs'tɛnsəbl̩〕 *adj.* 表面上的；假裝的【最常考】

—— 同 seeming

The *ostensible* reason for his trip to Greece was business, but it was actually a vacation.

他到希臘表面上的理由是出差，但其實是度假。

pallid 〔'pælɪd〕 *adj.* 蒼白的；無光澤的

—— 同 pale , bloodless , wan , sallow , white

After being sick in bed for a week, Jane still looked *pallid*.

臥病在床一星期後，珍的臉色看起來仍然蒼白。

perpetual 〔pə'pɛtʃuəl〕 *adj.* 永久的

—— 同 everlasting , unceasing , constant , unending

The seemingly *perpetual* rain made us all depressed.

這看起來下不停的雨讓大家都感到沮喪。

Exercise ▷ *Fill in the blanks.*

1. That exclusive boutique is filled with beautiful _____ that I could never afford.

2. The government began an _____ into possible vote fraud in the election.

3. The dentist _____ the child into the examining chair with promises of a free toy.

4. Through _____ research, scientists found a drug that would treat the disease.

5. Doug's _____ lying has made us distrust everything he says.

【解答】1. garments   2. inquiry   3. lured   4. meticulous   5. perpetual

plunge 〔plʌndʒ〕*v.* 跳進 ——同 submerge , dive , descend , dip , sink
On a hot summer day, I like nothing better than ***plunging*** into a cool swimming pool.
在炎熱的夏日裡，我最喜歡的事莫過於跳進涼爽的游泳池內。

principal 〔ˈprɪnsəpl̩〕*adj.* 主要的
——同 chief , foremost , prime , main , leading
The ***principal*** aim of this plan is to find a way to help students improve their study habits.
這計畫的主要目標是找出方法，來幫助學生改善讀書習慣。

quibble 〔ˈkwɪbl̩〕*n.* ①模稜兩可的話 ②挑毛病
——同 2. a petty distinction , an irrelevant objection
I hope you don't think this is a ***quibble***, but I have an objection.
我希望你不要以爲我是在挑毛病，不過我還是反對。

rampant 〔ˈræmpənt〕*adj.* 蔓延的；猖獗的；猛烈的
——同 widespread , rife , uncontrollable , excessive
You cannot allow children to run ***rampant*** through the museum.
你不能任小孩子在博物館內胡亂奔跑。

reluctant 〔rɪˈlʌktənt〕*adj.* 不情願的
——同 unwilling , loath , averse , hesitant
Bert was ***reluctant*** to tell his mother the washing machine was broken again. 柏特不願告訴母親洗衣機又故障了。

retreat 〔rɪˈtrit〕*v.* 撤退 ——同 withdraw , recede , draw back
The soldiers ***retreated*** to their camp in the hills.
士兵們撤回到他們在山丘上的營地。

sanction 〔ˈsæŋkʃən〕*n.* ①批准 ②制裁
——同 1. confirmation , permission 2. boycott , penalty
The city government gave its ***sanction*** to the library to build a new wing. 市政府批准圖書館興建新的分館。

setback 〔ˈsɛtˌbæk〕 *n.* 挫折；後退 ——同 backslide , defeat

Our building plans suffered a ***setback*** when a strong typhoon destroyed our building site.

強力颱風摧毀了工地，使得我們興建大樓的計畫遭到停擺。

smear 〔 smɪr 〕 *v.* 塗抹；弄髒；中傷

——同 stain , besmirch , smudge

The children played outside and ***smeared*** mud all over their clothes, faces and hands.

孩子們在外面玩耍，衣服、臉和手都沾滿泥巴。

spur 〔 spɝ 〕 *v.* 刺激 ——同 incite , arouse , instigate , stir up

Her coach's encouragement helped ***spur*** Heather to run faster and win the race.

教練的鼓勵刺激了海德，使她跑得更快獲得優勝。

∗∗stringent 〔ˈstrɪndʒənt〕 *adj.* 嚴厲的【最常考】

——同 strict , exacting , severe , forceful , rigorous

The military is famous for its ***stringent*** regulations of dress and behavior. 軍隊以嚴格的服裝和行為規範著稱。

surpass 〔 səˈpæs 〕 *v.* 凌駕 ——同 excel , outdo , exceed

Tommy studied so hard that he ***surpassed*** all the other students in his class.

湯米非常用功，因此成績凌駕班上其他同學。

∗thrall 〔 θrɔl 〕 *n.* 奴隸【常考】 ——同 slave , serf , bondsman

The peasant farmers were the ***thralls*** of the lord of the castle.

這些農夫是堡主的奴隸。

timid 〔ˈtɪmɪd〕 *adj.* 膽怯的 ——同 fearful , cowardly , shy

The tiny kitten was very ***timid***, and too afraid to approach us.

這隻小貓非常膽小，極度害怕而不敢靠近我們。

unassuming 〔͵ʌnə'sumɪŋ 〕 *adj.* 謙虛的
—— 同 modest , retiring , reserved , humble
Don't be fooled by his *unassuming* manner; he is really a very proud man. 別被他謙虛的態度給騙了，他這個人其實很驕傲。

valiant 〔'væljənt 〕 *adj.* 勇敢的
—— 同 dauntless , brave , courageous , gallant , valorous
The doctor's *valiant* efforts finally saved the child's life.
醫生無畏的努力終於挽救了孩子的性命。

* **wan** 〔 wɑn 〕 *adj.* 蒼白的【常考】
—— 同 pale , pallid , colorless , bloodless , ashen
Tony looked so *wan* and tired that I knew something must be wrong. 湯尼看起來如此蒼白與疲憊，我知道一定出事了。

yoke 〔 jok 〕 *n.* 軛；束縛 —— 同 bond , chain , link , tie , union
The farmer put a *yoke* on the oxen's necks and began to plow his fields. 農夫把軛套在牛的脖子上，開始耕田。

Exercise ▷ *Fill in the blanks.*

1. The _____ spread of the disease caused panic among the people of the country.

2. Although she was _____ to go, Tina came to the Assassin concert with me.

3. There were many _____ in organizing the business conference, but we finally succeeded.

4. Allan, who is anything but _____, often strikes up conversations with complete strangers.

5. Although she is a very accomplished pianist, she has a very _____ personality.

【解答】 1. rampant   2. reluctant   3. setbacks   4. timid   5. unassuming

· List 4 · 難字分析

abbreviate 〔 ə'brivɪˌet 〕 v. 縮減

ab + brevi + ate
to + brief + make

— to make shorter

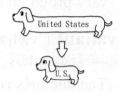

adjacent 〔 ə'dʒesn̩t 〕 adj. 鄰接的

ad + jac + ent
to + throw + adj.

— very close

alternative 〔 ɔl'tɜnətɪv 〕 n. 選擇

altern + ative
other + n., adj.

— a choice between two or among more than two things

avocation 〔ˌævə'keʃən 〕 n. 副業；嗜好

a + voc + ation
not + call + n.

— something one does in addition to his or her vocation and usually for pleasure

candidate 〔'kændəˌdet 〕 n. 候選人

cand + id + ate
white + adj. + person

— a person who seeks, or who has been proposed for a position, esp. in an election

contiguity 〔ˌkɑntə'gjuətɪ 〕 n. 鄰接

con + tig + uity
together + touch + n.

— nearness or contact

ingenuous 〔 ɪn'dʒɛnjʊəs 〕 *adj.* 率直的

in +	gen	+ uous
not +	produce +	adj.

— simple

oblivious 〔 ə'blɪvɪəs 〕 *adj.* 忘記的；不注意的

obliv + ious
forget + adj.

— forgetful or unmindful

ostensible 〔 ɑs'tɛnsəbl̩ 〕 *adj.* 表面上的；假裝的

os +	tens	+ ible
ob		
before +	stretch +	adj.

— seeming or pretended, but perhaps not really true

reluctant 〔 rɪ'lʌktənt 〕 *adj.* 不情願的

re +	luct	+ ant
against +	struggle +	adj.

— opposed in mind to do something

sanction 〔'sæŋkʃən 〕 *n.* ①批准 ②制裁

sanct + ion
sacred + n.

— approval; a formal action or punishment ordered when a law or rule is broken

stringent 〔'strɪndʒənt 〕 *adj.* 嚴厲的

string + ent
draw tight + adj.

— rigidly controlled

 TEST ▸ 2

請由 (A)～(D) 中選出和畫線部分意義最相近的字。

1. This program is <u>aptly</u> suited to students with low English proficiency.

   (A) appropriately
   (B) interestingly
   (C) nominally
   (D) hopefully

2. The flood waters <u>abated</u> to reveal the destruction of the farmers' crops.

   (A) flowed
   (B) returned
   (C) subsided
   (D) increased

3. The <u>incessant</u> noise from the construction next to our house is giving me a headache.

   (A) clamorous
   (B) boring
   (C) intermittent
   (D) continual

4. The wind made an <u>eerie</u> sound as it blew through the trees.

   (A) strange
   (B) pleasant
   (C) quiet
   (D) long

5. The military planned a joint land and air <u>raid</u> of the enemy capital.

   (A) retreat
   (B) attack
   (C) treaty
   (D) exercise

6. Relief workers <u>deplored</u> the lack of sanitation in the refugee camps.

   (A) increased
   (B) lamented
   (C) alleviated
   (D) reduced

7. Health officials are worried about the <u>inordinate</u> number of mosquitoes this year.

   (A) excessive
   (B) level
   (C) arrogant
   (D) surprising

8. Whoever <u>perpetrated</u> this crime was clever enough to not leave any clues.

   (A) discovered
   (B) acknowledged
   (C) committed
   (D) solved

9. His apartment building and mine are <u>adjacent</u>.

(A) adjoining
(B) distant
(C) identical
(D) unique

10. Our club was <u>unanimous</u> in voting Helen to be club president.

(A) unaware
(B) hesitant
(C) blatant
(D) united

11. The children <u>wallowed</u> in the muddy water along the shore of the river.

(A) marched
(B) slept
(C) rolled (around)
(D) stood

12. I could tell Rebecca had just entered the room because I could not mistake her <u>strident</u> voice.

(A) operatic
(B) shrill
(C) reticent
(D) hollow

13. The agar-agar will make the mixture slowly <u>coagulate</u>.

(A) separate
(B) cool
(C) boil
(D) congeal

14. Hester is known for her <u>jocular</u> teasing of her pupils.

(A) humorous
(B) malicious
(C) unwarranted
(D) mundane

15. The police found a <u>discrepancy</u> in the two suspects' stories.

(A) inconsistency
(B) correlation
(C) theme
(D) interest

16. An <u>ostensible</u> gift to the mayor turned out to be a bribe.

(A) alleged
(B) generous
(C) innocent
(D) ignoble

17. The antagonism between the two groups finally <u>ignited</u> violence between them.

(A) discouraged
(B) provoked
(C) spread
(D) smoldered

18. The two men were <u>ostracized</u> from their home village.

(A) banished
(B) deleted
(C) sickened
(D) encouraged

19. Terrance could not <u>efface</u> the terrible memory from his mind.

    (A) recount
    (B) oversee
    (C) expunge
    (D) understand

20. We had only a <u>nebulous</u> idea of how car engines worked.

    (A) precise
    (B) hazy
    (C) refined
    (D) exclusive

21. We want to address any <u>quibbles</u> you may have about the new office policy.

    (A) interests
    (B) suggestions
    (C) interpretations
    (D) objections

22. Be careful not to <u>smear</u> grease on your clothes when you change the oil in your car.

    (A) remove
    (B) pour
    (C) smudge
    (D) immerse

23. The hero was <u>valiant</u>, and all the women swooned at his feet.

    (A) stupid
    (B) courageous
    (C) malodorous
    (D) pompous

24. European <u>sanctions</u> would cripple our county's economy.

    (A) boycotts
    (B) trade
    (C) disasters
    (D) policies

25. The two frogs <u>plunged</u> into the pond to escape the boys trying to capture them.

    (A) skimmed
    (B) fled
    (C) dove
    (D) emerged

【解答】

1. A	2. C	3. D	4. A	5. B	6. B	7. A	8. C	9. A	10. D
11. C	12. B	13. D	14. A	15. A	16. A	17. B	18. A	19. C	20. B
21. D	22. C	23. B	24. A	25. C					

📋 **LIST ▸ 5**

**abet 〔 ə'bɛt 〕 *v.* 唆使；幫助【最常考】

——同 aid , assist , support , encourage

Norman was arrested for ***abetting*** the crime because he allowed the robbers to hide in his house.

諾曼因共犯罪被逮捕，因為他讓搶匪窩藏在他家裡。

* adjunct 〔'ædʒʌŋkt 〕 *n.* 附屬物；伴隨物【常考】

——同 appendix , addition , supplement , complement , accessory

The school president believed that a small garden would be a pleasing ***adjunct*** to the school grounds.

校董認為美麗的小花園可以用來襯托校園。

* altitude 〔'æltə‚tjud 〕 *n.* 高度【常考】   ——同 height , elevation

Mountain climbers often carry oxygen tanks because the air is very thin at high ***altitudes***.

登山者通常會攜帶氧氣筒，因為在極高的地帶空氣相當稀薄。

* archaic 〔 ɑr'keɪk 〕 *adj.* 古老的【常考】

——同 ancient , antique , outdated , obsolete , old

The only source of heat in this old house was an ***archaic*** coal stove.   這棟舊房子內唯一的供熱來源是個古老的煤爐。

banish 〔'bænɪʃ 〕 *v.* 放逐   ——同 exile , dismiss , expel , deport

The ex-president was ***banished*** from his country for life.

前任總統被放逐，終生不得再返回祖國。

canvass 〔'kænvəs 〕 *v.* ①拉票 ②遊說 ③討論

——同 1. solicit votes 2. solicit , beg 3. discuss , examine

Each mayoral candidate sent people to ***canvass*** various areas of the city.   每位市長候選人都派出人馬，到市內各地拉票。

**coalition〔͵koəˈlɪʃən〕*n.* 聯合【最常考】
　　——同 union , alliance , league
　A ***coalition*** of farmers' groups demanded more government support. 農民團體聯盟要求政府給予更多支持。

*conceive〔kənˈsiv〕*v.* 構想【常考】　——同 devise , frame
　The commandos ***conceived*** a complicated plan to rescue the kidnapped diplomat. 　*commando〔kəˈmando〕*n.* 突擊隊
　突擊隊構想出一個複雜的計畫，來拯救被綁架的外交官。

*contract〔kənˈtrækt〕*v.* 收縮【常考】　——同 shrink , narrow , reduce
　The cold weather made the cement in the sidewalk ***contract*** until it finally cracked.
　寒冷的天氣使得人行道的水泥收縮，最後終於龜裂。

deadlock〔ˈdɛd͵lɑk〕*n.* 停頓；僵持　——同 bottleneck , impasse
　The peace talks reached a ***deadlock*** and nothing could be decided. 和平談判陷入僵局，無法做出任何決定。

deride〔dɪˈraɪd〕*v.* 嘲弄　——同 laugh at , mock , sneer , taunt
　You should not ***deride*** children for their failures; you should encourage them to try again.
　你不該嘲弄孩子的失敗，應該鼓勵他們再嘗試。

**discrete〔dɪˈskrit〕*adj.* 個別的；分離的【最常考】
　　——同 separate , distinct , discontinuous
　The different sections of the city are actually quite ***discrete*** and each has its own characteristics.
　這城市內的不同地區事實上相當獨立，各有各的特色。

*elaborate〔ɪˈlæbərɪt〕*adj.* 精巧的【常考】
　　——同 intricate , delicate , painstaking , complicated
　The wedding dress was very ***elaborate*** and took many weeks to make. 這套婚紗的設計非常精細，費時許多星期來製作。

enhance〔ɪnˈhæns〕v. 加強

——同 intensify , strengthen , heighten , advance , augment

This new fax machine will **enhance** interoffice communications.　這部新的傳真機將加強辦公室間的通訊。

ethnology〔ɛθˈnɑlədʒɪ〕n. 民族學

——同 study of races

Dr. Henderson is a famous expert on Asian **ethnology**.
韓德森博士是著名的亞洲民族學專家。

facsimile〔fækˈsɪməlɪ〕n. 摹寫；複製

——同 likeness , duplicate , copy , replica

Gordon's painting was an almost perfect **facsimile** of the original.　戈登的畫簡直像原作的翻版。

Exercise 〉 *Fill in the blanks.*

1. Mr. Warren was arrested for _____ enemy soldiers.

2. In some cultures, criminals are _____ from the community and forced to live in the wilderness.

3. Because none of us could _____ of a better idea, we all agreed to Sally's plan.

4. A suggestion to bring in a mediator broke the _____ between the workers' union and company management.

5. Charlie bought a machine that is supposed to _____ the sound quality of his computer.

【解答】 1. abetting　2. banished　3. conceive　4. deadlock　5. enhance

foible 〔 'fɔɪbl̩ 〕 *n.* 缺點；弱點
—— 同 weakness , shortcoming , whimsy
Talking too much is one of Jack's *foibles* that I find a little annoying. 我覺得饒舌是傑克讓人感到厭煩的小缺點之一。

gasp 〔 gæsp 〕 *v.* 喘息 —— 同 pant , puff , heave
Anna *gasped* for breath after she swam up from the bottom of the pool. 安娜從池底游上水面後喘氣呼吸。

haphazard 〔 'hæp'hæzəd 〕 *adj.* 偶然的；隨便的
—— 同 accidental , incidental , unplanned , unorganized
Ethan made a *haphazard* attempt to find his lost watch, but gave up after only few minutes.
伊森嘗試隨便找找他遺失的錶，但沒幾分鐘後就放棄了。

illicit 〔 ɪ'lɪsɪt 〕 *adj.* 非法的 —— 同 illegal , illegitimate
The *illicit* sale of alcohol to minors is becoming a problem in our area. 非法販賣酒類給未成年人成為本地的問題。

* **incredulous** 〔 ɪn'krɛdʒələs 〕 *adj.* 懷疑的【常考】
—— 同 skeptical , doubtful , distrustful , suspicious , dubious
Melissa was *incredulous* that Sam would remember to pay this month's bills on time.
梅麗莎懷疑山姆是否會記得準時付這個月的帳單。

** **insatiable** 〔 ɪn'seʃɪəbl̩ 〕 *adj.* 貪婪的【最常考】
—— 同 greedy , voracious
Nothing seemed to satisfy Brian's *insatiable* appetite.
似乎沒有東西可以滿足布萊恩貪婪的口腹之慾。

jubilant 〔 'dʒublənt 〕 *adj.* 喜悅的
—— 同 overjoyed , rejoicing , enraptured , elated
We were *jubilant* at the news that Carla had been accepted at the university. 知道卡拉獲准入大學，我們都感到喜悅。

languid 〔ˈlæŋgwɪd〕 *adj.* 無精神的

　　—同 weak , weary , sluggish , inert , lethargic , drooping

The incredible summer heat and humidity made us all feel *languid*. 夏天超乎想像的熱氣與濕度，讓大家都覺得無精打采。

* **lust** 〔lʌst〕 *n.* 欲望【常考】

　　—同 desire , sensuality , avarice , carnality

The *lust* he felt for her seemed to take over his entire thought process. 他對她的愛慾似乎佔據了他所有的思緒。

** **malice** 〔ˈmælɪs〕 *n.* 怨恨【最常考】　　—同 spite , ill will , animosity

After their argument, the *malice* between Teri and Fred seemed to grow. 爭吵之後，泰瑞和弗瑞德間的怨恨似乎又加深了。

metropolitan 〔ˌmɛtrəˈpɑlətn̩〕 *adj.* 大都市的

　　—同 civil , urban , city-wide

Shanghai is one of the largest *metropolitan* areas in the world. 上海是世界上最大的大都會之一。

nefarious 〔nɪˈfɛrɪəs〕 *adj.* 邪惡的

　　—同 heinous , wicked , vicious , villainous , evil , atrocious

The bomber's *nefarious* deed destroyed many innocent lives. 轟炸員邪惡的行為摧毀了許多無辜的性命。

obscene 〔əbˈsin〕 *adj.* 猥褻的

　　—同 indecent , filthy , foul , lewd , dirty

The protesters shouted some *obscene* remarks at the police officers. 抗議人士向警官叫喊一些猥褻的詞語。

* **outburst** 〔ˈaʊtˌbɝst〕 *n.* 爆發【常考】

　　—同 eruption , explosion , blowup

A sudden *outburst* of fighting among rival soccer fans developed into a riot.

一場突發的對立足球迷間的鬥毆，演變成了暴動。

＊panacea 〔ˌpænəˈsiə〕 *n.* 萬靈藥【最常考】

　　——同 cure-all , universal remedy

Although this drug will help some cancer patients, it is not a
panacea. 雖然這藥可幫助一些癌症患者，但卻不是萬靈藥。

patricide 〔ˈpætrɪˌsaɪd , ˈpetrɪ- 〕 *n.* 弒父罪

When a will was discovered near the man's dead body,
patricide was suspected.
當男屍旁的遺囑被發現時，人們便懷疑這是一椿弒父案。

＊perplex 〔 pəˈplɛks 〕 *v.* 使困惑【常考】

　　——同 puzzle , baffle , bewilder , confound

We were *perplexed* by John's peculiar behavior.
我們對約翰奇異的行徑感到困惑。

Exercise ＞ *Fill in the blanks.*

1. I was ＿＿＿＿＿＿ that Paul had actually drawn the sketch
   because it was not like his style.

2. Tess was exhausted, and each of her steps seemed more
   ＿＿＿＿＿＿ than the last.

3. Although the two of them have petty arguments frequently,
   there is no real ＿＿＿＿＿＿ between them.

4. The subway system covers the entire ＿＿＿＿＿＿ area of
   Washington DC.

5. We were all ＿＿＿＿＿＿ as to how to repair the microwave
   oven.

【解答】1. incredulous　2. languid　3. malice　4. metropolitan　5. perplexed

* **priority** 〔 praɪˈɔrətɪ 〕 *n.* ①在前 ②優先權【常考】
—— 同 1. antecedent 2. preference , greater importance
Getting food to the famine victims is a ***priority*** for the relief
workers. 提供飢荒難民食物是救難人員的首要工作。

* **quiescent** 〔 kwaɪˈɛsn̩t 〕 *adj.* 安靜的【常考】
—— 同 still , motionless , fixed , stationary
Stan stared for hours at the ***quiescent*** scene of the Japanese
rock garden. 史丹觀賞寧靜的日本岩石花園景色達數小時。

random 〔ˈrændəm 〕 *adj.* 隨便的；無目的的
—— 同 casual , haphazard , fortuitous , unplanned
It was hard to find the CD I wanted because the store clerks
had put all the CD's in ***random*** order.
想找到我要的 CD 很困難，因為店員把所有的 CD 隨便擺放。

retrospect 〔ˈrɛtrəˌspɛkt 〕 *n.* 回顧
—— 同 reminiscence , reflection , remembrance , review
This movie is a ***retrospect*** on the life of Sun Yat-sen.
這部電影對孫逸仙的一生作了回顧。

** **reverberate** 〔 rɪˈvɝbəˌret 〕 *v.* 回響【最常考】
—— 同 echo , rebound , resound
The music coming from the great organ ***reverberated*** through
the entire church. 從大風琴傳出的音樂聲在整座教堂回響。

* **sanitary** 〔ˈsænəˌtɛrɪ 〕 *adj.* 衛生的【常考】
—— 同 hygienic , clean , sterilized , germfree , safe
Hospitals must keep everything ***sanitary*** to prevent the spread
of germs. 醫院裡所有的東西都必須保持衛生，以杜絕病菌滋生。

sever 〔ˈsɛvɚ 〕 *v.* 切斷 —— 同 separate , cut off , cleave
The road workers accidentally ***severed*** a water pipe.
馬路工人不小心切斷了一條水管。

smudge 〔 smʌdʒ 〕 *n.* 污點　　——同 smear, soil, blotch, stain

You have a *smudge* of chocolate on your shirt.

你的襯衫上沾了巧克力的污點。

squander 〔'skwɑndə 〕 *v.* 浪費　　——同 waste, dissipate

Kevin was broke because he had *squandered* all his money
gambling. 凱文破產了，因為他把所有的錢浪費在賭博上。

stripe 〔 straɪp 〕 *n.* 條紋　　——同 line, streak, band

Eric bought a new shirt that has green and yellow *stripes* on it.

艾瑞克買了一件黃綠條紋相間的新襯衫。

surplus 〔'sɝplʌs 〕 *n.* 剩餘

——同 excess, remainder, oversupply

The farmer decided to sell some of his corn *surplus* instead
of storing it. 農夫決定將部分剩餘的玉米出售而不庫存。

*tantamount 〔'tæntə,maʊnt 〕 *adj.* 相等的【最常考】

——同 equivalent, equal

The wages workers earn in that factory are *tantamount* to
nothing. 那家工廠工人的收入幾乎是零。

tint 〔 tɪnt 〕 *n.* 色彩　　——同 hue, tinge

Norma would like her new car to have a green *tint*.

諾馬想要一部綠色的新車。

uncanny 〔 ʌn'kænɪ 〕 *adj.* 不可思議的

——同 fantastic, mysterious, eerie, unearthly, weird

Walter has the *uncanny* ability to know when the boss is
going to call a meeting.

瓦特有不可思議的能力，能知道老闆何時要召開會議。

﹡**vanquish**〔'væŋkwɪʃ〕*v.* 克服【最常考】

——同 crush , conquer , overcome , overwhelm

The Roman army was very strong and **vanquished** peoples in Europe, Africa and the Middle East.

羅馬軍隊極爲強大，征服了歐洲、非洲及中東的民族。

wane〔wen〕*v.* 虧缺 ——同 decrease , lessen , ebb

The moon **wanes** to a thin crescent every month.

月亮每月會漸虧爲下弦月。 ﹡crescent〔'krɛsn̩t〕*n.* 新月

﹡**zealot**〔'zɛlət〕*n.* 狂熱者【最常考】

——同 devotee , fan , partisan , believer

Many religious **zealots** will do nearly anything to gain converts. 許多宗敎狂熱者會無所不用其極來吸收信徒。

﹡convert〔'kɑnvɜt〕*n.* 皈依者

Exercise > *Fill in the blanks.*

1. In _____, I realized that I had been wrong in ending my friendship with Julie.

2. He was a careless worker, and the machine he was working with suddenly _____ his hand.

3. The resemblance between the two men is absolutely _____.

4. Genghis Khan _____ most of Asia, establishing the Mongol Empire.

5. Mr. Harris is a _____ when it comes to the idea of cleanliness.

【解答】1. retrospect　2. severed　3. uncanny　4. vanquished　5. zealot

· List 5 · 難字分析

adjunct 〔ˈædʒʌŋkt 〕 *n.* 附屬物；伴隨物

ad + junct
| |
to + join

— a thing added to something else, but secondary or not essential to it

altitude 〔ˈæltəˌtjud 〕 *n.* 高度

alt + itude
| |
high + n.

— height

elaborate 〔 ɪˈlæbərɪt 〕 *adj.* 精巧的

e + labor + ate
ex | |
| | |
out + work + adj.

— worked out with much care and in great detail

facsimile 〔 fækˈsɪməlɪ 〕 *n.* 摹寫；複製

fac + simile
| |
do + like

— exact reproduction or copy

illicit 〔 ɪˈlɪsɪt 〕 *adj.* 非法的

il + lic + it
in | |
| | |
not + allow + adj.

— not allowed by law

incredulous〔ɪn'krɛdʒələs〕*adj.* 懷疑的

in + cred + ulous — showing doubt or disbelief
| | |
not + *believe* + *adj.*

insatiable〔ɪn'seʃɪəbl̩〕*adj.* 貪婪的

in + sati + able — that cannot be satisfied
| | |
not + *full* + *able to*

nefarious〔nɪ'fɛrɪəs〕*adj.* 邪惡的

ne + fari + ous — very wicked
| | |
not + *speak* + *adj.*

panacea〔ˌpænə'siə〕*n.* 萬靈藥

pan + acea — remedy for all diseases
| |
all + *cure, remedy*

retrospect〔'rɛtrəˌspɛkt〕*n.* 回顧

retro + spect — the act of looking back towards
| | the past
backward + *look*

sanitary〔'sænəˌtɛrɪ〕*adj.* 衛生的

san + it(y) + ary — free from danger to health
| | |
healthy + *n.* + *adj.*

📖 LIST ▸ 6

abiding 〔 ə'baɪdɪŋ 〕 *adj.* 永久的；持續性的

—— 同 lasting , perpetual , enduring , continual , never-ending

Her *abiding* love for painting led her to teach art to children.

對繪畫的永久愛好使她走向兒童美教之途。

∗admonish 〔 əd'mɑnɪʃ 〕 *v.* 勸告【最常考】

—— 同 advise , reprove

The teacher *admonished* the students for their rude behavior in class. 老師勸誡學生課堂上的魯莽行為。

amass 〔 ə'mæs 〕 *v.* 積聚；收集

—— 同 collect , gather , accumulate , heap , aggregate

After twenty years, Jill had *amassed* a huge collection of foreign coins. 二十年來吉兒已收藏了許多外國硬幣。

archive 〔 'ɑrkaɪv 〕 *n.* 檔案；紀錄

—— 同 record , file , chronicle , annals

The library has a historical map *archive* that many historians find very interesting.

許多歷史學家認為該圖書館的史學地圖集非常有趣。

∗banter 〔 'bæntɚ 〕 *v.* 嘲弄【最常考】

—— 同 joke , tease , deride , jeer , ridicule

We *bantered* for a few minutes before going into the meeting.

我們開了一陣子玩笑才去開會。

∗ captivity 〔 kæp'tɪvətɪ 〕 *n.* 監禁【常考】

—— 同 imprisonment , confinement , bondage

The years the playwright spent in *captivity* made him love freedom even more. 監禁數年使劇作家更愛好自由。

* **coherent** 〔koˈhɪrənt〕 *adj.* ①一致的 ②黏在一起的【常考】

—— 同 1. logical , consistent , rational , orderly 2. adhesive, tenacious

Mary had become so feverish that nothing she said was
coherent. 瑪麗的高燒嚴重得使她語無倫次。

conciliatory 〔kənˈsɪlɪəˌtorɪ〕 *adj.* 安撫的

—— 同 reconciliatory , pacificatory , placatory

After their argument, Patrick made a ***conciliatory*** gesture by
sending Jane flowers. 吵架後，派屈克藉著送花的舉動來安撫珍。

contrast 〔ˈkɑntræst〕 *n.* 差異；對照

—— 同 difference , opposition , disparity , dissimilarity

The ***contrast*** between my opinions and my brother's is
striking. 我和哥哥的意見差異相當大。

****dearth** 〔dɝθ〕 *n.* 缺乏【最常考】   —— 同 lack , shortage , scarcity

There is a ***dearth*** of parking places in Taipei.
台北缺乏停車位。

* **derivative** 〔dəˈrɪvətɪv〕 *n.* ; *adj.* 衍生之物（的）【常考】

—— 同 (*n.*) development , outgrowth , byproduct

This type of dance is a ***derivative*** of the traditional dancing
found in Chinese opera.
該舞蹈是從中國傳統京劇身段中衍生來的。

disdain 〔dɪsˈden〕 *v.* 輕蔑   —— 同 despise , scorn , spurn

Rebecca ***disdains*** the idea of having to arrive home by
10:00 PM. 芮貝卡對晚上十點前必須回家的想法嗤之以鼻。

elapse 〔ɪˈlæps〕 *v.* 經過；消逝

—— 同 pass , slip away , glide by , lapse

Years ***elapsed*** before Tony and Paula saw each other again.
經過數年後，湯尼和寶拉再度見面。

enigma 〔 ɪˋnɪgmə 〕 *n.* 謎

——同 puzzle , riddle , mystery

Philosophers enjoy thinking about *enigmas* that seem impossible to understand. 哲學家喜歡思考難以理解的謎。

etiquette 〔ˋɛtɪkɛt 〕 *n.* 禮節

——同 manners , formalities , decorum

Every culture has its own rules of table *etiquette*.
每種文化都有自己的餐桌禮儀。

* faction 〔ˋfækʃən 〕 *n.* 黨派【常考】

——同 clique , sect , party , denomination

Disputes between different *factions* of the party finally led to its fall. 黨內派系的鬥爭終於導致黨的瓦解。

Exercise > *Fill in the blanks.*

1. When our mothers met, they _____ about all the embarrassing things we had done as children.

2. Some people oppose keeping animals in _____.

3. Pauline _____ working for such a corrupt company, so she quit her job.

4. During the dinner party, you will be expected to follow rules of proper _____.

5. A conservative _____ broke with the main party and formed a new political party.

【解答】1. bantered   2. captivity   3. disdained   4. etiquette   5. faction

foliage 〔'folɪɪdʒ 〕 *n.* 樹葉　——圓 leaves , leafage

In fall, I like to visit the mountains because the *foliage* there turns such vivid colors.

在秋天，我喜歡去山區，因為那裡的樹葉會變成很鮮豔的顏色。

gauge 〔 gedʒ 〕 *v.* 測量

——圓 measure , estimate , evaluate , rate , assess

Our boss *gauges* how productive our department is through the sales of computers every month.

老闆以每月電腦的銷售量，來估計本部門的生產力。

* **harass** 〔'hærəs , hə'ræs 〕 *v.* 侵擾【常考】

——圓 trouble , disturb , annoy , plague , pester , vex

The manager *harassed* the new salesperson until he quit.

經理不斷地折磨新來的銷售員，直到他離職為止。

* **imbibe** 〔 ɪm'baɪb 〕 *v.* 吸入【常考】

——圓 drink , absorb , suck , swallow , receive

Ellis invited me to *imbibe* some of his expensive wine after dinner. 晚餐後，艾利斯邀我品嚐一些他的高級葡萄酒。

indemnify 〔 ɪn'dɛmnə,faɪ 〕 *v.* 賠償

——圓 secure , save , compensate , reimburse , remunerate

The government promised to *indemnify* the victims of the restaurant fire. 政府允諾賠償餐廳火災的受害者。

insert 〔 ɪn's3t 〕 *v.* 插入　——圓 inset , inject , stuff in

The doctor *inserted* a small tube into the patient's stomach to feed him. 醫生以小管插入病人的胃來餵食。

* **judicious** 〔 dʒu'dɪʃəs 〕 *adj.* 明智的【常考】

——圓 sensible , sage , sagacious , wise

I believe Laura is very *judicious* as she saves her money in the bank. 我認為蘿拉很明智，因為她把錢存在銀行裡。

lateral 〔ˈlætərəl 〕 *adj.* 側面的　——同 side, flanking, sideward
The *lateral* sides of the house were made of brick, while the front and back were wooden.
這棟房子的側邊是磚造的，而前後卻是木製的。

****malign** 〔 məˈlaɪn 〕 ① *v.* 誹謗　② *adj.* 有害的【最常考】
——同 1. defame, libel, disparage　2. harmful, malignant, vicious
His *malign* actions were finally punished by the judge.
他的惡行終究被法官懲處。

migrate 〔ˈmaɪgret 〕 *v.* 移居　——同 journey, travel
In the 1800's many Americans *migrated* west to find land for farming.　1800 年代，許多美國人往西遷徙找尋農耕地。

munificent 〔 mjuˈnɪfəsn̩t 〕 *adj.* 慷慨的
——同 generous, bounteous, liberal, beneficent, bountiful
The old man's *munificent* donation to the hospital was highly appreciated.　老人對醫院慷慨的捐贈贏得高度感謝。

negative 〔ˈnɛgətɪv 〕 *adj.* 否定的
——同 refusing, denying, dissenting
Carol's *negative* response meant that she did not want to go camping with them.　卡蘿的否定答覆表示她不想和他們去露營。

obscure 〔 əbˈskjur 〕 *adj.* 模糊的；微暗的
——同 faint, shadowy, gloomy, veiled, blurred
At sunset, we saw the *obscure* figure of a person entering the building.　在日落時，我們看到一個朦朧的身影進入大樓。

outcry 〔ˈaʊtˌkraɪ 〕 *n.* 叫喊
——同 clamor, tumult, shout, exclamation
There was an *outcry* against the banning of the book.
該書遭禁引起了一陣反對聲浪。

panorama 〔,pænəˈræmə 〕 *n.* 全景
——同 scene , vista , sight , view
From the top of this building you can see a wonderful
panorama of New York City.
從這棟建築物的樓頂，你可以看到紐約市美麗的全景。

* **persistent** 〔 pəˈzɪstənt , -ˈsɪst- 〕 *adj.* 持續性的【常考】
——同 lasting , immovable , immutable , insistent , persevering
She was *persistent* in her search for her lost puppy.
她一直在找尋遺失的小狗。

poll 〔 pol 〕 *n.* 投票　　——同 survey
A *poll* of city residents showed that over half of them
approved of building a new park.
市民投票顯示，超過半數的人同意設立新公園。

Exercise ＞ *Fill in the blanks.*

1. A newspaper questionnaire _____ readers' opinions
   on the proposed nuclear plant.

2. During our camping trip we were constantly _____
   by swarms of mosquitoes.

3. The fishermen's boats approached the docks, heavy with
   the day's _____ catch.

4. The town down in the valley appeared _____ in the
   dim light of the moon.

5. Our class conducted a _____ to measure students'
   approval of the president.

【解答】1. gauged　2. harassed　3. munificent　4. obscure　5. poll

* **probity** 〔ˈprobətɪ〕 *n.* 正直；廉潔【常考】

—— 同 integrity , honesty , uprightness , rectitude

The lawyer's clients always appreciated the **probity** with which she represented their cases.

該律師的客戶對她受理案件時的廉潔表現，均表讚賞。

** **quixotic** 〔kwɪksˈɑtɪk〕 *adj.* 幻想的；不實際的【最常考】

—— 同 visionary , unrealistic , whimsical , crazy

Everyone thinks he is a **quixotic** dreamer because he hopes to one day live in a space station.

每個人都認為他是個不切實際的幻想家，竟夢想有一天能居住在外太空。

rankle 〔ˈræŋkl̩〕 *v.* 使心痛 —— 同 irritate , fester , gall

It **rankles** me that Scott never apologizes when he does something wrong. 史考特從不認錯道歉，真是令我心痛。

reminiscence 〔ˌrɛməˈnɪsn̩s〕 *n.* 回憶

—— 同 memory , remembrance , recollection

Diana shared her **reminiscences** of her trip around the world with me. 黛安娜和我分享她環遊世界的回憶。

reverence 〔ˈrɛvərəns〕 *n.* 尊敬

—— 同 respect , honor , adoration , veneration , worship

The memorial statue was erected out of **reverence** for the founder of the country. 該紀念雕像是為了向建國者致敬而豎立的。

sapient 〔ˈsepɪənt〕 *adj.* 有智慧的

—— 同 wise , intelligent , sage , sagacious , knowledgeable

If you follow her **sapient** advice, you will be sure to succeed.

如果你遵照她明智的建言，你一定能成功。

severe 〔səˈvɪr〕 *adj.* 嚴厲的 —— 同 strict , harsh , tough , rigid

In some countries, the penalty for theft is very **severe**.

在某些國家，竊盜罪的刑罰是相當嚴厲的。

snarl〔snɑrl〕*v.* 咆哮 ——同 growl , grumble

When the guard dog ***snarled***, the man got so scared that he didn't move. 當守衛犬咆哮時，該名男子嚇得不敢動彈。

* **squash**〔skwɑʃ〕*v.* 壓扁【常考】

——同 crush , mash , squeeze , flatten

The children's ball rolled out into the street and was ***squashed*** by a passing car. 孩子們的球滾到馬路上，被一輛行駛過的車給壓扁了。

** **strive**〔straɪv〕*v.* 努力【最常考】 ——同 endeavor , strain , struggle

Once you choose your goal in life, you should ***strive*** to achieve it. 一旦你選擇了人生目標，就該努力去達成。

surreptitious〔ˌsɝəp'tɪʃəs〕*adj.* 秘密的

——同 stealthy , furtive , sneaky , secret

The reporter was told that ***surreptitious*** bribes were being given to officials. 該名記者被告知秘密賄款給了官員。

tap〔tæp〕① *v.* 輕敲 ② *n.* 龍頭

——同 1. pat , knock , rap , strike 2. faucet , valve , outlet

Peter ***tapped*** on Clair's window to get her attention as he walked by her office.

彼得經過克萊兒的辦公室時，輕敲窗戶引起她的注意。

* **tyro**〔'taɪro〕*n.* 初學者；新手【常考】

——同 beginner , novice , learner

Otis' computer class is for older ***tyros*** who are terrified of using a computer. 歐提的電腦課程是開給懼怕使用電腦的年老初學者。

ulterior〔ʌl'tɪrɪə〕*adj.* 隱秘的 ——同 hidden , secret , concealed

Do you think Dean has any ***ulterior*** motives in buying me a new microwave oven?

你認爲狄恩買新的微波爐給我，是有什麼隱秘的動機嗎？

vapid 〔'væpɪd〕 *adj.* 無味的；無趣的

—— 同 insipid , flavorless , flat , uninteresting

Ethan loves kung-fu movies, but Joe thinks they are just *vapid* entertainment.

伊森喜歡功夫電影，但喬卻認爲那是無趣的娛樂。

wanton 〔'wɑntən〕 *adj.* 放縱的；胡亂的

—— 同 lewd , loose , lustful , reckless , wild

The youths showed their *wanton* disrespect for the law by drinking in public.

這些年輕人公然飲酒，表現他們對法律的蔑視。

* **zenith** 〔'zinɪθ〕 *n.* 頂點【常考】

—— 同 top , summit , peak , apex , pinnacle , acme

After climbing for days, the mountain climbers reached the *zenith*. 攀爬數天後，這些登山者抵達到山頂。

Exercise > *Fill in the blanks.*

1. The entertaining, _____ novel I have just read was hard to put down.

2. I love listening to my grandmother's _____ about life when she was a young woman.

3. Angela _____ for perfection in everything she does.

4. Some people find vegetarian diets _____ and soon give them up.

5. Joyce is an actress at the _____ of her career.

【解答】1. quixotic   2. reminiscences   3. strives   4. vapid   5. zenith

· List 6 · 難字分析

admonish 〔 əd'manɪʃ 〕 *v.* 勸告

ad + mon + ish
to + advise + v.

—— give a mild warning or a gentle reproof

coherent 〔 ko'hɪrənt 〕 *adj.* ①一致的 ②黏在一起的

co + her + ent
con
together + stick + adj.

—— being naturally or reasonably connected; sticking together

derivative 〔 də'rɪvətɪv 〕 *n.* ; *adj.* 衍生之物（的）

de + riv + ative
from + river + adj., n.

—— something coming from another; not original

elapse 〔 ɪ'læps 〕 *v.* 經過；消逝

e + lapse
ex
out + slip

—— (of time) to pass away

judicious 〔 dʒu'dɪʃəs 〕 *adj.* 明智的

judic + ious
judge + adj.

—— having or showing sound judgment

migrate 〔'maɪgret 〕 v. 移居

migr + ate
remove + make

—— to move from one place to another

munificent 〔 mju'nɪfəsn̩t 〕 adj. 慷慨的

muni + fic + ent
public service + do + adj.

—— very generous in giving

panorama 〔ˌpænə'ræmə 〕 n. 全景

pan + orama
all + view

——wide and complete view

reminiscence 〔ˌrɛmə'nɪsn̩s 〕 n. 回憶

re + min + iscence
again + think + n.

—— the act of remembering or recollecting past experiences

surreptitious 〔ˌsɜ˞əp'tɪʃəs 〕 adj. 秘密的

sur + rept + itious
super		
over + creep + adj.

—— done secretly or stealthily

TEST ▶ 3

請由 (A)～(D) 中選出和畫線部分意義最相近的字。

1. These materials are <u>adjuncts</u> to the main text that will be used in class.
   - (A) requirements
   - (B) decorations
   - (C) necessities
   - (D) supplements

2. While digging for the house's foundation, the workers discovered several <u>archaic</u> tools.
   - (A) reliable
   - (B) ancient
   - (C) apparent
   - (D) artistic

3. Although he was <u>derided</u> by the other boys, Joe continued his ballet classes.
   - (A) revered
   - (B) taunted
   - (C) ignored
   - (D) misunderstood

4. The pathetic dog she found on the street had not eaten in days and had an <u>insatiable</u> appetite.
   - (A) slight
   - (B) voracious
   - (C) particular
   - (D) distinct

5. The manager wants a <u>facsimile</u> of the document you sent to the office in Tokyo.
   - (A) copy
   - (B) relative
   - (C) record
   - (D) memo

6. The newspaper reporter uncovered the CEO's <u>illicit</u> dealings with the Mafia.
   - (A) superficial
   - (B) illegal
   - (C) surprising
   - (D) obvious

7. The priest gave the young people a speech about the evils of <u>lust</u>.
   - (A) enjoyment
   - (B) reciprocity
   - (C) carnality
   - (D) living

8. A <u>nefarious</u> plot to gas bomb the legislature was discovered by the federal police.
   - (A) atrocious
   - (B) humble
   - (C) irrelevant
   - (D) nascent

9. One <u>priority</u> in becoming an industrialized nation is developing a large supply of skilled labor.

    (A) afterthought
    (B) interest
    (C) relation
    (D) antecedence

10. I can't believe you <u>squander</u> all your free time playing video games.

    (A) enjoy
    (B) spend
    (C) waste
    (D) save

11. The country's <u>abiding</u> love for its founder can be seen in the many memorial statues around the country.

    (A) enduring
    (B) fluctuating
    (C) normative
    (D) superior

12. This kind of tree has dense <u>foliage</u> and provides a lot of shade in the summer.

    (A) bark
    (B) branches
    (C) flowers
    (D) leafage

13. You cannot be <u>haphazard</u> about doing scientific research.

    (A) dedicated
    (B) ignorant
    (C) silly
    (D) unorganized

14. The sunglasses Marsha bought have a slight blue <u>tint</u> in the frame.

    (A) bend
    (B) tinge
    (C) light
    (D) line

15. It is an <u>enigma</u> why she would want to go on a date with that ill-mannered boy.

    (A) surprise
    (B) joy
    (C) mystery
    (D) excuse

16. Dan advised me to make a <u>conciliatory</u> gesture to Linda after the disagreement we had last night.

    (A) responsible
    (B) definite
    (C) placatory
    (D) humble

17. Do you believe that not revealing the truth is <u>tantamount</u> to lying?

    (A) equivalent
    (B) enhanced
    (C) superior
    (D) related

18. The entire family treated my grandmother with special <u>reverence</u>.

    (A) veneration
    (B) curiosity
    (C) understanding
    (D) fear

19. After the earthquake, the insurance company did not have the funds to <u>indemnify</u> all the insured victims.

    (A) protect
    (B) identify
    (C) remunerate
    (D) locate

20. Walter asked that his friends join him in <u>imbibing</u> in one of his vineyards' wines.

    (A) drinking
    (B) smelling
    (C) observing
    (D) pouring

21. Club members elected Jack Gates to be the club treasurer because they felt he was a man of <u>probity</u>.

    (A) wealth
    (B) intelligence
    (C) creativity
    (D) rectitude

22. Superman <u>squashed</u> the steel rod with a single stomp of his foot.

    (A) mashed
    (B) created
    (C) damaged
    (D) softened

23. The photographer used her camera to capture the beautiful <u>panorama</u> of the Hong Kong skyline.

    (A) buildings
    (B) people
    (C) flavor
    (D) vista

24. Joan made a <u>surreptitious</u> run to the bank from her office during work hours.

    (A) obvious
    (B) quick
    (C) stealthy
    (D) unnecessary

25. The quiet gathering suddenly turned into a <u>wanton</u> party when Alan and his friends arrived.

    (A) reserved
    (B) wild
    (C) undesirable
    (D) boring

【解答】

1. D	2. B	3. B	4. B	5. A	6. B	7. C	8. A	9. D	10. C
11. A	12. D	13. D	14. B	15. C	16. C	17. A	18. A	19. C	20. A
21. D	22. A	23. D	24. C	25. B					

LIST ▸ 7

abolish〔əˈbalɪʃ〕*v.* 廢除　──同 annul, abrogate, wipe out
In the United States, slavery was ***abolished*** during the Civil War.　美國的蓄奴制度在南北戰爭時廢除了。

adopt〔əˈdɑpt〕*v.* ①接受；採用　②收養
──同 1. embrace, accept　2. foster, take in
Our company has ***adopted*** the practice of allowing workers more flexible hours.
本公司已採行讓員工有更多彈性上班時數的辦法。

amateur〔ˈæməˌtʃur〕*n.* 業餘者
──同 nonprofessional, dilettante, hobbyist
This tennis competition is for ***amateurs*** only; no professionals are allowed to participate.
該網球比賽只提供給業餘者；職業選手不准參加。

**arduous〔ˈardʒuəs〕*adj.* 費力的【最常考】
──同 laborious, toilsome, onerous, strenuous, difficult
Because construction work can be very ***arduous***, few people want that kind of job.
因爲建築工作可能會很辛苦，所以很少人想從事這行業。

barren〔ˈbærən〕*adj.* 不毛的
──同 unproductive, infertile, sterile, desolate
Many people moved away from the village because the farmland there had become ***barren***.
許多人搬離該村莊，因爲那裡的土地已貧瘠。

*carve〔karv〕*v.* 刻【常考】　──同 cut, sculpture, slice
The sculptor ***carved*** a figure of a sitting boy out of stone.
這名雕刻家用石頭刻了一尊站立的男童像。

coin 〔 kɔɪn 〕 *v.* 鑄造；編造　——同 create , invent , mold , fabricate
Physicists call that particle a "quark," a nonsense word
coined by a famous Irish author.
物理學家稱該粒子爲「夸克」，這字沒有任何含義，是一位著名的愛爾
蘭作家編造出來的。

contrive 〔 kən'traɪv 〕 *v.* 構想；設計
　——同 devise , construct , design , concoct , fabricate
The children *contrived* a pulley to lift things into their tree
house.　這些小孩設計了一個滑輪，將東西吊進樹上的屋子。
＊pulley 〔'pʊlɪ 〕 *n.* 滑輪

coy 〔 kɔɪ 〕 *adj.* 嬌羞的　——同 bashful , reserved , shy
He was charmed by the young woman's *coy* smile.
他被這名年輕女子嬌羞的笑容迷住了。

decay 〔 dɪ'ke 〕 *v.* 衰退；腐爛　——同 rot , decline , degenerate
Their family situation *decayed* to the point where they
argued with each other all the time.
他們的家庭狀況惡化到大家無時無刻都在爭吵。

＊**descent** 〔 dɪ'sɛnt 〕 *n.* 降落【常考】　——同 fall , drop , comedown
The plane's *descent* was very rough, and many of the
passengers were frightened.　飛機猛然降落，許多乘客都嚇壞了。

disgust 〔 dɪs'gʌst 〕 *v.* 使厭惡　——同 nauseate , sicken , offend
The smell of rotten fish *disgusts* me.
腐壞的魚的味道令我作噁。

elastic 〔 ɪ'læstɪk 〕 *adj.* 彈性的　——同 flexible , pliable , adaptable
Most bathing suits are made of an *elastic* material that
allows the suit to stretch.
大部分的泳衣是由彈性質料製成，使得泳衣具伸縮性。

enlist〔ɪn'lɪst〕v. 入伍；徵募

── 同 enroll, engage, join, sign up, register

Gary did not want to **enlist** in the army, but he felt it was his duty. 蓋瑞並不想入伍，但他覺得他有義務。

eulogy〔'julədʒɪ〕n. 頌辭；頌揚

── 同 compliment, glorification, tribute, commendation

Mr. Garth gave a long **eulogy** about their achievements in the research. 葛斯先生對他們的研究成果大大地頌揚了一番。

fake〔fek〕n. 贋品

── 同 copy, fraud, imitation, phony

You can tell that watch is a **fake** because the words carved on the back are misspelled.

你可以看出這錶是贋品，因為刻在背面的字拼錯了。

> **Exercise** Fill in the blanks.

1. Mainland China has decided to _____ a five-day work week.

2. The _____ desert is not an inviting place for people to live.

3. Sam's and Mary's mutual friends _____ a plan to get the two of them out on a date.

4. The smell of cigarette smoke really _____ me.

5. Merchants in the night market have every kind of name brand _____ you can think of.

【解答】1. adopt 2. barren 3. contrived 4. disgusts 5. fake

foolproof 〔'ful,pruf 〕 *adj.* 極簡單的；安全無比的
——同 certain , guaranteed , infallible

Jenny has a *foolproof* plan to get Colin's hat back from Billy.

珍妮有個簡單的法子，可把柯林的帽子從比利那兒拿回來。

gaunt 〔 gɔnt 〕 *adj.* 骨瘦如柴的；憔悴的
——同 bony , lean , haggard

Many people criticize fashion designers for using *gaunt* models to display their clothes.

許多人批評服裝設計師以骨瘦如柴的模特兒來展示服裝。

* **harsh** 〔 harʃ 〕 *adj.* 嚴厲的；（天氣）惡劣的【常考】
——同 rough , severe , stern

Some people from Taiwan cannot adjust to the *harsh* winters in Canada.　一些來自台灣的人無法適應加拿大的嚴冬。

* **imitate** 〔'ɪmə,tet 〕 *v.* 模仿【常考】
——同 mimic , copy , ape , simulate

When my sister and I were very young, my sister would *imitate* everything I did.

在我和妹妹還小的時候，她會模仿我的一舉一動。

* **inquisitive** 〔 ɪn'kwɪzətɪv 〕 *adj.* 好奇的；好問的【常考】
——同 curious , inquiring , questioning , prying

Harriet's *inquisitive* mind led her to become a research scientist.

海瑞特的好奇心使她成爲一名從事研究的科學家。

insinuate 〔 ɪn'sɪnju,et 〕 *v.* 暗示
——同 suggest , hint , imply

Are you *insinuating* that I am the one who stole Andy's radio?

你在暗示是我偷了安迪的收音機嗎？

* **jurisdiction**〔͵dʒurɪsˋdɪkʃən〕*n.* 管轄權；裁判權【常考】

   ——同 judicial right , prerogative , legal right

Once the thief's car went across the state border, our state police had no *jurisdiction* to follow him.

一旦竊賊的車越過州界，本州的警方便無權跟蹤他。

* **latent**〔ˋletn̩t〕*adj.* 潛在的；潛伏的【最常考】

   ——同 concealed , hidden , veiled , lurking , underlying

The *latent* cause of crime is often poverty.

貧窮常是犯罪的潛在因子。

laud〔lɔd〕*v.* 褒獎；讚美　——同 praise , extol , compliment

Dr. Harris' fellow researchers *lauded* her thirty years of work in the laboratory.

海瑞斯博士的研究員同事，讚揚她三十年來對實驗室的付出。

* **malleable**〔ˋmælɪəbl̩〕*adj.* 順從的【常考】

   ——同 flexible , moldable , tractable , impressionable

When children are young, their minds are very *malleable*.

當孩子還小時，其思想相當地順從。

* **millennium**〔məˋlɛnɪəm〕*n.* 一千年【常考】

   ——同 one thousand years

In the year 2000, we will reach the beginning of a new *millennium*. 到了公元二○○○年時，我們將再展開新的一千年。

murmur〔ˋmɝmɚ〕*v.* 喃喃低語　——同 mumble , mutter , grumble

Carl *murmured* something that none of us heard clearly.

卡爾嘀咕數語，沒人聽清楚他講了什麼。

* **negligible**〔ˋnɛglədʒəbl̩〕*adj.* 不足取的；無關緊要的【常考】

   ——同 unimportant , insignificant , trifling , petty

The wind was so light that it had only a *negligible* effect on the outside temperature. 這風這麼弱，對外面的溫度起不了大作用。

✱✱obsess 〔 əb'sɛs 〕 *v.* 迷戀；著魔【最常考】

——同 haunt , besiege , beset

Professor Thompson has been ***obsessed*** with the history of ancient Egypt for more than twenty years.

湯普森教授醉心古埃及歷史已有二十多年。

outing 〔'aʊtɪŋ 〕 *n.* 遠足 ——同 excursion , expedition , pleasure trip

Our class went on an ***outing*** to the countryside where we had a picnic lunch. 我們班到鄉下去遠足野餐。

✱paradoxical 〔,pærə'dɑksɪk! 〕 *adj.* 矛盾的【常考】

——同 contradictory

Sam had a very ***paradoxical*** personality; he was very shy, but often outgoing, too. 山姆的個性矛盾；他很害羞，但又蠻外向。

✱perspective 〔 pɚ'spɛktɪv 〕 *n.* 觀點；正確的眼光【常考】

——同 attitude , way of looking

What is your ***perspective*** on the problems in today's schools, Harriet? 海瑞特，妳對當今校園的問題有何看法？

> **Exercise** ⟩ *Fill in the blanks.*

1. The teacher's _____ criticism made the little boy cry.

2. My parrot can _____ Michael Jackson singing "Bad."

3. He was a weak, _____ man with no will of his own.

4. Dr. Kimble became _____ with finding the one-armed man who had killed his wife.

5. This book tells a story from the _____ of a ten-year-old child.

【解答】1. harsh 2. imitate 3. malleable 4. obsessed 5. perspective

porcelain (ˈpɔrslɪn) *n.* 瓷器 ——同 china

Edith enjoys collecting fine ***porcelain*** from around the world.
伊蒂絲喜歡收集世界各地的精緻瓷器。

* **prodigal** (ˈprɑdɪgḷ) *adj.* 浪費的【常考】

——同 extravagant , wasteful

Randy's ***prodigal*** spending usually leaves him broke at the end of each month. 倫迪花錢揮霍，使得他每逢月底常一毛不剩。

quota (ˈkwotə) *n.* 配額

——同 allocation , portion , proportion , ration

The factory had a ***quota*** of refrigerators that they had to make every work day. 工廠對每日的冰箱生產量有配額。

rapture (ˈræptʃɚ) *n.* 狂喜

——同 ecstasy , delight , exaltation

His ***rapture*** at seeing his newborn daughter could be seen on his face. 見到初生女兒時的狂喜，在他的臉上展露無遺。

remnant (ˈrɛmnənt) *n.* 殘屑

——同 small piece , shred , remainder , residue

These few trees are the only ***remnants*** of a great forest that once grew here. 這幾株樹是此地從前的大森林僅餘留的。

* **reverse** (rɪˈvɝs) *v.* ①倒轉 ②取消；廢棄【常考】

——同 1. invert , turn back 2. alter , overthrow , upset

Janet ***reversed*** the car into the garage.
珍娜將車子倒回車庫裡。

satirical (səˈtɪrɪkḷ) *adj.* 諷刺的

——同 bitter , cynical , ironical , sarcastic , sardonic

Satirical comedies about politics are very popular television shows in Taiwan. 諷刺政治的電視喜劇在台灣廣受歡迎。

* **seethe** 〔 sið 〕 *v.* 沸騰【常考】　　——同 boil , surge , churn , fizz

The pot of stew on the stove *seethed* until it nearly boiled over. 爐子上的燉鍋一直沸騰到將近煮乾爲止。

sentry 〔'sɛntrɪ 〕 *n.* 哨兵

——同 watch , guard , sentinel , watchman , patrol

The *sentry* stopped the two men and demanded to see their identification. 哨兵攔下這兩名男子，並要求看他們的證件。

* **shabby** 〔'ʃæbɪ 〕 *adj.* 破舊的【常考】

——同 run-down , frayed , ragged , tattered , poor

The poor old woman only had a *shabby* sweater to keep her warm. 這名貧窮的老婦人只有一件破舊的毛衣禦寒。

sneak 〔 snik 〕 *v.* 溜走　　——同 slink , slip

The three boys tried to *sneak* into the principal's office that night. 這三個男孩試圖在那晚溜進校長的辦公室。

* **squeeze** 〔 skwiz 〕 *v.* 壓榨；緊握【常考】

——同 compress , wring , grip , crush , clutch

The little boy was frightened and *squeezed* his father's hand tightly. 小男孩嚇得緊握著父親的手。

tardy 〔'tɑrdɪ 〕 *adj.* 緩慢的　　——同 overdue , late , slow

If you are *tardy* in paying your electric bill, there may be a late fee added to your bill.

如果你遲繳電費，可能你的帳單上又會增加遲繳的罰款。

torment 〔 tɔr'mɛnt 〕 *v.* 使痛苦

——同 afflict , torture , agonize , distress , rack

Mathew was *tormented* by the thought that he would not pass the JCEE. 馬修爲考不上大學的想法所苦。

　* JCEE = Joint College Entrance Exam

vaporize 〔'vepə͵raɪz 〕 v. 蒸發

—— 同 evaporate

The water *vaporized* very quickly because of the heat of the sun. 太陽的熱氣使得水迅速地蒸發了。

warrant 〔'wɔrənt 〕 n. 令狀；授權書

—— 同 assurance , authority , sanction , commission , guarantee

The police officers who came to the house had a *warrant* for John's arrest. 來訪的警官提了拘票要逮捕約翰。

zigzag 〔'zɪgzæg 〕 adj. 鋸齒狀的；曲折的

—— 同 winding , devious

Take care when driving on this *zigzag* mountain road.
在這曲折的山路上開車要當心。

Exercise > *Fill in the blanks.*

1. Our department has surpassed our _____ of required sales for the third month in a row.

2. We bought some carpet _____ to cover the floor in our dorm room.

3. I hope you aren't going to wear that _____ pair of pants to the party!

4. Students who are _____ for class will be given demerits.

5. The artist had painted many colorful, _____ lines on the canvas.

【解答】1. quota   2. remnants   3. shabby   4. tardy   5. zigzag

· List 7 · 難字分析

amateur 〔'æmə͵tʃʊr 〕 *n.* 業餘者

amat + eur
love + person

— a person who engages in some art, sport, etc. for the pleasure of it rather than for money

eulogy 〔'julədʒɪ 〕 *n.* 頌辭；頌揚

eu + log + y
well + speak + n.

— speech or writing in praise of a person, event or thing

inquisitive 〔 ɪn'kwɪzətɪv 〕 *adj.* 好奇的；好問的

in + quisit + ive
into + seek + adj.

— inclined to ask many questions or seek information

insinuate 〔 ɪn'sɪnju͵et 〕 *v.* 暗示

in + sinu + ate
into + bend + v.

— to hint or suggest indirectly

jurisdiction 〔͵dʒʊrɪs'dɪkʃən 〕 *n.* 管轄權；裁判權

juris + dict + ion
law + speak + n.

— administration of justice; legal authority

malleable〔'mælɪəb!〕*adj.* 順從的

malle + able
|　　|
hammer + adj.

— easily trained or adapted

millennium〔mə'lɛnɪəm〕*n.* 一千年

mill + enni + um
|　　|　　|
thousand + year + n.

— any period of one thousand years

negligible〔'nɛglədʒəb!〕*adj.* 不足取的；無關緊要的

neg + lig + ible
|　　　|　　|
　　lect　　|
|　　　|　　|
not + choose + able to

— not significant or important enough to be worth considering

paradoxical〔ˌpærə'dɑksɪk!〕*adj.* 矛盾的

para + dox + ical
|　　|　　|
contrary to + opinion + adj.

— having the nature of, or expressing a paradox

perspective〔pɚ'spɛktɪv〕*n.* 觀點；正確的眼光

per + spect + ive
|　　|　　|
through + look + n.

— a specific point of view in understanding or judging things

torment〔tɔr'mɛnt〕*v.* 使痛苦

tor + ment
|　　|
twist + v.

— to cause great physical pain or mental anguish in

📋 LIST ▸ 8

aboriginal 〔ˌæbəˈrɪdʒənḷ 〕 *adj.* 土著的
——同 native , indigenous , primeval , primitive
More and more people are beginning to appreciate the
beauty of ***aboriginal*** works of art.
越來越多的人開始欣賞原住民的工藝之美。

advent 〔ˈædvɛnt 〕 *n.* 來臨 ——同 approach , arrival , coming
The ***advent*** of Michael Jackson's first album excited pop
music fans. 麥克・傑克森的第一張專輯問世時，使流行樂迷很興奮。

ambivalence 〔 æmˈbɪvələns 〕 *n.* ①矛盾 ②猶豫
——同 1. conflict , contradiction 2. equivocation , uncertainty
The government's ***ambivalence*** to the problem of corruption
is only allowing the problem to get worse.
政府對貪污問題的矛盾作法，只會令問題更嚴重。

* **annals** 〔ˈænəlz 〕 *n.* 年鑑【常考】 ——同 chronicle , history , archive
The widespread destruction caused by this typhoon will be
in the ***annals*** of the nation's history.
這個颱風所造成的大規模破壞，將被載入該國的史冊裡。

** **arid** 〔ˈærɪd 〕 *adj.* 乾燥的【最常考】
——同 dry , parched , waterless , moistureless
It is difficult to grow fruit in ***arid*** desert areas.
在乾燥的沙漠地帶種植水果有困難。

* **barrier** 〔ˈbærɪɚ 〕 *n.* 障礙【常考】
——同 obstacle , impediment , hindrance , handicap
His poor test scores were a ***barrier*** to his entering college.
他考試成績不理想將是入大學的障礙。

blasphemous 〔'blæsfɪməs 〕 *adj.* 褻瀆上帝的

—— 同 impious , sacrilegious , profane , irreverent

His book was considered **blasphemous** and thus banned.
他的書被認爲褻瀆上帝，因而遭禁。

cataclysm 〔'kætəˌklɪzəm 〕 *n.* 大災禍

—— 同 disaster , catastrophe , calamity , devastation , destruction

The **cataclysm** that destroyed Pompeii was the eruption of a
nearby volcano. 鄰近火山的爆發是摧毀龐貝的大災禍。

* **coincide** 〔ˌkoɪn'saɪd 〕 *v.* ①同時發生 ②符合；一致【常考】

—— 同 1. synchronize 2. accord , harmonize , correspond

Laura's and my ideas about how to improve our office
coincide. 在改進辦公室方面，蘿拉與我的意見一致。

* **concoct** 〔 kan'kakt 〕 *v.* 創造；調和【常考】　—— 同 invent , devise

Paul is in the kitchen **concocting** delicious new dishes.
保羅正在廚房裡調製新佳餚。

* **controversy** 〔'kantrəˌvɝsɪ 〕 *n.* 爭論【常考】

—— 同 argument , dispute , quarrel , conflict , contention

There is some **controversy** over the extreme violence in
movies and television programs today.
現今電影和電視節目中的極度暴力，引起了爭論。

deceptive 〔 dɪ'sɛptɪv 〕 *adj.* 欺騙的

—— 同 misleading , deceitful , false , delusive , fake

To avoid detection, the criminal left **deceptive** clues for the
police to find. 爲了躲避偵察，罪犯留下錯誤的線索給警方。

* **designate** 〔'dɛzɪgˌnet 〕 *v.* ①指派 ②命名【常考】

—— 同 1. assign , appoint , delegate 2. name , label , entitle

The captain **designated** three soldiers to lead the troops.
艦長指派三名士兵來率領部隊。

disillusion 〔͵dɪsɪˈluʒən〕 v. 使幻滅

—— 同 disenchant , break the spell

I was ***disillusioned*** by the failure of the computer program.

電腦程式的失敗使我的幻想破滅。

*elicit 〔ɪˈlɪsɪt〕 v. 引出【最常考】

—— 同 evoke , extract , bring out , derive , draw out , educe

No one could ***elicit*** any response from the reticent little girl.

沒有人能引誘那沉默的小女孩回答。　 *reticent 〔ˈrɛtəsn̩t〕 adj. 沉默的

enmity 〔ˈɛnmətɪ〕 n. 敵意

—— 同 hostility , hatred , animosity , antagonism , rancor

The ***enmity*** between John and Kirk has been festering for

years. 約翰和寇克間的敵意已積聚多年。　 *fester 〔ˈfɛstɚ〕 v. 積恨

Exercise 〉 *Fill in the blanks.*

1. The _____ of computers has drastically changed the
   way information is stored and shared.

2. A tall _____ had been set up around the refugee
   camp to prevent escape.

3. The _____ surrounding the murder case ensured that
   it received considerable television coverage.

4. She was _____ to discover that her idol was really a
   drug-using, arrogant jerk.

5. The new tax law _____ protests from many people.

【解答】1. advent　 2. barrier　 3. controversy　 4. disillusioned　 5. elicited

euphonious 〔 ju'fonɪəs 〕 adj. 悅耳的

—同 melodious , harmonious , mellifluous , dulcet

The *euphonious* sound of Carrie's cello playing always puts me at ease. 凱莉悅耳的大提琴演奏總讓我心曠神怡。

**fallacious 〔 fə'leʃəs 〕 adj. 錯誤的【最常考】

—同 incorrect , erroneous

Many people have the *fallacious* belief that touching someone with AIDS will infect them.

許多人誤以為和愛滋病患接觸就會被傳染。

fluffy 〔'flʌfɪ 〕 adj. 毛茸茸的　—同 downy , cottony

Nick's favorite toy was a *fluffy* teddy bear his grandmother had given him. 尼克最喜歡的玩具是祖母給他的絨毛玩具熊。

gelatinous 〔 dʒə'lætənəs 〕 adj. 膠狀的

—同 gluey , glutinous , gummy , jelly-like , sticky , viscous

A *gelatinous* substance in seaweed is used to make ice cream smooth and creamy. 海藻中的膠質被用來使冰淇淋滑溜和乳化。

* hatch 〔 hætʃ 〕 v. 孵【常考】　—同 breed , incubate , bring forth

The chickens on our farm are *hatching* more baby chicks than they did last year. 我們農場的雞所孵出的小雞比去年還多。

* immense 〔 ɪ'mɛns 〕 adj. 龐大的【常考】

—同 huge , massive , gigantic , tremendous , colossal , stupendous

During her trip to Egypt, Jane was amazed at the *immense* size of the ancient Pyramids. ＊pyramid 〔'pɪrəmɪd 〕 n. 角錐

在埃及之旅中，珍被古金字塔的龐大所懾。

**indigenous 〔 ɪn'dɪdʒənəs 〕 adj. ①本地的 ②天生的【最常考】

—同 1. native , endemic , original　2. innate , inborn

Taiwan is trying to protect the island's *indigenous* plant and animal life. 台灣正努力保護島上的本地植物和動物。

* **inspect** 〔 ɪn'spɛkt 〕 *v.* 調查【常考】

—— 同 investigate , scan , survey , check , examine

The police sent a detective to ***inspect*** the scene of the crime.
警方派了一名探員去調查犯罪現場。

juvenile 〔'dʒuvənḷ , 'dʒuvənaɪl 〕 *adj.* 少年的；幼稚的

—— 同 immature , adolescent , junior , young

Nelson's teacher was tired of his ***juvenile*** behavior and sent him to the principal for punishment.
尼爾森的老師受夠了他的幼稚行為，將他送給校長去處罰。

launch 〔 lɔntʃ 〕 *v.* 發射

—— 同 propel , discharge , send off , dispatch , set afloat

Large amounts of special fuel are needed to ***launch*** a rocket into space. 發射火箭上太空需要大量的特殊燃料。

mallet 〔'mælɪt 〕 *n.* 木槌 —— 同 wooden hammer

Many cooks use ***mallets*** to pound meat to make it more tender.
許多廚師使用木槌來敲肉使它軟化。

** **mimic** 〔'mɪmɪk 〕 *v.* 模仿【最常考】

—— 同 copy , simulate , resemble , mirror , imitate

Some birds, like parrots, can ***mimic*** human speech.
有一些鳥類，像是鸚鵡，會模仿人類說話。

mushroom 〔'mʌʃrum 〕 *v.* 急速發展

—— 同 grow , spread , boom , expand , flourish , spring up

The use of alternative energy sources has ***mushroomed*** in the last few years. 替代性能源的使用在近幾年急速成長。

nibble 〔'nɪbḷ 〕 *v.* 細咬

—— 同 gnaw , bite , munch , nip , peck , pick at

Yvonne ***nibbled*** on some carrot sticks as a snack.
伊芳細咬胡蘿蔔條，當作是在吃零食。

outlast 〔 aʊt'læst 〕 v. 比…持久；比…活得久

—同 outlive , survive , last longer than

The tree you plant today will **outlast** you, and your grandchildren.

今日你所種植的樹將會存活得比你、你的孫子還久。

* **paramount** 〔 'pærə‚maʊnt 〕 adj. 最高的；最重要的 【常考】

—同 supreme , dominant , superior , preeminent , foremost

The president is the **paramount** political figure in the country. 總統是一國中政治地位最高的人物。

perspire 〔 pɚ'spaɪr 〕 v. 流汗 —同 sweat

After jogging for ten miles, Carla was **perspiring** heavily.

慢跑十哩之後，卡拉汗流如注。

Exercise Fill in the blanks.

1. The children's mouths gaped in awe at the sight of the _____ dinosaur skeletons.

2. The locals are worried about the rise in _____ delinquency in their country.

3. When you _____ a ship for the first time, it is traditional to break a bottle of champagne on the bow.

4. When learning a foreign language, it is helpful to _____ the pronunciation of a native speaker.

5. Jane goes crazy when her husband _____ on her ear lobes.

【解答】 1. immense   2. juvenile   3. launch   4. mimic   5. nibbles

* **portable** 〔ˈpɔrtəbḷ〕 *adj.* 可攜帶的；手提的【常考】

—— 同 movable , conveyable , easily carried , handy

Wanda is considering buying a *portable* computer for her work. 汪妲正考慮要買部手提式電腦來處理工作。

* **proficient** 〔 prəˈfɪʃənt 〕 *adj.* 熟練的【常考】

—— 同 skillful , expert , dexterous , competent , adept

Derrick is the most *proficient* typist in our typing class.
德瑞克是本打字班技術最熟練的打字員。

psyche 〔ˈsaɪkɪ 〕 *n.* 精神；靈魂 —— 同 mind , soul , spirit

Gary found the study of people's *psyches* a fascinating subject. 蓋瑞認為研究人的精神是門有趣的學科。

relegate 〔ˈrɛləˌget 〕 *v.* ①移管；委託 ②放逐

—— 同 1. consign , commit , assign , refer 2. eject , expel

The captain *relegated* some of the less important duties to his junior officers. 艦長將一些較不重要的任務，移交給年輕的軍官。

remote 〔 rɪˈmot 〕 *adj.* 遙遠的 —— 同 distant , faraway , far-off

Ned grew up on a farm in a *remote* area of the country.
奈德在該國一偏遠地區的農場裡長大。

revert 〔 rɪˈvɝt 〕 *v.* 恢復

—— 同 go back , turn back , backslide , regress , resume

After exercising diligently for two weeks, Ken finally *reverted* to his old lazy ways.
勤勞運動兩星期後，肯恩最後又恢復原來的惰性。

scaly 〔ˈskelɪ 〕 *adj.* 鱗狀的 —— 同 flaky , scurfy

The snake's skin was *scaly* and dry, not wet and slimy as I had thought.
這隻蛇的皮乾燥又有鱗片，不是我原先以為的濕濕黏黏的。

shady 〔ˈʃedɪ〕 *adj.* ①陰暗的 ②可疑的

——同 1. dim , shaded 2. fishy , suspicious , untrustworthy

I don't trust Victor; he is always involved in **shady** deals.

我不信任維克特；他總是涉及可疑的勾當。

snobbish 〔ˈsnɑbɪʃ〕 *adj.* 勢利的

——同 arrogant , high-hat , pretentious , snooty , priggish , haughty

Everyone was annoyed by his **snobbish** attitude.

每個人都對他勢利的態度反感。

stag 〔stæg〕 *n.* 雄鹿　——同 male deer

We were impressed by the size of the **stag's** antlers.

這隻雄鹿頭角的尺寸讓我們印象深刻。　＊antler 〔ˈæntlɚ〕 *n.* 鹿角

suffuse 〔səˈfjuz〕 *v.* 布滿

——同 spread over , fill , bathe , pervade , permeate

When she opened the heavy curtains, light suddenly **suffused** the room.　當她拉開厚重的窗簾時，房間內突然充滿了光線。

suspense 〔səˈspɛns〕 *n.* 懸疑

——同 uncertainty , ambiguity , doubt , anxiety , expectancy

Tara enjoys the **suspense** in mystery novels.

塔拉喜歡推理小說的懸疑。

tarnish 〔ˈtɑrnɪʃ〕 *v.* 使晦暗

——同 discolor , taint , blacken , blemish , darken , dim

People often buy stainless steel eating utensils because they do not **tarnish**.　人們常買不銹鋼的餐具，因爲不會變黑。

＊**torrent** 〔ˈtɔrənt〕 *n.* 急流【常考】　——同 rapid stream , gush

The **torrent** of water turned our little boat over and we had to swim to the shore.

急流將我們的小船翻覆，因此我們必須游回岸上。

undermine 〔͵ʌndɚˋmaɪn 〕 *v.* 破壞

——同 impair , sabotage , disable , weaken , subvert

The president was worried that his vice president was trying to *undermine* his power. 總統擔憂副總統正企圖倒戈。

variation 〔͵vɛrɪˋeʃən 〕 *n.* 變化

——同 alteration , change , deviation , diversity , difference

Mark doesn't like any *variation* in his diet; he eats the same thing every day.

馬克不喜歡變化飲食；他每天都吃同樣的東西。

* **wary** 〔ˋwɛrɪ 〕 *adj.* 小心的【常考】

——同 cautious , heedful , careful

After being bitten by a stray dog, Gail was *wary* of all dogs.

被野狗咬傷後，蓋爾對所有的狗都心存戒備。

> **Exercise** *Fill in the blanks.*

1. Dr. Green is a _____ surgeon, so you should not be nervous about his operating on you.

2. After the failure of several new economic policies, the government _____ back to its former policy.

3. The _____ of not knowing if I have been accepted at the university is making me crazy!

4. People's fear of injections is _____ the possible effectiveness of the new vaccine.

5. You should be _____ when walking around campus alone at night.

【解答】1. proficient　2. reverted　3. suspense　4. undermining　5. wary

·List 8· 難字分析

aboriginal 〔͵æbə'rɪdʒənḷ〕 *adj.* 土著的

ab	+ orig	+ in	+ al
from	+ rise	+ n.	+ adj.

— existing from the beginning or from earliest days

ambivalence 〔æm'bɪvələns〕 *n.* ①矛盾 ②猶豫

ambi	+ val	+ ence
both	+ strong	+ n.

— simultaneous conflicting feelings toward a person or thing;
a feeling of uncertainty about something due to a mental conflict

blasphemous 〔'blæsfɪməs〕 *adj.* 褻瀆上帝的

blas	+ phem	+ ous
hurt	+ speak	+ adj.

— having the habit of speaking against God or things considered holy

coincide 〔͵koɪn'saɪd〕 *v.* ①同時發生 ②符合；一致

co	+ in	+ cide
con		
together	+ on	+ fall

— to occur at the same time; to be identical

designate 〔'dɛzɪg͵net〕 *v.* ①指派 ②命名

de	+ sign	+ ate
down	+ mark	+ v.

— to name for an office or duty; to refer to by a distinguishing name

euphonious 〔ju'fonɪəs〕 *adj.* 悅耳的

eu	+ phon	+ ious
well	+ sound	+ adj.

— pleasant in sound

fallacious 〔 fə'leʃəs 〕 *adj.* 錯誤的

> fall + aci + ous
> |　　|　　|
> err +　n. +　*adj.*

　　— containing or based on false reasoning

juvenile 〔'dʒuvən̩ , 'dʒuvənaɪl 〕 *adj.* 少年的；幼稚的

> juven + ile
> |　　　|
> young + *adj.*

　　— young or youthful

paramount 〔'pærə,maʊnt 〕 *adj.* 最高的；最重要的

> par + a　+ mount
> |　　|　　　|
> per　ad　　|
> |　　|　　　|
> by + to +　hill

　　— of chief concern or importance; supreme

perspire 〔 pɚ'spaɪr 〕 *v.* 流汗

> per　 + spire
> |　　　|
> through + breathe

　　— to give forth a characteristic salty moisture through the pores of skin

relegate 〔'rɛlə,get 〕 *v.* ①移管；委託 ②放逐

> re　+ leg + ate
> |　　|　　|
> away + send + *v.*

　　— to assign to a class; to assign to an inferior position

suffuse 〔 sə'fjuz 〕 *v.* 布滿

> suf　+ fuse
> |　　　|
> sub　　|
> |　　　|
> under + pour

　　— to cover or overspread, esp. with a color or liquid

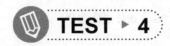

請由 (A)～(D) 中選出和畫線部分意義最相近的字。

1. Mr. Saunders enjoys studying astronomy, but he is only an <u>amateur</u> in the field.

  (A) expert
  (B) student
  (C) hobbyist
  (D) spectator

2. Many <u>eulogies</u> of Dr. Sun Yat-sen have been written in both the East and the West.

  (A) stories
  (B) biographies
  (C) reports
  (D) commendations

3. Vivian placed the beautiful roses in a <u>porcelain</u> vase on the table.

  (A) plastic
  (B) wooden
  (C) crystal
  (D) china

4. We will have to be very quiet if we are going to <u>sneak</u> past the guard undetected.

  (A) slip
  (B) crawl
  (C) march
  (D) dance

5. Calvin's letter <u>insinuated</u> that he and Jean might be getting engaged.

  (A) hinted
  (B) expressed
  (C) denied
  (D) ensured

6. The two scientists' research results were surprisingly <u>paradoxical</u>.

  (A) contradictory
  (B) harmonious
  (C) unrelated
  (D) interesting

7. Looking at the sign in a mirror <u>reverses</u> all the letters, so everything looks backwards.

  (A) clarifies
  (B) explodes
  (C) inverts
  (D) jumbles

8. In a confession of love, Ernest revealed his <u>latent</u> feelings for Jessica.

  (A) unrealistic
  (B) shallow
  (C) muddled
  (D) hidden

9. It is <u>fallacious</u> to say that all Americans share the same beliefs.

(A) logical
(B) suspicious
(C) simple
(D) erroneous

10. Potatoes, <u>indigenous</u> to South America, are now grown all over the world.

(A) introduced
(B) native
(C) cultivated
(D) proximal

11. He was overwhelmed by the <u>rapture</u> of returning to his home country after thirty years in exile.

(A) delight
(B) disappointment
(C) confusion
(D) astonishment

12. We watched as an eagle made the <u>descent</u> to its nest.

(A) way
(B) materials
(C) drop
(D) location

13. Keith felt a certain <u>ambivalence</u> about seeing his long-lost father after eighteen years.

(A) certainty
(B) uncertainty
(C) curiosity
(D) interest

14. A <u>gelatinous</u> material protects frog eggs from drying out before they hatch.

(A) crystalline
(B) jelly-like
(C) encrusted
(D) living

15. The dry desert wind had made their skin become dry and <u>scaly</u>.

(A) flaky
(B) tanned
(C) wrinkled
(D) ugly

16. Computer users have <u>coined</u> many new terms that are beginning to be used in people's everyday conversations.

(A) created
(B) reused
(C) deleted
(D) calculated

17. The membership fee to this club is a <u>negligible</u> amount.

(A) ridiculous
(B) trifling
(C) large
(D) surprising

18. If the Three Gorges dam that is being planned ever bursts, it will be an enormous <u>cataclysm</u> for China.

(A) boost
(B) achievement
(C) catastrophe
(D) setback

19. The boy concocted a story about another child who had broken the neighbor's window with a baseball.

    (A) learned
    (B) fabricated
    (C) retold
    (D) found

20. Coffee sales have mush-roomed as a result of the current popularity of coffee houses.

    (A) declined
    (B) fluctuated
    (C) flourished
    (D) leveled off

21. The death of North Korea's paramount leader, Kim Il-Sung, brought confusion to the country.

    (A) reticent
    (B) conservative
    (C) long-lived
    (D) supreme

22. The art museum's opening turned out to be a gathering of snobbish art critics.

    (A) pretentious
    (B) learned
    (C) gifted
    (D) dull

23. There was no enmity between us, so we were able to reach an agreement on the sale of the property.

    (A) friendship
    (B) relationship
    (C) animosity
    (D) interest

24. We spent the afternoon polishing brass door knobs and plaques that had become tarnished.

    (A) shiny
    (B) discolored
    (C) rusted
    (D) oily

25. Dr. Harris believes that computers are the most influential development of this millennium.

    (A) one thousand years
    (B) one hundred years
    (C) fifty years
    (D) ten thousand years

【解答】

1. C   2. D   3. D   4. A   5. A   6. A   7. C   8. D   9. D   10. B
11. A   12. C   13. B   14. B   15. A   16. A   17. B   18. C   19. B   20. C
21. D   22. A   23. C   24. B   25. A

LIST ▶ 9

abruptly 〔 əˈbrʌptlɪ 〕 *adv.* 突然地
——同 suddenly , rudely , precipitately , unexpectedly , rashly
Diana ***abruptly*** left the party, not telling anyone where she was going. 黛安娜突然離開宴會，沒告訴任何人她要去哪裡。

⁂adverse 〔 ədˈvɝs 〕 *adj.* 反對的【最常考】
——同 opposing , hostile , contrary , antagonistic
Margaret is ***adverse*** to the idea of spending the next month living in this old apartment.
瑪格麗特反對下個月住在這棟舊公寓裡。

amble 〔ˈæmbḷ 〕 *v.* 漫步 ——同 ramble , roam , stroll
Tony ***ambled*** through the forest for hours before realizing he was lost. 湯尼在森林裡漫步數小時後才發現自己迷路了。

arithmetical 〔ˌærɪθˈmɛtɪkḷ 〕 *adj.* 算術的
——同 mathematical , computational , numerical
Our math teacher asked all the students to find the ***arithmetical*** solution to the problem.
我們的數學老師要求所有的學生找出這個問題的算法。

⁂augment 〔 ɔgˈmɛnt 〕 *v.* 增大【最常考】 ——同 increase , multiply
The rezoning of school districts ***augmented*** our school's student body by 150 new students.
學區的重劃使本校的學生人數增加了一百五十人。

⁎barter 〔ˈbɑrtɚ 〕 *v.* 以物易物【常考】 ——同 exchange , trade
The poor peasants ***bartered*** almost everything they owned for boat tickets to America.
貧窮的農夫幾乎把所有的家當，拿來換往美國的船票。

brim 〔 brɪm 〕① *n.* 邊緣 ② *v.* 充滿

——同 1. edge , rim , brink , verge

Her eyes ***brimmed*** with tears after the little boy took away her toy. 小男孩把她的玩具拿走後,她就熱淚盈眶。

cascade 〔 kæs'ked 〕*n.* 小瀑布 ——同 waterfall

The Hawaiian Islands have many beautiful ***cascades*** hidden in the forests. 在夏威夷島上的森林裡,隱藏了許多美麗的小瀑布。

categorize 〔'kætəgə,raɪz 〕*v.* 分類

——同 classify , sort , group , systemize , rank

The platypus is hard to ***categorize*** because it secretes milk like a mammal, but it also lays eggs. ＊platypus 〔'plætəpəs 〕*n.* 鴨嘴獸
要將鴨嘴獸歸類有困難,因爲牠旣像哺乳類會分泌乳汁,但又會產卵。

＊**collaborate** 〔 kə'læbə,ret 〕*v.* ①合作 ②通敵【常考】

——同 1. cooperate , coproduce , affiliate 2. conspire , collude

The two authors ***collaborated*** on this book about European history. 這兩位作家合力著作這本歐洲歷史的書籍。

concord 〔'kankɔrd , 'kaŋ- 〕*n.* 和諧;一致

——同 accord , agreement , harmony , concert , unanimity

We hope that one day all the people will live in ***concord*** with one another. 我們希望有朝一日,所有的人都能和睦相處。

decipher 〔 dɪ'saɪfə 〕*v.* 解讀 ——同 make out , decode

The code the enemy used was so complicated that we could not ***decipher*** it. 敵人所用的密碼過於複雜,我們無法解讀。

desolate 〔'dɛsḷɪt 〕*adj.* 荒涼的

——同 barren , dreary , solitary , waste , lonely

After the drought, the farmer's fields were ***desolate*** tracts of dust. 乾旱之後,農人的田裡盡是荒涼的塵跡。

dismal 〔ˈdɪzml̩〕 *adj.* 憂鬱的；陰沉的 ——同 gloomy , depressing

Ernie lived in a ***dismal*** part of town, with decrepit buildings and a high crime rate. ＊decrepit〔dɪˈkrɛpɪt〕*adj.* 破舊的

厄尼住在鎮上的黑暗地帶，裡頭是破舊的建築物與高犯罪率。

＊**eligible** 〔ˈɛlɪdʒəbl̩〕*adj.* 合格的【常考】

——同 qualified , fit , suitable

Your good grades have made you ***eligible*** for a scholarship to study at the university.

你優異的成績使你有資格領取獎學金進入大學。

＊**empirical** 〔ɛmˈpɪrɪkl̩〕*adj.* 經驗的；實驗的【常考】

——同 experimental , observed , pragmatic , perceptual

The new drug could not be used without more ***empirical*** evidence of its effectiveness.

在其效用尚未有更多實證以前，這種新藥不能使用。

Exercise ⟩ *Fill in the blanks.*

1. In the middle of the piano concert, Dennis _____ got up and left.

2. If you fill your cup to the _____, the coffee will spill over the sides when you lift it.

3. The books in this library are _____ by subject matter.

4. It was difficult to _____ exactly what the professor had meant.

5. Tina will have been working here for a year next week and will be _____ for a raise.

【解答】1. abruptly   2. brim   3. categorized   4. decipher   5. eligible

evacuate 〔 ɪ'vækjʊˌet 〕 *v.* 撤離；清除
—— 同 depart, withdraw, empty, purge, remove
People were *evacuated* from the building because of the
bomb threat. 由於受到炸彈的恐嚇，人們已被疏離該大樓。

falter 〔 'fɔltɚ 〕 *v.* 猶豫；動搖
—— 同 hesitate, totter, stammer, stutter, waver
The demand for new cars has not *faltered* in the past few
years. 對新車的需求這些年來未曾動搖過。

* **forecast** 〔 for'kæst 〕 *v.* 預測【常考】
—— 同 predict, foresee, forebode, foretell, prophesy
The weather bureau is *forecasting* rain for most of the
island tomorrow. 氣象局預測明天全島幾乎都會降雨。

gem 〔 dʒɛm 〕 *n.* 寶石　—— 同 jewel, precious stone
Sheila's new ring has a beautiful blue *gem* in it.
席拉的新戒指上有顆美麗的藍寶石。

* **haul** 〔 hɔl 〕 *v.* 拖拉【常考】
—— 同 draw, pull, drag, tow, tug
The bags of dry cement were too heavy for one person to
haul. 這幾袋水泥太重，一個人是拖不來的。

* **imminent** 〔 'ɪmənənt 〕 *adj.* 迫切的；即將來臨的【常考】
—— 同 coming, impending, approaching, near, close at hand
The high school seniors were excited about their *imminent*
graduation. 這些中學高年級生很興奮他們即將要畢業了。

indigent 〔 'ɪndədʒənt 〕 *adj.* 貧乏的
—— 同 poor, impoverished, poverty-stricken, destitute, needy
The nuns tried to help the *indigent* peasants find homes and
food. 這些尼姑試圖幫貧困的農人尋求住所和食物。

installment 〔 ɪnˈstɔlmənt 〕 *n.* ①分期付款 ②裝設
——同 1. chapter , division 2. installation , setting up , positioning
Because Mary doesn't have a lot of money, she is paying for her car in monthly ***installments***.
由於瑪麗的錢不多，所以她每月分期付款來繳車費。

* **keen** 〔 kin 〕 *adj.* 鋒利的；敏銳的【常考】
——同 piercing , sharp , edged , cutting
Even though my grandfather is old, his mind is still ***keen***.
雖然祖父已年邁，他的頭腦依然敏銳。

** **leap** 〔 lip 〕 *v.* 跳躍【最常考】 ——同 jump , hop , spring
The children ***leaped*** excitedly into the swimming pool.
孩子們興奮地跳入游泳池裡。

* **mammoth** 〔ˈmæməθ 〕 *adj.* 龐大的【常考】
——同 titanic , immense , gigantic , colossal , gargantuan
The Great Wall of China is the most ***mammoth*** wall ever made by humans.　中國的萬里長城是人類建造過最龐大的城牆。

* **miniature** 〔ˈmɪnɪətʃɚ 〕 *adj.* 小的【常考】
——同 minute , tiny , petite , diminutive , minuscule
Wendy likes to collect ***miniature*** furniture for her doll house.
溫蒂喜歡爲她的娃娃屋收集小型的傢俱。

muster 〔ˈmʌstɚ 〕 *v.* 集合 ——同 gather , assemble , convene
Although Albert was tired, he ***mustered*** all his strength to finish swimming his race.
雖然亞伯特已疲倦，他仍集中所有的力量游完比賽。

nimble 〔ˈnɪmbḷ 〕 *adj.* 敏捷的；靈巧的 ——同 spry , agile , brisk
When my grandmother does embroidery, her hands are very ***nimble***.　祖母做起刺繡來雙手靈巧的很。
　　* embroidery 〔 ɪmˈbrɔɪdərɪ 〕 *n.* 刺繡

* **obstacle** 〔ˈɑbstəkl̩〕 *n.* 障礙【常考】

——同 barrier , hindrance , obstruction , impediment

A lack of education is an ***obstacle*** to getting a good job.
教育程度不夠是謀求高職的障礙。

* **outlet** 〔ˈaʊtˌlɛt〕 *n.* 出口【常考】

——同 exit , opening , vent , escape , egress

The water flowed out of the cave through a small ***outlet***.
水從一個小小的出口流出洞穴。

****parody** 〔ˈpærədɪ〕 *n.* 諷刺詩文【最常考】

——同 burlesque , caricature , travesty , lampoon , satire

The book *Animal Farm* is a ***parody*** of the rise of communism
in Russia. 動物農莊一書諷刺俄國的共產制度。

Exercise > *Fill in the blanks.*

1. Many economists have _____ an increase in inflation
   in the near future.

2. We knew a thunderstorm was _____ as we could
   hear the rumbling of thunder growing louder.

3. That _____ beggar sitting on the bench over there
   was once a wealthy man.

4. China plans to build a _____ dam that will flood the
   famous Three Gorges.

5. The children's _____ feet quickly dashed across the
   stones in the stream.

【解答】1. forecasted 2. imminent 3. indigent 4. mammoth 5. nimble

pertinent (ˈpɝtṇənt) *adj.* 貼切的【最常考】   *v.* pertain

—— 同 appropriate , apt , relevant , to the point , proper

I think the information in this book is **pertinent** to the
report you are writing. 我認為此書的資料和你要寫的報告很貼切。

profound (prəˈfaʊnd) *adj.* 深奧的

—— 同 deep , unfathomed , serious , abysmal

The **profound** differences of opinion between Mona and her
father hurt their relationship.
夢娜和父親間意見上的鴻溝，傷害了他們的關係。

rash (ræʃ) *adj.* 輕率的   —— 同 heedless , indiscreet , reckless

Don't be **rash** in accepting money you know you cannot
repay. 不要輕率地接受你無法償還的錢。

render (ˈrɛndɚ) *v.* 給予；表現【常考】

—— 同 give , deliver , supply , perform , present

All the people in the neighborhood **rendered** their
assistance in looking for the lost child.
所有的鄰居皆施予援助，尋找失蹤的兒童。

revoke (rɪˈvok) *v.* 取消；廢除

—— 同 abolish , annul , rescind , retract , invalidate

After Jason was caught driving drunk, his driving license
was **revoked**. 被抓到酒醉開車後，傑森的駕照便被吊銷了。

scan (skæn) *v.* 審查；掃描   —— 同 examine , survey , look over

Dana **scanned** the classroom to see if she had left her keys
there. 黛娜檢查了教室，看看是否把鑰匙給忘在那兒了。

sheath (ʃiθ) *n.* 鞘   —— 同 scabbard , case , envelope

After the battle, the knight put his sword in its **sheath**.
打鬥過後，騎士把劍收入鞘內。

smash 〔 smæʃ 〕 *v.* 使破碎　——同 mash , shatter , break into pieces

In a fit of anger, Lorraine **smashed** a vase on the ground.

一氣之下，羅琳將花瓶打破在地上。

socket 〔 ˈsɑkɪt 〕 *n.* 插座；凹處

——同 receptacle , outlet , hole , pit , cavity

Will you plug the lamp into the **socket** in that wall?

請你把燈插到那牆上的插座好嗎？

* **stagger** 〔 ˈstægɚ 〕 *v.* 蹣跚；搖晃【常考】

——同 falter , totter , waver , sway , teeter

After drinking too much beer, Alex **staggered** out of the pub.

在喝了很多啤酒之後，亞歷士就搖搖晃晃地走出了酒吧。

stunt 〔 stʌnt 〕 *v.* 阻礙　——同 retard , cramp , check

A diet without nutritious foods will **stunt** a child's normal growth. 缺乏營養食物的飲食會阻礙兒童的正常生長。

suspicious 〔 səˈspɪʃəs 〕 *adj.* 懷疑的

——同 doubtful , incredulous , uncertain , skeptical , dubious

Alaina was **suspicious** of Bart going out alone so late at night.

艾蓮娜懷疑巴特；這麼晚了還要獨自出門。

tart 〔 tɑrt 〕 *adj.* 酸的；辛辣的

——同 acid , sharp , piquant , cutting , pungent

The lemon juice in this drink gives it a slightly **tart** flavor.

檸檬汁使這飲料產生微酸的味道。

tortuous 〔 ˈtɔrtʃuəs 〕 *adj.* 扭曲的

——同 spiral , winding , crooked , twisting , coiled

The **tortuous** road wound up the mountain until it finally reached Joseph's house.

這彎曲的道路沿山盤繞，直到約瑟夫的家。

underscore 〔͵ʌndɚ'skor 〕*v.* 強調;畫底線

—— 同 underline , emphasize , stress , accent

The recent fires in businesses ***underscore*** the need for business owners to follow fire codes.

最近營業場所的火災,強調了業者遵守防火條例的必要性。

* **vehement** 〔'viəmənt 〕*adj.* 激烈的;熱情的【常考】

—— 同 violent , forceful , passionate , fervent , ardent

With a ***vehement*** "NO!" Roger denied that he had broken the television set. 羅傑以一聲激烈的「不」,否認了是他弄壞電視機。

wavering 〔'wevərɪŋ 〕*adj.* 搖擺的;猶豫的

—— 同 swinging , swaying , hesitant , hesitate , tottery

The baby's first steps toward her father were ***wavering*** ones.

這個小嬰兒剛開始走向她的父親時,是搖搖晃晃的。

Exercise ⟩ *Fill in the blanks.*

1. The oranges on the table are too _____, so nobody will eat any of them.

2. Taxes are _____ to the government to pay for public projects.

3. The country's economic growth was _____ by a high inflation rate.

4. Two _____ men entered the bar and began asking how they could purchase guns.

5. We were all surprised by her _____ rejection of Mr. Clark's gift.

【解答】1. tart   2. rendered   3. stunted   4. suspicious   5. vehement

·List ⑨· 難字分析

augment 〔 ɔgˊmɛnt 〕 *v.* 增大

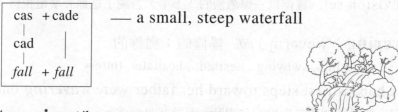

aug + ment —— to enlarge
increase + *v.*

cascade 〔 kæsˊked 〕 *n.* 小瀑布

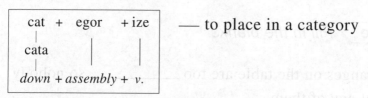

cas + cade —— a small, steep waterfall
cad
fall + fall

categorize 〔ˊkætəgəˏraɪz 〕 *v.* 分類

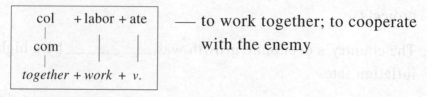

cat + egor + ize —— to place in a category
cata
down + assembly + *v.*

collaborate 〔 kəˊlæbəˏret 〕 *v.* ①合作 ②通敵

col + labor + ate —— to work together; to cooperate
com   with the enemy
together + work + *v.*

desolate 〔ˊdɛsḷɪt 〕 *adj.* 荒涼的

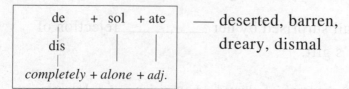

de + sol + ate —— deserted, barren,
dis   dreary, dismal
completely + alone + *adj.*

eligible 〔'ɛlɪdʒəbḷ 〕 *adj.* 合格的

```
    e  +  lig  +  ible        —— legally or normally qualified
    |      |      |
    ex     |      |
    |      |      |
  out + choose + able to
```

evacuate 〔 ɪ'vækju͵et 〕 *v.* 撤離;清除

```
    e  +  vac + uate          —— to empty; to withdraw or depart
    |      |      |               from
    ex     |      |
    |      |      |
  out + empty +  v.
```

imminent 〔'ɪmənənt 〕 *adj.* 迫切的;即將來臨的

```
    im  +  min  + ent         —— likely to come soon
    |       |      |
    in      |      |
    |       |      |
  upon + project + adj.
```

pertinent 〔'pɝtṇənt 〕 *adj.* 貼切的

```
    per    +  tin + ent       —— having some connection
     |        |     |            with the matter at hand
  thoroughly + hold + adj.
```

suspicious 〔 sə'spɪʃəs 〕 *adj.* 懷疑的

```
   sus  + (s)pici + ous       —— showing or expressing suspicion
    |        |       |
   sub       |       |
    |        |       |
  under +   look   + adj.
```

📅 LIST ▸ 10

* abstract 〔'æbstrækt〕① *adj.* 抽象的 ② *n.* 摘要【常考】

— 同 1. symbolic , imaginary , conceptual

　　　2. summary , epitome , outline

Brian thinks that ***abstract*** modern art is more expressive than traditional art.

布萊恩認為，抽象的現代藝術比傳統藝術更富含意。

* advocate 〔'ædvə,ket〕*v.* 提倡【常考】

— 同 recommend , propose , uphold , espouse , promote

Some of the economists ***advocated*** ending the national health plan. 有些經濟學家提議停止全民健保方案。

amenity 〔 ə'mɛnətɪ 〕*n.* 舒適

— 同 comforts , cordiality , amiability , pleasance

This luxury hotel has all the ***amenities*** you could ever want.

這家豪華飯店提供一切你所想要的舒適。

* aroma 〔 ə'romə 〕*n.* 芳香【常考】

— 同 fragrance , scent , odor , perfume , savor , bouquet

The ***aroma*** of the curry that John was cooking filled the apartment. 約翰烹調的咖哩香味充滿了整棟公寓。

austere 〔 ɔ'stɪr 〕*adj.* 嚴厲的

— 同 stern , strict , severe , ascetic , astringent

Kyle had a hard time adjusting to the ***austere*** life in the military. 凱爾難以適應嚴厲的軍中生活。

bead 〔 bid 〕*n.* 珠子 — 同 drop , pellet , ball

Rhonda wore a beautiful necklace made of amber ***beads***.

蓉姐戴了一條琥珀珠子做的美麗項鍊。 * amber 〔'æmbə 〕*n.* 琥珀

* **brisk** 〔 brɪsk 〕 *adj.* 活潑的；敏捷的【常考】
—— 同 lively , spirited , vigorous , frisky , nimble
We took a ***brisk*** walk around the park for a little exercise.
我們繞著公園快走作一些運動。

celebrated 〔'sɛləbretɪd 〕 *adj.* 著名的
—— 同 famous , well-known , noted , famed , prominent
Albert Einstein is the most ***celebrated*** physicist of the last one
hundred years. 亞伯特・愛因斯坦是過去一百年內最著名的物理學家。

* **collide** 〔 kə'laɪd 〕 *v.* 碰撞【常考】 —— 同 bump , crash , clash
Some scientists think an asteroid ***collided*** with Earth and
killed the dinosaurs. * asteroid 〔'æstə,rɔɪd 〕 *n.* 小行星
有些科學家認為，是一小行星碰撞上地球，摧毀了恐龍。

concur 〔 kən'kɝ 〕 *v.* 同意；一致 —— 同 agree , assent , coincide
I think everyone ***concurred*** that the rapid transit system was a
disappointment. 我認為所有人都會同意捷運是個失敗之作。

* **conventional** 〔 kən'vɛnʃənl 〕 *adj.* 傳統的【常考】
—— 同 orthodox , customary , formal , traditional
Fiona thought a ***conventional*** vacation would be boring, so
she decided to climb Mt. Everest.
費歐娜認為傳統的度假太無趣，所以她決定去爬艾佛勒斯峰。

declivity 〔 dɪ'klɪvətɪ 〕 *n.* 傾斜 —— 同 decline , drop , descent
The economy's ***declivity*** in the past few months has many
people worried. 在過去幾個月來的經濟下滑讓許多人很擔憂。

destitute 〔'dɛstə,tjut 〕 *adj.* 極窮困的
—— 同 poor , stripped , broke
Few merchants want to set up shops in this ***destitute***
neighborhood. 很少商人想在這貧困的地區開商店。

disorient 〔 dɪs'orɪˌɛnt 〕 *v.* 使迷失方向

—— 同 confuse

The thick fog *disoriented* the hikers, and the whole group got lost. 濃霧使健行者迷失了方向，整支隊伍都迷路了。

* eliminate 〔 ɪ'lɪməˌnet 〕 *v.* 去除【常考】

—— 同 exclude , eradicate , eject , remove , get rid of

The doctor told me to *eliminate* more fat and salt from my diet. 醫生要我多去除飲食中的脂肪和鹽分。

enchase 〔 ɛn'tʃes 〕 *v.* 鑲嵌；鏤刻

—— 同 engrave

Chris had the locket *enchased* and put on chain so he could present it to Lisa.

克里斯將盒式小墜子作了雕刻，並串在鍊子上，以便送給麗莎。

* locket 〔'lɑkɪt 〕 *n.* 盒式小墜子

Exercise ⟩ *Fill in the blanks.*

1. Greenpeace is an organization that _____ environmental protection.

2. Ms. Jasper's garden was filled with the _____ of roses.

3. Violet enjoys a _____ swim in the morning.

4. After _____ methods failed, they tried a more experimental approach.

5. Don was _____ from the race for cheating.

【解答】1. advocates　2. aroma　3. brisk　4. conventional　5. eliminated

eventual 〔 ɪˈvɛntʃʊəl 〕 *adj.* 最後的

—— 同 ultimate , final , at last , consequent , succeeding

The *eventual* result of all her years of studying was a Ph.D. in economics. 她讀書多年的最終結果，是拿到了經濟學博士。

farce 〔 fɑrs 〕 *n.* 鬧劇

—— 同 travesty , burlesque , fiasco , buffoonery , mockery

Traffic laws in this city are a *farce* because no one follows them and they are not enforced.

該市的交通規則是個笑話，因爲既無人遵守也無人執法。

* **foremost** 〔ˈforˌmost 〕 *adj.* 主要的【常考】

—— 同 leading , primary , chief , uppermost , prime

Our company's *foremost* export is computer keyboards.

本公司主要的出口產品是電腦鍵盤。

* **genetic** 〔 dʒəˈnɛtɪk 〕 *adj.* 遺傳的【常考】

—— 同 innate , hereditary , inherited , genic

Otto's green eyes are *genetic*; his mother and father both have green eyes. 奧圖的綠眼珠是遺傳的，他的父母都是綠眼珠。

* **haven** 〔ˈhevən 〕 *n.* 避難所【常考】   —— 同 refuge , shelter , asylum

This coffee shop is my *haven* from the noise of the city.

這家咖啡店是我躲離城市喧囂的避難所。

* **immobile** 〔 ɪˈmobl̩ 〕 *adj.* 靜止的【常考】

—— 同 immovable , motionless

Richard's right arm was *immobile* after the car crash.

車禍後，理查的右臂癱瘓了。

* **indiscriminate** 〔ˌɪndɪˈskrɪmənɪt 〕 *adj.* 不加區別的【常考】

—— 同 random , heterogeneous , chaotic , miscellaneous

The *indiscriminate* shots of the soldiers killed dozens of innocent civilians. 士兵全面的掃射殺死了許多無辜的老百姓。

* **institute** 〔'ɪnstə,tjut〕① *v.* 開始 ② *n.* 學會；研究所【常考】
   ——同 1. start , commence , originate 2. society , college
   This company will *institute* a new policy of customer service. 該公司將啓用新的服務顧客的措施。

‡ **ken** 〔kɛn〕*n.* 知識範圍【最常考】　　——同 knowledge , scope
   I'm afraid that astrophysics is quite beyond my *ken*.
   我恐怕天體物理學超出我的知識範圍外。

* **lease** 〔lis〕① *v.* 租 ② *n.* 租約【常考】
   ——同 1. rent , hire , demise 2. leasehold , contract
   The *lease* on our apartment runs out next month.
   我們公寓的租約下月就到期了。

mandatory 〔'mændə,torɪ〕*adj.* 強制性的
   ——同 obligatory , compulsory , required , commanding , imperative
   It is *mandatory* that all high school students take a biology class before they graduate.
   所有中學生畢業前，都必須修習生物這門課。

* **minuscule** 〔mɪ'nʌskjul〕*adj.* 微小的【常考】
   ——同 tiny , small , minute
   The difference between these two neckties is so *minuscule* that I can't tell them apart. 這兩條領帶的差異微乎其微，我無從分辨。

mutation 〔mju'teʃən〕*n.* 突變；變化
   ——同 change , variation , metamorphosis , transformation
   Because of the radiation from the nuclear power plant, *mutations* were found in fish in a nearby lake.
   由於核能電廠的輻射，鄰近湖裡的魚出現了突變。

nomadic 〔no'mædɪk〕*adj.* 游牧的　　——同 wandering , roving
   Nomadic desert peoples often rely on camels to transport their goods. 沙漠的游牧民族常仰賴駱駝來運貨。

obstinate 〔ˈɑbstənɪt 〕 *adj.* 頑固的

——同 stubborn , headstrong , unyielding , pertinacious , pig-headed

George's **obstinate** refusal to play with the other children ruined the birthday party.

生日派對因喬治堅持不和其他的孩子玩而搞砸了。

outlying 〔 aʊtˈlaɪɪŋ 〕 *adj.* ①在外的 ②偏遠的

——同 1. outer , exterior 2. distant , remote , far-off

The city's **outlying** areas are served by the subway system.

該市的外圍地帶有地鐵設備。

parsimonious 〔ˌpɑrsəˈmonɪəs 〕 *adj.* 吝嗇的；節儉的

——同 miserly , frugal , excessively stingy , thrifty

Grandmother's **parsimonious** lifestyle left plenty of money in the bank.

祖母節儉的生活方式留下一大筆錢在銀行裡。

Exercise　*Fill in the blanks.*

1. The UN declared the town a safe _____, and no troops were allowed to enter there.

2. After spending eight hours cleaning the house, Alton lay _____ on the sofa.

3. Attendance at the meeting is _____ for all employees.

4. Mongolians are traditionally a _____ people.

5. Mr. Hansen's contributions to the church were _____ at best.

【解答】1. haven　2. immobile　3. mandatory　4. nomadic　5. parsimonious

perturb 〔 pɚ'tɝb 〕 *v.* 擾亂；使煩惱
——同 disturb , upset , harass , distress , bother
Alice was *perturbed* that no one helped clean the dishes.
愛麗絲很煩惱沒有人幫她洗碗盤。

portrait 〔'portret 〕 *n.* 肖像
——同 painting , image , picture , likeness , depiction
A huge *portrait* of the former king hung in the main hallway of
the palace.   宮殿的前廊上掛著一幅前國王的肖像。

* **prognosis** 〔 prɑg'nosɪs 〕 *n.* 預斷【常考】
——同 forecast , prediction
What is the doctor's *prognosis* for your illness?
醫生對你病情的預斷如何？

ratify 〔'rætə,faɪ 〕 *v.* 批准
——同 endorse , sanction , confirm , admit , validate
The legislature is voting to *ratify* a new fire safety bill.
立法院正要票決批准新的防火安全條款。

** **renegade** 〔'rɛnɪ,ged 〕 *n.* 叛徒【最常考】
——同 traitor , betrayer , defector , apostate , turncoat
A group of *renegades* planned to take over the town.
一群叛徒計畫要接管這城鎮。

revolt 〔 rɪ'volt 〕 *n.* 叛變
——同 uprising , rebellion , mutiny , revolution
There was nothing the king feared more than a *revolt* among
his noblemen.   這位國王最懼怕的事，莫過於貴族的叛變。

scanty 〔'skæntɪ 〕 *adj.* 不足的   ——同 scant , meager , inadequate
The army's *scanty* food supplies were not enough to feed all of
the starving villagers.   該軍隊短缺的糧秣不夠餵飽所有飢餓的村民。

* **sheen** 〔 ʃin 〕 *n.* 光澤【常考】　——同 light , gleam , luster , shine

The bright **sheen** of the horse's coat showed that it was healthy. 這隻馬毛皮閃亮的光澤顯示出牠很健康。

sole 〔 sol 〕 ① *adj.* 唯一的；單獨的　② *n.* 底部

——同 1. single , unique , exclusive , individual　2. bottom

After wearing the same pair of shoes for a year, Darren found that the **soles** of his shoes were worn out.

戴倫同一雙鞋穿了一整年後，發現鞋底都磨破了。

stale 〔 stel 〕 *adj.*　①不新鮮的　②陳腐的

——同 1. musty , spoiled　2. flat , trite , hackneyed , vapid

This bread was left on the counter overnight and now it's **stale**.

這麵包被擺在櫃檯上一夜，現在已不新鮮了。

sublime 〔 sə'blaɪm 〕 *adj.*　高貴的；卓越的

——同 noble , majestic , excellent , magnificent , lofty , heavenly

After reading this **sublime** book, I wanted to meet the author.

讀完這本鉅作後，我真想認識作者。

* **sustenance** 〔 'sʌstənəns 〕 *n.*　①維持　②食物【常考】

——同 1. subsistence , maintenance　2. edibles , food

During their wilderness survival training, the soldiers learned to find **sustenance** in the forest.

在野外求生訓練中，士兵們學習從森林裡尋找食物。

tease 〔 tiz 〕 *v.* 嘲弄　——同 taunt , mock , banter , chaff

Betty always **teases** her younger brother.

貝蒂老是嘲弄她的弟弟。

touchy 〔 'tʌtʃɪ 〕 *adj.*　暴躁的　——同 irritable , bad-tempered

Be nice to Elaine. She is a little **touchy** about losing the bike race. 對伊蓮好一點。她輸了單車比賽，脾氣有點暴躁。

undomesticated ﹝͵ʌndə´mɛstɪ͵ketɪd﹞ *adj.* 未馴服的

——同 wild , feral , untamed

A herd of ***undomesticated*** horses lives on the island, running freely and ignoring people.

這島上住著一群野馬，牠們自由奔跑，無視人們的存在。

vehicle ﹝´viɪkḷ﹞ *n.* ①車輛 ②傳達媒介

——同 1. transportation , automobile , car 2. a means of conveying

Mozart used music as a ***vehicle*** to express his emotion.

莫札特以音樂為媒介來傳達他的情感。

weave ﹝wiv﹞ *v.* ①編織 ②編造

——同 1. interlace , interlock 2. compose , make up

My uncle is a great storyteller who can ***weave*** wonderful tales about imaginary places.

我叔叔是個說故事高手，他可以編造出虛構地方的奇妙故事。

Exercise ▷ *Fill in the blanks.*

1. As a wedding present, Jane paid to have her niece's wedding _____ painted.

2. Some saw Frank Lloyd Wright as an architectural _____, others, a genius.

3. The room had been closed up for months and when the door was opened, it had a _____ smell.

4. Stop _____ the dog or he might bite you.

5. Don't be so _____ over a little joke.

【解答】1. portrait　2. renegade　3. stale　4. teasing　5. touchy

List 10   難字分析

declivity 〔 dɪ'klɪvətɪ 〕 *n.* 傾斜

de	+	cliv	+	ity
down	+	bend	+	*n.*

—— a downward slope

destitute 〔'dɛstə,tjut 〕 *adj.* 極窮困的

de	+	stitute
away	+	stand

—— living in complete poverty

disorient 〔 dɪs'orɪ,ɛnt 〕 *v.* 使迷失方向

dis	+	ori	+	ent
away	+	rise	+	*v.*

—— to cause to lose one's bearings

eliminate 〔 ɪ'lɪmə,net 〕 *v.* 去除

e +	limin	+	ate
ex			
out +	threshold	+	make

—— to take out

indiscriminate 〔,ɪndɪ'skrɪmənɪt 〕 *adj.* 不加區別的

in +	dis	+	crimin	+	ate
not +	apart	+	separate	+	*adj.*

—— not based on careful selection

mandatory 〔'mændə,torɪ〕 *adj.* 強制性的

mand + at(e) + ory
order + v. + adj.

— containing or carrying a command

obstinate 〔'ɑbstənɪt〕 *adj.* 頑固的

ob + stin + ate
against + stand + adj.

— unreasonably determined to have one's own way

prognosis 〔prɑg'nosɪs〕 *n.* 預斷

pro + gnos + (s)is
before + know + n.

— forecast of the probable course of a disease

renegade 〔'rɛnɪ,ged〕 *n.* 叛徒

re + neg + ade
again + deny + person

— person who abandons his religion or party

sustenance 〔'sʌstənəns〕 *n.* ①維持 ②食物

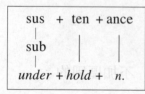

— support; food

TEST ▶ 5

請由 (A)～(D) 中選出和畫線部分意義最相近的字。

1. Taking a second job would <u>augment</u> your salary considerably.
   (A) increase
   (B) stabilize
   (C) ensure
   (D) nullify

2. Our neighborhood <u>mustered</u> a small group of volunteers to help clean up the park.
   (A) hired
   (B) dismissed
   (C) elected
   (D) assembled

3. Pablo Picasso's work had a <u>profound</u> effect on the 20th century modern art.
   (A) relative
   (B) precursory
   (C) deep
   (D) neutral

4. I don't think these apples are ripe yet because they taste so <u>tart</u>.
   (A) sweet
   (B) salty
   (C) rotten
   (D) sour

5. After the rainstorm, I <u>leaped</u> over puddles to avoid getting my new shoes wet.
   (A) stomped
   (B) crawled
   (C) slid
   (D) jumped

6. Tommy made a statement that was very <u>pertinent</u> to the discussion.
   (A) relevant
   (B) interesting
   (C) generous
   (D) evaluated

7. The accident resulted in his hipbone dislocating from its <u>socket</u>.
   (A) outlet
   (B) muscle
   (C) cavity
   (D) protuberance

8. The support of Diana's parents for her medical career never <u>wavered</u>.
   (A) hesitated
   (B) reliable
   (C) understood
   (D) forced

9. Although it was an <u>austere</u> lifestyle, becoming a monk appealed to Christopher.
   (A) fulfilling
   (B) demeaning
   (C) ascetic
   (D) extravagant

10. His pretending to be concerned for her welfare was a <u>farce</u>.
    (A) entertainment
    (B) mockery
    (C) preamble
    (D) fantasy

11. None of us were <u>adverse</u> to stopping over at Hawaii during our flight across the Pacific Ocean.
    (A) encouraged
    (B) observed
    (C) contrary
    (D) enthusiastic

12. The two countries were in <u>concord</u> over how to deal with their trade deficit.
    (A) harmony
    (B) disagreement
    (C) conflict
    (D) resolution

13. Many countries are <u>ratifying</u> environmental protection legislation.
    (A) justifying
    (B) negotiating
    (C) endorsing
    (D) filing

14. The bus turned the corner at a dangerous speed and <u>collided</u> with an oncoming car.
    (A) avoided
    (B) deflected
    (C) crashed
    (D) raced

15. Tommy always throws his dirty clothes on the floor in an <u>indiscriminate</u> manner.
    (A) orderly
    (B) severe
    (C) particular
    (D) random

16. Ted found the Grand Canyon a beautiful place, but Deborah thought it was <u>desolate</u> and boring.
    (A) plentiful
    (B) barren
    (C) minuscule
    (D) humdrum

17. Katherine grew tired of her <u>nomadic</u> lifestyle and decided to finally settle down.
    (A) exotic
    (B) luxurious
    (C) wandering
    (D) reserved

18. We heard a <u>sublime</u> singing voice coming from the apartment upstairs.
    (A) shrill
    (B) deep
    (C) curious
    (D) heavenly

19. With the threat of flooding, townspeople were asked to <u>evacuate</u> their homes and find higher ground.
   (A) depart
   (B) fortify
   (C) evaluate
   (D) move

20. The Smiths' mobile home they travel the country in has all the <u>amenities</u> of a regular house.
   (A) comforts
   (B) appliances
   (C) appearances
   (D) inconveniences

21. The parts of a circuit board are so <u>minuscule</u> that you need a magnifying glass to see them clearly.
   (A) specialized
   (B) charged
   (C) complicated
   (D) tiny

22. Albert was <u>obstinate</u> in refusing to throw away his old typewriter and buy a computer.
   (A) unyielding
   (B) wavering
   (C) obnoxious
   (D) old-fashioned

23. After the school discovered the student had cheated on all his exams, they <u>revoked</u> his diploma.
   (A) reexamined
   (B) annulled
   (C) punished
   (D) prohibited

24. The continued <u>declivity</u> of the US dollar against the Japanese yen has worried several economists.
   (A) decline
   (B) stabilization
   (C) influx
   (D) export

25. Police officers investigating the case admitted the evidence against the suspect was too <u>scanty</u> to convict him.
   (A) unreliable
   (B) insufficient
   (C) bizarre
   (D) perfect

【解答】

1. A	2. D	3. C	4. D	5. D	6. A	7. C	8. A	9. C	10. B
11. C	12. A	13. C	14. C	15. D	16. B	17. C	18. D	19. A	20. A
21. D	22. A	23. B	24. A	25. B					

LIST ▶ 11

abstruse 〔 æb'strus 〕 *adj.* 深奧的；難懂的
——同 incomprehensible , profound , recondite , enigmatic , obscure
I could not understand the scientist's *abstruse* explanation of the chemical reaction.
我無法了解科學家對於這種化學反應所做的深奧解釋。

aerate 〔'eə,ret 〕 *v.* 使暴露於空氣中　——同 air (out)
This plant will do much better if you *aerate* the soil before you place it in the pot.
在你把土放進花盆前，要先讓它接觸空氣，這樣植物會長得比較好。

**amiable 〔'emɪəbḷ 〕 *adj.* 親切的；和藹的【最常考】
——同 agreeable , good-natured , kind-hearted , affable
There is an *amiable* old couple who run a small grocery store on the corner.　有對和藹的老夫婦在街角經營一家小雜貨店。

*array 〔 ə're 〕 *n.* ①陳列　②裝扮【常考】
——同 1. display , order , arrangement　2. garb , attire , dress
There was a huge *array* of delicious fruits on the dinner table.　餐桌上擺了許多好吃的水果。

**authentic 〔 ɔ'θɜntɪk 〕 *adj.* 眞正的【最常考】
——同 real , genuine , actual , factual , veritable
This restaurant has tasty Vietnamese food that is *authentic*.
這家餐廳有道地而且好吃的越南菜。

*beam 〔 bim 〕 *n.* ①橫樑　②光線【常考】
——同 1. girder , joist , support　2. gleam , radiation , ray , glow
A *beam* fell from the building under construction, killing a worker.　這棟建築物在施工期間，有根橫樑掉落；砸死了一名工人。

* **brittle** 〔'brɪtḷ 〕*adj.* 易碎的【常考】
　——同 breakable , fragile , frangible
The frames of his glasses were so old that they became
brittle and cracked.　他眼鏡的框架十分老舊，變得易碎又脆弱。

cement 〔 sə'mɛnt 〕① *v.* 結合　② *n.* 水泥；接合劑
　——同 1. join , unite , adhere , stick , glue　2. glue , adhesive , paste
The bench at the bus stop was *cemented* to the sidewalk.
公車站牌旁邊的長椅被固定在人行道上。

colonize 〔'kɑlə‚naɪz 〕*v.* 殖民　——同 settle , populate , found
Many scientists have predicted that people from Earth will
one day *colonize* Mars.
許多科學家預測，地球上的人類有一天會到火星上殖民。

condemn 〔 kən'dɛm 〕*v.* 譴責　——同 blame , denounce , censure
The Mayor *condemned* the violent behavior of street gangs.
市長譴責街頭幫派的暴力行為。

convert 〔 kən'vɝt 〕*v.* 改變　——同 change , alter , make over
The old town courthouse was *converted* into a shopping
arcade.　城裡這棟古老的法院被改建為商店街。
　* arcade 〔 ɑr'ked 〕*n.* 有騎樓的街道

decompose 〔‚dikəm'poz 〕*v.* 腐爛；分解
　——同 decay , rot , dissolve , disintegrate , corrupt
The dead leaves on the ground *decompose* to form new soil
that helps the trees grow.
地面上的枯葉會進行分解，形成新的土壤，有助於樹木的生長。

* **deter** 〔 dɪ'tɝ 〕*v.* 妨礙；阻止【常考】
　——同 restrain , hinder , discourage
Spending time in jail did not *deter* them from continuing
their illicit trade.　身陷牢獄並不妨礙他們繼續從事非法交易。

disparage〔dɪˈspærɪdʒ〕v. 輕視；毀謗

——同 degrade, depreciate, belittle, speak evil of

Tim's father **disparaged** his studies, calling them meaningless.

提姆的父親批評他的研究，認為他的研究沒有意義。

* elite〔ɪˈlit〕① n. pl. 精英分子；名流 ② adj. 最優秀的【常考】

——同 1. cream, nobility　2. selected, best, exclusive, first-class

The country's **elite** own the greatest percentage of the country's wealth.

該國的精英分子擁有國家大部分的財富。

entail〔ɪnˈtel〕v. 需要

——同 require, necessitate, involve, call for, demand

Being an astronaut **entails** many long hours of training, and lots of scientific knowledge.

想成為太空人，必須經過長期的訓練，並具備豐富的科學知識。

Exercise *Fill in the blanks.*

1. Could you explain the stock market to me without using _____ terms?

2. The museum has several pieces of _____ Tang dynasty porcelain on display.

3. The lampshade had become _____ with age.

4. The Lees _____ their back porch into an enclosed sun room.

5. Planning a traditional wedding ceremony _____ a lot of work and time.

【解答】1. abstruse　2. authentic　3. brittle　4. converted　5. entails

evolution 〔͵ɛvə'luʃən 〕 *n.* 進化；進展
—— 同 development , growth , progress , maturation
The *evolution* of television into the most important means of communication was rapid.
電視成為最重要的傳播媒體，其進展的速度是非常快的。

fasten 〔'fæsn̩ 〕 *v.* 繫緊 —— 同 bind , tie , attach
Wait for me; I have to *fasten* my shoelaces. 等等我，我綁一下鞋帶。

* **foretell** 〔 for'tɛl 〕 *v.* 預測【常考】
—— 同 predict , forecast , foresee , foreshadow , portend
An old man who lives on the hill claims he can *foretell* the future. 有位住在山上的老人宣稱他可以預測未來。

* **genuine** 〔'dʒɛnjuɪn 〕 *adj.* 真正的【常考】
—— 同 real , authentic , actual
Janet took the diamond to the jeweler and found that it was *genuine*. 珍娜把鑽石拿到珠寶商那裡，結果發現是真品。

* **hazard** 〔'hæzəd 〕 *n.* 危險【常考】 —— 同 danger , risk , peril
Bumpy roads with many potholes are a *hazard* to motorcycle drivers. * bumpy 〔'bʌmpɪ 〕 *adj.* 崎嶇不平的   pothole 〔'pɑt͵hol 〕 *n.* 坑洞
崎嶇不平而且坑坑洞洞的道路，對於機車駕駛人而言，十分危險。

** **immune** 〔 ɪ'mjun 〕 *adj.* 免疫的【最常考】
—— 同 free , exempt , unaffected
This vaccine will make you *immune* to the measles.
這種疫苗會讓你對麻疹免疫。
* vaccine 〔'væksin 〕 *n.* 疫苗   measles 〔'mizl̩z 〕 *n. pl.* 麻疹

* **indispensable** 〔͵ɪndɪs'pɛnsəbl̩ 〕 *adj.* 不可或缺的【常考】
—— 同 necessary , essential , requisite , needed , vital
The detective would not investigate a case without his *indispensable* assistant, Dr. Watson.
這位偵探如果少了不可或缺的助手 —— 華生醫師，他就不想調查案子。

* **intact** 〔 ɪn'tækt 〕 *adj.* 完整的【常考】 ——同 whole , unscathed

Few of the houses in the town were left *intact* after the large earthquake. 經過大地震之後，城裡的房子很少有完整無損的。

kidnap 〔'kɪdnæp 〕 *v.* 綁架 ——同 carry off , abduct , capture

The three men tried to *kidnap* the wealthy businessman, but were not successful. 那三名男子想要綁架富商，但並沒有得逞。

legendary 〔'lɛdʒənd,ɛrɪ 〕 *adj.* ①傳說的 ②著名的
——同 1. fictitious , mythical , fabled
　　　　2. celebrated , renowned , famous

The writings of the *legendary* author were prized by book collectors everywhere.
這位名作家的作品受到各地書籍收藏家的讚賞。

* **maneuver** 〔 mə'nuvɚ 〕 *n.* ①演習 ②策略【常考】
——同 1. deployment , movement , operation
　　　　2. tactic , scheme , strategy

The three-point-turn is the hardest *maneuver* you must perform in the driving test.
駕駛測驗中，三點轉彎是你必須做的最難動作。

* **minute** 〔 mə'njut , maɪ- 〕 *adj.* 微小的【常考】
——同 minuscule , tiny

Several *minute* cracks had begun to appear in the glass of the window. 窗上的玻璃已開始出現一些細微的裂痕。

mythical 〔'mɪθɪkl̩ 〕 *adj.* ①神話的 ②虛構的 *n.* myth
——同 1. fabulous , mythological
　　　　2. imaginary , made-up , fabricated

The most famous *mythical* animal is the unicorn.
神話中最有名的動物是獨角獸。

nominal 〔ˈnɑmənḷ 〕 *adj.* ①名義上的 ②些許的

——同 1. formal , ostensible , titular 2. small , minimal

Though Mr. Green was the ***nominal*** leader of the group, we made many decisions on our own.

雖然格林先生是這個團體名義上的領導者，我們還是自已做了許多決定。

obstruct 〔 əbˈstrʌkt 〕 *v.* 妨礙

——同 hinder , impede , retard , hamper , block

A large tree that had fallen on the road ***obstructed*** the vehicular traffic. 倒在路上的大樹妨礙了車輛的交通。

* outmoded 〔 aʊtˈmodɪd 〕 *adj.* 過時的【常考】

——同 obsolete , old-fashioned , out of date , behind the times

My aunt still drives an ***outmoded*** car from the 1970's and will not trade it in.

我姑媽還是開那部七〇年代的舊車，不願意用舊車抵購新車。

* particle 〔ˈpɑrtɪkḷ 〕 *n.* 分子；微粒【常考】

——同 atom , mite , molecule , speck , bit

Particles of coal in the air make everything look gray.

空氣中的碳屑使得每樣東西看起來都是灰色的。

| **Exercise** | *Fill in the blanks.* |

1. Taiwan's recent history is an example of the ＿＿＿＿＿ of a democracy.

2. The prophet had ＿＿＿＿＿ the coming of a savior.

3. Ken is an ＿＿＿＿＿ part of the party's leadership.

4. The insect is too ＿＿＿＿＿ to see with the naked eye.

5. After the newspaper's computer system broke down, they had to use their ＿＿＿＿＿ equipment to print the paper.

【解答】1. evolution   2. foretold   3. indispensable   4. minute   5. outmoded

* **peruse** 〔 pəˈruz 〕 *v.* 精讀【常考】 —— 同 read , study

My father *perused* the instruction manual before setting up the stereo. 我父親在組裝音響之前，有仔細閱讀說明書。

* manual 〔ˈmænjʊəl 〕 *n.* 手冊

portray 〔 porˈtre 〕 *v.* 描述；飾演

—— 同 describe , depict , sketch , represent , delineate

In this movie, the actor *portrays* a lawyer who discovers a plot to kill the president.

在這部電影中，男主角飾演一位律師，他發現了一樁謀殺總統的陰謀。

* **prohibitive** 〔 proˈhɪbɪtɪv 〕 *adj.* 禁止的；嚇阻的【常考】

—— 同 forbidding , proscriptive , restrictive , suppressive

The *prohibitive* prices in that store keep everyone but the richest people from going in.

那家店價格十分嚇人，除了有錢人之外，大家都不敢進去。

** **raze** 〔 rez 〕 *v.* 消除；破壞【最常考】 —— 同 demolish , level , tear down

The entire city was *razed* to the ground by the powerful typhoon. 這整個都市都被強烈颱風夷為平地。

renovate 〔ˈrɛnəˌvet 〕 *v.* 革新

—— 同 renew , refresh , recreate , reform , restore

The government provided money to the museum to *renovate* its dinosaur collection. 政府提供經費給博物館，更新其恐龍的收集品。

rhythm 〔ˈrɪðəm 〕 *n.* 節奏 —— 同 beat , tempo , cadence

The *rhythm* of the drums in the music made everyone want to get up and dance. 音樂中鼓聲的節奏，讓大家都想站起來跳舞。

* **scarcely** 〔ˈskɛrslɪ 〕 *adv.* 幾乎不；僅僅【常考】

—— 同 hardly , barely

I had *scarcely* begun to talk when Robert interrupted me.

我才剛要開口，羅伯特就打斷了我的話。

* **sheer**〔ʃɪr〕*adj.* 完全的【常考】 ——同 utter , absolute , entire

The look on her face when she saw the dead body was one of *sheer* horror.　當她看到屍體時，臉上的表情是全然的恐懼。

* **solemn**〔'saləm〕*adj.* 嚴肅的；莊嚴的【常考】

——同 grave , serious

The memorial service for the people who had died in the bombing was *solemn*.

為爆炸中喪生的人所舉辦的紀念儀式，十分莊嚴肅穆。

* **stalk**〔stɔk〕① *v.* 潛近 ② *n.* 莖【常考】

——同 1. creep , shadow , tail 2. stock , axis , stem

After all the corn was picked, all that remained in the field was the *stalks*.　所有玉米都採收完了，田裡只剩下莖。

submarine ①〔ˌsʌbmə'rin〕*adj.* 海底的
② 〔'sʌbməˌrin〕*n.* 潛水艇

——同 1. undersea , underwater 2. underwater craft

The marine scientist collected several *submarine* plants to see if they could be raised as food.

海洋科學家收集了好幾種海洋植物，想看看是否可以作食物來培植。

* **swamp**〔swɑmp〕① *n.* 沼澤 ② *v.* 淹沒；壓制【常考】

——同 1. bog , marsh , mire 2. flood , overwhelm , drench , submerge

The *swamp* is full of dangerous poisonous snakes.
沼澤裡充滿了危險的毒蛇。

* **tedious**〔'tidɪəs〕*adj.* 乏味的【常考】

——同 wearisome , dull , boring

Although Patty loves going fishing, her brother thinks it is a *tedious* pastime.

雖然佩蒂很喜歡釣魚，但她哥哥卻認為那是種無聊的消遣。

tractable 〔'træktəbl̩ 〕 *adj.* 溫馴的 ——同 docile , obedient , tame
After his bottle, the baby was quite ***tractable*** and slept for
most of the afternoon.
嬰兒喝完奶後，變得十分溫馴，下午大部分的時間都在睡覺。

unevenly 〔 ʌn'ivənlɪ 〕 *adv.* 不平均地
——同 roughly , unfairly , unequally , disparately
Tom had never made a cake before, and he spread the icing
on it very ***unevenly***.　＊icing〔'aɪsɪŋ 〕 *n.* 糖衣；糖霜
湯姆沒做過蛋糕，所以他抹在蛋糕上的糖霜十分不均勻。

vein 〔 ven 〕 *n.* ①靜脈 ②性情；氣質
——同 1. blood vessel , stream , current 2. temper , mood , character
When lifting weights, Greg's ***veins*** pop out on his forehead.
當葛瑞格舉起重物時，他額頭上的靜脈就會浮現。

wed 〔 wɛd 〕 *v.* ①結婚 ②結合
——同 1. marry , espouse 2. join , unite , ally , combine
Allen and Naomi are to ***wed*** the Saturday after next.
艾倫和娜娥蜜下下星期六要結婚了。

Exercise 〉 *Fill in the blanks.*

1. I'd like to ＿＿＿＿＿＿ all of the brochures before making
   my decision.

2. The store is being ＿＿＿＿＿＿ and will reopen in a week.

3. After the ＿＿＿＿＿＿ graduation ceremony, all of the
   students were ready to celebrate.

4. That dog is ＿＿＿＿＿＿ only when its owner is around.

5. Wealth is spread very ＿＿＿＿＿＿ among the population
   of the country.

【解答】1. peruse　2. renovated　3. solemn　4. tractable　5. unevenly

· List 11 · 難字分析

abstruse 〔 æb'strus 〕 *adj.* 深奧的；難懂的

abs + truse
| |
away + push

—— difficult to understand

decompose 〔 ,dikəm'poz 〕 *v.* 腐爛；分解

de + com + pose
| | |
do the + together + put
opposite of

—— to break up into basic components

entail 〔 ɪn'tel 〕 *v.* 需要

en + tail
| |
into + cut

—— to make necessary

indispensable 〔 ,ɪndɪs'pɛnsəbl̩ 〕 *adj.* 不可或缺的

in + dis + pens + able
| | | |
not + apart + hang + able to

—— that cannot be neglected

legendary 〔 'lɛdʒənd,ɛrɪ 〕 *adj.* ①傳說的 ②著名的

leg + end + ary
| |
read + n. + adj.

—— of or told in a legend; famous

nominal 〔'nɑmənḷ 〕 *adj.* ①名義上的 ②些許的

nomin + al
name + *adj.*

—— in name only; very small

peruse 〔 pə'ruz 〕 *v.* 精讀

per + use
through + *use*

—— to read thoroughly

prohibitive 〔 pro'hɪbɪtɪv 〕 *adj.* 禁止的;嚇阻的

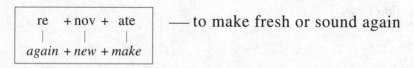

pro + hibit + ive
before + *have* + *adj.*

—— intended to prevent the use or misuse of something

renovate 〔'rɛnə,vet 〕 *v.* 革新

re + nov + ate
again + *new* + *make*

—— to make fresh or sound again

submarine ① 〔,sʌbmə'rin 〕 *adj.* 海底的
② 〔'sʌbmə,rin 〕 *n.* 潛水艇

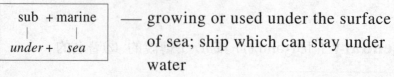

sub + marine
under + *sea*

—— growing or used under the surface of sea; ship which can stay under water

📓 LIST ▸ 12

* abundant 〔ə'bʌndənt〕*adj.* 豐富的；充裕的【常考】
　　——同 ample , sufficient , copious , profuse , prolific
There is *abundant* room for guests in my parents' house.
我父母的房子有足夠的空間可招待客人。

**affable 〔'æfəbl̩〕*adj.* 和藹的；溫柔的【最常考】
　　——同 amiable , approachable , friendly , genial , cordial
Tina is such an *affable* person that I look forward to going
to dinner with her this weekend.
蒂娜相當的溫柔，我很期待和她在這週末一起吃晚餐。

ample 〔'æmpl̩〕*adj.* 充足的
　　——同 abundant , sufficient , plentiful , expansive , spacious
Our yard has *ample* space to plant a few flowers and
vegetables.　我們的院子有充足的空間，可種植些花草和蔬菜。

arrogant 〔'ærəgənt〕*adj.* 傲慢的
　　——同 surly , haughty , presumptuous , overbearing , proud , pompous
I can't believe Eric was *arrogant* enough to say that he did
better than you.　我無法相信艾瑞克敢傲慢地說，他表現得比你好。

authorize 〔'ɔθə,raɪz〕*v.* 授權
　　——同 empower , accredit , approve , entitle , give authority
The strike was *authorized* by union leaders.
該罷工係由工會領袖所授權。

behold 〔bɪ'hold〕*v.* 注視　——同 look at , watch , observe
When we finally reached the mountaintop and looked down,
we *beheld* the most beautiful sight.
當我們終於爬上山頂往下看時，我們見到了最美的景色。

broach 〔 brotʃ 〕 *v.* 提出　——同 bring up , mention , propose

I don't think you should ***broach*** the subject of Oscar's divorce at the party.　我認為你不該在宴會上把奧斯卡離婚的事提出來。

censure 〔'sɛnʃᴪ 〕 *v.* 責難

——同 blame , chide , condemn , criticize , reproach

The people ***censured*** the officials in charge of fire safety.

民眾譴責主管火災安全的官員。

comic 〔'kamɪk 〕 *adj.* 喜劇的　——同 funny , laughable , farcical

It was a ***comic*** play about a woman living in New York.

這是齣關於一位住在紐約的女人的喜劇。

condescend 〔,kandɪ'sɛnd 〕 *v.* 屈尊

——同 patronize , deign , demean oneself , submit

We were amazed that the queen would ***condescend*** to join us commoners for dinner.

我們都感到驚訝,皇后竟會屈尊和我們平民一起吃飯。

*convey 〔 kən've 〕 *v.* 傳達;輸送【常考】

——同 communicate , transport , reveal , forward

Long ago, American Indians used smoke signals to ***convey*** messages.　從前,美國的印地安人使用煙訊來傳遞消息。

decree 〔 dɪ'kri 〕 *v.* 命令　——同 command , prescribe , ordain

The mayor ***decreed*** that an official investigation of the city council's budget would begin immediately.

市長下令隨即展開對市議會預算的正式調查。

**disparity 〔 dɪs'pærətɪ 〕 *n.* 不一致;懸殊【最常考】

——同 discrepancy , gap , inequality , inequity , divergence

The ***disparity*** between the rich and the poor is growing rapidly in China.　中國的貧富懸殊急速地成長。

diurnal 〔 daɪˈɜ̩nl̩ 〕 *adj.* 每日的　—同 daily , quotidian

Martin closed his eyes, hoping the rooster wouldn't crow and signal the start of his **diurnal** chores.

馬丁閉上眼睛，希望公雞不要啼叫，告訴他又要開始每天的雜務。

drowsy 〔ˈdraʊzɪ 〕 *adj.* 昏昏欲睡的
　—同 sleepy , half-asleep , lethargic , sluggish

This cold medicine will make you feel **drowsy**, so don't drive after you take it.

這感冒藥會讓你覺得昏昏欲睡，所以服用之後不要開車。

eloquent 〔ˈɛləkwənt 〕 *adj.* 雄辯的；生動的
　—同 articulate , persuasive , silver-tongued , forceful , well-expressed

His speech requesting money for the library was so **eloquent** that everyone there made donations.

他為圖書館籌款的演講極為生動，在場的人都捐款了。

Exercise　*Fill in the blanks.*

1. Her ＿＿＿＿＿＿ personality made her popular with the students.

2. Did the manager ＿＿＿＿＿＿ the purchase of a new copier machine?

3. His ＿＿＿＿＿＿ response made all the people present laugh.

4. I am too ＿＿＿＿＿＿ to continue working on this report.

5. Everyone was moved by the ＿＿＿＿＿＿ performance of the actor.

【解答】1. affable　2. authorize　3. comic　4. drowsy　5. eloquent

entice 〔 ɪn'taɪs 〕 *v.* 引誘 ——同 lure , tempt , attract
The wonderful fragrance coming from the coffee shop *enticed*
me to enter. 從咖啡店內傳來的美味，誘使我進了店門。

* **exacerbate** 〔 ɪg'zæsə͵bet 〕 *v.* 加劇；激怒【常考】
——同 aggravate , intensify , sharpen , embitter
The hot summer weather always *exacerbates* Martha's bad
mood. 炎夏的天氣每每加劇瑪莎的壞脾氣。

fastidious 〔 fæs'tɪdɪəs 〕 *adj.* 苛求的
——同 hard to please , picky , fussy , meticulous
Mr. Wang is very *fastidious* about keeping his office spotlessly
clean. 王先生嚴格地要求，他的辦公室要保持得一塵不染。

* **forge** 〔 fɔrdʒ 〕 *v.* ①鑄造 ②仿冒【常考】
——同 1. create , hammer out 2. counterfeit , fake , feign
He was arrested for *forging* several thousand dollars worth of
checks. 他因為偽造價值數千元的支票而被捕。

germinate 〔'dʒɜmə͵net 〕 *v.* 發芽
——同 sprout , burgeon , bud , grow , vegetate
This type of flower needs a moist, cool environment to
germinate. 這種花要在濕涼的環境下才會發芽。

hallucination 〔 hə͵lusn̩'eʃən 〕 *n.* 幻覺
——同 fantasy , illusion , delusion , apparition
Drugs can often cause the user to have strange *hallucinations*.
毒品通常會讓使用者產生奇怪的幻覺。

****impale** 〔 ɪm'pel 〕 *v.* 刺穿【最常考】 ——同 transfix , pierce , stab
The severed heads of enemy soldiers were *impaled* on the
spears and placed outside the city gates.
敵軍的斷頭被穿在矛上，並擺在城門外頭。

indisputable〔͵ɪndɪˈspjutəbḷ〕*adj.* 不容爭辯的
——同 unquestionable , undeniable , obvious , evident , unmistakable
The scientist could not provide ***indisputable*** evidence that his
theory was correct.
科學家無法提出不容爭辯的證據，來說明他的理論是正確的。

intangible〔ɪnˈtændʒəbḷ〕*adj.* 摸不著的；無形的
——同 impalpable , imperceptible , immaterial , abstract
Although teaching is hard work, it has many ***intangible***
rewards.　教書雖然辛苦，但卻能得到許多無形的回報。

legislation〔͵lɛdʒɪsˈleʃən〕*n.* ①立法 ②法律
——同 1. lawmaking , codification 2. act , bill , regulation
This new ***legislation*** will protect consumers from unsafe
products.　這項新法將保護消費者不會買到危險的產品。

* manifestation〔͵mænəfɛsˈteʃən〕*n.* 顯示；證明【常考】
——同 demonstration , display , indication , revelation
The drop in his grades at school was a ***manifestation*** of his
depression.　他在校成績的滑落，顯示出他的心情沮喪。

miser〔ˈmaɪzɚ〕*n.* 守財奴 ——同 niggard , skinflint
That old ***miser*** wouldn't even pay the fare to ride the bus.
那位年老的守財奴甚至不肯花錢搭公車。

**nostalgia〔nɑˈstældʒɪə〕*n.* 鄉愁；懷舊之情【最常考】
——同 homesickness , regretfulness , reminiscence , longing
He was filled with ***nostalgia*** for his youth.
他對年輕時的歲月充滿懷舊之情。

**obtrusive〔əbˈtrusɪv〕*adj.* 莽撞的；冒失的【最常考】
——同 impertinent , interfering , forward , intrusive , pushy
Tony's ***obtrusive*** comments embarrassed everyone.
湯尼莽撞的言語令大家十分尷尬。

outrage ﹝'aʊt,redʒ﹞① *n.* 暴行 ② *v.* 激怒

——同 1. offense , violence , affront 2. anger , infuriate , madden

The citizens considered the proposed increase in taxes an *outrage*. 市民對於提議增稅感到十分憤怒。

patch ﹝pætʃ﹞① *n.* 細片 ② *v.* 修補

——同 1. small piece , shred , scrap 2. mend , fix , reinforce

Could you *patch* this hole in my pants?
你能幫我修補褲子上的破洞嗎？

＊**perverse** ﹝pə'vɜs﹞ *adj.* 倔強的；固執的【最常考】

——同 contrary , stubborn , self-willed , ungovernable , wayward

He was *perverse* in his insistence on building the house himself. 他很固執，堅持要自己蓋房子。

> **Exercise** Fill in the blanks.

1. Her allergies were ＿＿＿＿＿ by the cold wind.

2. Joan is a ＿＿＿＿＿ eater, and she never likes what I cook.

3. After the plant ＿＿＿＿＿, it will not be long before its flowers bloom.

4. It is difficult to describe ＿＿＿＿＿ ideas, such as love or morality.

5. My boss was such a ＿＿＿＿＿ that he refused to give us year-end bonuses.

【解答】1. exacerbated 2. fastidious 3. germinates 4. intangible 5. miser

* **posthumous** (ˈpɑstʃuməs) *adj.* 死後的【常考】
—— 同 happening after death , postmortem
This book is a ***posthumous*** volume of the writer's previously unpublished poems.
這本書收錄了該作家未發表的詩作，在其死後才出版。

* **proliferate** (proˈlɪfəˌret) *v.* 繁殖【常考】
—— 同 breed , multiply , increase , expand , escalate
The ivy vines ***proliferated*** and soon nearly covered the house.
長春藤不斷繁殖，很快就長滿了整棟房子。

* **prudent** (ˈprudṇt) *adj.* 謹慎的【常考】
—— 同 discreet , wise , careful
George does not think that buying a car now would be ***prudent***.
喬治認爲現在買車是不智之舉。

rebuff (rɪˈbʌf) *v.* 斷然拒絕   —— 同 refuse , reject , turn down
Penny ***rebuffed*** any offer of help in carrying the box up the stairs. 潘妮斷然拒絕，不要別人幫她把箱子搬到樓上。

renowned (rɪˈnaʊnd) *adj.* 有名的
—— 同 famous , eminent , celebrated , notable , well-known
Several ***renowned*** musicians will be performing in town this week. 本週有好幾位著名的音樂家要來城裡演奏。

ridicule (ˈrɪdɪkjul) *v.* 嘲笑
—— 同 mock , sneer at , scoff at , deride , make fun of
Children can be cruel in ***ridiculing*** other children for being different. 小孩子可能會殘忍地嘲笑其他異常的孩子。

* **scatter** (ˈskætɚ) *v.* ①驅散 ②散播【常考】
—— 同 1. disperse , disband , dissipate 2. spread , sprinkle , strew
The people in the square quickly ***scattered*** when they learned of the bomb threat. 當廣場上的人知道有炸彈的威脅時，便快速地疏散。

* **shift** 〔 ʃɪft 〕 v. 轉變【常考】 —— 同 vary , change , veer , switch

Oliver **shifted** his attention to the argument going on behind him. 奧利佛轉而注意別人在他背後的議論。

* **soothing** 〔'suðɪŋ 〕 adj. 緩和的【常考】

—— 同 comforting , calming , relieving , palliative

Some people feel that the sound of waves crashing on the beach is very **soothing**.
有些人覺得海浪衝擊海岸的聲音聽起來十分舒服。

stamina 〔'stæmənə 〕 n. 體力

—— 同 energy , vitality , vigor , endurance , strength

It takes a lot of **stamina** to be a marathon runner.
要成為馬拉松選手需要充沛的體力。

* **submerge** 〔 səb'mɝdʒ 〕 v. 浸入水中；淹沒【常考】

—— 同 sink , immerse , swamp , dip

Ethan enjoyed **submerging** himself in the cool water of the lake. 伊森喜歡浸在冰涼的湖水中。

sway 〔 swe 〕 v. 影響 —— 同 influence , control , direct

Betty tried to **sway** Mike over to her side of the argument.
貝蒂想要影響麥克來支持她這一邊的論點。

* **tedium** 〔'tidɪəm 〕 n. 沉悶【常考】 —— 同 boredom , dullness

The **tedium** of her job drove her to finally quit.
她的工作十分沉悶，最後她就把工作給辭了。

** **tranquil** 〔'træŋkwɪl 〕 adj. 寧靜的【最常考】

—— 同 serene , peaceful , quiet , placid , unperturbed

Ron and Martha walked until they found a **tranquil** spot to eat their picnic.
朗恩和瑪莎一直走，直到他們找到一處安靜的地方野餐。

* **unquenchable** 〔 ʌnˈkwɛntʃəbḷ 〕 *adj.* 無法滿足的【常考】

—— 同 insatiable , limitless , unsatisfied

His *unquenchable* desire for power finally led to his ruin.

他對權力毫無止境的慾望，最後造成了他的滅亡。

* **velocity** 〔 vəˈlɑsətɪ 〕 *n.* 速度【常考】

—— 同 speed , celerity

The *velocity* of a space rocket has to be immense to escape Earth's gravity.

太空火箭的速度必須快，才能擺脫地球的地心引力。

wedge 〔 wɛdʒ 〕 *v.* 擠；塞

—— 同 cram , stuff , squeeze , jam , thrust

She *wedged* a small piece of wood under the door to keep it from being blown shut by the wind.

她在門下塞一小塊木板，防止門因風吹而關上。

Exercise ⟩ *Fill in the blanks.*

1. He made a _____ decision to set aside some money in a retirement fund.

2. We felt no remorse for _____ the arrogant man.

3. There is a _____ spot on the hill where we can go to talk.

4. A seemingly _____ thirst can be a sign of diabetes.

5. Police use radar guns to measure the _____ of cars traveling on the highway.

【解答】1. prudent 2. ridiculing 3. tranquil 4. unquenchable 5. velocity

· List 12 · 難字分析

affable 〔 'æfəbḷ 〕 *adj.* 和藹的；溫柔的

af + fa + ble
ad ⎪ able
to + speak + able to

— pleasant and easy to talk to

condescend 〔 ‚kɑndɪ'sɛnd 〕 *v.* 屈尊

con + de + scend
together + down + climb

— to agree to do something beneath one's social rank

exacerbate 〔 ɪg'zæsəˌbet 〕 *v.* 加劇；激怒

ex + acerb + ate
out + sharp + make

— to increase the severity of; to aggravate

germinate 〔 'dʒɝməˌnet 〕 *v.* 發芽

germin + ate
bud + make

— to sprout

indisputable 〔 ‚ɪndɪ'spjutəbḷ 〕 *adj.* 不容爭辯的

in + dis + put + able
not + apart + think + able to

— that cannot be doubted

intangible 〔 ɪn'tændʒəb! 〕 *adj.* 摸不著的；無形的

in + tang + ible
| | |
not + touch + able to

— that cannot be touched

manifestation 〔 ˌmænəfɛs'teʃən 〕 *n.* 顯示；證明

mani + fest + ation
| | |
hand + strike + n.

— making clear and plain; an indication of the reality of something

obtrusive 〔 əb'trusɪv 〕 *adj.* 莽撞的；冒失的

ob + trus + ive
| | |
against + push + adj.

— inclined to push forward

posthumous 〔 'pɑstʃuməs 〕 *adj.* 死後的

post + hum + ous
| | |
after + ground + adj.

— coming or happening after death

submerge 〔 səb'mɝdʒ 〕 *v.* 浸入水中；淹沒

sub + merge
| |
under + sink

— to place under or cover with water

velocity 〔 və'lɑsətɪ 〕 *n.* 速度

veloc + ity
| |
fast + n.

— quickness of motion

TEST ▸ 6

請由 (A)～(D) 中選出和畫線部分意義最相近的字。

1. We all met at our favorite restaurant for an <u>amiable</u> lunch gathering.
   - (A) annual
   - (B) obligatory
   - (C) friendly
   - (D) responsible

2. How can you <u>condemn</u> the man if you don't have all the facts of the story?
   - (A) support
   - (B) denounce
   - (C) study
   - (D) measure

3. We were <u>deterred</u> from joining a local gang by the stern words of our teacher.
   - (A) encouraged
   - (B) violated
   - (C) discouraged
   - (D) analyzed

4. In Australia, wildfires burned out of control, <u>razing</u> entire communities.
   - (A) enflaming
   - (B) reviving
   - (C) mortifying
   - (D) destroying

5. Jasper made a <u>genuine</u> attempt to make up with Nora, but Nora refused his apology.
   - (A) diluted
   - (B) real
   - (C) timid
   - (D) forced

6. I was surprised to receive my bicycle <u>intact</u> after I lent it to Lyle.
   - (A) punctual
   - (B) damaged
   - (C) repainted
   - (D) unscathed

7. <u>Prohibitive</u> measures were taken to keep school children from being truant.
   - (A) illegal
   - (B) nominal
   - (C) restrictive
   - (D) superb

8. Darla went on a trip to Sydney for the <u>nominal</u> purpose of securing new business contacts.
   - (A) occasional
   - (B) ostensible
   - (C) burdensome
   - (D) necessary

9. Slick television advertisements <u>entice</u> consumers to buy a company's products.

(A) demand
(B) require
(C) lure
(D) refer

10. Why are you so <u>perverse</u> as to refuse to call your own father on his birthday?

(A) stubborn
(B) timid
(C) ridiculous
(D) predictable

11. With American university tuition so high, it seems only the moneyed <u>elite</u> can afford a higher education.

(A) upper class
(B) masses
(C) officials
(D) military

12. My offer to loan Sandy some money to help pay her phone bill was <u>rebuffed</u>.

(A) encouraged
(B) questioned
(C) refused
(D) negotiated

13. Plant and animal life are prolific in the warm, moist environment of the <u>swamp</u>.

(A) marsh
(B) desert
(C) plains
(D) forest

14. Victims had been <u>impaled</u> by sharp debris sent flying by the tornado.

(A) pounded
(B) suffocated
(C) stabbed
(D) crushed

15. Mosquitoes <u>proliferate</u> quickly in places where there is standing water.

(A) decline
(B) infect
(C) mutate
(D) multiply

16. Since the problem with the software is <u>minute</u>, you can continue to use it without worry.

(A) fundamental
(B) fortunate
(C) substantial
(D) slight

17. The bookcase was so full of books that you couldn't possibly <u>wedge</u> in another volume.

(A) remove
(B) slide
(C) replace
(D) cram

18. There were <u>scarcely</u> enough medical supplies available to treat all the disaster victims.

(A) barely
(B) surplus
(C) similarly
(D) literally

19. We have an <u>abundant</u> supply of strawberries every summer from our backyard strawberry patch.

    (A) copious
    (B) scant
    (C) profitable
    (D) delicious

20. After he became a famous movie star, he no longer <u>condescended</u> to do his own grocery shopping.

    (A) expected
    (B) hurried
    (C) deigned
    (D) neglected

21. After taking a ballet class, the professional football player appreciated the dancers' <u>stamina</u>.

    (A) endurance
    (B) grace
    (C) patience
    (D) aggression

22. The business tycoon knew that money would always <u>sway</u> people to see things his way.

    (A) terrorize
    (B) persuade
    (C) argue
    (D) send

23. If you should <u>broach</u> the subject of economics with her, I'm sure you two would have a lively discussion.

    (A) avoid
    (B) describe
    (C) repeat
    (D) mention

24. Charles' teacher was surprised by the <u>disparity</u> between the test scores from last semester and this semester.

    (A) equality
    (B) discrepancy
    (C) increase
    (D) decrease

25. For tonight's dinner party, my parents invited my <u>obtrusive</u> aunt who is always prying into other people's affairs.

    (A) unassuming
    (B) pushy
    (C) distant
    (D) subdued

【解答】

1. C   2. B   3. C   4. D   5. B   6. D   7. C   8. B   9. C   10. A
11. A   12. C   13. A   14. C   15. D   16. D   17. D   18. A   19. A   20. C
21. A   22. B   23. D   24. B   25. B

LIST ▸ 13

abuse〔əˈbjuz〕*v.* ①濫用 ②虐待
　　——同 1. misuse , misapply , mishandle　2. mistreat , maltreat
The child was ***abused*** by her parents for many years before
being rescued.　該兒童在獲救之前，已遭父母虐待多年。

* **affiliate**〔əˈfɪlɪˌet〕*v.* 使有密切關連【常考】
　　——同 associate , combine , connect , syndicate , merge
This bank is ***affiliated*** with other banks in the region.
這家銀行和該地區其他的銀行關係密切。

* **analogy**〔əˈnælədʒɪ〕*n.* 類似【常考】
　　——同 parallel , correspondence , similarity , comparison
She drew an ***analogy*** between the greed of bureaucracies and
the greed of individual people.
她指出官僚的貪婪與個人的貪心二者之間的相似處。
　＊bureaucracy〔bjuˈrɑkrəsɪ〕*n.* 官僚

article〔ˈɑrtɪkḷ〕*n.* ①文章 ②物品
　　——同 1. essay , story , report　2. item , object , thing
There were several ***articles*** in the store which he was
interested in buying.　這家店有些他有興趣購買的東西。

＊＊**autonomous**〔ɔˈtɑnəməs〕*adj.* 自治的【最常考】
　　——同 independent , sovereign , self-governing , self-ruling
The government considered creating an ***autonomous*** economic
region in the south.　政府考慮要在南方成立經濟自治區。

bellow〔ˈbɛlo〕*v.* 喊叫　——同 shout , yell , roar , bawl , scream
He ***bellowed*** loudly when the pile of books fell on his foot.
當成堆的書掉在他腳上時，他大聲地叫了起來。

brochure 〔 broˈʃur 〕 *n.* 小冊子
──〔同〕 pamphlet , booklet , leaflet , hand-out
The airport is a good place to get **brochures** on traveling in a city. 機場是取得都市旅遊手冊的好地方。

*** chaos** 〔ˈkeɑs 〕 *n.* 混亂【常考】　*adj.* chaotic
──〔同〕 complete disorder , confusion , turmoil , uproar , disorganization
The **chaos** caused by the fire in the apartment building made it difficult for firefighters to get to the fire.
火災在公寓大樓內所造成的混亂，使得消防人員難以救火。

commanding 〔 kəˈmændɪŋ 〕 *adj.* ①指揮的　②威嚴的
──〔同〕 1. controlling , decisive , dominant　2. forceful , authoritative
The politician's **commanding** presence drew many people to follow him. 那位政治家威嚴的儀態吸引許多人跟隨他。

*** condone** 〔 kənˈdon 〕 *v.* 寬恕【常考】
──〔同〕 forgive , excuse , pardon , wink at , overlook , let pass
I cannot **condone** the terrible thing you have done.
你做出如此可怕的事，我沒辦法原諒你。

︰convivial 〔 kənˈvɪvɪəl 〕 *adj.* 歡宴的；歡樂的【最常考】
──〔同〕 festive , jovial , gay , sociable , genial , companionable
The Christmas party was a **convivial** affair enjoyed by everyone. 聖誕舞會是大家所喜愛的歡樂活動。

deduce 〔 dɪˈdjus 〕 *v.* 推論　──〔同〕 infer , conclude , derive
From the clues the detective gathered, she **deduced** that Mr. Smith was the thief.
由那位偵探所蒐集的線索看來，她推論史密斯先生是小偷。

detest 〔 dɪˈtɛst 〕 *v.* 厭惡　──〔同〕 hate , abhor , despise
Sam **detests** the smell of gasoline. 山姆討厭汽油味。

* **disperse**〔dɪ'spɝs〕*v.* 驅散【常考】

——同 scatter , spread , distribute , diffuse , disseminate

The oil gradually **dispersed** over the surface of the water.

油逐漸在水面上擴散開來。

dual〔'djuəl〕*adj.* 雙重的

——同 duplex , twofold , double , binary , duplicate

The **dual** purpose stadium is for football and baseball.

這體育場兼具舉行橄欖球與棒球比賽的雙重功用。

* **elucidate**〔ɪ'lusə,det〕*v.* 闡明【最常考】

——同 explain , clarify , illuminate , illustrate , interpret

Could you **elucidate** the reasons why we need a
bigger house?

你能說明我們需要更大的房子的理由嗎？

Exercise ▷ *Fill in the blanks.*

1. Olga was sad to see that wild animals were _____ in
   Taipei.

2. My travel agent sent me several _____ about things
   to do in San Francisco.

3. After the major earthquake, everything was in _____.

4. The world's failure to stop the mass murders of people in
   Rwanda passively _____ it.

5. I _____ riding on buses on rainy days at rush hour.

【解答】1. abused   2. brochures   3. chaos   4. condoned   5. detest

entirely 〔 ɪnˈtaɪrlɪ 〕 *adv.* 完全地

—— 同 solely , completely , totally , wholly , all

This amazing picture is made ***entirely*** of flower petals.

這幅驚人的圖畫全部由花瓣所製成。

exact 〔 ɪgˈzækt 〕 *adj.* ①精確的 ②嚴厲的；嚴謹的

—— 同 1. accurate , correct , precise 2. strict , unequivocal

The official was very ***exact*** in his actions, following the rules
to the letter.　這位官員的行為非常嚴謹，他很嚴格地遵守規定。

* **fatigue** 〔 fəˈtig 〕 *n.* 疲乏【常考】

—— 同 tiredness , weariness , exhaustion

Fatigue makes you more likely to get sick.

疲勞會使你更容易生病。

* **feat** 〔 fit 〕 *n.* 功績；壯舉【常考】

—— 同 accomplishment , achievement , exploit

If you could just finish the marathon, that would be a ***feat***.

如果你能跑完這場馬拉松，那真是壯舉。

** **flagrant** 〔ˈflegrənt 〕 *adj.* 惡劣的；公然的【最常考】

—— 同 notorious , awful , dreadful , arrant , heinous

The townspeople protested the police officer's ***flagrant***
disregard for their rights.　鎮民抗議警員公然漠視他們的權利。

ghetto 〔ˈgɛto 〕 *n.* (少數民族的) 居住地　—— 同 segregated slum

Life for people living in the ***ghetto*** is difficult.

住在少數民族居住地的人，過著困苦的生活。

headway 〔ˈhɛdˌwe 〕 *n.* 進展

—— 同 progress , advance , improvement , furtherance

It was hard to make any ***headway*** up the mountain with the
heavy rain.　在大雨中，要往山上前進十分困難。

impartial 〔 ɪm'parʃəl 〕 *adj.* 公正的
—— 同 unbiased , fair , unprejudiced , candid

It is important that all judges be *impartial* in their decisions.

法官做決定時必須公正，這是非常重要的。

** **integrate** 〔 'ɪntə͵gret 〕 *v.* 整合【常考】
—— 同 fuse , synthesize , blend , assimilate , merge

The city planned to *integrate* all of the local football clubs into a citywide league.

該市計畫要整合當地所有的美式足球社團，成立全市的聯盟。

lenient 〔 'linɪənt 〕 *adj.* 寬容的　　—— 同 mild , tolerant , indulgent

He is worried that if he is too *lenient* with his children, they will be spoiled. 他很擔心如果對小孩太寬容，會寵壞他們。

** **manipulate** 〔 mə'nɪpjə͵let 〕 *v.* 操縱【常考】
—— 同 operate , handle , manage , control , conduct

This machine is very complicated and difficult to *manipulate*.

這部機器非常複雜，很難操縱。

mishap 〔 'mɪs͵hæp 〕 *n.* 不幸之事　　—— 同 mischance , misfortune

Rhoda had a small *mishap* on her way home from work today.

蘿達今天下班回家途中，出了一點小意外。

notwithstanding 〔 'natwɪθ'stændɪŋ 〕 *prep.* 雖然
—— 同 nevertheless , although , however , yet , despite

Notwithstanding the trouble the little kitten causes, Amy is glad to have it.

雖然小貓替艾美製造了一點小麻煩，她還是很高興能擁有牠。

occult 〔 ə'kʌlt 〕 *adj.* 神秘的　　—— 同 mystic , supernatural

The strange man claimed to have *occult* powers to communicate with spirits. 那個怪人宣稱他有神秘的力量，能和靈魂溝通。

outskirts〔'aut,skɜts〕 n. pl. 郊區

——同 suburbs, environs, surroundings

Warren likes living on the *outskirts* of town, where it is quieter and cleaner. 華倫喜歡住在較安靜而且乾淨的市郊。

pathway〔'pæθ,we〕 n. 小徑

——同 lane, route, way, course

There is a small *pathway* through the park that leads to the lake. 公園裡有條小徑可以通往湖。

petition〔pə'tɪʃən〕 v.; n. 請求

——同 (v.) request, appeal, beg; (n.) plea, request

Many homeowners *petitioned* the government to reduce property taxes. 許多屋主都要求政府降低財產稅。

Exercise *Fill in the blanks.*

1. Gail could not be an _____ juror in the trial because she knows the defendant.

2. The two clubs were _____ to form a single organization.

3. Mr. Smith is never _____ in grading our assignments.

4. Due to a mailing _____, our newspaper will not be able to run the crossword puzzle today.

5. A strange _____ organization has started meeting every Thursday in an abandoned building.

【解答】1. impartial 2. integrated 3. lenient 4. mishap 5. occult

posture〔ˈpɑstʃɚ〕*n.* ①姿勢　②狀態；情勢

——同 1. bearing , pose , stance　2. circumstances , condition , state

The little girl had the ***posture*** of a refined young lady.

那小女孩的舉止像個有敎養的小淑女。

prolong〔prəˈlɔŋ〕*v.* 延長

——同 extend , make longer , protract , lengthen

This new drug could ***prolong*** AIDS patients' lives by several

years.　這種新藥可延長愛滋病患者數年的生命。

prune〔prun〕*v.* 修剪　——同 cut , shear , trim

Scott ***pruned*** the bushes in front of the house.

史考特修剪屋前的灌木叢。

* **receptacle**〔rɪˈsɛptəkḷ〕*n.* 容器【常考】

——同 container , holder , repository

I could not find a ***receptacle*** large enough to hold all the

garbage we collected.

我找不到大的容器，可以裝得下我們所收集的垃圾。

repetition〔ˌrɛpɪˈtɪʃən〕*n.* 重覆

——同 repeating , reiteration , recurrence , reappearance

His constant ***repetition*** of the same song nearly drove us crazy.

他不斷唱著同一首歌，使我們幾乎要發瘋。

* **rift**〔rɪft〕*n.* 裂痕【常考】　——同 crack , cleft , fissure , split

The ***rift*** between them had grown too wide, so they decided to

divorce.　他們之間的裂痕太深，因此決定要離婚。

* **scent**〔sɛnt〕*n.* ①氣味；香味　②痕跡；線索【常考】

——同 1. fragrance , aroma , odor　2. spoor , track , trail

The police officers felt they were on the ***scent*** of a criminal.

警官認為他們已經掌握了罪犯的線索。

shrewd 〔 ʃrud 〕 *adj.* 精明的 ——同 clever , keen , astute
Jason's *shrewd* judgment helped him to choose the best stocks
to invest in. 傑森精明的判斷力，幫助他選擇了最好的股票投資。

sophisticated 〔 sə'fɪstɪˏketɪd 〕 *adj.* ①世故的 ②複雜的
——同 1. seasoned , worldly　2. complex , complicated , delicate
Everyone in the little country town was captivated by the
sophisticated man from the city.
小鎮裡的人，都被那位來自城裡的世故人士所迷惑。

* **staple** 〔'stepḷ 〕 ① *n.* 主要產物　② *adj.* 主要的【常考】
——同 1. major commodity , mainstay , necessity , essential
　　　2. main , primary
Grain is the *staple* of the local economy.
穀類是當地主要的經濟作物。

* **submit** 〔 səb'mɪt 〕 *v.* ①屈服　②提出【常考】
——同 1. surrender , yield , succumb　2. propose , state , turn in
The soldier finally *submitted* after being tortured by the
enemy. 那士兵終於向敵人的折磨屈服了。

* **swerve** 〔 swɝv 〕 *v.* 轉向【常考】 ——同 deviate , turn aside , veer
The car suddenly *swerved* into another car on the icy road.
那輛車在結冰的道路上突然轉向，撞上了另一部車。

** **teem** 〔 tim 〕 *v.* 充滿；富於【最常考】 ——同 swarm , abound
The river *teemed* with all sorts of fish.
那條河裡有各式各樣的魚。

transact 〔 træns'ækt 〕 *v.* 處理
——同 conduct , manage , carry on , execute
We are interested in *transacting* business with the new
company. 我們有興趣和那家新公司做生意。

* **unravel** 〔ʌn'ræv!〕 *v.* ①解開 ②闡釋；解決【常考】

　　——同 1. unwind , disentangle , undo　2. explain , interpret

　　It took many years before the police could ***unravel*** the murder mystery. 警方花了許多年才解決這宗謀殺疑案。

‡ **veneration** 〔‚vɛnə'reʃən〕 *n.* 尊敬【最常考】

　　——同 esteem , respect , admiration , awe , adoration

　　The people's ***veneration*** for the cruel leader was baffling. 人們對那位殘忍的領袖心存尊敬，令人十分不解。

* **wax** 〔wæks〕 *v.* 增大【常考】

　　——同 grow , increase , rise , mount , become larger

　　As the Lantern Festival approaches, the moon ***waxes*** until it is finally full. 隨著元宵節逼近，月亮也漸滿，直到正圓。

> **Exercise** ⟩ *Fill in the blanks.*

1. If you _____ your rose bushes, they will have more rose blooms.

2. The dance teacher had the students do four _____ of the dance combination.

3. Please _____ all application forms to the registrar's office.

4. The schoolyard was _____ with youngsters playing and talking.

5. To show their _____ for God, people are quiet when they enter a church.

【解答】 1. prune　2. repetitions　3. submit　4. teeming　5. veneration

·List 13· 難字分析

affiliate 〔 ə'fɪlɪ‚et 〕 *v.* 使有密切關連

af +	fil +	iate
ad		
to +	*son +*	*make*

— to connect or associate

analogy 〔 ə'nælədʒɪ 〕 *n.* 類似

ana +	log +	y
upon +	*speak +*	*n.*

— similarity in some respects
between things otherwise unlike

autonomous 〔 ɔ'tɑnəməs 〕 *adj.* 自治的

auto +	nom +	ous
self +	*govern +*	*adj.*

— self-governing

elucidate 〔 ɪ'lusə‚det 〕 *v.* 闡明

e +	lucid +	ate
ex		
out +	*bright +*	*make*

— to make clear

integrate 〔 'ɪntə‚gret 〕 *v.* 整合

in +	tegr +	ate
not +	*touch +*	*v.*

— to put or bring together into
a whole

lenient ﹝'liniənt ﹞ *adj.* 寬容的

leni + ent
mild + adj.

— not severe

manipulate ﹝ mə'nıpjə,let ﹞ *v.* 操縱

mani + pul + ate
hand + pull + v.

— to operate or handle with skill

petition ﹝ pə'tıʃən ﹞ *v.* ; *n.* 請求

pet + ition
seek + n.

— to request; a request

receptacle ﹝ rı'sɛptəkḷ ﹞ *n.* 容器

re + cept + acle
back + take + small

— container for keeping things in

sophisticated ﹝ sə'fıstı,ketıd ﹞ *adj.* ①世故的 ②複雜的

soph + ist + ic + ate + (e)d
wise + person + adj. + v. + adj.

— having learned the ways of the world; complex

📋 LIST ▶ 14

˟accede 〔 æk'sid 〕 *v.* 同意【最常考】

──同 agree , assent , consent , acquiesce , comply

Mr. Watson *acceded* to his students' request to delay the test for one day.

華生老師同意學生的要求，將考試延後一天。

˟affluent 〔'æfluənt 〕 *adj.* 豐富的；富裕的【最常考】

──同 abundant , rich , plentiful , opulent , wealthy

She lives in an *affluent* neighborhood in the southern part of the city.　她住在該市南方一處非常富裕的地區。

˟anarchy 〔'ænəkɪ 〕 *n.* 無政府狀態；混亂【最常考】

──同 chaos , disorder , misrule , lawlessness , confusion

The whole city was in *anarchy* when the attack began.

當攻擊開始時，全市都陷入混亂的狀態。

artificial 〔,ɑrtə'fɪʃəl 〕 *adj.* 人造的

──同 unnatural , man-made , false , affected , counterfeit , fake

The hotel decorated the dining room tables with *artificial* silk flowers.　這家旅館用絲質的人造花來裝飾餐桌。

available 〔 ə'veləbḷ 〕 *adj.* 可獲得的

──同 accessible , handy , ready , obtainable

Are there any applications *available* at this office?

這辦公室要徵人嗎？

benefactor 〔'bɛnə,fæktɚ 〕 *n.* 恩人；慈善家

──同 helper , patron , philanthropist , altruist , contributor

The gifts of a *benefactor* allowed Vera to attend university.

慈善家所送的禮物使薇拉能夠上大學。

brusque 〔 brʌsk , brusk 〕 *adj.* 魯莽的；唐突的

——同 abrupt , gruff

Professor Chen's ***brusque*** manner often intimidates new students.　陳教授魯莽的行為常使新生倍感威脅。

＊intimidate 〔 ɪn'tɪmə,det 〕 *v.* 威嚇

chap 〔 tʃæp 〕 *v.* 龜裂　——同 crack , roughen , slit open

The dry desert wind had painfully ***chapped*** his skin.

沙漠乾燥的風使他的皮膚產生疼痛的龜裂。

commemorate 〔 kə'mɛmə,ret 〕 *v.* 紀念；慶祝

——同 memorialize , celebrate , solemnize , honor

A dinner was held to ***commemorate*** the tenth anniversary of the company's founding.　我們舉辦晚宴慶祝公司成立十週年。

confer 〔 kən'fɝ 〕 *v.* ①商議 ②授予

——同 1. consult , discuss , deliberate 2. bestow , grant , award

The queen ***conferred*** the title of knight on John Wood.

女王授予約翰・伍德騎士的頭銜。

coordinate 〔 ko'ɔrdn,et 〕 *v.* 協調；使對等

——同 harmonize , equalize , accord , conform , adapt

A new traffic computer system was bought by the city to ***coordinate*** the stoplights on the main roads.

該市購買了新的交通電腦系統，調節主要道路的交通號誌。

＊defer 〔 dɪ'fɝ 〕 *v.* ①延期 ②服從【常考】

——同 1. delay , postpone , put off 2. comply , yield , abide by

You can ***defer*** payment on this furniture for only one week.

關於這件傢俱，你可以延期一星期再付款。

detrimental 〔,dɛtrə'mɛntḷ 〕 *adj.* 有害的

——同 harmful , injurious , deleterious , hurtful , prejudicial

Eating a high-fat, high-sodium diet is very ***detrimental*** to your health.　吃高脂、高鈉的飲食對健康十分有害。

* disposable〔dɪ'spozəbl̩〕*adj.* ①用完即丟的 ②可任意處置的

　　——同 1. throwaway , nonreturnable 2. available , free for use　　【常考】

If you want to help the environment, you should not use *disposable* plastic cups and plates.

如果想對環境有助益，就不該使用免洗的塑膠杯與塑膠盤。

* dubious〔'djubɪəs〕*adj.* 可疑的；懷疑的【常考】

　　——同 doubtful , suspicious , uncertain , skeptical , equivocal

We were *dubious* that Nadia would arrive at the meeting on time.　對於娜迪雅是否準時赴會，我們感到懷疑。

elude〔ɪ'lud〕*v.* 逃避

　　——同 escape , evade , avoid , dodge , shun

The thief was able to *elude* the police by disguising himself.

小偷化了裝，成功地躲過警察。

Exercise　*Fill in the blanks.*

1. That _____ plant looks almost real.

2. She met their polite questions with a _____ response.

3. A celebration _____ the founding of the Republic of China is held on October tenth.

4. The committee _____ the work of members from several departments.

5. Too much exposure to the sun can be _____ to your skin.

【解答】1. artificial　2. brusque　3. commemorating　4. coordinated
　　　　5. detrimental

* **entity** 〔ˈɛntətɪ 〕 *n.* 實體;存在【常考】
  ——同 thing , being , existence
  Some people perceive God as an all-powerful *entity* that is all
  around us. 有些人覺得上帝是萬能的,存在於我們身邊。

  exaggeration 〔 ɪgˌzædʒəˈreʃən 〕 *n.* 誇張
  ——同 overstatement , magnification , hyperbole , puffery , inflation
  Saying that we waited in line all day was an *exaggeration*; it
  was only forty minutes.
  說我們排隊等了一整天是有點誇張,我們只等了四十分鐘而已。

* **feasible** 〔ˈfizəbḷ 〕 *adj.* 可行的【常考】
  ——同 practicable , possible , achievable , attainable , probable
  The doctors wondered whether a heart transplant would be
  feasible with such an elderly patient.
  醫生懷疑替這位年老的病人進行心臟移植手術,不知是否可行。

* **fort** 〔 fɔrt 〕 *n.* 堡壘【常考】   ——同 fortress , stronghold
  The *fort* was guarded by hundreds of troops.
  這座堡壘有好幾百個軍隊駐守。

* **fossil** 〔ˈfɑsḷ 〕 *n.* 化石【常考】
  The dinosaur *fossil* was preserved for millions of years in the
  air-tight cave. 這個恐龍化石在密閉的洞穴裡已存在好幾百萬年。

  gingerly 〔ˈdʒɪndʒəlɪ 〕 *adv.* ; *adj.* 謹慎地
  ——同 (*adv.*) carefully , prudently , cautiously , warily , alertly
  She *gingerly* placed the sleeping baby in the crib so as not to
  wake him. 她小心地把熟睡的嬰兒放在嬰兒床上,以免吵醒他。

* **heed** 〔 hid 〕 *n.* 注意【最常考】   ——同 attention , notice , regard
  You should give *heed* to your grandmother's sound advice.
  你應該多注意祖母的忠告。

impassive 〔 ɪm'pæsɪv 〕 *adj.* 無感情的

—— 同 emotionless , apathetic , insensible , insensitive

Although Chris was screaming loudly at her, Mona's face remained ***impassive***.

雖然克里斯對夢娜高聲尖叫，她仍然面無表情。

* **induce** 〔 ɪn'djus 〕 *v.* 說服；誘使【常考】

—— 同 incite , persuade , urge , encourage , effect , cause

How do you think I could ***induce*** my parents to take us all out to dinner?

你認爲我該如何，才能說服我的父母帶我們出去吃晚餐？

intense 〔 ɪn'tɛns 〕 *adj.* 激烈的

—— 同 extreme , violent , sharp , keen , acute , excessive

After ***intense*** bargaining, the salesperson finally sold me the coat at the price I asked.

經過一番激烈的討價還價，售貨員終於以我要求的價錢把外套賣給我。

** **lethal** 〔'liθəl 〕 *adj.* 致命的【最常考】　　—— 同 fatal , deadly

A ***lethal*** gas was released in the subway car, killing many passengers.　地下鐵車廂裡瀰漫著致命的毒氣，許多乘客因而死亡。

* **mock** 〔 mɑk 〕 *v.* 模仿；嘲弄【常考】　　—— 同 ridicule , mimic , jeer

We laughed as he ***mocked*** David's strange way of walking.

當他模仿大衛奇怪的走路姿態時，大家看得哈哈大笑。

nourish 〔'nɝɪʃ 〕 *v.* 養育　　—— 同 nurture , foster , support , feed

Such a young puppy needs to be ***nourished*** with special puppy food.　像這麼小的狗需要餵一些特別的狗食。

occupy 〔'ɑkjə,paɪ 〕 *v.* 佔據　　—— 同 hold , invade , take

The German army ***occupied*** France during World War II.

二次大戰期間，德國軍隊佔領了法國。

outspoken〔aʊt'spokən〕*adj.* 坦白的

—— 同 frank , candid , unreserved , blunt , bluff

Roger is an *outspoken* supporter of environmental protection.

羅傑是個毫無保留的環保支持者。

patron〔'petrən〕*n.* 贊助者；顧客

—— 同 benefactor , supporter , backer , customer , client

The *patrons* of the restaurant appreciated the good service and the fine food.

餐廳的顧客十分欣賞那裡良好的服務與可口的食物。

petulant〔'pɛtʃələnt〕*adj.* 生氣的；難取悅的

—— 同 fretful , irritable , peevish , irascible , peppery

The child was *petulant* about having to share his toys with other children.

那個小孩十分生氣，因為他必須和其他孩子分享玩具。

Exercise *Fill in the blanks.*

1. Without any _____, Marge is the best cook in our family.

2. It is _____ to hire a computer consultant to modernize our office.

3. It was an _____ basketball game, with our team finally winning in the end.

4. You should _____ your mind as well as your body.

5. Pam's _____ nature makes her a good candidate to become a politician one day.

【解答】1. exaggeration 2. feasible 3. intense 4. nourish 5. outspoken

potent〔ˈpotn̩t〕*adj.* 有力的 ──同 powerful , strong , mighty
I'm afraid whiskey is too *potent* a drink for my taste.
恐怕威士忌酒太強了，不合我的口味。

* **prominent**〔ˈprɑmənənt〕*adj.* 卓越的【常考】
──同 eminent , outstanding , notable , distinguished , conspicuous
Mr. Smith is a *prominent* banker from New York City.
史密斯先生是來自紐約的一位傑出的銀行家。

* **puncture**〔ˈpʌŋktʃɚ〕*v.* 鑽孔；刺傷【常考】
──同 prick , pierce , make a hole in , penetrate , nick
The sharp piece of wood *punctured* her bare foot.
尖銳的木片刺傷了她赤裸的腳。

* **reciprocal**〔rɪˈsɪprəkl̩〕*adj.* 彼此的；互相的【常考】
──同 mutual , correlative , alternative , interchangeable , complementary
The two companies signed a *reciprocal* agreement promising
to share the costs of the project.
這兩家公司彼此簽訂合約，要共同分攤這項計畫的費用。

reproach〔rɪˈprotʃ〕*v.* 譴責
──同 censure , reprove , scold , chide , rebuke , blame
Mother *reproached* Tina for making such a rude remark.
媽媽責備汀娜，因為她言語粗魯。

* **rigid**〔ˈrɪdʒɪd〕*adj.* ①嚴格的 ②僵硬的【常考】
──同 1. strict , stern , austere 2. stiff , inflexible
The government food inspectors use *rigid* standards to check
food. 政府的食品檢查員檢查食物時，採取十分嚴格的標準。

schedule〔ˈskɛdʒul〕*n.* 時間表；計畫表
──同 timetable , agenda , catalogue , list , plan
We have a very busy *schedule* planned for tomorrow.
我們明天預定的時間表十分緊湊。

* **shrink** 〔 ʃrɪŋk 〕 v. 退縮【常考】
—— 同 contract , flinch , recoil , shrivel , dwindle
If you put that cotton shirt in the clothes dryer, it will **shrink**.
如果你把那件棉衫放到乾衣機裡，它可能會縮水。

* **soporific** 〔 ˌsopəˈrɪfɪk 〕 adj. 催眠的；令人想睡的【常考】
—— 同 hypnotic , sedative , dull , lethargic , torpid , wearisome
The principal's **soporific** speeches always put the students to
sleep. 校長具有催眠作用的演講讓學生都很想睡。

startle 〔ˈstartḷ 〕 v. 使驚嚇   —— 同 frighten , shock , astound
The sudden knock at the door **startled** me.
突然有人敲門，把我嚇了一跳。

subordinate 〔 səˈbɔrdṇɪt 〕 adj. 次要的；附屬的
—— 同 inferior , junior , lower , secondary
All of the colonel's **subordinate** officers were a little afraid
of him. 上校手下所有的軍官都有點怕他。   ＊colonel 〔ˈkɝnḷ 〕 n. 上校

swift 〔 swɪft 〕 adj. 快速的   —— 同 quick , rapid , fleet
Swift delivery of the package to San Francisco is necessary.
必須儘快將這包裹送到舊金山去。

temperament 〔ˈtɛmprəmənt 〕 n. 性情；氣質
—— 同 disposition , temper , nature , inclination , tendency
Sam's old brown horse has a good **temperament** and even
allows children to ride on his back.
山姆那匹棕色的老馬性情溫馴，甚至肯讓小孩子騎在牠的背上。

transient 〔ˈtrænʃənt 〕 adj. 短暫的
—— 同 temporary , ephemeral , momentary , short , brief , fleeting
Many young children have a **transient** phase when they suck
their thumb. 許多小孩都有一小段時期會吸吮拇指。

unrelenting 〔ˌʌnrɪˈlɛntɪŋ〕 *adj.* 無情的；堅決的
——同 hard , stern , merciless , rigorous , severe

The ***unrelenting*** wind finally blew down our tent.

無情的風最後把我們的帳篷吹倒了。

venom 〔ˈvɛnəm〕 *n.* 怨恨；毒液
——同 poison , spite , virulence , rancor , bitterness

You could hear ***venom*** in his voice as he argued.

當他在爭辯時，你可以聽到他的聲音裡充滿了怨恨。

welfare 〔ˈwɛlˌfɛr〕 *n.* 福利
——同 well-being , happiness , profit , benefit , prosperity

The school should always put the ***welfare*** of its students first.

學校應該永遠把學生的福利放在第一位。

Exercise > *Fill in the blanks.*

1. The most _____ feature of Paris is the Eiffel Tower.

2. Mike always _____ his dog when he misbehaves.

3. This express mail company guarantees _____ delivery of all packages.

4. University students are often just _____ residents in a city.

5. The _____ from the snakebite killed him within minutes.

【解答】 1. prominent   2. reproaches   3. swift   4. transient   5. venom

·List 14· 難字分析

affluent 〔'æfluənt 〕*adj.* 豐富的；富裕的

af + flu + ent
ad
to + flow + adj.

— plentiful; wealthy

anarchy 〔'ænəkɪ 〕*n.* 無政府狀態；混亂

an + arch + y
without + ruler + n.

— lack of government

benefactor 〔'bɛnə,fæktə 〕*n.* 恩人；慈善家

bene + fact +   or
well + do + person

— person who has given help, esp. financial help

commemorate 〔 kə'mɛmə,ret 〕*v.* 紀念；慶祝

com + memor + ate
together + remember + v.

— to honor the memory of a person or event

coordinate 〔 ko'ɔrdn̩,et 〕*v.* 協調；使對等

co + ordin + ate
com
with + order + make

— to bring into proper relation

detrimental 〔͵dɛtrə'mɛntļ〕 *adj.* 有害的

```
de  + tri + ment + al        — harmful
 |     |     |      |
away + rub +  n.  + adj.
```

exaggeration 〔 ɪg͵zædʒə'reʃən〕 *n.* 誇張

```
ex + ag +  ger  + ation      — description beyond the truth
      |
      ad
     |            |      |
out + to  + carry +  n.
```

feasible 〔'fizəbļ〕 *adj.* 可行的

```
feas +  ible                 — that can be done
 |       |
 do  + able to
```

soporific 〔͵sopə'rɪfɪk〕 *adj.* 催眠的；令人想睡的

```
sopori +  fic                — making sleepy
  |        |
sleep  + making
```

subordinate 〔 sə'bɔrdṇɪt〕 *adj.* 次要的；附屬的

```
sub  + ordin + ate           — placed below another in rank,
 |       |      |               importance, etc.
under + order + adj.
```

transient 〔'trænʃənt〕 *adj.* 短暫的

```
trans + ient                 — passing away with time
 |       |
across + going
```

TEST ▶ 7

請由 (A)～(D) 中選出和畫線部分意義最相近的字。

1. Don't forget to pack a few <u>articles</u> of warm clothing for your camping trip.

   (A) boxes
   (B) catalogues
   (C) items
   (D) suitcases

2. We passed the evening with wine and <u>convivial</u> conversation.

   (A) drunken
   (B) elusive
   (C) serious
   (D) genial

3. Immigrants in America have <u>dispersed</u> to all parts of the country.

   (A) returned
   (B) left
   (C) spread
   (D) responded

4. Professor Smith was glad to <u>elucidate</u> the topic he lectured on in class to us.

   (A) explain
   (B) repeat
   (C) preview
   (D) nullify

5. No <u>headway</u> was made between the armies during the peace talks.

   (A) delivery
   (B) treaty
   (C) fellowship
   (D) progress

6. After many years of practice, James can <u>manipulate</u> any machinery with ease.

   (A) break
   (B) build
   (C) handle
   (D) admire

7. Is there a <u>receptacle</u> to put this leftover food from the party in?

   (A) place
   (B) container
   (C) kitchen
   (D) cook

8. Teachers <u>petitioned</u> the Ministry of Education for better pay and smaller class sizes.

   (A) marched
   (B) entreated
   (C) bombed
   (D) criticized

9. John's <u>dubious</u> behavior made everyone think he was the one who started the rumor.

(A) suspicious
(B) superfluous
(C) silly
(D) surreptitious

10. The doctor received a prize for his <u>feat</u> in medicine.

(A) discovery
(B) contribution
(C) accomplishment
(D) generosity

11. <u>Unrelenting</u> news coverage of the war in Bosnia has made many people numb to the tragedies occurring there.

(A) poor
(B) continual
(C) insane
(D) youthful

12. I find economic reports rather <u>soporific</u> and a perfect cure for insomnia.

(A) fulfilling
(B) dull
(C) demeaning
(D) reliable

13. Police <u>acceded</u> to the kidnapper's demands in order to protect the safety of the kidnapped boys.

(A) acquiesced
(B) refused
(C) responded
(D) bargained

14. The nurse <u>gingerly</u> applied the medicine to the cut on the boy's leg.

(A) carefully
(B) quickly
(C) vigorously
(D) instinctively

15. Mr. Johnson is a regular <u>patron</u> at our golf course.

(A) client
(B) worker
(C) inspector
(D) person

16. Fighting among members led to a <u>rift</u> in the political party, which resulted in its decreased influence.

(A) split
(B) cohesion
(C) debate
(D) resolution

17. There are several possible <u>subordinate</u> causes of the bridge's collapse.

(A) surprising
(B) secondary
(C) misunderstood
(D) mysterious

18. Helen had never roller-skated before, and she suddenly lost control and <u>swerved</u> into a tree.

(A) wiggled
(B) jumped
(C) flew
(D) veered

19. People were afraid that without international intervention, the country would slip into <u>anarchy</u>.

    (A) oblivion
    (B) lawlessness
    (C) poverty
    (D) disease

20. Each person should be treated as an individual <u>entity</u>, not as a small part of a larger whole.

    (A) thought
    (B) center
    (C) idea
    (D) being

21. Dr. Lane prescribed a less <u>potent</u> medication for the patient after he had a bad reaction to a stronger drug.

    (A) powerful
    (B) complicated
    (C) desirable
    (D) dangerous

22. Water is the most important <u>staple</u> for human life.

    (A) related product
    (B) end result
    (C) basic item
    (D) luxury item

23. When she entered her office to work every morning, the expression on her face be-came <u>impassive</u> and detached.

    (A) hateful
    (B) joyful
    (C) lively
    (D) emotionless

24. George has the perfect <u>temperament</u> to be a kindergarten teacher.

    (A) disposition
    (B) simplicity
    (C) capability
    (D) education

25. Please send us a <u>brochure</u> about your new products.

    (A) pamphlet
    (B) statement
    (C) sample
    (D) evaluation

【解答】

1. C	2. D	3. C	4. A	5. D	6. C	7. B	8. B	9. A	10. C
11. B	12. B	13. A	14. A	15. A	16. A	17. B	18. D	19. B	20. D
21. A	22. C	23. D	24. A	25. A					

📋 LIST ▸ 15

‡‡accelerate 〔æk'sɛlə,ret 〕*v.* 加速【最常考】

── 同 hasten , expedite , speed up , quicken , precipitate

Anna pressed the gas pedal and **accelerated** down the highway.

安娜踩緊油門，在公路上加速行駛。 ＊pedal 〔'pɛdḷ〕*n.* 踏板

agenda 〔ə'dʒɛndə 〕*n.* 議程

── 同 program , schedule , timetable , list , calendar

What is on the company **agenda** for next week?

公司下星期的議程有什麼？

anguish 〔'æŋgwɪʃ 〕*n.* 痛苦

── 同 pain , suffering , torment , torture , agony

The child's death caused great **anguish** for the family.

這孩子的死爲家人帶來極大的痛苦。

ascertain 〔,æsə'ten 〕*v.* 確定

── 同 discover , find out , determine , make certain , identify

The cause of the problem with my computer was never **ascertained**. 我的電腦爲何出毛病一直無法確知。

asset 〔'æsɛt 〕*n.* 有價值之物；有用之物

── 同 advantage , aid , resource , benefit , boon

Rose has been a great **asset** to our company and we are sorry she is retiring.

蘿絲是本公司的可貴人才，我們很遺憾她即將要退休了。

‡‡avaricious 〔,ævə'rɪʃəs 〕*adj.* 貪心的【最常考】

── 同 greedy , covetous , rapacious , avid , acquisitive

The **avaricious** factory owner made his employees work like slaves. 貪心的工廠老闆讓他的員工像奴隸一樣地作工。

※※**benevolent** 〔 bəˈnɛvələnt 〕 *adj.* 仁慈的【最常考】

── 同 kindly , benign , generous , well-meaning , amiable

The ***benevolent*** queen was loved by all her subjects.

這位仁慈的皇后受到臣民的愛戴。

※**buckle** 〔ˈbʌkḷ 〕 *v.* ①扣住 ②彎曲【常考】

── 同 1. clasp , fasten 2. curve , bend , twist

You don't need to ***buckle*** your seat belt so tightly.

你不必把安全帶繫得這麼緊。

characteristic 〔ˌkærɪktəˈrɪstɪk 〕 *n.* 特徵；特色

── 同 quality , trait , peculiarity , idiosyncrasy , distinguishing feature

Bob's main ***characteristic*** is that he is very artistic.

具備藝術氣息是鮑勃最大的特色。

commence 〔 kəˈmɛns 〕 *v.* 開始 ── 同 begin , initiate , originate

Everyone in the stadium was impatiently waiting for the

concert to ***commence***. 體育館內的每個人都不耐煩地等著演唱會開始。

confiscate 〔ˈkɑnfɪsˌket 〕 *v.* 沒收；充公

── 同 seize , commandeer , expropriate , take , dispossess

The stolen cellular phones were ***confiscated*** by the police after

the thief was caught. 小偷被抓後，警方將遭竊的行動電話沒收充公。

※※**copious** 〔ˈkopɪəs 〕 *adj.* 豐富的；大量的【最常考】

── 同 abundant , plentiful

Helen always puts ***copious*** amounts of sugar in her morning

cup of coffee. 海倫早上喝咖啡時，總是放了大量的糖。

deflect 〔 dɪˈflɛkt 〕 *v.* 使偏斜；使偏離

── 同 deviate , divert , swerve , turn aside , avert , swing

Light colors ***deflect*** the heat of the sun, so in summer, you

should wear light colored clothes.

淺的顏色會使太陽的熱力偏斜，所以在夏天時，你該穿淺色的服裝。

deviate ('divɪ,et) v. 脫離

—同 stray , diverge , swerve , divert , separate , divagate

If you *deviate* from this mountain trail, you are likely to get lost. 如果你走離這條山徑，很可能會迷路。

* disposition (,dɪspə'zɪʃən) n. ①氣質；性情 ②配置【常考】

—同 1. character , temperament , temper

2. arrangement , distribution

David's quiet *disposition* makes him suited to being a librarian. 大衛的性情文靜，適合作圖書館員。

emancipation (ɪ,mænsə'peʃən) n. 解放

—同 release , liberation , setting free , enfranchisement , manumission

The *emancipation* of young people's minds is necessary for them to be creative.

要讓年輕人有創意，必須解放他們的思想。

Exercise ⟩ *Fill in the blanks.*

1. There are three meetings on my _____ tomorrow so it will be difficult for me to meet you for lunch.

2. We _____ the cause of the malfunction in the elevator.

3. He is a _____ man who always helps the poor.

4. What are the _____ of French cuisine?

5. Abraham Lincoln is famous for ordering the _____ of the slaves in America.

【解答】1. agenda 2. ascertained 3. benevolent 4. characteristics
5. emancipation

ephemeral 〔 ə'fɛmərəl 〕 *adj.* 短暫的【最常考】
── 同 short-lived , temporal , momentary , transient , fleeting
Although she knew the happiness of the moment was
ephemeral, she cherished it.
雖然她知道此刻的歡愉是短暫的，但是她珍惜它。

exalt 〔 ɪg'zɔlt 〕 *v.* 提高【常考】   ── 同 elevate , lift up , raise
In 18th century Europe, science was *exalted* as the greatest
achievement of human beings.
在十八世紀的歐洲，科學被捧為人類最偉大的成就。

feeble 〔'fibl 〕 *adj.* 虛弱的   ── 同 weak , infirm , invalid
Rebecca's long illness left her *feeble* and pale.
長期的病痛讓芮貝卡虛弱又蒼白。

fortify 〔'fɔrtə,faɪ 〕 *v.* 加強
── 同 encourage , reassure , strengthen , reinforce
Our coach *fortified* our team's confidence with inspiring
words.   教練以鼓舞的言辭加強本隊的信心。

glare 〔 glɛr 〕① *n.* 強光 ② *v.* 瞪視
── 同 1. blaze , strong light , very harsh light 2. gaze , stare
Mr. Gordon *glared* at Tommy for insulting him.
戈登先生因為湯米侮辱他，所以瞪了他一眼。

henceforth 〔,hɛns'forθ 〕 *adv.* 從此以後
── 同 from now on , from this time on , hence , henceforward
Our club will *henceforth* be known as "The Music Lover's
Club." 今後我們的社團就叫「愛樂社」。

impeccable 〔 ɪm'pɛkəbl 〕 *adj.* 無瑕疵的；無過失的【最常考】
── 同 faultless , flawless , stainless , refined , perfect
Let Clara help you pick out a dress to buy; she has
impeccable taste. 讓克拉拉幫你挑件衣服來買；她的品味錯不了的。

inept 〔 ɪnˈɛpt 〕 *adj.* ①笨拙的；無能的 ②不適當的
——同 1. awkward , clumsy , incompetent 2. improper , unfit
Stockholders protested that the chairman of the board was *inept* and should be replaced. 股東抗議董事長無能，應該被換下來。

* **interfere** 〔ˌɪntɚˈfɪr 〕 *v.* 干擾【常考】
——同 intervene , meddle , interpose , disrupt , conflict
Dan was worried that the time he spent in the office was *interfering* with his family life.
丹擔心他花在辦公室的時間，會干擾他的家庭生活。

lethargic 〔 lɪˈθɑrdʒɪk 〕 *adj.* 昏睡的
——同 drowsy , languid , sluggish , listless , sleepy
I feel very *lethargic* this morning; maybe I have the flu.
我今早覺得昏昏欲睡；也許我是感冒了。

mendicant 〔ˈmɛndɪkənt 〕 *n.* 乞丐 ——同 beggar , pauper
The streets around the temple were filled with *mendicants* hoping for the generosity of worshipers.
寺廟周邊的街道佈滿了乞丐，他們渴望信徒能慷慨施捨。

* **modify** 〔ˈmɑdəˌfaɪ 〕 *v.* 修正；減緩【常考】 ——同 change , alter
The doctor *modified* the dose of the medicine to only one pill a day. 醫生把藥量調減為每日一顆。

****novice** 〔ˈnɑvɪs 〕 *n.* 初學者；新手【最常考】
——同 beginner , apprentice
Paula is only a *novice* golfer, so don't make fun of her.
寶拉不過是高爾夫球新手，所以別取笑她。

optical 〔ˈɑptɪkl̩ 〕 *adj.* 視覺的 ——同 visual , ocular
The long lines in the wallpaper had the *optical* effect of making the ceiling appear higher.
壁紙上的直線具有視覺的效果，它可讓天花板顯得更高。

* **overly** 〔′ovɚlɪ 〕 *adv.* 過度地【常考】

　　——同 too , excessively , overmuch , exceedingly , immoderately ,
　　　　unduly

You shouldn't be *overly* worried about taking an airplane
for the first time.

你實在不必爲第一次搭飛機而過度操心。

pending 〔′pɛndɪŋ 〕 *adj.* 未決定的；審理中的

　　——同 undecided , unresolved , unsettled , undetermined

Everyone is nervous about the *pending* exam results.

每個人都爲尚未揭曉的考試成績感到緊張。

pharmaceutical 〔,fɑrmə′sjutɪkl̩ , -′su- 〕 *n.* 藥

　　——同 drug , medicine , physic , elixir , prescription

Many people think the *pharmaceutical* industry charges
excessively high prices.　許多人認爲製藥商的索價過高。

Exercise 〉 *Fill in the blanks.*

1. The child's legs were ＿＿＿＿＿＿ from his illness and
could not carry him.

2. With ＿＿＿＿＿ accuracy, Joe answered all the questions.

3. The company had to ＿＿＿＿＿ its work force by laying
off half the workers.

4. When it comes to camping, Jacob is only a ＿＿＿＿＿.

5. She found his ＿＿＿＿＿ polite manner very annoying.

【解答】1. feeble　2. impeccable　3. modify　4. novice　5. overly

posterity 〔 pɑs'tɛrətɪ 〕 *n. pl.* 子孫；後代

——同 offspring , progeny , descendants , future generations

It is very important to preserve historical artifacts for *posterity*. 為後代子孫保存歷史文物很重要。

＊artifact 〔'ɑrtɪˌfækt 〕 *n.* 古器物

prank 〔 præŋk 〕 *n.* 惡作劇 ——同 joke , trick , frolic , jest

Warren often plays *pranks* on his older brother.
華倫時常對他的哥哥惡作劇。

prompt 〔 prɑmpt 〕 ① *adj.* 即時的；立刻的 ② *v.* 激勵；促使

——同 1. quick , rapid , punctual , on time 2. motivate

I want to thank you for the *prompt* delivery of your report.
我要感謝你即時送來報告。

recital 〔 rɪ'saɪtḷ 〕 *n.* ①朗誦 ②獨奏會

——同 1. retelling , narration 2. concert , musicale

The entire family went to hear Laura's piano *recital*.
全家人都去聽蘿拉的鋼琴獨奏會。

＊**reproduce** 〔ˌriprə'djus 〕 *v.* ①複製 ②繁殖【常考】

——同 1. duplicate , copy 2. proliferate , breed

The scientists tried to *reproduce* the results of the experiment.
科學家試著要複製實驗的結果。

＊**rigor** 〔'rɪgɚ 〕 *n.* 嚴厲【常考】 ——同 harshness , austerity

Aaron was happy he would not have to endure the *rigor* of
military life any more. 亞倫很高興不必再忍受嚴厲的軍中生活。

＊＊**scope** 〔 skop 〕 *n.* 範圍【最常考】

——同 range , field , sphere , extent , compass

The *scope* of Chinese history spans five thousand years.
中國歷史的範圍橫跨五千年。

* **shrub** 〔 ʃrʌb 〕 *n.* 灌木【常考】 ——同 scrub , bush , hedge

   Peter decided to plant ***shrubs*** in front of his house.

   彼得決定在家門前種植灌木。

* **sort** 〔 sɔrt 〕① *n.* 種類 ② *v.* 分類【常考】

   ——同 1. class , kind , variety 2. classify , arrange , assort

   Machines are used to ***sort*** the mail by city.

   機器被用來將郵件依照城市分類。

   stately 〔'stetlɪ 〕 *adj.* 莊嚴的

   ——同 majestic , grand , imposing , magnificent , lordly

   The queen lived at the top of the hill in a ***stately*** palace.

   皇后住在山丘頂上莊嚴的皇宮裡。

* **subsequent** 〔'sʌbsɪ,kwɛnt 〕 *adj.* 其後的【常考】

   ——同 following , succeeding , ensuing , latter , later

   Each of our ***subsequent*** letters to each other was longer than the one before. 我們之後寫給對方的每封信，都比前一封來得長。

   symbolize 〔'sɪmbḷ,aɪz 〕 *v.* 象徵

   ——同 represent , indicate , signify , typify , mean , betoken , imply

   The image of a bald eagle is used to ***symbolize*** the United States. 禿鷹像被用來象徵美國。

   temperate 〔'tɛmprɪt 〕 *adj.* ①溫和的 ②節制的

   ——同 1. mild , pleasant 2. restrained , moderate

   He told me to be ***temperate*** in my spending or I'd be short of money soon. 他勸我花錢節制點，否則我很快就會沒錢。

* **transparent** 〔 træns'pɛrənt 〕 *adj.* 透明的【常考】

   ——同 sheer , clear , diaphanous , see-through

   The material that dress is made of is practically ***transparent***.

   那衣服的質料幾乎是透明的。

ᕽ untenable 〔 ʌnˈtɛnəbḷ 〕 *adj.* 難獲支持的；站不住腳的【最常考】

——同 indefensible , insupportable , inconsistent , illogical

How can he possibly defend such ***untenable*** thinking?

這種站不住腳的想法，他如何辯護得了？

verdict 〔ˈvɝdɪkt 〕 *n.* 裁決

——同 decision , judgment , finding , decree , opinion

Everyone in the courtroom anxiously awaited the ***verdict*** in the case.

法庭裡的每個人都焦急地等待案件的裁決。

whiskers 〔ˈhwɪskɚz 〕 *n. pl.* 腮鬚

——同 beard , mustache , sideburns , goatee

Martha has tried many times to get Ralph to shave off his ***whiskers***. 瑪莎試了好幾次要瑞夫刮掉他的絡腮鬍。

Exercise ⟩ *Fill in the blanks.*

1. She kept the photo album for the sake of _____.

2. The _____ of our study includes subjects from all walks of life.

3. The wooden cross, an ancient instrument of torture, came to _____ the Christian religion.

4. Nora's arguments were _____ to her real motives.

5. He lost the debate because his arguments were so _____.

【解答】1. posterity 2. scope 3. symbolize 4. transparent 5. untenable

· List 15 · 難字分析

accelerate 〔 æk'sɛlə,ret 〕 *v.* 加速

ac +	celer +	ate
ad		
to +	*quick +*	*v.*

—— to move faster

benevolent 〔 bə'nɛvələnt 〕 *adj.* 仁慈的

bene +	vol +	ent
well +	*wish +*	*adj.*

—— inclined to do good

confiscate 〔'kɑnfɪs,ket 〕 *v.* 沒收；充公

con +	fisc +	ate
with +	*treasury +*	*make*

—— to seize for the public treasury

deviate 〔'divɪ,et 〕 *v.* 脫離

de +	vi +	ate
away +	*way +*	*make*

—— to turn away

disposition 〔,dɪspə'zɪʃən 〕 *n.* ①氣質；性情 ②配置

dis +	pos +	ition
apart +	*put +*	*n.*

—— one's nature; management of affairs

emancipation 〔 ɪ͵mænsə'peʃən 〕 *n.* 解放

e	+	man	+	cip	+	ation		— setting free
ex							
out	+	hand	+	take	+	*n.*	

ephemeral 〔 ə'fɛmərəl 〕 *adj.* 短暫的

| ep | + | hemer | + | al | — lasting for a very short time |
| upon | + | day | + | *adj.* | |

posterity 〔 pɑs'tɛrətɪ 〕 *n. pl.* 子孫;後代

| poster | + | ity | — future generations |
| after | + | *n.* | |

subsequent 〔 'sʌbsɪ͵kwɛnt 〕 *adj.* 其後的

| sub | + | sequ | + | ent | — coming after |
| under | + | follow | + | *adj.* | |

transparent 〔 træns'pɛrənt 〕 *adj.* 透明的

| trans | + | par | + | ent | — that can be seen through |
| through | + | appear | + | *adj.* | |

untenable 〔 ʌn'tɛnəbḷ 〕 *adj.* 難獲支持的;站不住腳的

| un | + | ten | + | able | — that cannot be held |
| not | + | hold | + | able to | |

📋 LIST ▸ 16

accessible 〔 æk'sɛsəbḷ 〕 *adj.* 可接近的；可得到的

—— 同 approachable, available, reachable, obtainable, at hand

The products in this store are too expensive, so they are not very ***accessible*** to poor people.

這家店的東西太貴，所以窮人不太買得起。

* **aggravate** 〔'ægrə,vet 〕 *v.* ①加重；惡化 ②激怒【常考】

—— 同 1. increase, intensify 2. annoy, irritate

His asthma was ***aggravated*** by the heavy pollution.

嚴重的污染使他的氣喘惡化。　 * asthma 〔'æsmə, 'æzmə 〕 *n.* 氣喘

annul 〔 ə'nʌl 〕 *v.* 使無效；取消

—— 同 invalidate, abolish, cancel, rescind, abrogate

Their marriage was ***annulled*** by the court after only three weeks.　才不過三星期，法院便判他們的婚姻失效。

aspect 〔'æspɛkt 〕 *n.* ①外觀 ②觀點；方面

—— 同 1. look, appearance, countenance

　　　2. respect, facet, point of view

There is also the business ***aspect***, which we have not yet considered.　還有生意上的觀點我們還沒考慮到。

avenge 〔 ə'vɛndʒ 〕 *v.* 報仇

—— 同 revenge, retaliate, take vengeance, requite, get even with

All she could think about was ***avenging*** her brother's wrongful death.　她所能想的，就是為她弟弟的枉死報仇。

benign 〔 bɪ'naɪn 〕 *adj.* 親切的

—— 同 amiable, complaisant, gracious

We were beginning to wonder if Mr. Ford was as ***benign*** as he seemed.　我們開始懷疑福特先生是否像他表面一樣親切。

* bulky 〔'bʌlkɪ 〕*adj.* 大型的；龐大的【常考】

　　——同 enormous , massive

This box is too ***bulky*** for me to carry up the stairs alone.

這箱子太大，我無法一個人搬上樓。

chaste 〔 tʃest 〕*adj.* 貞節的　　——同 virtuous , pure , undefiled

Most societies expect women to be ***chaste***, while they allow men their freedom.

大部分的社會要求女性要貞節，但卻允許男性放縱。

commensurate 〔 kə'mɛnʃərɪt , -'mɛnsə- 〕*adj.* 相稱的；適當的

　　——同 proportional , equivalent , appropriate , suitable , adequate

Everyone felt that the punishment set by the judge was ***commensurate*** with the crime committed.

每個人都覺得，法官對該罪所判的刑罰恰到好處。

* conflict 〔'kɑnflɪkt 〕*n.* 衝突；爭鬥【常考】

　　——同 discord , struggle , battle , combat , clash , collision

The ***conflict*** between the two countries dragged on for years and claimed many lives.

這兩國間的鬥爭延續數年，剝奪了許多人命。

cordial 〔'kɔrdʒəl 〕*adj.* 眞誠的

　　——同 sincere , ardent , genial , hearty

I want to thank you for the ***cordial*** invitation; I would be delighted to come.

我要感謝你誠摯的邀請，我將欣然前往參加。

defraud 〔 dɪ'frɔd 〕*v.* 詐取；欺騙

　　——同 cheat , swindle , bamboozle , trick , beguile , delude

It was discovered that the politician was ***defrauding*** his constituents.　這名政客欺騙選民的事，被揭露了出來。

　　*constituent 〔 kən'stɪtʃuənt 〕*n.* 選民

detergent 〔 dɪ'tɝdʒənt 〕 *n.*; *adj.* 清潔劑；清潔的
—同 (*n.*) cleaner ; (*adj.*) cleaning , detersive
We use a powerful ***detergent*** to clean the oil off the floor.
我們用強力的清潔劑將地板上的油洗乾淨。

* **devour** 〔 dɪ'vaʊr 〕 *v.* 吞食；狼吞虎嚥【常考】   —同 gorge , gulp
After swimming all day long, the children ***devoured*** their
dinner and immediately fell asleep.
游泳一整天後，孩子們狼吞虎嚥地吃著晚餐，很快便入睡了。

disregard 〔,dɪsrɪ'gɑrd 〕 *v.* 忽視
—同 ignore , neglect , overlook , slight , omit , pass over
The teacher ***disregarded*** the students' pleas to postpone the
test one more day. 學生要求將考試延後一天，但老師不予理會。

embark 〔 ɪm'bɑrk 〕 *v.* 上（船、飛機）
—同 board ship , take ship , put on board , go aboard
We ***embarked*** the luxurious cruise ship to begin our trip
around the world. 我們登上豪華的遊艇，展開環遊世界之旅。

Exercise ⟩ *Fill in the blanks.*

1. Very few buildings in Taipei have been made _____
   to wheelchair-bound people.

2. I want to buy simple, light furniture, not _____
   furniture like that.

3. She insisted that their relationship remain _____.

4. We watched the man in the movie being _____ by a
   dinosaur.

5. Our ship is about to _____ passengers; we had better
   hurry.

【解答】 1. accessible   2. bulky   3. chaste   4. devoured   5. embark

epidemic 〔͵ɛpə'dɛmɪk 〕① *adj.* 傳染的；蔓延的 ② *n.* 流行病
——同 1. prevalent , pandemic , rampant 2. outbreak , plague , pestilence
The popularity of KTVs in Taiwan is *epidemic*.
台灣的 KTV 旋風蔓延不斷。

exasperate 〔 ɛg'zæspə͵ret , ɪg- 〕*v.* 激怒
——同 annoy , enrage , irritate , anger , infuriate , inflame
The little child's constant questions *exasperated* the baby-sitter.
這小孩不斷地提問題，激怒了褓母。

****feign** 〔 fen 〕*v.* 假裝【最常考】 ——同 simulate , pretend , counterfeit
Although I found the boss' story boring, I had to *feign* interest.
雖然我覺得老闆的故事很無聊，但我必須假裝有趣。

found 〔 faʊnd 〕*v.* 建立 ——同 establish , set up , constitute
The women's help group *founded* the first home for battered
women in the city. *battered 〔'bætəd 〕*adj.* 受虐的
婦女救援會在本市建立了第一家受虐婦女的收容所。

****glib** 〔 glɪb 〕*adj.* 能言善道的【最常考】
——同 loquacious , eloquent , fluent
Michael is surprisingly *glib* for a five-year-old child.
對一個五歲小孩而言，邁可實在是能言善道。

herald 〔'hɛrəld 〕*n.* 傳令者；使者
——同 bearer of tidings , crier , messenger
In the past, a *herald* would walk through the streets shouting
the town news for everyone to hear.
在以前，傳令的人會走遍街道，大聲宣傳鎮上的新聞給大家聽。

****impediment** 〔 ɪm'pɛdəmənt 〕*n.* 障礙【最常考】
——同 barrier , block , difficulty , encumbrance , hindrance
Violence in the legislature is an *impediment* to real democracy.
國會內的暴力，是邁向眞正民主的障礙。

* **inevitable** 〔 ɪnˈɛvətəbḷ 〕 *adj.* 無法避免的【常考】
　　——同 unavoidable , inescapable , determined , certain
Robert had to face the ***inevitable*** truth that he would have to repeat eighth grade.
羅伯特必須面對這無法逃避的事實，那就是他得重讀八年級。

* **interior** 〔 ɪnˈtɪrɪɚ 〕 *n.* ; *adj.* 內部（的）【常考】　　——同 inside
Helen decided to redecorate the ***interior*** of her house.
海倫決定重新裝潢她家的內部。

* **liability** 〔 ˌlaɪəˈbɪlətɪ 〕 *n.* 責任【常考】　　——同 responsibility , duty
According to our contract, the landlord's ***liability*** includes repairing any broken furnishings.
根據我們的合約，房東的責任包括修理任何故障的設備。
　　＊furnishings 〔ˈfɝnɪʃɪŋz 〕 *n. pl.* （房間的）陳設品

marshal 〔ˈmarʃəl 〕 *v.* 整頓
　　——同 align , arrange , deploy , dispose , order , organize
People were ***marshaled*** into shelters during the air raid drill.
防空演習時，民眾被安排進入避難所。

modulate 〔ˈmadʒəˌlet 〕 *v.* 調整
　　——同 adjust , modify , adapt , regulate , reconcile
Don't try to ***modulate*** your voice to make it higher; it sounds fine naturally.　別試著調高你的聲音；自然的就可以了。

* **noxious** 〔ˈnakʃəs 〕 *adj.* 有害的；有毒的【常考】
　　——同 injurious , harmful , poisonous , pernicious , unhealthy
Suddenly, ***noxious*** fumes began to pour out of the engine of the bus.　突然間，毒氣開始從公車的引擎裡冒出來。

* **offspring** 〔ˈɔfˌsprɪŋ 〕 *n. pl.* 子孫【常考】
　　——同 descendants , posterity , progeny , heirs , successors
Jean's green eyes were passed down to all three of her ***offspring***.
珍的三個子孫都遺傳了她的綠眼睛。

* **oversight**〔'ovɚ‚saɪt〕 *n.* 疏忽【常考】

—— 同 inattention , omission , negligence , disregard , carelessness

Due to an ***oversight*** by the electrician, every time this light is turned on, a fuse is blown. * fuse〔fjuz〕*n.* 保險絲

由於電工的疏失，這燈只要一開，保險絲就燒壞。

peak〔pik〕*n.* 山頂

—— 同 mountaintop , hilltop , summit , pinnacle , apex , crest

The ***peak*** of the mountain is covered with snow all year round.

這座山的山頂終年被雪所覆蓋。

phase〔fez〕*n.* 階段

—— 同 condition , level , step , stage , state

Everyone is excited to be finished with the final ***phase*** of the project. 該計畫的最後階段已完成，每個人都感到很興奮。

Exercise ▷ *Fill in the blanks.*

1. Soccer players are famous for _____ injuries to induce a time out.

2. A poor work environment is an _____ to worker productivity.

3. It is _____ that he will quit his job at that company.

4. The TV satellite signal was _____ so that only viewers with a special decoder could receive the signal.

5. The manager's ignorance of employees' dissatisfaction with company policy was an _____ that led to a serious problem.

【解答】1. feigning   2. impediment   3. inevitable   4. modulated   5. oversight

precarious 〔 prɪˈkɛrɪəs 〕 *adj.* 不確定的；危險的【最常考】

—— 同 uncertain , doubtful , hazardous , dangerous , insecure

After losing three business contracts, Bill felt that he was in a *precarious* position at work.

在失去三筆生意上的合約後，比爾覺得他的工作危險不保。

promulgate 〔 prəˈmʌlget 〕 *v.* 發佈【最常考】

—— 同 publish , proclaim

The cult *promulgates* a message of peace and love, but you have to follow the cult's leader.　＊cult 〔 kʌlt 〕 *n.* 教派

該教派宣揚愛與和平的訊息，但是你必須服從該教的領袖。

purify 〔ˈpjʊrəˌfaɪ 〕 *v.* 淨化【常考】　　—— 同 clarify , cleanse , refine

Travelers to less developed countries can buy tablets to *purify* local drinking water.　遊客到落後國家時，可以買藥來淨化當地的飲水。

reckless 〔ˈrɛklɪs 〕 *adj.* 魯莽的

—— 同 careless , rash , heedless , foolhardy , impetuous

The police officer pulled him over for *reckless* driving.

他開車橫衝直撞，被警察攔了下來。

request 〔 rɪˈkwɛst 〕 *v.* 請求

—— 同 ask for , beseech , call for , demand , entreat , solicit

Jessica was not feeling well, so she *requested* the day off from work.　潔西卡身體不舒服，所以她請求休假。

rip 〔 rɪp 〕 *v.* 撕裂　　—— 同 tear , split , rend , slit

A nail sticking out of the wooden bench *ripped* my new pants.

板凳上突出的釘子將我的新褲子扯破了。

scorch 〔 skɔrtʃ 〕 *v.* 燒焦；使乾枯　　—— 同 char , singe , brown

The forest fire *scorched* hundreds of acres of trees.

森林大火燒焦了數百英畝的樹木。

shudder 〔ˈʃʌdɚ〕 *v.* 發抖

——同 quiver , tremble , shake , quake , vibrate , shiver

The sound of the dog's howling made him *shudder*.

這隻狗的吠聲令他發抖。

soundproof 〔ˈsaʊndˌpruf〕 *adj.* 隔音的

——同 impermeable to noise

To make good quality recordings, you should tape in a *soundproof* recording booth.

想製作高品質的錄音，必須在隔音的錄音室進行。

* **static** 〔ˈstætɪk〕 *adj.* 靜態的【常考】

——同 still , inert , inactive , fixed , motionless , stationary

The population of this small town has been *static* for years.

這小鎮的人口已經有好幾年沒有成長。

* **subside** 〔səbˈsaɪd〕 *v.* ①平靜 ②下沉；退落【常考】

——同 1. abate , quiet down , diminish 2. sink , go down

After a few seconds, the minor earthquake had *subsided*.

數秒之後，這小地震平靜了下來。

* **symmetry** 〔ˈsɪmɪtrɪ〕 *n.* 對稱【常考】

——同 correspondence , proportion , evenness

Artists use *symmetry* in their paintings to make them appear balanced. 藝術家作畫時會利用對稱，以使作品看起來均衡。

tempo 〔ˈtɛmpo〕 *n.* 節奏 ——同 rhythm , pace , speed

It was hard for the musicians to keep the quick *tempo* in the music. 要樂師維持樂曲中這麼快的節奏很困難。

travail 〔ˈtrævel〕 *n.* 辛勞 ——同 labor , task , struggle , pains

After much *travail*, the house was finally finished and the family moved in. 經過千辛萬苦，房子終於蓋好，這戶人家搬了進去。

verify 〔'vɛrə,faɪ〕 v. 證實

——同 confirm , attest , authenticate , prove , substantiate

The tests **verified** the doctor's diagnosis of heart disease.

檢查結果證實了醫生所下的心臟病診斷無誤。

vernacular 〔və'nækjələ〕 n. ; adj. 方言（的）

——同 (n.) tongue , dialect , argot , slang

Although we lived in the village for two years, we never mastered the local **vernacular**.

雖然我們在鎮上住了兩年，但從沒學會當地的方言。

* wholesome 〔'holsəm〕 adj. 有益健康的【常考】

——同 healthful , salutary , beneficial , nourishing , salubrious

She feels that regular exercise has a **wholesome** effect on her mind as well as her body. 她覺得規律的運動有益她身心的健康。

Exercise ▷ *Fill in the blanks.*

1. The sky diver hung in a _____ position because her parachute had caught in a tree.

2. A new campaign _____ the benefits of a vegetarian diet.

3. If our factory's output remains _____, we will sustain great losses.

4. The artist was struck by the beautiful _____ of her features.

5. She survived the _____ of the boat trip to America, but died upon her arrival in the new country.

【解答】 1. precarious   2. promulgates   3. static   4. symmetry   5. travail

· List 16 · 難字分析

accessible 〔 æk'sɛsəbḷ 〕 *adj.* 可接近的；可得到的

ac + cess + ible	— that can be approached or
ad	entered
to + go + able to	

— that can be approached or entered

aggravate 〔 'ægrə,vet 〕 *v.* ①加重；惡化 ②激怒

ag + grav + ate	— to make worse; to annoy
ad	
to + heavy + make	

— to make worse; to annoy

commensurate 〔 kə'mɛnʃərɪt , -'mɛnsə- 〕 *adj.* 相稱的；適當的

| com + mensur + ate | — in the right proportion; |
| together + measure + adj. | appropriate |

— in the right proportion; appropriate

epidemic 〔 ,ɛpə'dɛmɪk 〕 ① *adj.* 傳染的；蔓延的 ② *n.* 流行病

epi + dem + ic	— spreading rapidly among many
among + people + adj.	people in the same place for a
	time; an epidemic disease

— spreading rapidly among many people in the same place for a time; an epidemic disease

exasperate 〔 ɛg'zæspə,ret , ɪg- 〕 *v.* 激怒

| ex + asper + ate | — to irritate or annoy very much |
| fully + rough + make | |

— to irritate or annoy very much

impediment〔ɪm'pɛdəmənt〕*n.* 障礙

im + pedi + ment
in + foot + n.

—— something that hinders

inevitable〔ɪn'ɛvətəbḷ〕*adj.* 無法避免的

in + e + vit + able
ex
not + out + empty + able to

—— that cannot be avoided
or evaded

modulate〔'mɑdʒə,let〕*v.* 調整

mod + ul + ate
manner + n. + make

—— to adjust or adapt to the proper
degree

precarious〔prɪ'kɛrɪəs〕*adj.* 不確定的；危險的

prec + arious
pray + adj.

—— uncertain; unsafe

promulgate〔prə'mʌlget〕*v.* 發佈

pro + mulg + ate
before + people + make

—— to publish or make known
officially

symmetry〔'sɪmɪtrɪ〕*n.* 對稱

sym + metr + y
together + measure + n.

—— right correspondence of parts

TEST ▶ 8

請由 (A)～(D) 中選出和畫線部分意義最相近的字。

1. Our meeting will <u>commence</u> as
   soon as Mr. Hatchet arrives
   with the blueprints.
   (A) adjourn
   (B) continue
   (C) liven up
   (D) begin

2. Sal is so <u>inept</u> in the kitchen
   that he doesn't even know
   how to boil water.
   (A) reliable
   (B) irresponsible
   (C) incompetent
   (D) gifted

3. The use of force to subdue the
   protesters will only <u>aggravate</u>
   the situation.
   (A) relieve
   (B) modify
   (C) intensify
   (D) alleviate

4. I enjoy shopping at that store
   because the store clerks are all
   so <u>cordial</u>.
   (A) punctual
   (B) handsome
   (C) friendly
   (D) knowledgeable

5. Teachers in the school will
   <u>confiscate</u> any hand-held
   video games found on campus.
   (A) return
   (B) enjoy
   (C) destroy
   (D) seize

6. His <u>pending</u> lawsuit will deter-
   mine whether he will be able
   to keep his business or not.
   (A) decisive
   (B) preliminary
   (C) unsettled
   (D) disastrous

7. Police promised a <u>commensu-
   rate</u> reward for any information
   about the serial killer.
   (A) criminal
   (B) pathetic
   (C) royal
   (D) appropriate

8. A strange measles <u>epidemic</u>
   broke out on college campuses
   across the country.
   (A) cure
   (B) mystery
   (C) outbreak
   (D) recurrence

9. Gary has come as the <u>herald</u> of good news; he is the father of a newborn baby girl.

  (A) doctor
  (B) hearer
  (C) recorder
  (D) messenger

10. In America, April 1 is called April Fool's Day; it is a day when people play <u>pranks</u> on one another.

  (A) tricks
  (B) poems
  (C) games
  (D) songs

11. He was a <u>reckless</u> young man who never listened to his family's advice.

  (A) devoted
  (B) religious
  (C) foolhardy
  (D) evil

12. When I kicked the soccer ball toward the goal, it hit the goal post and was <u>deflected</u> to the right.

  (A) received
  (B) located
  (C) diverted
  (D) found

13. My mother made sure we children had a <u>wholesome</u> dinner every evening.

  (A) nourishing
  (B) attractive
  (C) fragrant
  (D) exotic

14. Residents complained about the <u>noxious</u> fumes coming from the fertilizer factory.

  (A) pleasant
  (B) poisonous
  (C) thick
  (D) strange

15. The skiers <u>accelerated</u> down the steep slope, and many had trouble stopping at the bottom of the hill.

  (A) quickened
  (B) slowed
  (C) fell
  (D) panicked

16. My iron was too hot and I managed to <u>scorch</u> the sleeve of my favorite shirt.

  (A) burn
  (B) inflate
  (C) flatten
  (D) ignite

17. Ned's <u>recital</u> of a poem for English class became a disaster when he suddenly forgot all the words.

  (A) writing
  (B) retelling
  (C) translation
  (D) transition

18. What was the judge's <u>verdict</u> regarding the bribery case?

  (A) information
  (B) decision
  (C) interpretation
  (D) history

19. Alice chose a career in environmental protection because she knew the field was more than an <u>ephemeral</u> fad.
    (A) fleeting
    (B) popular
    (C) endemic
    (D) regulated

20. Florida's <u>temperate</u> winter climate makes it popular with elderly people, who often move there upon retirement.
    (A) rainy
    (B) mild
    (C) breezy
    (D) harsh

21. The first <u>phase</u> of this operation is the most delicate, and the patient must be monitored carefully.
    (A) percentage
    (B) stage
    (C) action
    (D) price

22. Too much sleep can actually make you feel <u>lethargic</u>.
    (A) energetic
    (B) sluggish
    (C) stupid
    (D) happy

23. After this year's successful city-wide art festival, the city is planning to hold <u>subsequent</u> art festivals.
    (A) following
    (B) larger
    (C) innovative
    (D) profitable

24. Please <u>disregard</u> the last fax we sent you; it contained some wrong information and we are sending a correction.
    (A) attend
    (B) remember
    (C) resend
    (D) ignore

25. Under this guarantee, the cost of any repairs to the microwave oven during the first year of use is the manufacturer's <u>liability</u>.
    (A) promise
    (B) prerequisite
    (C) responsibility
    (D) purchase

【解答】

1. D	2. C	3. C	4. C	5. D	6. C	7. D	8. C	9. D	10. A
11. C	12. C	13. A	14. B	15. A	16. A	17. B	18. B	19. A	20. B
21. B	22. B	23. A	24. D	25. C					

📋 LIST ▸ 17

**aggressive 〔 ə'grɛsɪv 〕 *adj.* ①侵略的 ②積極的【最常考】

——同 1. hostile , belligerent 2. ambitious , energetic , competitive

Dogs that are abused by their owners may become *aggressive* in self-defense. 遭主人虐待的狗在自衛時，可能會變得具侵略性。

**anonymous 〔 ə'nɑnəməs 〕 *adj.* 匿名的【最常考】

——同 unnamed , unsigned , nameless , incognito , pseudonymous

The informer received several *anonymous* threats on his life. 告密者接到幾次匿名的恐嚇，要對他的生命不利。

*aspiration 〔 ,æspə'reʃən 〕 *n.* 渴望；抱負【常考】　——同 desire

After years of hard work and study, her *aspiration* to become an astronaut came true.

經過幾年的努力與用功，她想成爲太空人的抱負終於實現。

averse 〔 ə'vɝs 〕 *adj.* 反對的；不情願的

——同 opposed , loath , reluctant , unwilling , antipathetic

Some older people do not like today's rapidly changing technology because they are *averse* to change.

有些年長的人不喜歡日新月異的科技，因爲他們不願作改變。

boisterous 〔 'bɔɪstərəs 〕 *adj.* 喧鬧的

——同 noisy , clamorous , disorderly , unruly , rowdy , rambunctious

A *boisterous* crowd of teenagers suddenly entered the restaurant. 一群喧鬧的青少年突然進入了餐廳。

chatterbox 〔 'tʃætɚ,bɑks 〕 *n.* 喋喋不休的人

——同 talkative person

It was known by everyone in school that Lucy was a big *chatterbox*. 露西在學校是衆所皆知的大嘴巴。

* **commission**〔kə'mɪʃən〕n. 任務【常考】 ——同 duty, mission
It is the sales department's **commission** to improve sales by twenty percent this year.
將銷售量提高百分之二十是營業部本年度的任務。

conform〔kən'fɔrm〕v. 遵守
——同 comply, follow, obey, yield, adapt
Students must **conform** to the dress code or risk being expelled. 學生必須遵守服裝規定，否則恐怕會遭開除。

* **corpulent**〔'kɔrpjələnt〕adj. 肥胖的【常考】 ——同 fat, obese
Although she was not thin, she was not **corpulent** either.
她雖然不瘦，但也不算肥胖。

* **culminate**〔'kʌlmə,net〕v. 達到高潮；最後成為【常考】
——同 climax, conclude, end up
The riots **culminated** in the looting of over a hundred stores.
暴動最後變成搶劫，有上百家商店遭殃。

* **deft**〔dɛft〕adj. 靈巧的【常考】 ——同 skillful, nimble, proficient
The pianist's **deft** fingers moved rapidly up and down the keyboard. 鋼琴家靈巧的手指在琴鍵上迅速地來回移動。

diabolic〔,daɪə'bɑlɪk〕adj. 邪惡的；殘酷的
——同 evil, devilish, fiendish, demonic, wicked
The terrorists' **diabolic** plan was discovered in time to prevent them from carrying it out.
恐怖份子的邪惡計畫及時被發現，遭到了阻止。

disrupt〔dɪs'rʌpt〕v. 使分裂；使中斷
——同 upset, disorganize, disturb, break up, interrupt
I am sorry to **disrupt** your meeting, but you have an important phone call. 我很抱歉打斷你的會議，但你有通重要的電話。

＊dumbfounded 〔 ˌdʌmˈfaʊndɪd 〕 *adj.* 驚訝得說不出話的【最常考】

—— 同 speechless , stunned , thunderstruck , startled , staggered

He was ***dumbfounded*** at hearing the news that he was going to be a father.

當他聽到就要做爸爸的消息時，他驚訝得說不出話來。

＊embellish 〔 ɪmˈbɛlɪʃ 〕 *v.* 裝飾；渲染【常考】

—— 同 ornament , decorate , embroider , adorn

My father often ***embellishes*** the size of the fish he caught when he tells us about his fishing trips.

當父親去釣魚時，他常會加油添醋說他釣的魚有多大。

epitome 〔 ɪˈpɪtəmɪ 〕 *n.* 典型

—— 同 archetype , model

Diane's talent and years of hard practice made her the ***epitome*** of a perfect dancer.

黛安的天份加上多年的努力練習，使她成爲傑出舞蹈家的典型。

Exercise ❭ *Fill in the blanks.*

1. His _____ were many and very ambitious.

2. Janice is _____ to having a career in government.

3. The children at the playground were very _____.

4. Her _____ was to organize a trade meeting between the two companies.

5. The meeting was _____ by the entrance of several angry union members.

【解答】1. aspirations　2. averse　3. boisterous　4. commission　5. disrupted

* **exceed** 〔 ɪk'sid 〕 *v.* 超過【常考】 ——同 transcend , surpass , excel

The number of guests at the party *exceeded* the number of chairs available. 宴會上的客人數目超過椅子的數量。

ferocious 〔 fə'roʃəs 〕 *adj.* 殘忍的

——同 cruel , brutal , savage , mean , rapacious

When the poachers tried to take the lion cubs, the mother became *ferocious* and attacked them.

當偷獵者要抓走小獅子時，母獅變得兇暴並攻擊他們。

fowl 〔 faʊl 〕 *n.* 家禽 ——同 bird

Although the farmer raised many kinds of *fowl*, the highest demand was for his chickens.

雖然農夫養了多種家禽，但雞的需求量最大。

gloomy 〔'glumɪ 〕 *adj.* ①陰暗的 ②沮喪的

——同 1. dim , dark 2. depressed , cheerless , sullen , moody

Suddenly a thick fog rolled in, making the forest *gloomy* and cold. 突然間起了一陣濃霧，讓森林變得又暗又冷。

****hail** 〔 hel 〕 *n.* ; *v.* 稱讚；歡呼【最常考】 ——同 praise , acclaim

His new play has received much *hail* from critics and theatergoers. 他的新劇作受到評論家及戲劇愛好者高度的讚賞。

heredity 〔 hə'rɛdətɪ 〕 *n.* 遺傳

——同 congenital traits , genetics , inheritance

Heredity determines the color of your hair and eyes.

遺傳決定你的頭髮與眼睛的顏色。

impending 〔 ɪm'pɛndɪŋ 〕 *adj.* 逼近的

——同 approaching , coming , hovering , imminent , nearing

Ellen was nervous about the *impending* meeting with her boss.

艾倫對即將和上司見面感到緊張。

infallible 〔 ɪnˈfæləbḷ 〕 *adj.* 絕無錯誤的

── 同 unerring , unimpeachable , foolproof , irreproachable , perfect

Little children think their parents are ***infallible***.

幼兒認爲父母絕不會犯錯。

intermittent 〔 ˌɪntəˈmɪtṇt 〕 *adj.* 間歇的

── 同 fitful , off-and-on , recurrent , periodic , alternate

The couple's ***intermittent*** arguments gradually became more and more serious. 那對夫妻斷斷續續的爭論已逐漸越演越烈。

intimidate 〔 ɪnˈtɪməˌdet 〕 *v.* 威脅

── 同 frighten , dishearten , terrify , browbeat

Jane tried to ***intimidate*** her roommate into quitting her constant smoking. 珍想威脅她的室友不要繼續抽煙。

lid 〔 lɪd 〕 *n.* 蓋子   ── 同 cover , top , cap

Put the ***lid*** on that jar of jelly, or else the ants will get in it.

把果醬的蓋子蓋上，否則螞蟻會爬進去。

martial 〔 ˈmɑrʃəl 〕 *adj.* 軍事的；好戰的

── 同 military , soldierly , warlike , belligerent , combative

His ***martial*** mentality has made him many enemies.

他好戰的心理爲他樹立了不少敵人。

* **moist** 〔 mɔɪst 〕 *adj.* 潮濕的【常考】   ── 同 damp , humid , dank , wet

Don't store bread in a ***moist*** place or it will start to mold.

別把麵包貯藏在潮濕的地方，否則會長霉。

ominous 〔 ˈɑmənəs 〕 *adj.* 不吉利的

── 同 unfavorable , baleful , unpromising , threatening

The morning we were planning to go to the beach, ***ominous*** dark clouds suddenly began to roll in. *roll in* 大量出現

那天早晨我們正打算要去海邊，結果就開始出現大量不祥的烏雲。

overstatement 〔'ovɚ'stetmənt 〕 *n.* 誇大

—— 同 exaggeration , magnification , overclaiming , overdoing

To say that John and Barry hate each other is an **overstatement**; they just don't get along well.

說約翰和貝利兩人彼此憎恨，那是誇大其辭，他們只是合不來。

* peculiar 〔 pɪ'kjuljɚ 〕 *adj.* 奇特的【常考】

—— 同 strange , odd , queer , eccentric , idiosyncratic

Jane has a **peculiar** habit of turning her glass around three times before she takes a drink.

珍有個很奇特的習慣，喝飲料之前，她會把玻璃杯轉三圈。

phenomenal 〔 fə'namənḷ 〕 *adj.* 異常的

—— 同 abnormal , uncommon , unusual , extraordinary , exceptional

No one could have predicted the **phenomenal** success of rap music. 沒有人料想得到，饒舌音樂會離奇地成功。

Exercise ⟩ *Fill in the blanks.*

1. Tom _____ our expectations in the math test.

2. My grandmother, who lives in a countryside village, raises many kinds of _____ .

3. The dog grew _____ after being abused by its owner.

4. Mr. Griggs is a feared teacher because of his _____ ideas of discipline.

5. We heard the _____ howl of a dog before we entered the abandoned house.

【解答】1. exceeded 2. fowl 3. ferocious 4. martial 5. ominous

precaution ﹝ prɪˋkɔʃən ﹞ *n.* 預防　──同 prevention
Sky diving is a very dangerous sport, and you must take
every ***precaution*** to prevent injury.
高空跳傘是種非常危險的運動，必須做好防備，以避免受到傷害。

prone ﹝ pron ﹞ *adj.* 傾向於；易於　──同 inclined , disposed
Betty is careful to always carry a parasol because her fair
skin is ***prone*** to sunburn.　＊parasol ﹝ˋpærəˌsol ﹞ *n.* 陽傘
貝蒂總是十分小心，常隨身攜帶陽傘，因爲她美麗的皮膚很容易曬傷。

＊**quaint** ﹝ kwent ﹞ *adj.*　①奇特的　②古色古香的【常考】
──同 1. curious , fanciful , charming　2. gothic , artful , antique
In the little shop on the corner, Rex found a ***quaint*** little
teapot in the shape of a turtle.
雷克斯在街角的那家小店裡，發現一個奇特的烏龜形狀小茶壺。

＊**recluse** ﹝ˋrɛklus ﹞ *n.* 隱士【最常考】　──同 hermit , eremite
The ***recluse*** chose to live in a small stone cottage in the
forest.　那位隱士選擇住在森林裡小小的石屋中。

＊**regime** ﹝ rɪˋʒim ﹞ *n.* 政權【常考】　──同 government , rule
Many citizens are questioning the current ***regime***'s ability
to govern effectively.
許多人民懷疑當今執政者是否有能力有效率地治理國家。

rustic ﹝ˋrʌstɪk ﹞ *adj.* 農村的；質樸的　──同 rural , homespun
Jack's grandparents live in a ***rustic*** farmhouse in the
countryside.　傑克的祖父母住在鄉下的農舍裡。

＊**scourge** ﹝ skɝdʒ ﹞ *n.* 災害；天譴【常考】　──同 affliction , plague
When preparing her taxes, Martha always declares taxes the
scourge of poor, honest citizens.
瑪莎在準備稅金時總會說，稅是窮苦而誠實的人民極大的災難。

sideways (ˈsaɪdˌwez) *adv.* 斜向一邊地

—同 sidewards , obliquely , laterally , edgeways

Please straighten that picture; it is slanting *sideways* to the right. 麻煩你把那幅畫扶正，它向右邊傾斜。

sovereign (ˈsɑvrɪn) *adj.* 至高無上的 —同 supreme

The Constitution is seen as the *sovereign* law of the land.
憲法被視為國家至高無上的法律。

spot (spɑt) *v.* 認出；看見

—同 see , recognize , discern

I *spotted* the golf ball hidden in the high grass.
我看到藏在草叢中的高爾夫球了。

* **stationary** (ˈsteʃənˌɛrɪ) *adj.* 靜止的【常考】

—同 immobile , static

The strange light moving through the sky suddenly became *stationary* for several minutes.
橫越天際的奇怪光線，突然靜止了好幾分鐘。

* **subsidiary** (səbˈsɪdɪˌɛrɪ) *adj.* 輔助的【常考】

—同 supplementary

A *subsidiary* committee was formed to discuss the effects of toxic wastes on the local wildlife.
組織輔助委員會是要討論有毒的廢料對當地野生生物的影響。

symposium (sɪmˈpozɪəm) *n.* 討論會

—同 panel , colloquium

The university held a *symposium* to discuss the situation facing women entering male-dominated careers.
那所大學舉辦了一場討論會，探討女性在進入以男性為主的工作時，所面臨的情況。

traverse〔'trævɚs〕*v.* 橫貫；橫越

—— 同 cross , pass through , pass over , go over , go across

It took the group three weeks to *traverse* the many miles of
desert. 這群人花了三個星期的時間，才橫越好幾哩的沙漠。

unwind〔ʌn'waɪnd〕*v.* 解開

—— 同 disentangle , unravel , untwine , untwist , uncoil

The dog was so tangled in his chain that he couldn't *unwind*
himself from it. 那隻狗被牢牢地用鍊子栓住，牠自己解不開。

˚˚versatile〔'vɝsətl , -taɪl〕*adj.* 多才多藝的【最常考】

—— 同 variable , resourceful , multifaceted , many-sided , all-round

Carl is such a *versatile* actor that he can perform comedy one
minute and tragedy the next.

卡爾是個多才多藝的演員，他可以演一分鐘的喜劇，下一分鐘就演悲劇。

wiggle〔'wɪgl̩〕*v.* 擺動 —— 同 shake , wriggle , wag , squirm

The little kitten *wiggled* in my arms to get down and play.

小貓在我的懷裡動個不停，想下去玩。

Exercise ⟩ *Fill in the blanks.*

1. Watch out for Naomi; she is _____ to be clumsy and
   knock things over.

2. What a _____ tea set you have!

3. The drought was a _____ on the local farmers' livelihood.

4. The university offered a _____ on immigration laws.

5. This outfit is very _____; it can be casual or formal.

【解答】 1. prone　2. quaint　3. scourge　4. symposium　5. versatile

List 17 · 難字分析

anonymous 〔ə'nɑnəməs〕 *adj.* 匿名的

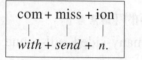

— without a name

commission 〔kə'mɪʃən〕 *n.* 任務

com + miss + ion
with + send + n.

— that which a person is authorized to do for another

corpulent 〔'kɔrpjələnt〕 *adj.* 肥胖的

corp + ulent
body + adj.

— very fat

embellish 〔ɪm'bɛlɪʃ〕 *v.* 裝飾；渲染

em + bell + ish
in + fine + make

— to decorate or improve by adding detail

epitome 〔ɪ'pɪtəmɪ〕 *n.* 典型

epi + tome
upon + cut

— something or somebody that perfectly displays a type

heredity 〔hə'rɛdətɪ〕 *n.* 遺傳

hered + ity
heir + n.

— tendency of living things to pass their characteristics on to offspring

infallible 〔 ɪnˈfæləbḷ 〕 *adj.* 絕無錯誤的

> in + fall +   ible
> | | |
> *not* + *err* + *able to*

—— incapable of error

intermittent 〔 ˌɪntəˈmɪtṇt 〕 *adj.* 間歇的

> inter   + mitt + ent
> | | |
> *between* + *send* + *adj.*

—— occurring from time to time;
stopping and starting at intervals

stationary 〔ˈsteʃənˌɛrɪ 〕 *adj.* 靜止的

> sta   + tion + ary
> | | |
> *stand* + *n.* + *adj.*

—— not moving

subsidiary 〔 səbˈsɪdɪˌɛrɪ 〕 *adj.* 輔助的

> sub   + sid + iary
> | | |
> *under* + *sit* + *adj.*

—— supplementary; serving to assist

symposium 〔 sɪmˈpozɪəm 〕 *n.* 討論會

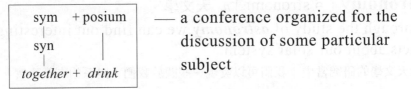

—— a conference organized for the
discussion of some particular
subject

versatile 〔ˈvɝsətɪl , -taɪl 〕 *adj.* 多才多藝的

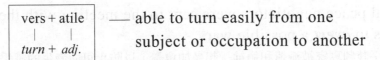

—— able to turn easily from one
subject or occupation to another

📖 LIST ▸ 18

* accommodation 〔 ə͵kɑmə'deʃən 〕 *n.* ①適應；調整
②（ *pl.* ）住宿【常考】
——同 1. adaptation , compliance , conformity 2. board , lodging
We had to make *accommodations* for the possibility of rain for
the outdoor wedding. 我們必須為戶外婚禮做些調整，因為可能會下雨。

agility 〔 ə'dʒɪlətɪ 〕 *n.* 敏捷   ——同 nimbleness
With grace and *agility*, the ice skaters glided past the judges
during their performance.
溜冰者在表演中，優雅又敏捷地滑過裁判的面前。

animate 〔'ænə͵met 〕 *v.* 賦予生命；使有活力   ——同 liven , inspire
The refreshing swim in the lake *animated* us after we had been
exhausted by working out in the hot sun. 在戶外炎熱的太陽下，
工作到筋疲力竭後，到湖裡游游泳真是令人神清氣爽，使我們又充滿活力。

assail 〔 ə'sel 〕 *v.* 攻擊   ——同 attack , assault
The rival political candidates *assailed* each other's character
throughout the campaign.
敵對的政黨候選人在整個競選活動中，互相攻擊對方的人格。

astronomy 〔 ə'strɑnəmɪ 〕 *n.* 天文學
Through the study of *astronomy* we can find out interesting
facts about our solar system.
從天文學的研究當中，我們可以發現一些關於我們太陽系的有趣事實。

avert 〔 ə'vɝt 〕 *v.* ①防止 ②轉移
——同 1. avoid , preclude , fend off 2. turn aside , turn away
Several peace negotiators were sent to the meeting with the
leaders to *avert* a possible war.
數位和平談判專家被派遣和領袖一起參加會議，以防止可能發生的戰爭。

* **bequeath** 〔 bɪ'kwið 〕 *v.* 遺留【常考】
—— 同 hand down , leave , pass on
Gordon **bequeathed** all his money and belongings to his wife.
戈登把所有的錢和財產遺留給他的妻子。

bunch 〔 bʌntʃ 〕 *n.* ①束 ②群集
—— 同 1. bundle , bouquet , clump 2. crowd , group
Eve went out into the field and picked a **bunch** of wild flowers.
伊芙到野外去摘了一束野花。

* **commodity** 〔 kə'mɑdətɪ 〕 *n.* 商品；物品【常考】
—— 同 good , merchandise
The chief **commodity** of our local economy is rice.
本地經濟的主要商品是稻米。

confound 〔 kɑn'faʊnd , kən- 〕 *v.* 使驚訝
—— 同 amaze , astonish , startle , astound , surprise , puzzle
All the mathematicians were **confounded** by the brilliance of
the ten-year-old math genius.
所有的數學家都對這個年僅十歲的數學天才的聰明感到驚訝。

corrode 〔 kə'rod 〕 *v.* 腐蝕；損害
—— 同 eat away , erode , corrupt , rust , impair , deteriorate
Rust had **corroded** so much of the metal door that it had to be
replaced. 這扇鐵門有太多地方都被鐵銹腐蝕了，所以必須把它換掉。

curb 〔 kɝb 〕 *v.* 抑制；控制【最常考】 —— 同 control , check , restrain
Although he was dieting, he could not **curb** his appetite for
pizza. 雖然他正在節食，但還是無法抑制想吃披薩的慾望。

* **defy** 〔 dɪ'faɪ 〕 *v.* 蔑視；違抗【常考】
—— 同 confront , despise , disregard
The private **defied** the colonel's orders and started to attack
when he should have retreated.
這個士兵違抗上校的命令，在他應該撤退時開始進攻。

diaphanous 〔 daɪˋæfənəs 〕 adj. 透明的

——同 transparent , sheer , limpid , see-through

A *diaphanous* curtain hung over the window, letting light into the room.

窗戶上掛著透明的窗簾，讓光線能夠透進房間裡。

dissect 〔 dɪˋsɛkt 〕 v. ①解剖 ②分析

——同 1. anatomize , cut apart , lay open 2. investigate , scrutinize

Our biology class is going to *dissect* frogs this week.

我們的生物課本週將要解剖青蛙。

duplicate 〔ˋdjupləkɪt , -͵ket 〕 adj. 複製的；相同的

——同 identical , copied , double , corresponding , twofold

Do you have any *duplicate* keys for the front door?

你有前門的複製鑰匙嗎？

Exercise ⟩ *Fill in the blanks.*

1. The sleepy dog became _____ upon seeing its owner.

2. I hereby _____ all my worldly possessions to my daughter, Christina.

3. The origin of the meteorite _____ the astronomers.

4. Her _____ dress caused a scandal at the restaurant.

5. Our bank keeps _____ copies of all documents in computer files.

【解答】1. animated 2. bequeath 3. confounded 4. diaphanous 5. duplicate

effigy 〔'ɛfədʒɪ 〕*n.* 肖像 ——㊐ dummy , icon , caricature
The protesters carried an *effigy* of the president wearing a
gold crown in front of the legislature.
抗議者拿著一幅總統戴著金冠的肖像，到立法院前抗議。

emblem 〔'ɛmbləm 〕*n.* 標誌；徽章 ——㊐ sign , symbol , hallmark
The company's *emblem* was an eagle in flight grabbing a
banner with the company's name on it.
這家公司的標誌是一隻飛翔的老鷹，抓著一面旗幟，上面寫著公司名稱。

* **epoch** 〔'ɛpək 〕*n.* 時代【常考】 ——㊐ period , era , age , time
Children think of the *epoch* of the dinosaurs as the most
fascinating time in history.
孩子們認為恐龍時代是歷史上最令人著迷的時代。

* **fertile** 〔'fɜtḷ 〕*adj.* 肥沃的；多產的【常考】
——㊐ rich , productive , fruitful , prolific , yielding
The land in the valley is the most *fertile* land for growing
crops. 山谷裡的那塊土地是種植農作物最肥沃的土地。

* **fracture** 〔'fræktʃə 〕*v.* ; *n.* 破裂【常考】
——㊐ break , crack , rupture
Sophie *fractured* bones in both her legs in the car accident.
那場車禍使蘇菲雙腿骨折。

glowing 〔'gloɪŋ 〕*adj.* ①明亮的 ②讚揚的
——㊐ 1. beaming , luminous 2. complimentary , laudatory
Although it was night, the brightly *glowing* city lights made it
look like day. 雖然是晚上，但都市裡明亮的燈光使得市區看起來像白天。

illegitimate 〔͵ɪlɪ'dʒɪtəmɪt 〕*adj.* 不合法的 ——㊐ illegal
Although the general's power was *illegitimate*, no one had
the military strength to stop him.
雖然將軍的權力不合法，卻沒有人有軍事力量去制止他。

imperative 〔 ɪmˋpɛrətɪv 〕 *adj.* 必要的
——同 necessary , required , indispensable
It is *imperative* that you get to the meeting on time with those computer disks. 你一定要帶著那些電腦磁碟片，準時去參加會議。

* **intervene** 〔 ͵ɪntɚˋvin 〕 *v.* 干涉；介入【常考】
——同 involve , mediate
No one *intervened* to help the woman when her purse was being stolen in the store.
當那位婦人的錢包在店裡被偷時，沒有人出面幫助她。

limp 〔 lɪmp 〕 ① *adj.* 疲倦的；無力的 ② *v.* 跛行
——同 1. weak , worn out 2. hobble , halt
After he pulled the child up the cliff with a rope, his arms fell *limp* with exhaustion.
在用繩子把那個小孩從懸崖拉上來之後，他的手臂因為疲倦而變得無力。
* cliff 〔 klɪf 〕 *n.* 懸崖　　fall 〔 fɔl 〕 *v.* 變成
exhaustion 〔 ɪgˋzɔstʃən 〕 *n.* (極度的) 疲憊

marvel 〔 ˋmɑrvḷ 〕 *n.* 奇蹟　——同 wonder , miracle , prodigy
The *marvel* of modern technology allows us to communicate with almost anyone, anywhere in the world.
現代科技的奇蹟，讓我們幾乎能和世界上任何地方的人通話。

* **molten** 〔 ˋmoltṇ 〕 *adj.* 熔化的【常考】　——同 melted , fused , liquefied
Molten lava poured out of the volcano and flowed in the direction of the village.
熔化的熔岩從火山口噴出來，並朝著村子的方向流動。

** **omnipotent** 〔 ɑmˋnɪpətənt 〕 *adj.* 全能的【最常考】
——同 almighty , all-powerful , supreme , puissant
In ancient times, the emperor was *omnipotent*, and no one would defy him. 古時候帝王是全能的，沒有人能違抗他。

overt 〔o'vɜt〕 *adj.* 明顯的 ——同 apparent, obvious, manifest
The *overt* hostility between Gwen and Rachel made everyone at the party very uncomfortable.
葛雯與瑞秋之間明顯的敵意，使得宴會裡的每一個人都不自在。

pedestal 〔'pɛdɪstḷ〕 *n.* 底座；基礎
——同 support, foundation, base, stand, foot
The *pedestal* that the statue rested on was beginning to crack.
這座雕像的底座開始出現裂縫。

philanthropic 〔,fɪlən'θrɑpɪk〕 *adj.* 慈善的；博愛的
——同 humanitarian, charitable, benevolent, altruistic
Mr. North was famous for his *philanthropic* donations to society. 諾斯先生以他對社會的慈善捐獻而聞名。

⁑predatory 〔'prɛdə,torɪ, -,tɔrɪ〕 *adj.* 肉食的；掠奪的【最常考】
——同 predacious, ravaging, voracious, plundering, pillaging
Wolves are one of the *predatory* animals that live in this region of the country. 狼是該國這個地區的肉食性動物之一。

Exercise *Fill in the blanks.*

1. An _____ of the president was burned by protesters.

2. That couple is so _____ that they have ten children.

3. The lawyer proved that Mr. Johnson's claim to the money was _____.

4. As ugly as he is, it's a _____ he can ever get a date.

5. The _____ threats by the military prevented the president from acting independently.

【解答】1. effigy 2. fertile 3. illegitimate 4. marvel 5. overt

prop 〔 prɑp 〕 *v.* 支撐 ——同 support , uphold , brace

We used a pile of books to ***prop*** the door open.

我們用一堆書把門撐開著。

pseudonym 〔 'sjudn̩‚ɪm , 'su- 〕 *n.* 筆名【最常考】

——同 pen name

Allen used a ***pseudonym*** when writing the essays for the magazine. 艾倫為雜誌撰文時使用筆名。

* **reciprocate** 〔 rɪ'sɪprə‚ket 〕 *v.* 回報【常考】

——同 repay , return , requite , retaliate

I hope one day we can ***reciprocate*** your kindness and invite you over to our house for dinner.

我希望有一天我們能回報你的親切，並請你來家裡吃晚餐。

reckon 〔 'rɛkən 〕 *v.* 認為 ——同 think , suppose , consider

I ***reckon*** the problem with today's teenagers is that they don't care about the consequences of their actions.

我認為當今青少年的問題在於，他們不在乎自己的行為會導致什麼後果。

rescind 〔 rɪ'sɪnd 〕 *v.* 廢止

——同 revoke , repeal , recall , annul , abrogate

The outdated law forbidding dancing was finally ***rescinded***.

禁止跳舞的落伍法令終於被廢除了。

ritual 〔 'rɪtʃuəl 〕 *n.* 儀式 ——同 rite , ceremony , service

Every culture has different ***rituals*** in a wedding ceremony.

每種文化在婚禮上都有不同的儀式。

* **scratch** 〔 skrætʃ 〕 *v.* ; *n.* 摩擦；抓癢【常考】 ——同 scrape , rub

A few minutes after the twig ***scratched*** my arm, my arm started to itch very badly. *twig 〔 twɪg 〕 *n.* 小樹枝

被小樹枝摩擦後沒幾分鐘，我的手臂便開始奇癢無比。

* **span** 〔 spæn 〕① *n.* 時間 ② *v.* 越過【常考】
  —— 同 1. duration , period 2. cross , extend across , range over
  During the ***span*** of my grandmother's life, many amazing
  changes and events have occurred.
  祖母的一生當中，發生了許多驚人的變化和事件。

stature 〔'stætʃɚ 〕*n.* 身高 —— 同 size , height
  Although he is short in ***stature***, he can run fast.
  雖然他身材短小，但他跑得很快。

* **subterranean** 〔,sʌbtə'renɪən 〕*adj.* 地下的【常考】
  —— 同 underground
  There are several very old ***subterranean*** tunnels beneath
  Beijing. 北京有一些很老舊的地下隧道。

succor 〔'sʌkɚ 〕*v.* 幫助 —— 同 aid , help , assist
  Few people are willing to devote themselves to ***succoring***
  those in need. 很少人願意致力幫助窮困的人。

symptom 〔'sɪmptəm 〕*n.* 徵兆 —— 同 sign , indication
  The doctor said that Harry had the ***symptoms*** of the measles.
  醫生說哈瑞有麻疹的徵兆。

* **tenacious** 〔 tɪ'neʃəs 〕*adj.* 緊抓的；堅持的【常考】
  —— 同 clinging , firm , inflexible , persevering , resolute
  The lawyer's ***tenacious*** support of her client impressed the
  jury. 這位律師對她的當事人始終支持到底，令陪審團印象深刻。

travesty 〔'trævɪstɪ , -vəstɪ 〕*n.* 滑稽化；曲解
  —— 同 mockery , ridiculous distortion , parody , burlesque
  The killing of the three innocent men by the government
  was a ***travesty*** of justice.
  政府處死這三個無辜的人，等於是曲解司法。

unwittingly 〔ʌn'wɪtɪŋlɪ〕 *adv.* 無心地；不知不覺地

——同 unintentionally , unknowingly , accidentally

Grace ***unwittingly*** helped the enemy by talking with a man who turned out to be a spy. 葛麗絲在不知不覺中幫助了敵人，因為她和一個男人談過話，而他竟是個間諜。

* **verse** 〔 vɝs 〕 *n.* 詩；韻文【常考】

——同 poetry , rhyme

Terrance had a wonderful story which he decided to write in ***verse***. 泰倫斯有一個非常棒的故事，他決定把它寫成詩。

* **wily** 〔'waɪlɪ〕 *adj.* 狡猾的【常考】

——同 cunning , sly , crafty , shrewd

The ***wily*** thief slipped out of the window without anyone knowing he had been in the building.

狡猾的小偷從窗戶偷偷溜出去，沒有人知道他來過這棟大樓。

Exercise ⟩ *Fill in the blanks.*

1. The sign was _____ up by a pile of bricks.

2. To _____ for the beautiful gift her sister had given her, she cooked a lavish meal for her sister.

3. I could tell by Nora's _____ that the mosquitoes were biting her too.

4. The bank was _____ loaning money to insolvent companies.

5. His _____ mind is always coming up with some new scheme to make more money.

【解答】 1. propped   2. reciprocate   3. scratching   4. unwittingly   5. wily

ᐧ List 18 ᐧ 難字分析

accommodation 〔 ə͵kɑmə'deʃən 〕 n. ① 適應；調整
② (*pl.*) 住宿

ac +	com +	mod	+ ation
ad			
to +	*together* +	*manner* +	*n.*

—— adjustment; room and board

agility 〔 ə'dʒɪlətɪ 〕 n. 敏捷

ag +	il(e) +	ity
act +	*adj.* +	*n.*

—— quickness in movement

diaphanous 〔 daɪ'æfənəs 〕 *adj.* 透明的

dia +	phan +	ous
through +	*appear* +	*adj.*

—— that can be seen through

duplicate 〔'djupləkɪt , -͵ket 〕 *adj.* 複製的；相同的

du +	plic +	ate
two +	*fold* +	*adj.*

—— corresponding exactly

effigy 〔'ɛfədʒɪ 〕 n. 肖像

ef +	fig	+ y
ex		
out +	*fashion* +	*n.*

—— representation of a person

illegitimate 〔͵ɪlɪˈdʒɪtəmɪt〕 *adj.* 不合法的

il + leg + itim + ate
in
not + law + most + adj.

— contrary to law or rules

omnipotent 〔ɑmˈnɪpətənt〕 *adj.* 全能的

omni + potent
all + powerful

— all powerful

philanthropic 〔͵fɪlənˈθrɑpɪk〕 *adj.* 慈善的；博愛的

phil + anthrop + ic
love + man + adj.

— kind and helpful; benevolent

pseudonym 〔ˈsjudn͵ɪm , ˈsu- 〕 *n.* 筆名

pseudo + (o)nym
false + name

— pen name

rescind 〔rɪˈsɪnd〕 *v.* 廢止

re + scind
back + cut

— to revoke or cancel

subterranean 〔͵sʌbtəˈrenɪən〕 *adj.* 地下的

sub + terr + anean
under + earth + adj.

— lying beneath the earth's surface

TEST ▶ 9

請由 (A)～(D) 中選出和畫線部分意義最相近的字。

1. This play opening has been <u>hailed</u> as the city's social event of the year.
   - (A) forgotten
   - (B) lauded
   - (C) overruled
   - (D) solidified

2. If you do not <u>conform</u> to the rigid requirements of the workplace, you will be fired.
   - (A) improve
   - (B) trivialize
   - (C) comply
   - (D) negotiate

3. Eric watched the earthworms <u>wiggle</u> on the pavement after the rainstorm.
   - (A) jump
   - (B) swim
   - (C) dart
   - (D) squirm

4. Coffee is becoming an even more important <u>commodity</u> in the world market.
   - (A) price
   - (B) good
   - (C) beverage
   - (D) plant

5. Scientists are trying to understand <u>heredity</u> by mapping human DNA.
   - (A) genetic make-up
   - (B) psychology
   - (C) thinking processes
   - (D) behavior

6. Riding a <u>stationary</u> bicycle is a good way for people who live in cities to exercise.
   - (A) mountain
   - (B) static
   - (C) lightweight
   - (D) expensive

7. Because she has exercised her whole life, my grandmother still has a lot of <u>agility</u>.
   - (A) mobility
   - (B) stiffness
   - (C) muscularity
   - (D) health

8. The acrobats seemed to <u>defy</u> gravity with their feats of strength and agility.
   - (A) exemplify
   - (B) toy
   - (C) question
   - (D) disregard

9. Dr. Banner considered the Scientific Revolution the beginning of a new <u>epoch</u>.

(A) era
(B) year
(C) idea
(D) example

10. Her <u>deft</u> feet leapt from stone to stone in the stream, while I fell on the first slippery rock I stepped on.

(A) tiny
(B) muscular
(C) handy
(D) nimble

11. Economists said it was an <u>overstatement</u> to say that the stock market was overheating.

(A) inaccuracy
(B) overture
(C) exaggeration
(D) plot

12. Fed up with the evils of modern society, the man moved to the woods and became a <u>recluse</u>.

(A) hermit
(B) reporter
(C) farmer
(D) salesman

13. This poem, though <u>anonymous</u>, is very famous.

(A) unsigned
(B) short
(C) boring
(D) detailed

14. Although Walter did not break his leg falling from the tree, he did <u>fracture</u> his arm.

(A) crush
(B) crack
(C) dislocate
(D) cure

15. She explained to the doctor that her headaches were <u>intermittent</u>, and none lasted for more than ten minutes.

(A) painful
(B) off-and-on
(C) allergy-induced
(D) frequent

16. In a communist system, the central government is virtually <u>omnipotent</u>.

(A) valuable
(B) all-knowing
(C) widespread
(D) all-powerful

17. He kept a <u>tenacious</u> hold on the rope the rescue workers were using to pull him out of the cavern.

(A) tentative
(B) delicate
(C) inconstant
(D) firm

18. How <u>imperative</u> is it that this package arrive by Monday?

(A) likely
(B) fortunate
(C) necessary
(D) ridiculous

19. We used our canoes to traverse the river at its narrowest point.

    (A) swim
    (B) detour
    (C) cross
    (D) drive

20. Salt water can corrode the metal of your automobile's body.

    (A) strengthen
    (B) electrify
    (C) deteriorate
    (D) season

21. Even housecats have predatory instincts, which will drive them to chase mice and insects in the home.

    (A) predacious
    (B) survival
    (C) tribal
    (D) protective

22. Wedding ceremonies are full of cultural and religious rituals.

    (A) costumes
    (B) rites
    (C) experiences
    (D) agreements

23. Our organization is dedicated to succoring victims of disasters in need of food and medicine.

    (A) reporting
    (B) transporting
    (C) helping
    (D) locating

24. The Odyssey was composed in verse by the Greek poet Homer.

    (A) poetry
    (B) novel form
    (C) song
    (D) Greek

25. The record store was swamped with a phenomenal number of telephone calls asking when the new album would be in stock.

    (A) small
    (B) recent
    (C) regular
    (D) extraordinary

【解答】

1. B	2. C	3. D	4. B	5. A	6. B	7. A	8. D	9. A	10. D
11. C	12. A	13. A	14. B	15. B	16. D	17. D	18. C	19. C	20. C
21. A	22. B	23. C	24. A	25. D					

📖 LIST ▸ 19

accomplice 〔 ə'kɑmplɪs 〕*n.* 共犯
—— 同 accessory , confederate , abettor , assistant , helper
Darryl was arrested for being an *accomplice* in the robbery.
達利爾因搶劫共犯的罪名而被逮捕。

∗agitate 〔'ædʒə,tet 〕*v.* 激動；擾亂【最常考】
—— 同 upset , stir , excite , provoke , disturb
The teacher was *agitated* by the students' constant talking in
class.　課堂上學生不斷交談，使老師情緒受擾。

antagonistic 〔 æn,tægə'nɪstɪk 〕*adj.* 敵對的
—— 同 hostile , opposed , contentious , averse , at odds
The group is *antagonistic* towards the building of an
incinerator in the community.　該團體反對在社區內興建焚化爐。
　∗incinerator 〔 ɪn'sɪnə,retə 〕*n.* 焚化爐

assay 〔 ə'se 〕*v.* 分析
—— 同 analyze , assess , evaluate , inspect , appraise
Inspectors were sent to *assay* the damage caused by the bomb.
巡官被派往分析炸彈所造成的損害。

∗ aviator 〔'evɪ,etə 〕*n.* 飛行員【常考】　—— 同 pilot , airman , flier
Her grandfather was one of the first *aviators* in the British
military.　她的祖父是英國軍隊中最早的飛行員之一。

∗ bereave 〔 bə'riv 〕*v.* 剝奪；喪失【常考】
—— 同 deprive , rob , strip , dispossess , divest
The refugees were *bereaved* of any hope by the dreary camps
they were forced to live in.
被迫住在這樣陰暗的營地，難民已被剝奪了希望。

burnish 〔ˈbɜnɪʃ 〕 *v.* 磨亮;擦亮

——同 brighten , buff , shine , smooth , furbish

The soldier **burnished** the decorative sword from his dress uniform. 這名士兵將裝飾用的刀在制服上磨亮。

chef 〔 ʃɛf 〕 *n.* 廚師 ——同 cook

The **chef** created wonderful dishes from various international cuisines. 這名廚師從各國的烹調法中創造出佳餚來。

* **communal** 〔ˈkɑmjunḷ , kəˈmjunḷ 〕 *adj.* 自治的;共有的【常考】

——同 collective , communistic , general , public , shared

This dorm has **communal** showers and toilets.

這間宿舍有公共的衛浴設備。

* **confront** 〔 kənˈfrʌnt 〕 *v.* 面對【常考】

——同 face , encounter , cope with

She was **confronted** with the problem of having to commute for two hours to her new job. 新工作使她面臨通勤兩小時的問題。

couch 〔 kautʃ 〕 ① *v.* 表達 ② *n.* 床;睡椅

——同 1. express , phrase , utter , frame , set forth 2. bed , cot , pallet

You should **couch** your request to Mr. Wang in a flattering way. 你應該以奉承的方式向王先生表達請求。

currency 〔ˈkɜənsɪ 〕 *n.* 貨幣 ——同 money , bills , coins

When people go to a foreign country, they are often confused when using the local **currency**.

人們出國後,常因使用當地貨幣而感到困惑。

* **dehydrate** 〔 diˈhaɪdret 〕 *v.* 使乾燥;脫水【常考】

——同 dry , dehumidify , desiccate , drain

The air on airplanes is very dry and can easily **dehydrate** you.

飛機上的空氣非常乾燥,很容易使你失去水分。

diffidence 〔 'dɪfədəns 〕 *n.* 羞怯【最常考】

—— 同 timidity , bashfulness , shyness , meekness

Her ***diffidence*** made public speaking very difficult for her.
由於羞怯，演講對她來說十分困難。

disseminate 〔 dɪ'sɛməˌnet 〕 *v.* 傳播；宣傳【常考】

—— 同 broadcast , propagate , spread , circulate

There are many different media to ***disseminate*** the news.
有許多不同的媒體報導新聞。

duration 〔 djʊ'reʃən 〕 *n.* 持續；期間

—— 同 term , period , continuance , persistence

During the ***duration*** of the pregnancy, a woman should not drink alcohol or smoke.
婦女在懷孕期間不應喝酒或抽煙。

Exercise ⟩ *Fill in the blanks.*

1. If you are _____ towards Ms. Muriyama, you will never convince her of your opinion.

2. They were left _____ by the death of their parents.

3. The buckle on his belt was _____ so that it shone brightly.

4. Ron _____ Jason about his alleged drug abuse.

5. I think her _____ towards Edward is only feigned.

【解答】1. antagonistic   2. bereft   3. burnished   4. confronted   5. diffidence

embody 〔 ɪm'bɑdɪ 〕 *v.* 具體化

—— 同 substantiate , incorporate , express

This book *embodies* that scientist's life work.

這本書具體呈現出該科學家畢生的心血。

equation 〔 ɪ'kweʒən , -ʃən 〕 *n.* 方程式；相等

—— 同 balance , parallel , equivalence , equality

This *equation* calls for us to use both multiplication and addition. 這道方程式需要使用乘法和加法。

excerpt 〔'ɛksɝpt 〕 *n.* 選錄

—— 同 selection , extract , quote , citation , passage

Our English teacher read an *excerpt* from Shakespeare's Hamlet. 我們的英文老師唸了一段莎士比亞的哈姆雷特。

** **fervent** 〔'fɝvənt 〕 *adj.* 熱烈的【常考】

—— 同 zealous , enthusiastic , impassioned , ardent , fervid

Kenny is a *fervent* basketball fan, watching every game he can on TV. 肯尼是個狂熱的籃球迷，每場電視轉播他都看。

** **fragile** 〔'frædʒəl 〕 *adj.* 易碎的【常考】

—— 同 breakable , brittle , frail , delicate , flimsy

Be careful with that vase; it is very *fragile*.

小心那個花瓶，它非常易碎。

gorge 〔 gɔrdʒ 〕 ① *n.* 峽谷 ② *v.* 吞食

—— 同 1. canyon , ravine 2. devour , surfeit

Taroko *Gorge* is famous for its natural beauty.

太魯閣峽谷以自然美景聞名。

heyday 〔'he,de 〕 *n.* 全盛時期 —— 同 golden age , prime , zenith

During its *heyday*, Hollywood was the center of glamour in America. 好萊塢在全盛時期，曾是美國的魅力中心。

imperious 〔 ɪmˋpɪrɪəs 〕 *adj.* 高傲的

—— 同 haughty , arrogant , oppressive , arbitrary

The *imperious* principal handed out cruel punishments for even the most innocent offenses.

這名高傲的首長對最無心的冒犯，也施以殘酷的懲罰。

* *hand out* 給予 　innocent 〔ˋɪnəsn̩t 〕 *adj.* 無惡意的

offense 〔 əˋfɛns 〕 *n.* 犯規；犯罪

inaugurate 〔 ɪnˋɔgjə‚ret 〕 *v.* 就職 　—— 同 install , induct

When the government *inaugurated* the new mayor, there was much celebrating in the city.

新市長就職時，城裡辦了許多慶祝活動。

infectious 〔 ɪnˋfɛkʃəs 〕 *adj.* 傳染的

—— 同 contagious , catching , spreading , transmittable

Chicken pox is an *infectious* disease that many children contract. 水痘是許多兒童都會感染的傳染病。

literacy 〔ˋlɪtərəsɪ 〕 *n.* 能力；教養

—— 同 education , knowledge

May works at a special education center which focuses on adult *literacy*.

梅在一個以培訓成人爲宗旨的特教中心任職。

* mason 〔ˋmesn̩ 〕 *n.* 泥水匠【常考】 　—— 同 bricklayer

The *mason* began to mix the cement that would hold the bricks together. 泥水匠開始攪拌使磚黏固的水泥。

* monitor 〔ˋmɑnətɚ 〕 *v.* 監視【常考】

—— 同 watch , oversee , supervise

This machine will *monitor* the patient's heart.

這部機器將可監看病人的心臟。

* **omnipresent** 〔͵ɑmnɪ'prɛzn̩t〕 *adj.* 無所不在的【常考】

　　——同 all-present , ubiquitous

Christians believe that God is ***omnipresent***, and so everything you do is seen by God.

基督徒以爲神是無所不在的，因此你的一舉一動上帝都知道。

* **overtake** 〔͵ovɚ'tek〕 *v.* 追上【常考】

　　——同 reach , catch up with , pass

In the last seconds of the race, my uncle's horse ***overtook*** the lead horse to win the race.

在比賽的最後幾秒，我叔叔的馬追上領先的馬隻，贏得比賽。

philology 〔fɪ'lɑlədʒɪ〕 *n.* 語言學　——同 linguistics

She finds French ***philology*** to be a fascinating subject.

她覺得法語學是個有趣的科目。

precipice 〔'prɛsəpɪs〕 *n.* 斷崖　——同 cliff , bluff , crag

A single guard rail was all that kept us from falling down the ***precipice***. 單邊護欄是使我們免於墜崖的唯一屏障。

Exercise ▷ *Fill in the blanks.*

1. Everyone in class had to memorize an ＿＿＿＿＿＿ from the play we were studying.

2. She had a ＿＿＿＿＿＿ belief that one day he would return.

3. The boss' ＿＿＿＿＿＿ attitude drove half of the office staff to quit.

4. It has been one year since the president was ＿＿＿＿＿＿.

5. The red sports car ＿＿＿＿＿＿ us and then crashed into an oncoming car.

【解答】1. excerpt　2. fervent　3. imperious　4. inaugurated　5. overtook

predicament 〔 prɪˈdɪkəmənt 〕 *n.* 困境
——同 dilemma , quandary , plight
Being invited to two weddings on the same day was quite a
predicament for Saul.
同一天受邀參加兩場婚禮使索爾陷入困境。

propagate 〔ˈprɑpəˌget 〕 *v.* ①繁殖 ②傳播
——同 1. breed , multiply , raise 2. disseminate , spread
With warm temperatures and plenty of rain, the plants
propagated quickly.
暖和的溫度和充足的雨水使植物生長迅速。

recur 〔 rɪˈkɝ 〕 *v.* 再發生   ——同 repeat , occur again
After you have had the chicken pox, it is very unlikely to
recur. 出過水痘後，極不可能再感染。

rescue 〔ˈrɛskju 〕 *v.* 救援   ——同 save , help
The brave firefighter rushed into the burning house to *rescue*
the little boy. 勇敢的救火員衝入火海拯救小男孩。

* **rival** 〔ˈraɪvḷ 〕 *n.* 對手【常考】
——同 competitor , challenger , antagonist , foe , opponent
The mayor's political *rival* was set to win the election.
市長的政敵積極運作贏得選舉。

** **scrub** 〔 skrʌb 〕 *v.* 擦洗【最常考】   ——同 scour , wash , cleanse
This pot is very dirty, so you will have to *scrub* hard to get it
clean. 這壺很髒，所以你要用力把它擦洗乾淨。

* **simultaneous** 〔ˌsaɪmḷˈtenɪəs , ˌsɪmḷ- 〕 *adj.* 同時的【常考】
——同 concurrent , at the same time
There was a *simultaneous* broadcast of the president's speech
on all three channels. 總統演說在三台同步播映。

* **sparse** 〔 spɑrs 〕 *adj.* 稀疏的；稀少的【常考】

　　——同 scanty , scarce , few and far between

My aging father's hair is getting *sparser*.

我父親的頭髮隨年紀增長而日漸稀疏。

staunch 〔 stɔntʃ , stɑntʃ 〕 *adj.* 忠實的

　　——同 firm , loyal , faithful , steadfast

Mr. Whithers has been my *staunch* ally in all my years as a
politician.　惠勒先生在我從政期間，一直是我的忠實同盟。

* **subtle** 〔 'sʌtḷ 〕 *adj.* 精巧的；淡的【常考】

　　——同 delicate , dainty , elusive , refined

There is a *subtle* taste of ginger in this dish.

這道菜中有淡淡的薑味。

* **synthetic** 〔 sɪn'θɛtɪk 〕 *adj.* 人造的【常考】

　　——同 artificial , man-made , unnatural

Today, many clothes are made of *synthetic* fibers.

現在許多衣服是由人造纖維所製成。

tenor 〔 'tɛnɚ 〕 *n.* 主旨　——同 gist , significance , meaning , import

His speech was so confusing that no one got the *tenor* of
what he had said.　他的演說相當混亂，所以無人聽懂主題。

treacherous 〔 'trɛtʃərəs 〕 *adj.* ①危險的　②不忠的

　　——同 1. dangerous , perilous　2. traitorous , unfaithful , unreliable

Our journey through the jungle will be a *treacherous* one.

我們此次的叢林之旅將十分危險。

* **turbulent** 〔 'tɝbjələnt 〕 *adj.* 混亂的；狂暴的【常考】

　　——同 agitated , riotous , violent , tumultuous

As the storm approached, the sea grew more and more
turbulent.　當暴風雨逼近時，海水變得越來越洶湧。

unwonted 〔 ʌn'wʌntɪd 〕 adj. 不習慣的；不尋常的

—— 同 not used , unaccustomed , unusual

He found her **unwonted** excitement for the baseball game very strange. 她對棒球比賽不尋常的熱衷，令他感到十分詭異。

*vindicate 〔 'vɪndə,ket 〕 v. 辯護【常考】

—— 同 justify , defend , assert , acquit , excuse

She felt that winning the tennis championship **vindicated** her defeat in previous years.

她覺得贏得這次的網球冠軍，已為她前幾年的失敗雪恥了。

wince 〔 wɪns 〕 v. 畏縮

—— 同 shrink back , recoil , draw back , flinch

Paul **winced** when the nurse gave him the shot.

當護士要幫保羅打針時，他畏畏縮縮的。

Exercise ⟩ *Fill in the blanks.*

1. The electricity going out in the middle of the party was quite a _____ for the host.

2. The students were excited about the basketball game between their school and its _____.

3. The couple's apartment had only _____ furnishings.

4. Just tell me the _____ of the story, not the details.

5. She _____ her failure on the quiz by studying hard and passing the final exam.

【解答】1. predicament 2. rival 3. sparse 4. tenor 5. vindicated

· List 19 · 難字分析

accomplice 〔 ə'kɑmplɪs 〕 *n.* 共犯

ac +	com	+ plice
ad		
to +	*together+*	*fold*

—— helper or companion in wrongdoing

antagonistic 〔 æn,tægə'nɪstɪk 〕 *adj.* 敵對的

ant	+ agon(y) +	ist	+ ic
anti			
against +	*struggle +*	*person +*	*adj.*

—— acting in opposition

dehydrate 〔 di'haɪdret 〕 *v.* 使乾燥；脫水

de +	hydr +	ate
dis		
away +	*water+*	*make*

—— to remove water from a substance

diffidence 〔 'dɪfədəns 〕 *n.* 羞怯

dif +	fid +	ence
dis		
apart +	*trust +*	*n.*

—— shyness

disseminate 〔 dɪ'sɛmə,net 〕 *v.* 傳播；宣傳

dis +	semin +	ate
apart +	*seed +*	*make*

—— to scatter far and wide

infectious〔ɪnˈfɛkʃəs〕*adj.* 傳染的

in +	fect +	ious	— containing disease
in +	make +	adj.	

philology〔fɪˈlɑlədʒɪ〕*n.* 語言學

philo +	log +	y	— study of the development of
love +	speak +	n.	language or of particular languages

precipice〔ˈprɛsəpɪs〕*n.* 斷崖

pre +	cipice	— steep cliff
before +	head	

predicament〔prɪˈdɪkəmənt〕*n.* 困境

pre +	dica +	ment	— difficult or unpleasant situation
before +	speak +	n.	from which escape seems difficult

simultaneous〔ˌsaɪml̩ˈtenɪəs , ˌsɪml̩-〕*adj.* 同時的

simul +	taneous	— happening or done at the same time
same +	adj.	

vindicate〔ˈvɪndəˌket〕*v.* 辯護

vin +	dic +	ate	— to show or prove the truth of
wine +	speak +	v.	something that has been attacked
			or disputed

LIST ▶ 20

accretion 〔 əˈkriʃən , æˈkriʃən 〕 *n.* 增大

——同 increase , augmentation , enlargement , extension

A thick *accretion* of dust covered everything in the old house.

增生的厚重灰塵將舊房子裡的所有東西都覆蓋住了。

agrarian 〔 əˈgrɛrɪən 〕 *adj.* 農業的

——同 agricultural , arable , rural , rustic

Agrarian regions in the country are poorer than industrial ones. 該國的農業地區比工業地區貧窮。

antedate 〔ˈæntɪˌdet , æntɪˈdet 〕 *v.* 提前；先於

——同 precede , predate , antecede

Printing in China *antedated* European printing by hundreds of years. 中國的印刷術比歐洲早了幾百年。

* assert 〔 əˈsɝt 〕 *v.* 斷言；堅持【常考】

——同 affirm , declare , claim , allege , avow

He *asserted* his innocence in the crime.

他堅持他在這樁案件中是無辜的。

avid 〔ˈævɪd 〕 *adj.* 熱望的；貪婪的

——同 desirous , ardent , zealous , eager , keen

My father is an *avid* golfer and goes to the golf course every weekend.

我父親是個狂熱的高爾夫球玩家；他每個週末都去球場。

* beseech 〔 bɪˈsitʃ 〕 *v.* 懇求【常考】

——同 implore , entreat , plead , solicit , beg

She *beseeched* her husband to be lenient with their child.

她懇求丈夫對孩子寬大點。

* **burrow** 〔 'bɝo 〕 *n.* 洞穴【常考】 ——同 hole , tunnel

The wild rabbit we had been watching suddenly ran into its *burrow*. 我們觀察的那隻野兔突然跑進洞穴裡了。

** **chicanery** 〔 ʃɪ'kenərɪ 〕 *n.* 欺騙；詭計【最常考】

——同 deception , trickery , fraud , subterfuge

The principal punished the boys for their *chicanery* in hiding all the chalk.
校長懲罰這些男孩，因爲他們使詭計將所有的粉筆都藏起來。

* **compact** 〔 kəm'pækt 〕 ① *adj.* 簡潔的 ② *v.* 壓緊【常考】
——同 1. concise , brief , terse 2. cram , condense , pack , squeeze

The steamroller *compacted* the asphalt to make the new road surface. 壓路機將柏油壓緊，製造新的路面。

*asphalt 〔 'æsfɔlt , -fælt 〕 *n.* 柏油

** **congenial** 〔 kən'dʒinjəl 〕 *adj.* 意氣相投的【最常考】
——同 compatible , kindred , agreeable , pleasing , harmonious

She had a *congenial* chat with her new next-door neighbor.
她和隔壁的新鄰居聊得很投機。

coverage 〔 'kʌvərɪdʒ 〕 *n.* 報導範圍
——同 reportage , reporting , description , broadcasting

The international news *coverage* of the event was extensive.
國際間對此事件的新聞報導很多。

curfew 〔 'kɝfju 〕 *n.* 宵禁 ——同 deadline , restriction

We were prevented from attending any parties by the dorm's strict *curfew*. 由於宿舍門禁時間嚴格，我們無法參加任何的舞會。

curtail 〔 kɝ'tel 〕 *v.* 削減 ——同 reduce , diminish , decrease

To *curtail* your desire for cigarettes, try munching on carrot sticks. 爲了減低你對香煙的慾望，試試嚼一嚼胡蘿蔔。

‡**deity** 〔'diətɪ〕 *n.* 神【最常考】

—同 god , divine , being

Townsfolk gather at this temple to worship the local *deity*.

鎮民聚集在這座廟膜拜地方上的神。

dilapidated 〔də'læpə,detɪd〕 *adj.* 荒廢的；破舊的

—同 run-down , decaying , ruined , ramshackle , tumble-down

With his small salary, all he could afford was a *dilapidated*,
little apartment.

以他微薄的薪水，他只能付得起破舊的小公寓。

‡**dissent** 〔dɪ'sɛnt〕 *v.* 不同意【最常考】

—同 disagree , disapprove , object

No one dared to *dissent* when the king made a decision.

沒有人敢不同意國王的決定。

Exercise ▷ *Fill in the blanks.*

1. The artist enjoyed capturing the beauty of _____
   scenes on canvas.

2. She _____ that she could be relied upon for
   assistance after the river overflowed its banks.

3. I _____ you to save our town from economic ruin.

4. The government must _____ spending to reduce the
   deficit.

5. Several of the legislators _____ when the premier
   announced the new policy.

【解答】1. agrarian   2. asserted   3. beseech   4. curtail   5. dissented

dwelling (ˈdwɛlɪŋ) *n.* 住處
——同 residence , abode , habitation , lodging , domicile
Caves actually make very practical, well-insulated *dwellings*
for people.　＊insulate (ˈɪnsə‚let , ˈɪnsjʊ-) *v.* 隔離
對人類而言，洞穴實際上是相當實用、隱蔽的住所。

embrace (ɪmˈbres) *v.* ①擁抱　②包含
——同 1. hug , clasp , cuddle　2. cover , include , comprise
This new law *embraces* the rights of children as well as those
of the elderly.　這條新的法律包含兒童及老年人的權利。

equity (ˈɛkwətɪ) *n.* 公正；公平
——同 fairness , impartiality , justice , justness , equitableness
Equity for all citizens is the goal of our society.
讓全民平等是我們社會的目標。

＊**excessive** (ɪkˈsɛsɪv) *adj.* 過度的【常考】
——同 immoderate , extreme , inordinate , exorbitant
Excessive smoking will shorten your life drastically.
過度的吸煙會嚴重縮短壽命。　＊drastically (ˈdræstɪkəlɪ) *adv.* 嚴重地

feud (fjud) *n.* 不和；夙怨　——同 hostility , enmity , rancor
A *feud* between Romeo's and Juliet's families forced them to
meet in secret.　羅密歐和茱麗葉兩家的夙怨，迫使他們得偷偷相會。

fragrant (ˈfregrənt) *adj.* 芳香的　——同 aromatic ,
sweet-smelling , ambrosial , perfumed , odorous , balmy
Norma planted several *fragrant* plants and flowers in her
rooftop garden.　諾瑪在她的屋頂花園裡種了幾種芳香的花草。

genteel (dʒɛnˈtil) *adj.* 優雅的　——同 elegant , courteous , urbane
Her *genteel* manners impressed everyone at the dinner party.
她優雅的儀態讓晚宴中的每個人印象深刻。

* **hibernate** 〔ˈhaɪbɚˌnet〕 *v.* 冬眠【常考】　——同 lie dormant
  Bears eat enormous amounts of food, so they can live off their
  fat when they **hibernate**. *＊live off* 以～維生
  熊攝取了大量的食物,所以在冬眠時可靠脂肪維生。

* **impermeable** 〔ɪmˈpɝmɪəbḷ〕 *adj.* 不滲透的【常考】
  ——同 hermetic , impassable , impenetrable , impervious
  The experiment called for a container that was **impermeable** to
  light. 這個實驗需要一個不透光的容器。

* **inferior** 〔ɪnˈfɪrɪɚ〕 *adj.* 劣質的【常考】　——同 minor , imperfect
  This **inferior** furniture may be cheaper, but it will not last long.
  這套劣質的傢俱也許比較便宜,但使用不了太久。

  intractable 〔ɪnˈtræktəbḷ〕 *adj.* 不聽話的;難駕馭的
  ——同 unmanageable , uncontrollable , headstrong , unyielding
  It was difficult for the bank teller to remain pleasant with such
  an **intractable** customer.
  面對這麼難應付的顧客,要銀行出納員保持親切實在有困難。

  loath 〔loθ〕 *adj.* 不願意的　——同 averse , reluctant
  Some little children are **loath** to take baths. 有些小孩不願意洗澡。

  masterful 〔ˈmæstɚfəl〕 *adj.* 專橫的　——同 authoritative
  When talking about business, his voice suddenly lowers and
  becomes more **masterful**.
  談到生意的時候,他的聲音突然壓低下來,而且變得更專橫。

* **monumental** 〔ˌmɑnjəˈmɛntḷ〕
  adj. ①紀念碑的 ②龐大的 ③不朽的【常考】
  ——同 1. serving as a monument 2. huge 3. significant , outstanding
  A **monumental** plaque was put up in the city hall to celebrate
  the city's 100-year anniversary. *＊plaque* 〔plæk〕 *n.* 匾額
  市府廳內掛了一紀念匾額,慶祝該市成立一百週年。

*obsolete (ˈɑbsəˌlit) adj. 過時的【最常考】

——同 outdated, outmoded

In today's world, computer models become **obsolete** in only a few years. 在現今的世界裡，電腦機型不消幾年就變過時。

* onerous (ˈɑnərəs) adj. 繁重的【常考】

——同 burdensome, heavy, toilsome, cumbersome, oppressive

Jack was given the **onerous** duty of cleaning out the elephants' stall at the zoo.

傑克被分派到動物園內清掃大象舍的繁重工作。

* overwhelm (ˌovəˈhwɛlm) v. 擊潰；壓倒【常考】

——同 conquer, defeat, overpower, overcome, beat

The poorly armed local soldiers were quickly **overwhelmed** by the stronger national troops.

缺乏戰備的地方兵很快就被強大的國軍給擊潰了。

Exercise ⟩ *Fill in the blanks.*

1. The police officer was reprimanded for _____ use of force in arresting the suspect.

2. The building cannot withstand a major earthquake because _____ materials were used in building it.

3. Hotel staff often have to deal with _____ customers.

4. His _____ attitude towards customers has lost our company many clients.

5. We were _____ with grief when we heard the sad news.

【解答】 1. excessive　2. inferior　3. intractable　4. masterful　5. overwhelmed

peek 〔 pik 〕 *v.* 偷看　——同 peep , glance , look

She *peeked* over her newspaper to get a better look at the handsome man.

她從報紙後偷看，想仔細瞧瞧這位英俊的男士。

propel 〔 prə'pɛl 〕 *v.* 推進　——同 push , thrust , impel

The wind *propelled* the sailboat through the water quickly.

風使帆船在水中快速推進。

* **resemble** 〔 rɪ'zɛmbl̩ 〕 *v.* 相似【常考】　——同 look like , parallel

Everyone says Gail really *resembles* her grandmother.

每個人都說姑兒長得很像她祖母。

* **roam** 〔 rom 〕 *v.* 漫步【常考】　——同 wander , range , ramble

After their argument, Heather *roamed* about the neighborhood to calm herself.

爭吵過後，海德在鄰近地區漫步，讓自己冷靜下來。

ruffian 〔 'rʌfɪən 〕 *n.* 惡棍；流氓

——同 villain , rascal , scoundrel , robber , miscreant

Two mean-looking *ruffians* sat at the bar, and glared at the people all around.

兩個面貌邪惡的流氓坐在吧檯，瞪著四周的人。

* **scrupulous** 〔 'skrupjələs 〕 *adj.* ①謹慎的　②正直的【常考】

——同 1. cautious , careful 2. upright , moral

Thomas is *scrupulous* about keeping his apartment spotlessly clean.　湯瑪士很謹慎地將他的公寓維持得一塵不染。

sip 〔 sɪp 〕 *v.* 啜飲　——同 drink , imbibe , taste

On summer evenings, we like to sit on the porch and *sip* cool drinks. 在夏天的夜晚，我們喜歡坐在走廊啜飲著冷飲。

* **porch** 〔 portʃ , pɔrtʃ 〕 *n.* 走廊

* **spawn** 〔spɔn〕*v.* 產生；產卵【常考】 ——同 generate , give birth to
The issue of capital punishment *spawned* a great debate among the students in the class.
死刑的話題在班上同學間產生了一場激烈的辯論。

steadfast 〔'stɛd,fæst〕*adj.* 堅定的
——同 firm , resolute , steady , faithful , determined
Although she knew it would take a lot of work, she was *steadfast* in striving to become a doctor.
雖然她明白這將花費許多心力，她仍立志要成為醫師。

subvert 〔səb'vɝt〕*v.* 顛覆；破壞 ——同 overthrow , overturn
Rumors about the teacher *subverted* her authority in the classroom. 有關老師的謠言破壞了她在班上的威信。

* **synopsis** 〔sɪ'nɑpsɪs〕*n.* 摘要【常考】 ——同 summary , digest
In Jane's report to her boss, she included a *synopsis* of the meetings she had attended.
在給老闆的報告內，珍附了一份有關她所參加的會議的摘要。

tension 〔'tɛnʃən〕*n.* 緊張 ——同 strain , pressure
The *tension* she felt while preparing for the interview caused her stomach to hurt. 在準備面試時所感到的緊張，讓她的胃又痛了。

trenchant 〔'trɛntʃənt〕*adj.* 尖刻的
——同 incisive , caustic , sharp , acerbic , biting
The advisor's *trenchant* comments are valued by the president.
顧問尖刻的批判受到總統的重視。

turmoil 〔'tɝmɔɪl〕*n.* 混亂
——同 disruption , tumult , disturbance , turbulence , commotion
The whole city was in *turmoil* after the gas explosion.
在氣爆之後，整個城市陷入混亂。

upheaval〔ʌpˈhivl̩〕n. 動亂
——同 cataclysm , disorder , disturbance , turmoil , revolution

The French Revolution was one of the great *upheavals* in history. 法國大革命是史上的大動亂之一。

vertigo〔ˈvɜtɪˌgo〕n. 暈眩
——同 dizziness , light-headedness

Mary suffers from *vertigo* every time she rides in a glass elevator. 瑪麗每次搭玻璃電梯時就會感到暈眩。

wistful〔ˈwɪstfəl〕adj. 渴望的
——同 wishful , desirous , yearning , longing , craving

David had a *wistful* look in his eyes whenever he talked about his days in college.

每當談及他的大學生涯時，大衛的眼睛裡便浮現了渴望的神情。

Exercise > *Fill in the blanks.*

1. The townspeople felt relieved when the _____ was arrested by the police.

2. The furniture in this house _____ the furniture in my grandmother's house.

3. The widely popular television series _____ public interest in Spanish flamenco dancing.

4. She was _____ in her belief that a cure would be found for the disease.

5. We were _____ about the time we had spent at the shore.

【解答】 1. ruffian 2. resembles 3. spawned 4. steadfast 5. wistful

·List 20· 難字分析

accretion ﹝ əˈkriʃən , æˈkriʃən ﹞ n. 增大

ac +	cret +	ion
ad		
to +	grow +	n.

— growth in size

agrarian ﹝ əˈgrɛrɪən ﹞ adj. 農業的

agr +	arian
field +	adj.

— of agriculture or farmers

congenial ﹝ kənˈdʒinjəl ﹞ adj. 意氣相投的

con +	gen +	ial
together +	produce +	adj.

— having the same tastes and temperament; pleasant

dilapidated ﹝ dəˈlæpəˌdetɪd ﹞ adj. 荒廢的；破舊的

di +	lapid +	at(e) +	ed
apart +	stone +	make +	adj.

— falling to pieces or into disrepair; shabby and neglected

hibernate ﹝ ˈhaɪbəˌnet ﹞ v. 冬眠

hibern +	ate
winter +	make

— to spend the winter in a dormant state

impermeable 〔 ɪmˋpɝmɪəbḷ 〕 adj. 不滲透的

im +	per +	me +	able
not +	through +	glide +	able to

—— that substances cannot pass through

intractable 〔 ɪnˋtræktəbḷ 〕 adj. 不聽話的；難駕馭的

in +	tract +	able
not +	draw +	able to

—— unruly or stubborn; hard to manage

monumental 〔 ˌmɑnjəˋmɛntḷ 〕 adj.
①紀念碑的　②龐大的　③不朽的

monu +	ment +	al
remind +	n. +	adj.

—— serving as a monument; very great; of lasting value

obsolete 〔 ˋɑbsəˌlit 〕 adj. 過時的

ob +	sol +	ete
against +	be accustomed +	adj.

—— no longer in fashion

synopsis 〔 sɪˋnɑpsɪs 〕 n. 摘要

syn +	op +	sis
together +	sight +	n.

—— a statement giving a brief, general review

 TEST ▶ 10

請由 (A)～(D) 中選出和畫線部分意義最相近的字。

1. The police decided that the suspect had <u>accomplices</u> in the crime.

(A) morals
(B) leaders
(C) assistants
(D) mistakes

2. His lecture was <u>couched</u> in so much scientific jargon that none of us understood him.

(A) performed
(B) recorded
(C) repeated
(D) phrased

3. Missionaries have been coming to the Far East for centuries to <u>propagate</u> Christianity.

(A) learn
(B) practice
(C) conservatize
(D) spread

4. Dave is an <u>avid</u> surfer and spends his summers at the beach.

(A) border-line
(B) professional
(C) listless
(D) zealous

5. The United Nations sent observers into the country to <u>monitor</u> the elections.

(A) observe
(B) officiate
(C) pardon
(D) select

6. What do you think is the fastest way to <u>disseminate</u> this information to the troops?

(A) receive
(B) broadcast
(C) motion
(D) guarantee

7. The shuttle astronauts reveled in the <u>unwonted</u> weightlessness they felt in outer space.

(A) bizarre
(B) humdrum
(C) slight
(D) unaccustomed

8. After studying <u>philology</u> for several years, she became a noted language scholar.

(A) philosophy
(B) linguistics
(C) anthropology
(D) grammar

9. Mrs. Green warned the boys not to try any more <u>chicanery</u> in the neighborhood.

   (A) playing
   (B) trickery
   (C) experiments
   (D) projects

10. Snakes are one kind of animal that <u>hibernates</u> through the cold winter.

    (A) finds sustenance
    (B) remains motionless
    (C) makes noise
    (D) lies dormant

11. After <u>assaying</u> the extensive flood, the president declared the area a national disaster area.

    (A) inspecting
    (B) watching
    (C) hearing
    (D) documenting

12. Everyone in the parochial little town thought the stranger was surely a <u>ruffian</u>.

    (A) executive
    (B) scoundrel
    (C) lawyer
    (D) do-gooder

13. This <u>dilapidated</u> car of yours should really go to the dump.

    (A) run-down
    (B) antique
    (C) inexpensive
    (D) unique

14. A <u>genteel</u> young man came to call on Margaret early this afternoon.

    (A) successful
    (B) sickly
    (C) cultured
    (D) intelligent

15. Special fuel is needed to <u>propel</u> a rocket into outer space.

    (A) navigate
    (B) break
    (C) thrust
    (D) burn

16. Many people felt that the country's single Olympic athlete <u>embodied</u> the hope of the entire nation.

    (A) substantiated
    (B) lifted
    (C) increased
    (D) destroyed

17. The teacher's comments written on my papers are always <u>trenchant</u>.

    (A) superfluous
    (B) morbid
    (C) restrictive
    (D) incisive

18. I am <u>loath</u> to drive my car during rush hour traffic.

    (A) encouraged
    (B) reluctant
    (C) invigorated
    (D) excited

19. For the finale of the fireworks display, dozens of fireworks were set for a simultaneous explosion.

(A) scattered
(B) prolonged
(C) concurrent
(D) spectacular

20. The soldier's treacherous intentions were discovered when a message to the enemy he sent was intercepted.

(A) traitorous
(B) convoluted
(C) simplistic
(D) revolutionary

21. The feud between the editors of the city's two largest newspapers was well known to everyone.

(A) empathy
(B) apathy
(C) friendship
(D) hostility

22. With the development of calculators, slide rules became obsolete mathematical tools.

(A) outdated
(B) new-tangled
(C) obvious
(D) favorite

23. In its heyday, the steam train was considered the fastest and most advanced mode of transportation.

(A) decline
(B) beginning
(C) prime
(D) advance

24. An accretion of calcium inside the water pipes is the cause of the low water pressure in this house.

(A) flow
(B) accumulation
(C) presence
(D) lack

25. When we went to the observation deck of the skyscraper, Janice suddenly had a spell of vertigo.

(A) pain
(B) dizziness
(C) blindness
(D) infection

【解答】

1. C	2. D	3. D	4. D	5. A	6. B	7. D	8. B	9. B	10. D
11. A	12. B	13. A	14. C	15. C	16. A	17. D	18. B	19. C	20. A
21. D	22. A	23. C	24. B	25. B					

📝 **LIST ▸ 21**

* **accumulate**〔 ə'kjumjə,let 〕*v.* 積聚【常考】

　—— 同 gather , amass , heap , pile , muster

After years of collecting stamps, Tina had ***accumulated*** several hundred stamps.

集郵多年之後，汀娜已積聚了好幾百張郵票。

ailment〔'elmənt 〕*n.* 疾病

　—— 同 disease , malady , illness , complaint , sickness

Ricardo is suffering from a rare skin ***ailment***.

理卡度患了一種罕見的皮膚病。

anthem〔'ænθəm 〕*n.* 聖歌；讚美詩

　—— 同 song , hymn , chorale , psalm , canticle

Many people think that America's national ***anthem*** is difficult to sing. 許多人認爲美國的國歌很難唱。

** **assiduous**〔 ə'sɪdʒʊəs 〕*adj.* 勤勉的【最常考】

　—— 同 industrious , diligent , laborious , persevering , persistent

Few of this company's employees are as ***assiduous*** as he is.

這家公司的職員很少有人像他一樣勤勉。

avouch〔 ə'vautʃ 〕*v.* 保證　—— 同 avow , affirm

Ms. Simms can ***avouch*** for John's business abilities.

席孟絲女士可以爲約翰的生意能力作保證。

* **bestow**〔 bɪ'sto 〕*v.* 給予【常考】

　—— 同 confer , present , donate , bequeath

The senator ***bestowed*** the award for teaching excellence on our eighth grade science teacher.

參議員將教學優良獎頒給我們八年級的自然老師。

bypass 〔 ˈbaɪˌpæs 〕 *v.* 迂迴；迴避
—— 同 avoid , circumvent , detour , pass around , skirt
Let's **bypass** this city; the traffic there is too heavy.
我們避開這個都市吧；那裡的交通太繁忙了。

chore 〔 tʃor 〕 *n.* 雜務 —— 同 task , job , assignment
Children should have household **chores** to help them learn
responsibility. 兒童應該要作家事，才能幫助他們培養責任感。

* **comparable** 〔 ˈkɑmpərəbl̩ 〕 *adj.* ①相似的 ②可比較的【常考】
—— 同 1. similar , akin 2. equivalent , as good as , equal
American rice is **comparable** to Asian rice, but it is slightly
different. 美洲稻米可媲美亞洲稻米；但仍有些微的差異。

congenital 〔 kənˈdʒɛnətl̩ 〕 *adj.* 天生的
—— 同 innate , inherent , inborn , inbred
The baby was born with a **congenital** heart defect.
這嬰兒一出生就有先天性心臟病。

cozy 〔 ˈkozɪ 〕 *adj.* 舒適的 —— 同 comfortable , snug , homey
After skiing all afternoon, they were happy to return to their
cozy cabin.
滑了一下午的雪後，他們快樂地回到舒適的小木屋。

delegate 〔 ˈdɛləˌget 〕 ① *n.* 代表 ② *v.* 委派作代表
—— 同 1. deputy , representative , agent , envoy 2. depute , designate
A **delegate** from the Norwegian government paid a visit to
the president. 挪威政府的代表拜訪了總統。

dilate 〔 daɪˈlet , dɪ- 〕 *v.* 膨脹
—— 同 widen , expand , swell , distend , inflate
When people are scared, their pupils **dilate**.
人害怕的時候，瞳孔會放大。 * pupil 〔 ˈpjupl̩ 〕 *n.* 瞳孔

* **dissolve** 〔 dɪ'zɑlv 〕 *v.* 溶解【常考】

　——同 melt , liquefy , thaw , flux

Anna *dissolved* a spoonful of sugar in her coffee.

安娜將一湯匙的糖溶在咖啡裡。

donate 〔'donet 〕 *v.* 捐贈

　——同 contribute , bestow , give , grant , gift

Mr. Ellis *donates* money to his old college every year.

艾利斯先生每年都捐款給母校。

dwindle 〔'dwɪndḷ 〕 *v.* 減少

　——同 decrease , diminish , lessen , fade , wane

Our country's natural resources are *dwindling*.

我們國家的天然資源正在減少。

Exercise *Fill in the blanks.*

1. Dust had _____ on the top of the refrigerator.

2. Praise was _____ on the scientist for her new genetic discovery.

3. Carol and I have _____ tastes in food.

4. During winter, my cat always likes to find a _____ place in the house to curl up and sleep.

5. Each of the member countries sent a _____ to the economic conference.

【解答】1. accumulated　2. bestowed　3. comparable　4. cozy　5. delegate

* **embryo** 〔'εmbrɪˌo 〕 *n.* 胚胎【常考】

A human ***embryo*** grows at an amazing rate.

人類的胚胎生長的速度很驚人。

* **equivalent** 〔 ɪ'kwɪvələnt 〕 *adj.* 相等的；相當的【常考】

——同 equal , tantamount , identical , same , interchangeable

Amazingly, his salary was almost ***equivalent*** to the boss's.

真令人驚訝，他的薪水幾乎和老闆一樣多。

* **expenditure** 〔 ɪk'spɛndɪtʃɚ 〕 *n.* 費用；開支【常考】

——同 expense , cost , payment , outlay

Have you calculated your ***expenditures*** for the trip to Hawaii?

你算過你到夏威夷旅遊的開銷了嗎？

* **fiasco** 〔 fɪ'æsko 〕 *n.* 慘敗【常考】

——同 failure , defeat , miscarriage

Unfortunately, the office party was a terrible ***fiasco***.

很不幸地，辦公室舞會舉辦失敗。

futile 〔'fjutḷ 〕 *adj.* 徒然的；無益的

——同 abortive , in vain , unsuccessful , unprofitable

Jane made a ***futile*** effort to persuade Tom to come with them to the movie. 珍勸湯姆和他們一起去看電影，但是遊說無效。

granular 〔'grænjəlɚ 〕 *adj.* 顆粒的

——同 grainy , gritty , sandy , granulated

My apartment building has a ***granular*** brown surface.

我住的公寓大樓有顆粒狀的棕色外層。

* **highlight** 〔'haɪˌlaɪt 〕 ① *n.* 要點；最精彩的部分 ② *v.* 強調【常考】

——同 1. best part , climax , focus , peak 2. underline , stress

Winning the award was the ***highlight*** of his career.

贏得該獎是他事業的顛峰。

**impervious 〔 ɪmˈpɝvɪəs 〕 *adj.* ①不能滲透的 ②無動於衷的

——同 1. impenetrable , impassable 　　　　　　　【最常考】

　　　　2. unmoved , unaffected , impassible

Although she was badly hurt, she seemed **impervious** to the pain. 雖然她傷得很嚴重，但對疼痛似乎無動於衷。

infiltrate 〔 ɪnˈfɪltret 〕 *v.* 滲透

——同 permeate , pervade , penetrate , spread to

The toxic chemicals **infiltrated** the water supply, polluting it. 這些有毒的化學物質滲透到水池裡，污染了水池。

* intricate 〔ˈɪntrəkɪt 〕 *adj.* 複雜的【常考】

——同 complicated , complex , elaborate , sophisticated , knotty

We all admired the **intricate** Chinese embroidery. 我們都很欣賞精細的中國刺繡。

lobby 〔ˈlɑbɪ 〕 *n.* ①大廳 ②遊說團

——同 1. entrance hall , foyer

　　　　2. pressure group , advocates , bloc

Free-trade advocates formed a **lobby** to pressure the government. 自由貿易的支持者組成一遊說團，向政府施壓。

maxim 〔ˈmæksɪm 〕 *n.* 格言

——同 adage , motto , proverb , dictum , gnome , aphorism

"Neither a borrower nor a lender be," was his **maxim** in life. 「不向人借錢，不借錢給人」是他的生活格言。

* morale 〔 moˈræl , moˈrɑl 〕 *n.* 士氣【常考】

——同 spirit , confident state of mind , nerve , faith

The **morale** of the troops declined after the defeat. 打敗仗後，軍隊的士氣低落。

* **onset** 〔'ɑn,sɛt 〕 *n.* 開始【常考】 ——同 initiation , beginning , outset

At the ***onset*** of pregnancy, many women feel nausea.

在開始懷孕的時候，許多婦女會感到噁心。

* nausea 〔'nɔʒə , 'nɔzɪə 〕 *n.* 噁心

overwrought 〔'ovə'rɔt 〕 *adj.* 過度疲勞的；過度興奮的

——同 overexcited , agitated , uncontrolled , wrought up , overworked

We were all ***overwrought*** by the extra work at the office.

因為辦公室內的額外工作，我們都感到過度疲勞。

peerless 〔'pɪrlɪs 〕 *adj.* 無與倫比的

——同 unique , unequaled , matchless , unbeatable , unrivaled

The ***peerless*** beauty of the pageant winner astonished everyone in the audience. 這位無與倫比的選美優勝者令在場的觀衆很驚艷。

* pageant 〔'pædʒənt 〕 *n.* 選美 (= *beauty contest*)

pillar 〔'pɪlə 〕 *n.* 支柱 ——同 pilaster , post , column , pedestal

Ancient Greek architecture used ***pillars*** extensively.

古希臘的建築廣泛地使用支柱。

Exercise *Fill in the blanks.*

1. There are often many hidden _____ in buying a house.

2. It is _____ for you to try to convince Victor that he is wrong.

3. The relationships within a large village can be very _____, and very delicate.

4. _____ was low after the team had lost fifteen games in a row.

5. Cancer can be difficult to detect at its _____.

【解答】 1. expenditures　2. futile　3. intricate　4. Morale　5. onset

* **precursor**〔prɪˈkɝsɚ〕 *n.* 先驅【常考】

——同 forerunner , predecessor , harbinger , pioneer , originator

The telegraph was a ***precursor*** to the modern telephone.
電報是現代電話的先驅。

propensity〔prəˈpɛnsətɪ〕 *n.* 傾向；習性

——同 tendency , inclination , leaning , bent , disposition

Taylor has a ***propensity*** to drink too much when he goes out.
泰勒出外時，有飲酒過度的習性。

redundancy〔rɪˈdʌndənsɪ〕 *n.* ①重覆 ②過多

——同 1. repetition , tautology　2. superabundance , superfluity

There was a ***redundancy*** of construction workers at this site.
這工地裡有過多的建築工人。

revenue〔ˈrɛvəˌnju〕 *n.* 收入

——同 income , interest , rewards , gain

Our company's ***revenues*** were up last year.
本公司去年的收入增加。

robust〔roˈbʌst〕 *adj.* 強壯的

——同 husky , muscular , athletic , hardy

After a long illness, he is now in ***robust*** health.
久病之後，他現在體魄強壯。

****scrutinize**〔ˈskrutn̩ˌaɪz〕 *v.* 細察【最常考】

——同 examine , scan , inspect , investigate , probe

The teacher ***scrutinized*** the students' reports for mistakes.
老師細察學生的報告改正錯誤。

sinuous〔ˈsɪnjʊəs〕 *adj.* 彎曲的；蜿蜒的　——同 winding

The seaweed left on the shore by the tide was long and
sinuous.　這些被潮水帶上岸的海藻長得長長彎彎的。

sojourn 〔'sodʒɝn 〕 *n.* 居留；寄居

——同 stay , stopover , visit , rest

They made a short ***sojourn*** in a small village on the coast.
他們在海岸邊的一個小村子住了一小段時間。

****stifle** 〔'staɪfl̩ 〕 *v.* 使窒息【最常考】

——同 choke , smother , suffocate , strangle

The noxious fumes ***stifled*** the subway car passengers.
有毒的氣體讓地下鐵的乘客窒息。

* **succinct** 〔 sək'sɪŋkt 〕 *adj.* 簡明的；簡潔的【常考】

——同 concise , terse , laconic , pithy , brief

The journalist wrote a ***succinct*** report on the murder
investigation. 記者針對謀殺案的調查寫了一篇簡潔的報導。

* **synthesize** 〔'sɪnθə,saɪz 〕 *v.* 綜合【常考】

——同 combine , amalgamate , construct , blend

The artist ***synthesized*** modern and traditional painting
techniques. 這位藝術家綜合了現代與傳統的繪畫技巧。

****tentative** 〔'tɛntətɪv 〕 *adj.* 試驗的【最常考】

——同 experimental , trial

For now, we will work with this ***tentative*** schedule for the
conference. 現在，我們將以此試驗性的時間表來進行會議。

throng 〔 θrɔŋ 〕 *n.* 群眾 ——同 crowd , mob , mass

A huge ***throng*** of people appeared for the new art exhibition.
有一大群人來看這場新的藝術展。

tutelage 〔'tutl̩ɪdʒ , 'tju- 〕 *n.* 教導

——同 teaching , instruction

Under Ms. Velance's ***tutelage***, Garret became fluent in French.
在法蘭絲女士的教導下，蓋瑞特的法文變得流利。

uphold〔ʌpˈhold〕v. ①維持 ②贊成；鼓勵

—— 同 1. maintain , sustain 2. approve , encourage

Democracy helps to **uphold** the freedom of the country's citizens. 民主政治有助維持國民的自由。

vestige〔ˈvɛstɪdʒ〕n. 遺跡

—— 同 trace , relic , remains , scrap

The reporter searched for a **vestige** of the destroyed village but she could find none.

這名記者去尋找這座被摧毀的村落的遺跡，但卻什麼都沒有找到。

yelp〔jɛlp〕v.（狗）吠叫

—— 同 cry , yammer , yap

The puppy **yelped** when I accidentally stepped on its paw.

當我不小心踏到小狗的腳時，牠叫了出來。

Exercise 〉 *Fill in the blanks.*

1. Everyone hoped the rapid transit system would be the _____ of orderly traffic flow in the future.

2. What is the main source of _____ for this city?

3. We followed a _____ trail through the forest which finally led back to our campsite.

4. The city had a _____ agreement with the contractor to build a new public square.

5. There was no _____ of human habitation on the island.

【解答】1. precursor   2. revenue   3. sinuous   4. tentative   5. vestige

∙ List 21 ∙ 難字分析

accumulate 〔 ə'kjumjə,let 〕 v. 積聚

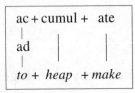

— to make or become greater in number or quantity

assiduous 〔 ə'sɪdʒʊəs 〕 adj. 勤勉的

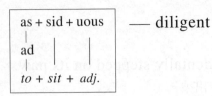

— diligent

congenital 〔 kən'dʒɛnətḷ 〕 adj. 天生的

con + genit + al
with + produce + adj.

— existing from or before birth

equivalent 〔 ɪ'kwɪvələnt 〕 adj. 相等的；相當的

equi + val + ent
equal + worth + adj.

— equal in value, amount, meaning

expenditure 〔 ɪk'spɛndɪtʃɚ 〕 n. 費用；開支

ex + pend + iture
out + hang + n.

— the amount of money, time, etc. expended

impervious 〔 ɪm'pɝvɪəs 〕 *adj.* ①不能滲透的 ②無動於衷的

im +	per +	vi +	ous
not +	through +	way +	adj.

— incapable of being passed through; not affected by

intricate 〔'ɪntrəkɪt 〕 *adj.* 複雜的

in +	tric +	ate
in +	obstacle +	adj.

— hard to follow or understand due to being full of complicated parts

precursor 〔 prɪ'kɝsɚ 〕 *n.* 先驅

pre +	curs +	or
before +	run +	person

— person or thing coming before

propensity 〔 prə'pɛnsətɪ 〕 *n.* 傾向;習性

pro +	pens +	ity
forward +	hang +	n.

— natural tendency

redundancy 〔 rɪ'dʌndənsɪ 〕 *n.* ①重覆 ②過多

red +	und +	ancy
again +	wave +	n.

— repetition; the state or quality of being excessive

revenue 〔'rɛvə,nju 〕 *n.* 收入

re +	ven +	ue
back +	come +	n.

— income

LIST ▶ 22

accuracy 〔'ækjərəsɪ 〕 *n.* 正確性
——同 authenticity , correctness , exactness , precision
Accuracy is very important when solving mathematical equations. 在解數學方程式時，準確性是相當重要的。

ajar 〔 ə'dʒɑr 〕 *adj.* 微開的
——同 slightly open , agape , gaping , unclosed
Because the door was left *ajar*, several mosquitoes entered the house.
因為門是微開的，所以有幾隻蚊子進到屋裡來。

* **anticipate** 〔 æn'tɪsə‚pet 〕 *v.* 期待【常考】
——同 expect , foresee , look forward to , hope for , await
I have been *anticipating* this trip to Europe all year long.
我一整年都在期待此次的歐洲之旅。

assuage 〔 ə'swedʒ 〕 *v.* 緩和
——同 ease , alleviate , allay , relieve , lessen , lighten
This medicine might *assuage* some of the pain caused by the wound.
這藥可緩和一下傷口所引起的疼痛。

* **awkward** 〔'ɔkwəd 〕 *adj.* 笨拙的【常考】
——同 clumsy , unskillful , inept , all thumbs , inexpert
First-time ice skaters are generally very *awkward* on the ice.
初次溜冰的人在冰上大都顯得很笨拙。

beverage 〔'bɛv(ə)rɪdʒ 〕 *n.* 飲料 ——同 drink , draught , liquid
This restaurant has a wide selection of *beverages*.
這家餐廳有許多飲料可供選擇。

** **chronic** 〔'krɑnɪk 〕 *adj.* 慢性的；長期的【最常考】
　　——〔同〕long-lasting , persistent , continuing , prolonged
　　My uncle suffers from ***chronic*** back pain. 我叔叔罹患慢性背痛。

** **compatible** 〔 kəm'pætəbḷ 〕 *adj.* 和諧的；相容的【最常考】
　　——〔同〕congenial , harmonious , agreeable , consonant , accordant
　　I don't think Patty's and Mike's personalities are ***compatible***.
　　我不認為佩蒂和邁克的個性合得來。

conglomeration 〔 kən,glɑmə'reʃən 〕 *n.* 聚集物；凝塊
　　——〔同〕assortment , accumulation , composite , mass , combination
　　The city is a ***conglomeration*** of different ethnic groups.
　　該城市是由不同種族的團體凝聚而成。

* **crafty** 〔'kræftɪ 〕 *adj.* 狡猾的【常考】
　　——〔同〕tricky , sly , guileful , wily
　　Fred thought up a ***crafty*** scheme to sneak into the bank at
　　night.　弗瑞德想到一個狡猾的計謀，要在半夜潛入銀行內。

* **crooked** 〔'krʊkɪd 〕 *adj.* ①彎曲的 ②不誠實的；行為不正的
　　——〔同〕1. bent , curved , hooked 2. deceitful , dishonest , crafty【常考】
　　The electric fan won't work because this blade is ***crooked***.
　　這電扇不會動，因為這個葉片已經彎曲。

deleterious 〔,dɛlə'tɪrɪəs 〕 *adj.* 有害的
　　——〔同〕harmful , baneful , dangerous , detrimental , baleful
　　Smoking has many ***deleterious*** effects on your health.
　　抽煙對健康有許多的害處。

** **distort** 〔 dɪs'tɔrt 〕 *v.* ①扭曲；變形 ②曲解；誤傳【最常考】
　　——〔同〕1. deform , misshape 2. misrepresent , falsify
　　This special mirror ***distorts*** your image to make you look
　　taller.　這面特殊的鏡子會使你的樣子變形，讓你看起來更高。

* **dormant** 〔'dɔrmənt 〕 *adj.* 蟄伏的；睡眠狀態的【常考】

　　——同 hibernating , inactive , inert , latent , slumbering

Flea eggs can lie ***dormant*** for years in your carpet.

跳蚤的卵可在地毯內蟄伏好幾年。

dungeon 〔'dʌndʒən 〕 *n.* 地牢　　——同 prison , jail , cell

Although the man was innocent, the king ordered that he be locked up in the ***dungeon***.

雖然這個人是清白的，但國王卻下令把他鎖在地牢裡。

** **dynamic** 〔 daɪ'næmɪk 〕 *adj.* 有活力的；活動的【最常考】

　　——同 energetic , vital , vigorous , driving , powerful

Our college has a ***dynamic*** student organization that many people participate in.

本學院有個活躍的學生會，許多學生都加入其中。

Exercise ＞ *Fill in the blanks.*

1. Other scientists questioned the ＿＿＿＿＿ of Dr. Walter's experiment results.

2. Her ＿＿＿＿＿ lateness has become annoying.

3. Fortunately, my next-door neighbors and I are quite ＿＿＿＿＿.

4. He suffered no ＿＿＿＿＿ effects from taking the medication.

5. Patty Lutz is a ＿＿＿＿＿ advocate for helping children raised in poverty.

【解答】1. accuracy　2. chronic　3. compatible　4. deleterious　5. dynamic

*emerge〔ɪ'mɝdʒ〕*v.* 出現；脫穎而出【最常考】
——同 come into prominence, appear, arise, come forth, spring up
He has *emerged* as the most promising novelist of his
generation.　他脫穎而出，成爲他那一代中最有潛力的小說家。

equivocal〔ɪ'kwɪvəkḷ〕*adj.* 模稜兩可的；不確定的
——同 ambiguous, vague, obscure, doubtful, ambivalent
She was *equivocal* about participating in the singing
performance.　她不確定要不要參加歌唱表演。

* exclusive〔ɪk'sklusɪv〕*adj.* ①唯一的　②高級的【常考】
——同 1. sole, only, unique　2. classy, aristocratic
Wendy and Joe went out to dinner at an *exclusive* restaurant
in the city.　溫蒂和喬到城裡一家高級的餐廳吃晚餐。

* fictitious〔fɪk'tɪʃəs〕*adj.* 虛構的；假想的【常考】
——同 imaginary, created, false, feigned
Ellen wrote a *fictitious* story about a dog which can talk.
艾倫寫了一篇虛構的故事，內容是關於一隻會說話的狗。

* framework〔'frem,wɝk〕*n.* 結構【常考】　——同 structure, plan
The *framework* of the building must be strong enough to
withstand a large earthquake.
這大樓的結構必須要強到能耐得住大地震。

grasp〔græsp〕*v.* ①抓住　②領會；瞭解
——同 1. grip, clasp, seize　2. understand, comprehend, perceive
Some principles in physics are not very easy to *grasp*.
物理學中有些原理讓人不易領會。

grudge〔grʌdʒ〕*n.* 怨恨　——同 resentment, enmity, aversion
Andrew held a *grudge* against his friend for having cheated
him.　安德魯因受朋友欺騙而對他存有怨恨。

hilarious 〔 həˈlɛrɪəs , hɪ- 〕 *adj.* 歡樂的；有趣的
—— 同 amusing , comic , funny , jolly , joyful , mirthful
The movie we saw last night was so *hilarious* that I couldn't stop laughing.　我們昨晚看的電影很有趣，所以我笑個不停。

impetus 〔ˈɪmpətəs 〕 *n.* 推進力；刺激
—— 同 stimulus , motivation , spur , push , incentive
The riots became a great *impetus* for the country to solve the problem of poverty.
這些暴動形成強大的助力，促使該國解決貧窮的問題。

* **intrigue** 〔 ɪnˈtrig 〕① *n.* 陰謀 ② *v.* 使感興趣【常考】
—— 同 1. plot , scheme , conspiracy　2. fascinate , interest
This mystery novel is full of surprises and *intrigue*.
這部推理小說充滿了驚險與陰謀。

intuition 〔ˌɪntjʊˈɪʃən 〕 *n.* 直覺　—— 同 insight , instinct
Martha's *intuition* told her that John was the man she had been looking for.　瑪莎的直覺告訴她，約翰正是她一直在尋找的人。

* **locomotion** 〔ˌlokəˈmoʃən 〕 *n.* 移動；位移【常考】
—— 同 movement
Walking is just one method of human *locomotion*.
走只是人類行進的方式之一。

* **meager** 〔ˈmigɚ 〕 *adj.* ①不足的 ②瘦的【常考】
—— 同 1. scanty , deficient , inadequate　2. skinny , emaciated , bony
Our grain supplies for this winter are *meager*.
我們今年冬天的穀藏不足。

morsel 〔ˈmɔrsəl 〕 *n.* 一小口；一點　—— 同 mouthful , bite , crumb
Henry looked in the refrigerator for a *morsel* to eat before dinner.　亨利往冰箱裡看，想找一點東西在晚餐前吃。

ooze 〔uz〕 v. 緩緩流出   ——同 drip , emit , leak , seep , dribble

Thick mud *oozed* from the cracks in the pavement when you walked on it.

當你走在人行道上時，混濁的泥巴會從裂縫中緩緩流出。

peevish 〔'pivɪʃ〕 adj. 易怒的

——同 irritable , captious , grumpy , touchy , ill-tempered

She had to listen to the *peevish* complaints of the man next to her on the bus. 她必須聽公車上鄰座男子憤怒的抱怨。

pinpoint 〔'pɪn,pɔɪnt〕 v. 明確指出

——同 locate , spot , distinguish , get a fix on , define

We used a compass to try and *pinpoint* our location.

我們使用羅盤測量並明確指出所在的方位。

Exercise	Fill in the blanks.

1. All she gave me was an _____ "Maybe," when I asked if she would come.

2. No one believed his _____ story about having met the Queen of England.

3. Ellen holds a _____ against Willis for stealing her clients at work.

4. The environmental movement has been an _____ for young people to choose "green" careers.

5. A green slime _____ from the pipes that led away from the fertilizer plant.

【解答】 1. equivocal   2. fictitious   3. grudge   4. impetus   5. oozed

** **predominant** 〔 prɪˋdɑmənənt 〕 *adj.* ①有勢力的 ②主要的

—— 同 1. sovereign , ruling　2. leading , capital , chief　　【最常考】

The **predominant** export of this area is pork.

這地區的主要輸出品是豬肉。

* **property** 〔ˋprɑpətɪ〕 *n.* ①財產 ②特性【常考】

—— 同 1. assets , possessions　2. quality , trait , characteristic

Hilda had inherited some **property** from her mother.

西達從母親那裡繼承了一些財產。

* **refine** 〔 rɪˋfaɪn 〕 *v.* ①精製 ②使優雅【常考】

—— 同 1. purify , clarify , cleanse　2. civilize , cultivate , perfect

Sugar is usually **refined** before it is packaged and sent to

stores.　糖在包裝送往商店前通常已先精製過。

remonstrate 〔 rɪˋmɑnstret 〕 *v.* 抗議

—— 同 object , protest , expostulate , take issue

She **remonstrated** with her boss about her co-worker's

undeserved raise.　她為同事不應得的加薪而向老闆抗議。

repentance 〔 rɪˋpɛntəns 〕 *n.* 悔恨

—— 同 regret , remorse , penitence , grief , guilt

The **repentance** she felt for hitting the child with her car

filled her heart.　她為開車撞傷孩子一事，心中充滿了悔恨。

* **reside** 〔 rɪˋzaɪd 〕 *v.* 居住【常考】　　—— 同 live , dwell , lodge , inhabit

My parents **reside** in a small, rural village.

我的父母親居住在一個小農村裡。

seasonably 〔ˋsiznəblɪ〕 *adv.* 合時宜地

—— 同 appropriately , fittingly , suitably

It was **seasonably** cold for that time of the year.

一年的那個時候正是寒冷。

* **sketch** 〔 skɛtʃ 〕 *n.* 素描；簡圖【常考】 ──同 draft , drawing

Bart drew a ***sketch*** of his neighborhood so that I would be able to find his house.

巴特畫了一張他家附近的簡圖，以便我能找到他家。

* **specimen** 〔'spɛsəmən 〕 *n.* 樣本【常考】 ──同 sample , example

The laboratory needs a blood ***specimen*** to test your cholesterol level. 檢驗室需要一些血液樣本來檢查你的膽固醇值。

＊cholesterol 〔 kə'lɛstə,rol 〕 *n.* 膽固醇

* **steer** 〔 stɪr 〕 *v.* 駕駛；引導【常考】

──同 direct , lead , conduct , pilot

I ***steered*** the car slowly out of the parking lot.

我將車慢慢地駛出停車場。

* **succumb** 〔 sə'kʌm 〕 *v.* ①屈服 ②死【常考】

──同 1. yield , give way , submit , give in , surrender 2. die

After many restless hours, she finally ***succumbed*** to sleep.

在不眠不休許多小時之後，她終於向睡眠屈服。

* **tepid** 〔'tɛpɪd 〕 *adj.* ①微溫的 ②不熱心的【常考】

──同 1. lukewarm , warmish 2. apathetic , unenthusiastic , indifferent

My grandmother hates to drink ***tepid*** coffee. 祖母討厭喝溫咖啡。

* **tremor** 〔'trɛmɚ 〕 *n.* 顫抖；震動【最常考】

──同 shaking , trembling , quivering , shivering , shudder , vibration

The ***tremor*** shook all the books off the shelves in the house.

這一震動將屋內架上的書都搖落了。

tycoon 〔 taɪ'kun 〕 *n.* 大亨；商業鉅子

──同 baron , capitalist , financier , merchant prince , mogul

The oil ***tycoons*** of Saudi Arabia are among the richest in the world. 沙國的石油大亨屬全世界最富有的人士。

upright (ˊʌpˌraɪt , ʌpˊraɪt) *adj.* 正直的

——同 honest , righteous , virtuous , honorable , conscientious

The people of the city believed the councilor was an ***upright*** citizen. 該市的人民相信這位議員是正直的公民。

＊councilor (ˊkaʊnsḷɚ) *n.* 議員

＊**vessel** (ˊvɛsḷ) *n.* ①容器 ②船【常考】

——同 1. container , utensil 2. boat , ship , craft

This clay ***vessel*** was used in ancient times to hold wine.

這陶器在古時候是用來盛酒的。

withhold (wɪðˊhold , wɪθ-) *v.* 保留；抑制

——同 reserve , retain , curb , repress

You should not ***withhold*** any information from the police in this investigation.

在此次調查中，你不該對警方保留任何消息。

Exercise ▷ *Fill in the blanks.*

1. In ＿＿＿＿＿＿ for his sins, he devoted his life to the church.

2. We ＿＿＿＿＿＿ to the children's request for ice cream.

3. The school principal ＿＿＿＿＿＿ with the teacher for unfair grading practices.

4. Several media ＿＿＿＿＿＿ met to discuss the possible uses of computers in future media displays.

5. Only one ＿＿＿＿＿＿ man stood up against the company's plans to buy up the villagers' homes.

【解答】1. repentance　2. succumbed　3. remonstrated　4. tycoons　5. upright

ᴸList 22 ᴸ 難字分析

anticipate 〔 æn'tɪsəˌpet 〕 *v.* 期待

anti	+ cip	+ ate
before	*+ take +*	*v.*

—— to look forward to

compatible 〔 kəm'pætəbḷ 〕 *adj.* 和諧的；相容的

com	+ pat	+ ible
together	*+ suffer +*	*able to*

—— able to exist together

conglomeration 〔 kənˌglɑmə'reʃən 〕 *n.* 聚集物；凝塊

con	+ glomer	+ ation
together	*+ ball of yarn +*	*n.*

—— mass of accumulated things

equivocal 〔 ɪ'kwɪvəkḷ 〕 *adj.* 模稜兩可的；不確定的

equi	+ voc	+ al
equal	*+ voice +*	*adj.*

—— having two or more meanings; uncertain

fictitious 〔 fɪk'tɪʃəs 〕 *adj.* 虛構的；假想的

fict	+ itious
feign	*+ adj.*

—— imaginary; not real

hilarious〔həˈlɛrɪəs , hɪ- 〕 *adj.* 歡樂的；有趣的

hilar + ious
| |
merry + adj.
— noisily merry

locomotion〔ˌlokəˈmoʃən 〕 *n.* 移動；位移

loco + mot + ion
| | |
place + move + n.
— motion or the power of moving from one place to another

predominant〔prɪˈdɑmənənt 〕 *adj.* ①有勢力的 ②主要的

pre + domin + ant
| | |
before + rule + adj.
— having more power or influence than others; chief

remonstrate〔rɪˈmɑnstret 〕 *v.* 抗議

re + monstr + ate
| | |
against + show + v.
— to say or plead in protest

succumb〔səˈkʌm 〕 *v.* ①屈服 ②死

suc + cumb
| |
sub
| |
under + lie down
— to give way to; to die

TEST ▶ 11

請由 (A)～(D) 中選出和畫線部分意義最相近的字。

1. A new highway was built to <u>bypass</u> the city in order to reduce the traffic in the city.
   - (A) intersect
   - (B) ignore
   - (C) speed
   - (D) avoid

2. <u>Dissolve</u> the baking powder in one cup of milk before adding it to the cake batter.
   - (A) remove
   - (B) cook
   - (C) liquefy
   - (D) ferment

3. After a <u>robust</u> hike through the woods, everyone was ready to relax in the cool lake.
   - (A) jocular
   - (B) leisurely
   - (C) thorough
   - (D) athletic

4. Our <u>sojourn</u> in the Hawaiian Islands was very pleasant and restful.
   - (A) flight
   - (B) walk
   - (C) message
   - (D) visit

5. The pediatric surgeon decided to operate on the <u>congenital</u> defect in the baby's lung.
   - (A) inborn
   - (B) serious
   - (C) recent
   - (D) unfortunate

6. The cave walls were <u>impervious</u> to the sounds of the outside world.
   - (A) porous
   - (B) impenetrable
   - (C) reliant
   - (D) affable

7. "Do to others as you would have them do to you," is a famous <u>maxim</u>.
   - (A) question
   - (B) malapropism
   - (C) aphorism
   - (D) conjunction

8. When my Aunt Gail visits my mother, they have a <u>propensity</u> to talk until very late.
   - (A) tendency
   - (B) mission
   - (C) proposal
   - (D) notification

9. Monica tried to <u>assuage</u> my nervousness about my driver's license test tomorrow.

(A) cultivate
(B) relieve
(C) restrict
(D) deny

10. Our company has developed a solid <u>framework</u> for expanding into foreign markets.

(A) plan
(B) idea
(C) measurement
(D) presentation

11. Mrs. Jones is such a hypo-condriac that she claims to suffer from a new <u>ailment</u> every week.

(A) sickness
(B) medication
(C) doctor
(D) x-ray

12. During the Middle Ages in Europe, powerful lords were the <u>predominant</u> class in society.

(A) ruling
(B) underling
(C) responsible
(D) intellectual

13. The bank's loan <u>fiasco</u> resulted in the closing of the bank.

(A) failure
(B) expansion
(C) success
(D) investigation

14. Tulip bulbs lay <u>dormant</u> during the winter and bloom in the spring.

(A) planning
(B) inactive
(C) growing
(D) dying

15. The baby bird's <u>meager</u> legs could barely hold its tiny frame.

(A) fat
(B) skinny
(C) long
(D) short

16. Donna has written up several <u>tentative</u> menus for next week's banquet for you to choose from.

(A) definitive
(B) unreliable
(C) trial
(D) substandard

17. The medical students had to examine <u>specimens</u> of human tissues under the microscope.

(A) samples
(B) imitations
(C) species
(D) vials

18. The president is a member of this <u>exclusive</u> golf club.

(A) classy
(B) average
(C) secret
(D) fortified

19. Archaeologists learn much about ancient cultures from finding <u>vestiges</u> of their civilizations.

   (A) memories
   (B) interpretations
   (C) experiences
   (D) relics

20. He refused to take our advice, trusting what he called his <u>intuition</u>.

   (A) ability
   (B) truth
   (C) instinct
   (D) belief

21. Many Americans think of lawyers as <u>crafty</u> and unscrupulous.

   (A) ingenious
   (B) fortunate
   (C) rich
   (D) sly

22. Don't leave the door <u>ajar</u> or the cat will come in the room.

   (A) agape
   (B) closed
   (C) unlocked
   (D) broken

23. <u>Chronic</u> inflation caused by economic reforms has made citizens weary of reform policies.

   (A) fluctuating
   (B) prolonged
   (C) shrinking
   (D) mediated

24. Alan's suggestion that we take a vacation in the desert received a <u>tepid</u> response.

   (A) definitive
   (B) surprising
   (C) unenthusiastic
   (D) nostalgic

25. Joy was worried our small sailing <u>vessel</u> would not make it to the other side of the river.

   (A) jar
   (B) cloth
   (C) waves
   (D) boat

【解答】

1. D	2. C	3. D	4. D	5. A	6. B	7. C	8. A	9. B	10. A
11. A	12. A	13. A	14. B	15. B	16. C	17. A	18. A	19. D	20. C
21. D	22. A	23. B	24. C	25. D					

📋 LIST ▸ 23

* accustom 〔 ə'kʌstəm 〕 *v.* 使習慣【常考】
—— 同 adapt , habituate , acquaint , familiarize
It takes time to **accustom** yourself to the lifestyle, manners
and food of a foreign country.
要習慣外國的生活方式、禮儀與食物，需要一段時間。

alert 〔 ə'lɜt 〕 *adj.* 機警的 —— 同 wary , watchful , vigilant
The guard at the gate kept **alert** for any signs of danger or
intrusion. 大門的守衛十分警覺，要注意是否有任何危險與侵入的跡象。

* apathetic 〔 ˌæpə'θɛtɪk 〕 *adj.* 冷淡的【最常考】
—— 同 indifferent , impassive , emotionless , cold , unconcerned
It is difficult to teach a child who is **apathetic** towards his
studies. 教導對功課不太在乎的孩子十分困難。

* assume 〔 ə'sum , ə'sjum 〕 *v.* ①認為 ②承擔【最常考】
—— 同 1. think , suppose , believe 2. shoulder , take over , accept
Parents must **assume** responsibility for their children's
actions in public. 父母必須對小孩在公共場所的行為負責。

bewilder 〔 bɪ'wɪldə 〕 *v.* 使困惑
—— 同 puzzle , confuse , confound , perplex
We were all **bewildered** by the strange message left on Tim's
phone answering machine.
對於提姆電話答錄機上奇怪的留言，我們都覺得十分困惑。

* blend 〔 blɛnd 〕 *v.* 混合【常考】
—— 同 mix , merge , combine , mingle , compound
To make this cake, you must first **blend** some sugar and butter.
要做這種蛋糕，必須先將一些糖和奶油混合。

chronological 〔͵krɑnə'lɑdʒɪkl̩〕*adj.* 依年代順序的
—同 consecutive , ordered , sequential , progressive
The history museum had a ***chronological*** display of the events
that led up to World War II. ****lead up to*** 逐漸進入；終將導致
歷史博物館依年代順序展示了導致二次世界大戰發生的事件。

* **congregation** 〔͵kɑŋgrɪ'geʃən〕*n.* 聚集；會眾；教友【常考】
—同 assembly , flock , multitude , throng , crowd
After the church service, many members of the ***congregation***
gathered to chat. 在教堂做完禮拜之後，許多教友聚集在一起聊天。

cram 〔kræm〕*v.* 填塞 —同 stuff , pack , jam
Rob ***crammed*** as many things as he could in his suitcase.
羅伯在手提箱裡拼命塞東西。

crimson 〔'krɪmzn̩〕*n.* 深紅色 —同 deep red
The gown she wore to the party was a stunning ***crimson***.
她參加宴會時，穿了一件漂亮的深紅色禮服。

****crucial** 〔'kruʃəl〕*adj.* 極重要的【最常考】
—同 momentous , essential , extremely important , vital
It was ***crucial*** that they got Bobby to the hospital in time.
他們將巴比及時送達醫院，這是十分重要的。

* **deliberately** 〔dɪ'lɪbərɪtlɪ〕*adv.* 故意地【常考】
—同 on purpose , knowingly , intentionally , willfully
The police suspected that someone had set the forest fire
deliberately. 警方懷疑有人故意在森林裡縱火。

* **dilute** 〔dɪ'lut , daɪ'lut〕*v.* 稀釋【常考】
—同 weaken , make thinner
The chef thought the soup was too thick, so she added some
water to ***dilute*** it.
主廚認為湯太濃了，所以加了一點水稀釋它。 *chef 〔ʃɛf〕*n.* 主廚

* **diverge** 〔 dəˈvɝdʒ , daɪ- 〕 v. 分歧【常考】

—— 同 split , separate , branch , divide , fork

Be careful not to take any of the paths that ***diverge*** from the main road. 要小心，不要走到大道旁的叉路。

dot 〔 dɑt 〕 v. 點綴

—— 同 spot , sprinkle , dabble , fleck , stud

Some young girls like to ***dot*** their i's with little hearts because they think it's cute. 有些年輕女孩寫「i」時，喜歡在上面打上心形的點，因為她們覺得那樣很可愛。

effrontery 〔 əˈfrʌntərɪ 〕 n. 厚顏無恥 —— 同 impudence

I don't believe he had the ***effrontery*** to use my car without asking me first.

我真不敢相信他會如此厚臉皮，不先問過我就開我的車。

Exercise ⟩ *Fill in the blanks.*

1. In a few days you will become _____ to the time difference between the countries.

2. Shirley was _____ about the accomplishments of her husband.

3. He _____ the spring roll filling and began to stuff the wrappers.

4. Clean water is _____ to many forms of life, including human life.

5. It was at that point that our lines of thought _____.

【解答】1. accustomed 2. apathetic 3. blended 4. crucial 5. diverged

* **emit** 〔 ɪˈmɪt 〕 *v.* 發射【常考】 *n.* emission
—— 同 give off , discharge , eject , cast out , shed , send forth
The sun *emits* light and heat, which allows life on our planet
to survive. 太陽發出光和熱，讓地球上的生物得以生存。

* **execute** 〔ˈɛksɪ͵kjut 〕 *v.* 執行【常考】
—— 同 carry out , enforce , enact
We will need everyone's help to *execute* such a difficult
plan. 要執行如此困難的計畫，我們需要大家的幫助。

expel 〔 ɪkˈspɛl 〕 *v.* 驅逐 —— 同 exile , dismiss , banish
The school *expelled* the student for cheating on the
semester exam. 學校因這名學生在考試時作弊而將他退學。

* **fiscal** 〔ˈfɪskl̩ 〕 *adj.* 財務的【常考】 —— 同 financial , monetary
The economist believed that a conservative *fiscal* policy
was best for the country.
那位經濟學家認為該國最好採取保守的財經政策。

frantic 〔ˈfræntɪk 〕 *adj.* 瘋狂的 —— 同 mad , frenetic , furious
We had a *frantic* day at the office; everything went wrong
at once. 今天我們辦公室裡十分瘋狂；有一度每樣事都不對勁。

gratify 〔ˈɡrætə͵faɪ 〕 *v.* 使滿足 —— 同 satisfy , content
She was *gratified* to know that her donation would go to
form a special scholarship.
當她知道她的捐贈將成立特別的獎學金時，覺得十分滿意。

grueling 〔ˈɡruəlɪŋ 〕 *adj.* 令人筋疲力盡的
—— 同 fatiguing , exhausting , grinding , strenuous , arduous
A marathon is a *grueling*, twenty-six mile race, generally
through a city. 馬拉松比賽是項令人筋疲力盡、長達二十六哩的賽
跑，通常賽跑的路線會貫穿全市。

hinder 〔ˈhɪndɚ〕 *v.* 阻礙 ——同 impede , retard

We were ***hindered*** from reaching the ancient temple by the thick jungle vines.

由於叢林藤蔓太濃密了，所以我們受到阻礙，無法到達那間古廟。

hurdle 〔ˈhɝdḷ〕 *n.* 障礙 ——同 hindrance , difficulty

Lack of openness in talking about sex is a ***hurdle*** in preventing the spread of AIDS.

由於大眾缺少公開談論性，因而阻礙了愛滋病防範工作的進行。

＊implement ① 〔ˈɪmpləmənt〕 *n.* 工具
② 〔ˈɪpləˌmɛnt〕 *v.* 實行【最常考】

——同 1. tool , instrument 2. execute , carry out , enact

Doctors use special ***implements*** to do the delicate work needed in surgery.

醫生使用特殊的工具，進行手術所必需的精密的工作。

＊ingenious 〔ɪnˈdʒinjəs〕 *adj.* 聰明的【最常考】 ——同 clever

Tony came up with an ***ingenious*** plan to keep his neighbor's dog out of his flower garden.

湯尼想到一個十分聰明的計畫，可以使鄰居的狗遠離他的花園。

＊intrinsic 〔ɪnˈtrɪnsɪk〕 *adj.* 本質的【最常考】

——同 essential , inherent

Curiosity is an ***intrinsic*** part of learning.

好奇是學習的本質。

lodge 〔lɑdʒ〕 ① *v.* 投宿 ② *n.* 小屋

——同 1. accommodate , put up , stay 2. cabin , cottage , hut , shelter

It is difficult to find an inexpensive place to ***lodge*** in New York City.

要在紐約市找一處便宜的住所十分困難。

✱✱meander 〔mɪˈændɚ〕 v. 蜿蜒【最常考】 ——同 wind, snake, stray
The small dirt road **meandered** through the nearby
countryside, finally ending at the lake.
那條小小的泥濘路蜿蜒穿過附近的鄉間，最後到達那座湖。

mortify 〔ˈmɔrtəˌfaɪ〕 v. 屈辱 ——同 humiliate, abash, shame
Many years ago, people were **mortified** at the idea of
divorce. 多年以前，提到離婚，大家會覺得那是件可恥的事。

✱opaque 〔oˈpek〕 adj. 不透明的；晦暗的【常考】
——同 obfuscated, dim, dull, lusterless
They fitted their house's windows with **opaque** glass for
privacy. 他們房子的窗戶裝有不透明的玻璃，以確保隱私。

✱penetrate 〔ˈpɛnəˌtret〕 v. 穿透【常考】
——同 pierce, perforate, impale, prick, go through, bore, stab
A diamond-tipped drill was used to **penetrate** the thick
layers of rock covering the oil deposit.
尖端鑲有鑽石的鑽孔機，被用來穿透覆蓋在石油沉積物上厚厚的岩層。
＊drill 〔drɪl〕 n. 鑽孔機　　deposit 〔dɪˈpazɪt〕 n. 沉積物

Exercise > *Fill in the blanks.*

1. The illegal immigrants were _____ from the country.

2. We were _____ when we heard the news of the train
   wreck.

3. It would _____ Ms. Smith to know that you enjoyed
   the gift she sent you.

4. With an _____ mind like hers, she is sure to succeed.

5. A steel rod from the car had _____ deep into her skin
   during the crash.

【解答】1. expelled　2. frantic　3. gratify　4. ingenious　5. penetrated

placid 〔'plæsɪd 〕 *adj.* 平靜的 ──同 serene , unruffled

The normally energetic child looked so *placid* sleeping on the chair. 那個平時活力充沛的孩子正睡在椅子上，看來十分平靜。

* **preeminent** 〔 prɪ'ɛmənənt 〕 *adj.* 優越的【常考】

──同 outstanding , superior , matchless , paramount , excellent

Dr. Cook is a *preeminent* scholar of ancient Indian history. 庫克博士是一位研究古印度史的傑出學者。

prophecy 〔'prɑfəsɪ 〕 *n.* 預言 ──同 forecast , prediction

The *prophecy* of a shepherd boy becoming king of the nation came true. 牧羊童會成為該國國王的預言實現了。

* **refute** 〔 rɪ'fjut 〕 *v.* 反駁【常考】 ──同 confute , controvert , disprove

Despite his efforts, Tom could not *refute* Kelly's claim that she was innocent.

雖然湯姆十分努力，仍無法反駁宣稱自己是清白的凱莉。

residual 〔 rɪ'zɪdʒuəl 〕 *adj.* 剩餘的

──同 leaving , remnant , remaining , leftover , extra , surplus

The *residual* paint was used to paint the next-door neighbor's garage. 剩餘的油漆被用來漆隔壁鄰居的車庫。

* **rotate** 〔'rotet 〕 *v.* 旋轉【常考】

──同 revolve , spin , swivel , turn , go round

The earth *rotates* on its axis once every twenty-four hours. 地球每二十四小時自轉一次。

seclude 〔 sɪ'klud 〕 *v.* 隔離

──同 separate , isolate , keep aloof , keep to oneself

The monks *seclude* themselves from society so as not to be distracted from their worship.

那些僧侶與社會隔絕，如此修行時才不會分心。

skim 〔 skɪm 〕 *v.* 略讀　——同 scan , glance through
I didn't have time to read the article, so I just ***skimmed*** it.
我沒時間讀那篇文章，所以我只是大略看一下而已。

* **specious** 〔'spiʃəs 〕 *adj.* 虛有其表的【常考】
——同 deceptive , fallacious , misleading , sophistic
The real estate agent gave her a ***specious*** description of the
apartment, which led her to believe it was in better condition
than it was.　那位不動產經紀人給她華而不實的描述，使她相信那間公寓
的情況比實際要好。

* **sterile** 〔'stɛrəl 〕 *adj.* 不能生育的；貧瘠的【常考】
——同 barren , infertile , arid , unfruitful
Exposure to large amounts of radiation can make a person
become ***sterile***.　暴露在大量的輻射下會使人不孕。

sullen 〔'sʌlɪn 〕 *adj.* 悶悶不樂的　——同 gloomy , melancholy
Robin has been in a ***sullen*** mood all week long.
羅賓一整個禮拜都悶悶不樂。

* **terminate** 〔'tɝmə‚net 〕 *v.* 終止【常考】　——同 stop , finish , expire
The company has decided to ***terminate*** your position as of
today.　公司已經決定要終止你的職務，你就做到今天爲止。

tribute 〔'trɪbjʊt 〕 *n.* 貢物；(表示敬意的) 禮物；頌辭
——同 gift , offering
Each of the television networks aired a ***tribute*** to the late
singing star.　每家電視台都向那位已故的歌星致敬。
* air 〔 ɛr 〕 *v.* 播送 (節目)

umpire 〔'ʌmpaɪr 〕 *n.* 仲裁人；裁判
——同 judge , moderator , referee , arbiter , arbitrator
Everyone booed the ***umpire*** for calling the runner safe when
he was obviously out.　* boo 〔 bu 〕 *v.* 向~作噓聲
大家都向裁判發出噓聲，因爲他判那位明顯已經出局的跑者安全上壘。

veteran 〔 ˈvɛtərən 〕 n. 老手

—— 同 master , professional , old hand

In the field of white water rafting, Bruce is a **veteran**.

在浪花上乘坐竹筏方面，布魯斯是個老手。　＊**white water** 浪花

vex 〔 vɛks 〕 v. 使苦惱

—— 同 annoy , agitate , irritate , provoke , afflict

The police seemed to be very **vexed** by the mysterious case of the jewelry theft.　警方對於神秘的珠寶竊案似乎十分苦惱。

withstand 〔 wɪθˈstænd , wɪð- 〕 v. 抵抗

—— 同 resist , stand up to , combat , confront , face

This building was constructed to **withstand** an earthquake of a magnitude of 7.5 on the Richter scale.

這棟建築物可以抵抗芮氏地震儀上的七點五級地震。

Exercise > Fill in the blanks.

1. The panel consisted of several _____ scholars and scientists.

2. The court _____ the case against the three men.

3. Used car salesmen are known for making _____ claims.

4. My father is an _____ for the local little league baseball games.

5. The excellent construction of the building _____ the earthquake.

【解答】1. preeminent　2. refuted　3. specious　4. umpire　5. withstood

·List 23· 難字分析

apathetic 〔͵æpə'θɛtɪk 〕 *adj.* 冷淡的

```
   a    +  path  + etic
   |       |       |
without + feeling + adj.
```
—— showing no interest

chronological 〔͵krɑnə'lɑdʒɪkḷ 〕 *adj.* 依年代順序的

```
chrono+  log  + ical
   |      |      |
 time  + study + adj.
```
—— in order of time

congregation 〔͵kɑŋgrɪ'geʃən 〕 *n.* 聚集；會眾；敎友

```
 con     + gregat + ion
   |        |        |
together + collect +  n.
```
—— a gathering of people or things

effrontery 〔 ə'frʌntərɪ 〕 *n.* 厚顏無恥

```
  ef   + front+ ery
  ex      |      |
away  + face  +  n.
```
—— shameless boldness

implement ① 〔'ɪmpləmənt 〕 *n.* 工具　② 〔'ɪmplə͵mɛnt 〕 *v.* 實行

```
im+ ple + ment
 |    |     |
in + full +  n.
```
—— tool or instrument for working with;
to carry out

penetrate 〔'pɛnə,tret 〕 *v.* 穿透

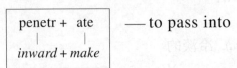
— to pass into

preeminent 〔 prɪ'ɛmənənt 〕 *adj.* 優越的

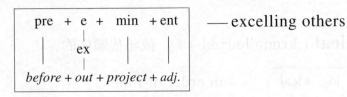
— excelling others

residual 〔 rɪ'zɪdʒʊəl 〕 *adj.* 剩餘的

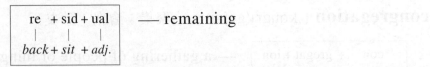
— remaining

terminate 〔'tɝmə,net 〕 *v.* 終止

```
termin + ate
   |      |
 limit + make
```
— to put an end to

veteran 〔'vɛtərən 〕 *n.* 老手

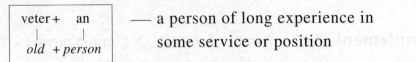
— a person of long experience in some service or position

📖 LIST ▸ 24

* acquisition 〔͵ækwə'zɪʃən 〕 *n.* 獲得【常考】

—— 同 obtainment , gaining , procurement , achievement , acquirement

The *acquisition* of knowledge was her goal in life.

獲得知識是她的人生目標。

** alien 〔'elɪən 〕① *adj.* 外國的；不同質的 ② *n.* 外國人【最常考】

—— 同 1. foreign , exotic　2. foreigner , stranger , outsider

All *aliens* must register with the government when entering the country.

進入該國時，所有的外國人都必須向政府登記。

** anthology 〔 æn'θɑlədʒɪ 〕 *n.* 選集【最常考】

—— 同 collection , analects , digest , compendium

That bookstore carries several *anthologies* of modern British literature.　那家書店裡有好幾本現代英國文學選集。

apparel 〔 ə'pærəl 〕 *n.* 衣服

—— 同 clothes , dress , attire , garment , costume

Children's *apparel* is located on the fifth floor of the department store.　童裝位於百貨公司的五樓。

* bias 〔'baɪəs 〕 *n.* 偏見【最常考】　—— 同 prejudice , partiality

The *bias* in favor of wealthy candidates makes the election process unfair.

在選舉的過程中，非常偏袒有錢的候選人，十分不公平。

blunder 〔'blʌndɚ 〕 *n.* 錯誤　—— 同 mistake , error , slip

Due to an apparent *blunder* at the tax office, Mr. Case was owed two thousand dollars by the government.

由於稅務局犯了明顯的錯誤，所以政府欠卡斯先生兩千元。

chubby 〔ˈtʃʌbɪ〕 *adj.* 圓胖的 ——同 plump , chunky
Since Vance doesn't exercise and eats fatty foods, he is
getting rather **chubby**.
由於方斯旣不運動而且又吃些高脂肪的食物，所以變得相當胖。

consistent 〔kənˈsɪstənt〕 *adj.* 一貫的；一致的
——同 regular , coherent , consonant , agreeing , compatible
The hospital's research on the disease was **consistent** with
the government laboratory's findings.
醫院對這種疾病的研究和政府實驗室裡的發現是一致的。

crate 〔kret〕 *v.* 包裝 ——同 pack , box , encase
We **crated** all of our furniture to be shipped to Seattle.
我們包裝了所有的傢俱，準備運往西雅圖。

creek 〔krik〕 *n.* 小溪 ——同 brook , rivulet , small river
A small **creek** flows beside my grandmother's house.
祖母的家旁邊有條小溪。

* **crude** 〔krud〕 *adj.* ①未加工的 ②粗魯的【常考】
——同 1. raw , unpolished , rough 2. uncouth , brutish
Crude oil must be refined before it can be used in a car
engine. 原油必須經過提煉，才能用在汽車引擎上。

delude 〔dɪˈlud〕 *v.* 欺騙 ——同 deceive , con , take in
You are **deluding** yourself if you think that she will be the
first to apologize.
如果你認爲她會最先道歉，那麼你就是在欺騙自己。

dim 〔dɪm〕 *adj.* 微暗的；模糊的 ——同 darkish , hazy
In a **dim** room in the back of the restaurant, an intense game
of poker was being held.
在餐廳後面陰暗的房間裡，正進行著激烈的撲克牌遊戲。

diversify 〔 dəˈvɝsəˌfaɪ , daɪ- 〕 *v.* 變化【最常考】

—— 同 vary , alter , branch out , transform

The lipstick company wanted to *diversify* into producing other cosmetics. 口紅公司想要有所改變，生產其他的化妝品。

doze 〔 doz 〕*v.* 打盹

—— 同 drowse , snooze , catnap , nap

Several of the students in the back row of the lecture hall were *dozing*. 在演講廳後排座位，有幾名學生正在打瞌睡。

emphatic 〔 ɪmˈfætɪk 〕 *adj.* 強調的；堅持的

—— 同 impressive , certain , definite , insistent , decided

Mother was *emphatic* in telling us that we must remember to look after our younger sisters.

媽媽一直強調，告訴我們一定要記得照顧妹妹們。

Exercise 〉 *Fill in the blanks.*

1. The museum's latest _____ are two paintings by Monet.

2. She suspected there was _____ in the company's hiring practices.

3. Our country's policy toward wildlife protection is _____ with international standards.

4. He continually _____ himself by thinking the situation will get better.

5. We were _____ in demanding better working conditions at the factory.

【解答】 1. acquisitions 2. bias 3. consistent 4. deludes 5. emphatic

eradicate〔ɪˈrædɪˌket〕v. 根除

——同 uproot , exterminate , extirpate , demolish , destroy , annihilate

The doctors hoped the new vaccination would **eradicate** the disease from the country. ＊vaccination〔ˌvæksn̩ˈeʃən〕n. 預防接種

醫生們希望這種新的疫苗接種可以把這種病從國內根除。

＊exemplary〔ɪgˈzɛmplərɪ〕adj. 模範的【常考】

——同 model , admirable

Henry proved to be an **exemplary** kindergarten teacher.

亨利成為一位模範的幼稚園老師。

explicit〔ɪkˈsplɪsɪt〕adj. 明白的

——同 distinct , definite , precise , specific , unambiguous

If you don't give Jim **explicit** directions, he will definitely get lost. 如果你給吉姆的指示不明確的話，他一定會迷路的。

figure〔ˈfɪgjɚ〕n. ①數字 ②身材

——同 1. digit , number 2. body , build , physique

Now that she is a banker, she has a six-**figure** income.

她是一位銀行家，收入有六位數字。

friction〔ˈfrɪkʃən〕n. ①摩擦 ②不合

——同 1. rubbing , scraping , attrition 2. animosity , bickering

The **friction** of the sandpaper on the wood smoothes out the surface of the wood. 砂紙摩擦木頭能使其表面變得十分平滑。

＊gravity〔ˈgrævətɪ〕n. ①嚴肅；嚴重 ②地心引力【常考】

——同 1. demureness , solemnity , seriousness

I don't think you understand the **gravity** of this situation.

我想你並不了解這情況的嚴重性。

guile〔gaɪl〕n. 奸詐；狡猾　——同 cunning , deception , trickery

A man of such **guile** is not to be trusted. 如此狡猾的人不值得信任。

hitherto 〔͵hɪðɚ'tu 〕 *adv.* 到目前爲止

—— 同 formerly , heretofore , so far , till now , up to now

The cause of this disease was **hitherto** unknown to scientists.

這種疾病的成因，到目前爲止科學家們仍然不知道。

hypnotize 〔'hɪpnə͵taɪz 〕 *v.* 催眠

—— 同 mesmerize , put in a trance , put to sleep

The psychiatrist **hypnotized** the patient to help him recall events in the past. 心理醫生催眠病人，幫助他想起過去發生的事情。

implicit 〔 ɪm'plɪsɪt 〕 *adj.* ①暗示的 ②絕對的【最常考】

—— 同 1. implied , latent , unspoken 2. absolute , steadfast

We assumed his open door was an **implicit** invitation for us to come in. 我們認爲他的門敞開，是邀我們進入的一種暗示。

ingredient 〔 ɪn'gridɪənt 〕 *n.* 成份；原料【常考】

—— 同 component , element , constituent , part

The **ingredients** for this dish are very expensive, so I do not make it often. 這道菜的材料很貴，所以我並不常做。

intrude 〔 ɪn'trud 〕 *v.* 闖入【常考】 —— 同 interlope , intervene

She accidentally **intruded** on a secret meeting being held in the copy room. 她很偶然地闖入在影印室裡進行的秘密會議。

lofty 〔'lɔftɪ , 'lɑftɪ 〕 *adj.* ①高的 ②高尚的

—— 同 1. high , tall 2. dignified , noble

He felt dizzy standing at such a **lofty** height overlooking the city. 站在如此高的高度俯瞰全市，他覺得有點暈眩。

meditate 〔'mɛdə͵tet 〕 *v.* 深思熟慮

—— 同 ponder , deliberate , muse , consider , ruminate , cogitate

The boss said she would **meditate** on my request for a raise.

老闆說關於我要求加薪的事她會多加考慮。

* **motif**〔moˈtif〕*n.* 主題【常考】

——同 theme , subject , topic , concept

In literature class we discussed the *motif* of death in a play of Shakespeare's.

在文學課中，我們討論一齣莎士比亞戲劇裡死亡的主題。

nadir〔ˈnedɚ〕*n.* 最低點

——同 bottom , lowest point , depths

The sudden death of his three children was the *nadir* of his life.　他三名小孩的猝死是他一生的最低潮。

* **pensive**〔ˈpɛnsɪv〕*adj.* 沉思的【常考】　——同 contemplative , meditative , ruminative , thoughtful , preoccupied

He grew more and more *pensive* as his wedding date approached.　隨著結婚日期日漸逼近，他變得越來越常沉思。

Exercise Fill in the blanks.

1. Lowell hoped the exterminator could _____ the rat infestation in his house.

2. He gave very _____ details in describing the scene.

3. It was his _____ that led him to the top of the business world, and it also led to his downfall.

4. We locked the door to keep people from _____ on us.

5. Jeremy's _____ mood made us wonder what was wrong with him.

【解答】1. eradicate　2. explicit　3. guile　4. intruding　5. pensive

plague〔 pleg 〕① *n.* 瘟疫；疫病 ② *v.* 困擾
——㊂ 1. epidemic , pandemic 2. annoy , bother , harass
A *plague* of cholera spread throughout the countryside,
killing hundreds of people. 霍亂在鄉間蔓延，造成數百人死亡。
＊cholera〔'kɑlərə〕*n.* 霍亂

premiere〔 prɪ'mɪr 〕*n.* 初演；首映 ——㊂ debut
Tickets to the *premiere* of the new Broadway show were
difficult to find. 這齣新的百老匯節目首演的入場券很難買到。

propitious〔 prə'pɪʃəs 〕*adj.* 順利的 ——㊂ fortunate , lucky
They decided the time was *propitious* for opening their own
clothing business. 他們認為那時候是他們服裝生意開張的最好時機。

regal〔'rigḷ〕*adj.* 帝王般的；堂皇的 ——㊂ royal , splendid
He had his house built in a *regal* style, so he could display his
wealth to his neighbors.
他把房子建造得富麗堂皇，如此便可以向鄰居展示他的財富。

＊＊**remuneration**〔 rɪ͵mjunə'reʃən 〕*n.* 酬勞；補償【最常考】
——㊂ award , compensation , pay , earnings , profit
A *remuneration* was given to passengers who had reservations
on the canceled flight. 預訂該被取消班次機位的旅客，可獲得賠償。

＊**secretion**〔 sɪ'kriʃən 〕*n.* 分泌【常考】
——㊂ releasing of a substance
Hormone *secretion* is controlled by a gland beneath the brain.
荷爾蒙分泌是由腦下垂體所控制。

soliloquy〔 sə'lɪləkwɪ 〕*n.* 獨白 ——㊂ monologue
The actor was nervous about forgetting his lines in the middle
of the *soliloquy*.
那位演員在唸獨白時，說到一半卻忘了台詞，令他十分緊張。

skip 〔 skɪp 〕*v.* ①跳 ②錯過

——同 1. leap, spring, jump, hop 2. omit, miss, pass over

I must have *skipped* that page when I was reading the magazine article. 當我閱讀雜誌的文章時，我一定是把那一頁漏掉了。

speckled 〔'spɛkḷd 〕*adj.* 有斑點的

——同 dotted, freckled, spotted, stippled, mottled

The puppy Dana brought home with her had *speckled* fur.
黛娜帶回家的小狗毛上有斑點。

* **stern** 〔 stɜn 〕*adj.* 嚴厲的【常考】 ——同 severe, strict, austere

Her overly *stern* parents refused to allow her to play on weekends. 她過度嚴厲的父母拒絕讓她在週末玩耍。

* **sultry** 〔'sʌltrɪ 〕*adj.* 悶熱的【最常考】

——同 stuffy, suffocating, sweltering, muggy, humid

The *sultry* heat kept us from leaving the comfort of our air conditioned house. 悶熱使我們不願離開舒適的冷氣房。

terse 〔 tɜs 〕*adj.* 簡明的

——同 succinct, concise, pithy, brief, laconic

This *terse* essay explains the relationship between poverty and crime. 這篇簡明的論文解釋了貧窮與犯罪之間的關係。

* **trickle** 〔'trɪkḷ 〕*v.* 滴下【常考】

——同 dribble, drip, drop, ooze, seep, stream

A small stream of water *trickled* off the roof to the ground.
有一小道水從屋頂滴落地面。

urbane 〔 ɜ'ben 〕*adj.* 有禮貌的

——同 polite, courteous, suave, mannerly, civil

An *urbane* politician is a rare find in these modern times.
有禮貌的政治家在現代已經很少見了。

* **viable** 〔'vaɪəbḷ 〕 *adj.* ①能生存的 ②可行的【常考】

——同 1. alive , living 2. practicable , feasible

Once the temperature drops below freezing, this plant will no longer be *viable*. 一旦溫度低於冰點，這棵植物就無法生存了。

vivacious 〔 vaɪ'veʃəs , vɪ- 〕 *adj.* 活潑的

——同 lively , animated , spirited , merry , vital , ebullient

Her grandson is a *vivacious* and curious little child.

她的孫子是個很活潑而且十分好奇的小孩。

wizened 〔'wɪznd 〕 *adj.* 枯萎的

——同 withered , shriveled , dried up , gnarled , wrinkled

At the end of the season, the field was full of *wizened* melons which would soon rot.

在產季末時，田野裡到處都是枯萎而且很快就會腐爛的甜瓜。

Exercise 〉 *Fill in the blanks.*

1. A _____ season of good weather gave the farmers a record crop yield.

2. The power company refused to make _____ to the companies that lost money during the power outage.

3. During the parade, several of the participants fainted in the _____ summer heat.

4. He answered her in short, _____ sentences.

5. My grandmother's _____ hands are still very nimble when she does her knitting.

【解答】1. propitious   2. remuneration   3. sultry   4. terse   5. wizened

⟨ List 24 ⟩ 難字分析

acquisition 〔͵ækwə'zɪʃən 〕 *n.* 獲得

ac + quisit + ion ── acquiring
|
ad
|
to + seek + n.

diversify 〔 də'vɝsə͵faɪ , daɪ- 〕 *v.* 變化

di　+ vers + ify ── to give variety to
|
dis
|
apart + turn + v.

emphatic 〔 ɪm'fætɪk 〕 *adj.* 強調的；堅持的

em +　pha　+ tic ── expressed with emphasis
|
in　+ show + adj.

eradicate 〔 ɪ'rædɪ͵ket 〕 *v.* 根除

e　+radic +　ate ── to tear out by the roots
|
ex
|
out + root + make

explicit 〔 ɪk'splɪsɪt 〕 *adj.* 明白的

ex + plic +　it ── clearly and fully expressed
|
out + fold + adj.

hypnotize 〔'hɪpnə,taɪz 〕 *v.* 催眠

hypno + tize
| |
sleep + *v.*

—— to put into a sleeplike condition

ingredient 〔 ɪn'gridɪənt 〕 *n.* 成份；原料

in + gred + ient
| | |
in + *walk* + *n.*

—— one of the parts of a mixture

propitious 〔 prə'pɪʃəs 〕 *adj.* 順利的

pro + pit + ious
| | |
before + *seek* + *adj.*

—— favorably inclined or disposed

secretion 〔 sɪ'kriʃən 〕 *n.* 分泌

se + cret + ion
| | |
apart + *separate* + *n.*

—— the production of some liquid material

soliloquy 〔 sə'lɪləkwɪ 〕 *n.* 獨白

soli + loquy
| |
alone + *speech*

—— speech by one individual

vivacious 〔 vaɪ'veʃəs , vɪ- 〕 *adj.* 活潑的

viv + acious
| |
live + *adj.*

—— full of life and animation

TEST ▶ 12

請由 (A)～(D) 中選出和畫線部分意義最相近的字。

1. The doctor instructed the child's parents to be <u>alert</u> to any bleeding from the stitches.
   - (A) ignorant
   - (B) watchful
   - (C) relaxed
   - (D) expectant

2. This television program is a presentation of the <u>chronlogical</u> development of lasers.
   - (A) scientific
   - (B) experimental
   - (C) creative
   - (D) historical

3. If the flavor of the curry is too strong, you can <u>dilute</u> it by adding more coconut milk.
   - (A) build it up
   - (B) water it down
   - (C) make it thick
   - (D) do it right

4. The light <u>emitted</u> by this lamp is not enough to read by.
   - (A) pulled back
   - (B) driven on
   - (C) given off
   - (D) made more

5. <u>Fiscal</u> difficulties have forced the company to reduce business.
   - (A) personnel
   - (B) financial
   - (C) structural
   - (D) management

6. Each trade has its own special <u>implements</u> designed for the trade's special requirements.
   - (A) tools
   - (B) measurements
   - (C) people
   - (D) education

7. For literature class, we have to read twelve poems from this poetry <u>anthology</u>.
   - (A) novel
   - (B) epic
   - (C) genre
   - (D) collection

8. The lawyer finally <u>refuted</u> the man's claim of innocence.
   - (A) believed
   - (B) enforced
   - (C) disproved
   - (D) cautioned

9. Anna was afraid the old woman's <u>prophecy</u> about her having a car accident would come true.

   (A) prediction
   (B) information
   (C) dream
   (D) idea

10. Grandmother loves to squeeze the baby's <u>chubby</u> cheeks.

    (A) plump
    (B) gaunt
    (C) long
    (D) red

11. Stan was a <u>specious</u> man, acting friendly to his boss, but really plotting behind his back.

    (A) encouraging
    (B) deceptive
    (C) artistic
    (D) enthusiastic

12. <u>Friction</u> between the two brothers at the party made us all feel uncomfortable.

    (A) drunkenness
    (B) ambiguity
    (C) animosity
    (D) friendship

13. After chemical pollutants had been dumped into the river, the water became <u>opaque</u>.

    (A) odorous
    (B) light
    (C) warm
    (D) not clear

14. Paul's obnoxious behavior towards the teacher showed his <u>effrontery</u> in the face of authority.

    (A) impudence
    (B) timidity
    (C) regularity
    (D) misunderstanding

15. You should <u>diversify</u> your experiences in life.

    (A) eliminate
    (B) vary
    (C) fortify
    (D) establish

16. Mr. Smith is a <u>veteran</u> of the stage, having spent the past forty years acting in the theater.

    (A) old hand
    (B) top hat
    (C) new kid
    (D) fine time

17. The young man finally came to realize the <u>gravity</u> of his crime.

    (A) mercifulness
    (B) indifference
    (C) secrecy
    (D) seriousness

18. The young child seemed to be <u>hypnotized</u> by the program on the television.

    (A) mesmerized
    (B) bored
    (C) excited
    (D) annoyed

19. Philosophers enjoy <u>meditating</u> on problems that seem to have no answers.

    (A) talking
    (B) musing
    (C) forgetting
    (D) writing

20. It was a long struggle for her to overcome the <u>nadir</u> of her life — her abusive childhood.

    (A) period
    (B) climax
    (C) depths
    (D) memory

21. The new theater company made its <u>premiere</u> with a performance of Shakespeare's Hamlet.

    (A) finale
    (B) debut
    (C) review
    (D) acting

22. Wanda is a <u>vivacious</u> woman who enjoys outdoor activities.

    (A) reserved
    (B) animated
    (C) intelligent
    (D) important

23. Shakespeare's plays are full of <u>soliloquies</u> which reveal characters' thoughts.

    (A) performances
    (B) rehearsals
    (C) verses
    (D) monologues

24. Sweat was <u>trickling</u> down the athlete's face after the race.

    (A) floating
    (B) dripping
    (C) swelling
    (D) rising

25. The <u>regal</u> giant redwood tree forests in California have impressed millions of visitors.

    (A) majestic
    (B) minute
    (C) unique
    (D) ancient

【解答】

1. B	2. D	3. B	4. C	5. B	6. A	7. D	8. C	9. A	10. A
11. B	12. C	13. D	14. A	15. B	16. A	17. D	18. A	19. B	20. C
21. B	22. B	23. D	24. B	25. A					

📋 LIST ▸ 25

* **acrid** 〔'ækrɪd〕*adj.* ①刻薄的 ②辛辣的；苦的【常考】
  —— 同 1. caustic , sarcastic , acrimonious 2. pungent , bitter
  The room was filled with a terrible **acrid** odor.
  這房間充滿了一種可怕的辛辣味。

* **alienate** 〔'eljən‚et〕*v.* 疏遠【最常考】
  —— 同 estrange , separate , turn away , break off , divorce
  In time, he **alienated** himself from his family and friends.
  他終究和他的家人朋友疏遠了。

* **appeal** 〔ə'pil〕*v.* ①吸引 ②懇求【常考】
  —— 同 1. attract , fascinate 2. implore , plead , request
  The new sports car model **appeals** to many car lovers.
  這款新型的跑車吸引許多愛車者。

* **astound** 〔ə'staʊnd〕*v.* 使驚駭【常考】
  —— 同 stun , astonish , shock , amaze , appall
  The magician **astounded** the crowd with his amazing magic
  tricks. 群眾對魔術師驚人的把戲大感震驚。

  bilateral 〔baɪ'lætərəl〕*adj.* 兩邊的
  —— 同 two-sided , symmetrical
  A **bilateral** trade agreement was signed by the leaders of
  the two countries.
  兩國領袖簽定雙邊貿易協定。

* **blunt** 〔blʌnt〕*adj.* ①鈍的 ②直率的【常考】
  —— 同 1. dull , pointless , unsharpened 2. plain-spoken , frank
  She was very **blunt** in telling Allen that he had no musical
  talent. 她很坦率地告訴亞倫他沒有音樂天份。

**cite 〔 saɪt 〕 *v.* 引用【最常考】

—— 同 quote , extract , allude to , adduce

Grace *cited* several famous historians in her essay.

葛麗絲在她的論文中，引述了幾位知名歷史學家的話。

**complement 〔'kɑmpləmənt 〕 *n.* 補充【最常考】

—— 同 companion , supplement , counterpart , rounding-off

The pudding she had made was a nice *complement* to the delicious meal she had served us.

她做的布丁是她所款待的美食中，美味的補充。

conspicuous 〔 kən'spɪkjuəs 〕 *adj.* 引人注目的

—— 同 obvious , remarkable , outstanding , notable , striking

Teresa is very *conspicuous* in a crowd because she dyed her hair purple. 因為泰瑞莎把頭髮染成紫色，所以在人群中十分引人注目。

crave 〔 krev 〕 *v.* 渴望 —— 同 long for , desire , aspire

She *craved* the simple life of the country.

她渴望鄉村簡單的生活。

crumb 〔 krʌm 〕 *n.* 小片 —— 同 bit , fragment , scrap

There were cookie *crumbs* all over the chair where Lester had been sitting. 雷斯特坐過的椅子上全是餅乾屑。

**deluge 〔'dɛljudʒ 〕 *n.* 大洪水【最常考】 —— 同 flood , inundation

A *deluge* of protest letters filled the senator's office after he made a remark insulting Asians. 在參議員發表侮辱亞洲人的言論之後，抗議的信件如洪水般湧入他的辦公室。

diminutive 〔 də'mɪnjətɪv 〕 *adj.* 小的 —— 同 small , little , tiny

The man grabbed the child begging on the roadside and shook his *diminutive* frame.

那男人抓住在路旁乞討的小孩，並搖晃他小小的身子。

****divert**〔 dəˈvɜt , daɪ- 〕*v.* ①轉向　②娛樂【最常考】

——同 1. deflect , turn aside　2. entertain , amuse

There were several signs to **divert** traffic from the parade path.　有幾個標誌將交通導離遊行的路線。

****dramatically**〔 drəˈmætɪkəlɪ 〕*adv.*　戲劇性地【最常考】

——同 theatrically , breathtakingly , excitingly

In the middle of the speech, he stopped **dramatically** and began to cry.　演講中途，他戲劇性地停了下來並開始哭泣。

empower〔 ɪmˈpaʊɚ 〕*v.* 賦予權力

——同 authorize , entitle , license , sanction , allow

This new law will **empower** women to sue their employers for discrimination.

這新的法律賦予婦女權力，可因雇主的歧視而控告他們。

Exercise　*Fill in the blanks.*

1. Many young people feel ＿＿＿＿＿＿ from their families and society.

2. Although the meat was tender, his knife was too ＿＿＿＿＿＿ to slice it.

3. The hat Amy bought was a nice ＿＿＿＿＿＿ to the dress her mother had given her.

4. The Swedish boy was very ＿＿＿＿＿＿ when traveling in China.

5. The child's ＿＿＿＿＿＿ hands were barely big enough to grasp the box.

【解答】1. alienated　2. blunt　3. complement　4. conspicuous　5. diminutive

* **erode** 〔ɪ'rod〕 *v.* 腐蝕【常考】

—— 同 abrade , consume , corrode , eat away , wear away

While the ocean *erodes* the beach in one section, it builds it up in another. 海侵蝕了海岸的這一頭，又會在另一處重建。

* **exempt** 〔ɪg'zɛmpt〕 *v.* 免除【常考】

—— 同 except , excuse , free , relieve , spare

The father explained to his son that he was not *exempt* from responsibility because he was rich.

父親向兒子解釋，不能因為他有錢，就可以免除責任。

filament 〔'fɪləmənt〕 *n.* 細絲

—— 同 thread , fiber , strand , string , wire , staple

When the *filament* in a light bulb breaks, the bulb is "burnt out." 當燈絲斷掉，燈泡就燒壞了。 * bulb 〔bʌlb〕 *n.* 電燈泡

* **fringe** 〔frɪndʒ〕 *n.* 邊緣【常考】 —— 同 edge , border , outskirts

There were several poor squatter settlements along the *fringes* of the city. 在城市的邊緣，有幾家貧窮的違章建築住戶。

* squatter 〔'skwɑtɚ〕 *n.* 違章建築住戶

* **graze** 〔grez〕 *v.* ①吃草 ②摩擦【常考】

—— 同 1. pasture , eat grass 2. scrape , abrade

The hill was dotted with cattle and sheep that were *grazing*.

山丘上點綴著吃草的牛羊。 * dot 〔dɑt〕 *v.* 點綴

gullible 〔'gʌləbḷ〕 *adj.* 易受騙的

—— 同 credulous , unsuspecting , easily taken in

It is amazing that at the age of thirty he is still so *gullible*.

以他三十歲的年紀還這麼容易受騙，真令人驚訝。

gulp 〔gʌlp〕 *v.* 吞食 —— 同 swallow , devour

The soldiers only had a few minutes to *gulp* down their dinners. 士兵們只有幾分鐘的時間可吃晚餐。

hoist 〔 hɔɪst 〕 *v.* 提升 —— 同 lift , raise , elevate
The sailors' arm muscles strained as they ***hoisted*** the main
sail of the ship. 當水手們揚起船上的主帆時，他們手臂的肌肉緊繃。
　＊strain 〔 stren 〕 *v.* 拉緊

＊＊**hypothesis** 〔 haɪ'pɑθəsɪs 〕 *n.* 假設【最常考】
—— 同 premise , presumption , proposition , conjecture , supposition
The scientist designed several experiments to test her
hypothesis. 科學家設計了幾個實驗來試驗她的假設。

＊**implore** 〔 ɪm'plor 〕 *v.* 懇求【常考】 —— 同 beg , beseech , entreat
The woman ***implored*** the soldiers to spare her family's
lives. 婦人懇求士兵饒了她家人的命。

＊**inhabitant** 〔 ɪn'hæbətənt 〕 *n.* 居民【常考】
—— 同 dweller , resident
The ***inhabitants*** of this community work together to prevent
crime in their neighborhood.
該社區的居民共同努力以防範鄰近地區的犯罪。

inundate 〔 'ɪnʌn,det , ɪn'ʌndet 〕 *v.* 淹水 —— 同 flood , deluge
The hospitals were ***inundated*** with victims of the subway
gas attack. 醫院裡充滿地鐵瓦斯中毒的受害者。

loiter 〔 'lɔɪtɚ 〕 *v.* 閒蕩 —— 同 loaf , dawdle , stray , linger , stroll
It is illegal to ***loiter*** in this park after hours.
下班後在這座公園裡遊蕩是不合法的。

morbid 〔 'mɔrbɪd 〕 *adj.* 不健康的；病態的
—— 同 sick , diseased , unsound , ailing
He has a ***morbid*** interest in the details of how the body
decomposes after death. ＊decompose 〔,dikəm'poz 〕 *v.* 腐爛
他對於人死後屍體如何腐化的細節，有一種病態的興趣。

* **motivate** (ˈmotəˌvet) *v.* 引起動機【常考】

　　—同 stimulate , induce , actuate , drive , inspire

The coach tried to *motivate* his team to take possession of the ball and make some baskets.

教練試著激發球隊取得控球權，並且投籃得分。

* **optimal** (ˈɑptəməl) *adj.* 最佳的【常考】

　　—同 optimum , prime , best , choicest , superlative

The patient's heart rate is well above the *optimal* rate.

這病人的心率是再好不過了。

* **perceptible** (pəˈsɛptəb!) *adj.* 可察覺的【常考】

　　—同 tangible , discernible , recognizable , detectable

There has been no *perceptible* change in the pollution levels in the city.　這城市污染的程度看不出變化來。

Exercise *Fill in the blanks.*

1. Wind and rain slowly _____ huge boulders into tiny stones.

2. Along the _____ of the park was a line of oak trees.

3. Rock climbers must _____ their entire body weight up cliffs with only their fingers and toes.

4. _____ of the small seaside town welcome tourists.

5. It was her love of animals that _____ her to become a veterinarian.

【解答】1. erode　2. fringe　3. hoist　4. Inhabitants　5. motivated

platform 〔'plæt,fɔrm 〕 *n.* ①講台 ②政綱
—— 同 1. podium , stage , stand 2. party line , policy
The candidate presented his election *platform* to the voters
in his speech. 候選人在演講中向選民表達他的政見。

preoccupation 〔 pri,ɑkjə'peʃən 〕 *n.* 專心；熱衷
—— 同 absorption , engrossment , immersion , abstraction
Her *preoccupation* with fabrics comes from her job as a
cloth merchant. 她熱衷於布織物乃因爲她的職業是布商。

prosaic 〔 pro'ze • ɪk 〕 *adj.* 枯燥的
—— 同 boring , hackneyed , stale , trite , flat , dull
The teacher had to read through thirty *prosaic* essays from
her students. 老師必須看三十篇學生寫的枯燥的論文。

* **rehabilitation** 〔,ri(h)ə,bɪlə'teʃən 〕 *n.* 恢復【常考】
—— 同 recovery , restoration , revival , betterment
After the car accident, it took many months for the
rehabilitation of her left leg.
交通意外之後，她的左腿花了好幾個月才恢復。

* **resolve** 〔 rɪ'zɑlv 〕 *v.* ①決定 ②分解【常考】
—— 同 1. decide , determine 2. separate , analyze
Mother told my sister and me to *resolve* our differences on
our own. 母親要我和妹妹自己解決我們的爭論。

routine 〔 ru'tin 〕 *n.* 例行公事   —— 同 drill , exercise
It took her a few weeks to learn the *routine* of her new job.
她花了幾個星期來學習新工作的例行公事。

* **secular** 〔'sɛkjələ 〕 *adj.* 世俗的【常考】
—— 同 worldly , earthly , profane
Kevin's parents decided to send him to a *secular* school
rather than a religious school.
凱文的雙親決定送他到普通學校就讀，而非宗教學校。

skyrocket 〔 skaɪˈrɑkɪt 〕 *v.* 暴漲

—— 同 rise rapidly , increase suddenly

After Andy Lau was seen wearing a pair of Levi's jeans, local sales of the jeans *skyrocketed*.

有人看到劉德華穿一條 Levi's 的牛仔褲之後，當地牛仔褲的銷售量便暴增。

****sphere** 〔 sfɪr 〕 *n.* 球體【最常考】

—— 同 orb , globe , ball

Scientists have proved that the earth is not a perfect *sphere*, but slightly egg-shaped.

科學家已經證明地球不是正圓形，而是有一點蛋形。

* **sticky** 〔ˈstɪkɪ 〕 *adj.* 黏的【常考】

—— 同 adhesive , gluey , gummy , clinging , gooey , tacky

The pack of gum became *sticky* after sitting in the sun for an hour. 在太陽下曝曬一小時後，這包口香糖已變黏了。

* **superiority** 〔 səˌpɪrɪˈɔrətɪ 〕 *n.* 卓越【常考】

—— 同 predominance , preeminence , supremacy , excellence

My grandfather believes in the *superiority* of Chinese herbal medicine. 祖父認為中藥較好。

* **textile** 〔ˈtɛkstḷ , -taɪl 〕 *adj.* 紡織的【常考】

—— 同 cloth , fabric , material

The *textile* industry is very important to our local economy.

紡織業對我們當地的經濟非常重要。

* **trigger** 〔ˈtrɪgɚ 〕 *v.* 引起【常考】

—— 同 cause , elicit , generate , give raise to , bring about , promote

The company president's announcement that there would be no year-end bonuses *triggered* worker complaints.

公司總裁宣布不發年終獎金，引起工人的抱怨。

urge 〔 ɝdʒ 〕 *v.* 催促 ——同 push , press , instigate

He *urged* Sabrina to continue her piano lessons.
他催莎比娜繼續上她的鋼琴課。

vibrate 〔ˈvaɪbret 〕 *v.* 震動
——同 tremble , quiver , oscillate , palpitate , pulsate

As he drew the bow across the violin strings, he felt them
vibrate. 當他將弓拉過小提琴的弦時，他感覺到它們在振動。

vociferous 〔 voˈsɪfərəs 〕 *adj.* 吵鬧的
——同 noisy , clamorous , shouting , loud , ranting

His *vociferous* pleas to the judge had no effect on his harsh
sentence. 他高聲向法官辯解，但對他嚴厲的刑罰仍無濟於事。

wobble 〔ˈwɑbḷ 〕 *v.* 動搖
——同 stagger , sway , shake , tremble , vibrate , waver

The little baby *wobbled* as she took her first steps.
這小嬰兒踏出她的第一步時，搖搖晃晃的。

> **Exercise** *Fill in the blanks.*

1. We found his _____ with movie stars boring.

2. That book was so _____ that I could only read five
   pages before I had to put it down.

3. Her daily _____ consisted of getting up in the
   morning, working until late, and coming home to sleep.

4. The price of coffee _____ after an exceptionally
   poor harvest.

5. The loud noise _____ panic among the people
   waiting in the doctor's office.

【解答】1. preoccupation 2. prosaic 3. routine 4. skyrocketed 5. triggered

⸱ List 25 ⸱ 難字分析

alienate 〔'eljən,et〕 *v.* 疏遠

alien + ate
| |
other + make

— to cause to become unfriendly
or indifferent

bilateral 〔baɪ'lætərəl〕 *adj.* 兩邊的

bi + later + al
| | |
two + side + adj.

— of or involving two sides

complement 〔'kɑmpləmənt〕 *n.* 補充

com   + ple + ment
| | |
together + fill + n.

— that which makes something
complete

conspicuous 〔kən'spɪkjuəs〕 *adj.* 引人注目的

con   + spic + uous
| | |
together + look + adj.

— attracting attention through
being unusual or remarkable

diminutive 〔də'mɪnjətɪv〕 *adj.* 小的

di   + min + utive
dis | |
|
apart + small + adj.

— much smaller than ordinary
or average

filament ('fɪləmənt) *n.* 細絲

fila + ment
　|　　　|
thread +　*n.*

—— a very slender thread of fiber

hypothesis (haɪ'pɑθəsɪs) *n.* 假設

hypo + thes + is
　|　　　|　　|
under + place + *n.*

—— an idea or suggestion put forward as a starting-point for reasoning or explanation

inhabitant (ɪn'hæbətənt) *n.* 居民

in + habit +　ant
　|　　|　　　|
in + dwell + person

—— a person that lives in some specific region

inundate ('ɪnʌnˌdet , ɪn'ʌndet) *v.* 淹水

in + und + ate
　|　　|　　|
into + wave + make

—— to cover with a flood

preoccupation (priˌɑkjə'peʃən) *n.* 專心；熱衷

pre + oc + cup + ation
　|　　|　　　|　　|
　　 ob
　|　　|　　　|　　|
before + at + seize +　*n.*

—— state of mind in which something takes up all a person's thoughts

vociferous (vo'sɪfərəs) *adj.* 吵鬧的

voci + fer + ous
　|　　|　　|
voice + carry + *adj.*

—— noisy

LIST ▸ 26

✲✲acrimonious〔ˌækrə'monɪəs〕*adj.* 尖刻的【最常考】
—— 同 bitter , sharp , caustic , harsh
While waiting in line at the tax office, Sam heard an
acrimonious man demanding a refund.
在稅務局排隊時，山姆聽到一名尖刻的男子在要求退費。

allegiance〔ə'lidʒəns〕*n.* 忠誠
—— 同 loyalty , fidelity , faithfulness , integrity
The soldiers promised their ***allegiance*** to their country.
這些士兵發誓要對國家忠心。

appease〔ə'piz〕*v.* 緩和；平息
—— 同 placate , mollify , calm , soothe , conciliate
The thieves ***appeased*** the guard dog with a bone and then
entered the house. 小偷以骨頭讓看守犬安靜下來，然後進入屋內。

✲astute〔ə'stjut〕*adj.* 機敏的；狡猾的【常考】
—— 同 shrewd , acute , canny , sagacious
She was an ***astute*** woman who understood the complexities
of the stock market.
她是個精明的女子，能了解股市的複雜運作。

badge〔bædʒ〕*n.* 徽章；象徵 —— 同 symbol , token , insignia
The boys all sewed their club ***badges*** on their school bags.
所有的男孩子都將他們社團的徽章縫在書包上。

blurred〔blɜd〕*adj.* 模糊的 —— 同 dim , indistinct , fuzzy
The pictures Adam took are all so ***blurred*** you can't tell
who is who in them.
亞當所拍的照片都一片模糊，你根本分不清誰是誰。

circumlocution 〔͵sɝkəmloˈkjuʃən 〕 *n.* 迂迴的說法

—— 同 paraphrase , periphrasis , indirectness

His speech is filled with **circumlocution** and few people can
listen to him for very long.

他講話總是兜圈子，所以沒有人能長時間聆聽。

combative 〔 kəmˈbætɪv 〕 *adj.* 好戰的；好鬥的

—— 同 aggressive , competitive , opposing , antagonistic

Sherman had no desire to get a job in the **combative** world of
investment companies.

雪曼並不想在投資公司這種競爭激烈的環境中工作。

constellation 〔͵kɑnstəˈleʃən 〕 *n.* 星座

—— 同 group of stars , stellar group

The Big Dipper is a large and easily identified **constellation**.

北斗七星是最大且最容易辨認的星座。

* convict 〔 kənˈvɪkt 〕 *v.* 定罪【常考】 —— 同 find guilty

The three men were **convicted** on robbery charges.

這三名男子因被控搶劫而遭定罪。

* crumble 〔ˈkrʌmbl̩ 〕 *v.* 粉碎；崩潰【常考】

—— 同 disintegrate , decompose , collapse , break up

The apartment building that had used sea sand in its
construction began to **crumble** after only a few weeks.

才過幾個星期，這棟以海砂建造的公寓大樓，就已經開始崩塌。

demise 〔 dɪˈmaɪz 〕 *n.* 終止；死亡 —— 同 death , extinction , end

His years of drug abuse finally led to his **demise**.

經年的藥物濫用終於導致他的死亡。

dire 〔 daɪr 〕 *adj.* 悲慘的；恐怖的 —— 同 appalling , dreadful

The consequences for forging a foreign passport are **dire**.

偽照外國護照的下場是很悲慘的。

divine 〔dəˈvaɪn〕 *adj.* 神聖的；神奇的

——同 sacred , holy , godly , religious

Many people believed in the ***divine*** healing powers of the waters of that spring. 許多人都相信那泉水的神奇療效。

* **drawback** 〔ˈdrɔˌbæk〕 *n.* 缺點【常考】

——同 deficiency , defect , disadvantage

The main ***drawback*** of this scanner is that it is slightly slower than other brands.

這掃描器的主要缺點是，它的速度比其他的廠牌稍慢。

emulate 〔ˈɛmjəˌlet〕 *v.* 模仿

——同 mimic , imitate , rival , compete with

The newly rich often try to ***emulate*** the old moneyed families of the country.

暴發戶常常試著要模仿國內的有錢人世家。

Exercise ⟩ *Fill in the blanks.*

1. An _____ businessman, he knew the way to get the company executive to sign the contract.

2. When I take off my glasses, my vision becomes _____.

3. If you do not have any evidence to support your case, the jury will not _____ the defendant of the crime.

4. Are there any _____ to building a house in this area?

5. While singing, he tries to _____ the voice of Frank Sinatra.

【解答】1. astute　2. blurred　3. convict　4. drawbacks　5. emulate

erotic〔ɪ'rɑtɪk〕*adj.* 色情的；性慾的
　　——同 carnal, lustful, sensual, amatory
She found it difficult to control the **erotic** desire she felt for
him. 她覺得要抑制對他的性慾很困難。

* **erratic**〔ə'rætɪk〕*adj.* 不穩定的；怪異的【常考】
　　——同 shifting, variable, capricious, abnormal
His **erratic** behavior led his teachers to believe he had
psychological problems. 他怪異的行徑使老師以爲他的心理有問題。

****exploit** ①〔ɪk'splɔɪt〕*v.* 利用　②〔'ɛksplɔɪt, ɪk'splɔɪt〕*n.* 功蹟
　　——同 1. utilize, use　2. achievement, accomplishment　【最常考】
In many countries, factory owners **exploit** their workers to
make profits for themselves.
在很多國家，工廠老闆利用工人爲他們自己賺取利益。

****expound**〔ɪk'spaʊnd〕*v.* 說明【最常考】
　　——同 explain, elucidate, describe, illustrate
In this book, the author **expounds** on his ideas of the perfect
democracy. 在這本書裡，作者說明他對眞正民主的看法。

filter〔'fɪltɚ〕① *v.* 過濾　② *n.* 過濾器
　　——同 1. filtrate, refine, screen, sieve, clarify　2. sifter, screen
This device **filters** drinking water to ensure its purity.
這個裝置可過濾飲用水，以確保它的純淨。

frolic〔'frɑlɪk〕*n.* 嬉戲　——同 fun and games
The children's summer afternoons were filled with happiness
and **frolic**. 孩子們的夏季午後充滿了快樂與嬉戲。

* **gregarious**〔grɪ'gɛrɪəs〕*adj.* 合群的【常考】
　　——同 sociable, companionable, affable
His **gregarious** personality allowed him a lively social life.
合群的個性使他擁有活躍的社交生活。

* hollow 〔ˋhɑlo 〕① *n.* 洞 ② *adj.* 空心的【常考】

—— 同 1. cavity , den , hole , pit 2. empty , void , vacant

The robber hid the money in the *hollow* of a tree.

搶匪把錢藏在樹洞裡。

** imply 〔ɪmˋplaɪ 〕*v.* 暗示【最常考】　—— 同 suggest , hint , connote

Are you *implying* that I am being greedy?

你是在暗示我很貪心嗎？

invalid 〔ˋɪnvəlɪd 〕*n.* 病弱者；病人　—— 同 sick person , patient

Her father is an *invalid* due to a serious stroke he suffered.

由於一次嚴重的中風，她的父親成了病人。

irrefutable 〔ɪˋrɛfjʊtəbḷ , ͵ɪrɪˋfjutəbḷ 〕*adj.* 難以反駁的

—— 同 indisputable , undeniable , unquestionable

The lawyer provided *irrefutable* evidence of her client's
innocence.　律師為她委託人的清白提出難以反駁的證據。

* juxtaposition 〔͵dʒʌkstəpəˋzɪʃən 〕*n.* 並列【常考】

—— 同 adjacency , vicinity , proximity , closeness

The museum's *juxtaposition* of modern art and classical art
made an interesting contrast.

博物館將現代與古典的藝術品並列在一起，構成了有趣的對比。

loophole 〔ˋlup͵hol 〕*n.* 漏洞

—— 同 means of escape , excuse , pretense

The politician used a *loophole* to avoid paying taxes on his
second house.　這名政客利用漏洞來避免繳納第二棟房屋的稅。

melancholy 〔ˋmɛlən͵kɑlɪ 〕*adj.* 憂鬱的

—— 同 sad , gloomy , downcast , depressed , dejected

His *melancholy* mood was caused by the loss of his job.

他憂鬱的情緒是因丟掉工作而引起。

* **monopoly** 〔 mə'nɑplɪ 〕 *n.* 壟斷【常考】

—— 同 exclusive possession , domination

The government is planning to end its *monopoly* on alcohol production. 政府計畫停止對製酒業的壟斷。

opulence 〔 'ɑpjələns 〕 *n.* 富裕；豪華

—— 同 luxury , affluence , wealth

Visitors are awed by the *opulence* of the royal palace.

遊客對皇宮的豪華都感到敬畏。

perennial 〔 pə'rɛnɪəl 〕 *adj.* 長年的；不斷的

—— 同 year-round , enduring , perpetual

The *perennial* problems of poverty are ones that every government must deal with.

長久以來貧窮的問題一直是每個政府所要面對的。

Exercise ▷ *Fill in the blanks.*

1. As she _____ on her theory of language development, we slowly began to understand.

2. The photographer placed a special light _____ over the lens of the camera.

3. Behind that hill is a little _____ where the children like to play hide-and-seek.

4. Grandmother insisted that she was not an _____ and proceeded to get out of bed.

5. The _____ song he sang moved everyone in the audience to tears.

【解答】1. expounded 2. filter 3. hollow 4. invalid 5. melancholy

plausible 〔'plɔzəbḷ〕 *adj.* 合理的；似真實的

——同 credible , probable , reasonable , tenable

It is *plausible* that George accidentally took my keys, but I might have just lost them.
有可能是喬治無意中拿了我的鑰匙，但也可能是我把它們弄丟了。

prerequisite 〔 pri'rɛkwəzɪt 〕 *n.* 先決條件；必要條件

——同 essential , must , necessity , requirement

Organic chemistry is a *prerequisite* for this advanced anatomy class. 要先修過有機化學，才能上這門高級解剖課。

proscribe 〔 pro'skraɪb 〕 *v.* 禁止 ——同 prohibit , outlaw , banish

Many individual freedoms were *proscribed* under the dictatorship. 在獨裁政權下，許多個人自由都遭到禁止。

rehearse 〔 rɪ'hɝs 〕 *v.* 預演 ——同 practice , prepare

The chorus *rehearsed* the song several times before the performance. 合唱團在演出前將這首歌排練了好幾次。

resonant 〔'rɛznənt〕 *adj.* 共鳴的；回音的

——同 resounding , echoing

We could hear the *resonant* "clang" of the church bell on the other side of town.
我們可以在城裡的另一頭，聽見教堂鐘聲的鏗鏘回音。

⁎⁎rudimentary 〔͵rudə'mɛntərɪ 〕 *adj.* 基本的【最常考】

——同 elementary , primary , fundamental

Michael lacks even the most *rudimentary* understanding of computers. 邁可連對電腦的基本認識都沒有。

secure 〔 sɪ'kjur 〕 ① *v.* 取得 ② *adj.* 安全的

——同 1. acquire , gain , obtain 2. sheltered , safe

After installing an alarm system, Jill felt her house was more *secure*. 裝了警報系統後，吉兒覺得家裡安全多了。

slander 〔'slændə-〕 *n.* 毀謗

—— 同 scandal , defamation , backbiting , smear

He decried the article in that magazine as *slander* on all public health officials.

他批評雜誌上的文章是對所有公共衛生官員的毀謗。

spinning 〔'spɪnɪŋ〕 *adj.* 旋轉的

—— 同 whirling , twirling , swirling , rotating

The children watched the *spinning* top travel across the floor.

孩子們看著旋轉的陀螺在地板上移動。

* stiff 〔 stɪf 〕 *adj.* 僵硬的【常考】

—— 同 hard , rigid , solid , tense , inflexible

As soon as she turned her car into traffic, her neck muscles grew *stiff*. 她一把車駛回車陣中，頸部又開始僵硬了。

supplant 〔 sə'plænt 〕 *v.* 取代

—— 同 replace , supersede , take over

Electronic products *supplanted* agricultural products as the country's top export. 電子產品取代農產品，成了該國最多的輸出品。

thaw 〔 θɔ 〕 *v.* 融解 —— 同 defrost , melt , dissolve

Angela took the meat out of the freezer to *thaw* it before cooking. 安琪拉將肉從冰箱中拿出，讓它在烹煮前解凍。

trim 〔 trɪm 〕 ① *adj.* 整齊的 ② *v.* 修剪

—— 同 1. neat , orderly 2. prune , cut , clip

Hester went to the beauty parlor to have her hair *trimmed*.

海斯特到美容院去修頭髮。

usurp 〔 ju'zɝp 〕 *v.* 奪取 —— 同 seize , expropriate

The military general *usurped* power from the president.

這名軍事將領從總統手中奪取政權。

vicinity 〔 vəˈsɪnətɪ 〕 *n.* 鄰近
—— 同 neighborhood , surroundings , proximity

The couple interested in buying the house asked if there was a grocery store in the *vicinity*.

這對有興趣買房子的夫婦，詢問鄰近是否有商店。

* **void** 〔 vɔɪd 〕 *adj.* ①空的 ②無效的【常考】
—— 同 1. bare , empty 2. ineffective , invalid

She discovered the insurance company had sent her a *void* check. 她發現保險公司開給她一張無效的支票。

wrath 〔 ræθ 〕 *n.* 憤怒
—— 同 vexation , choler , rage , anger

After not returning home until two o'clock in the morning, Sam had to face his father's *wrath*.

山姆一直到凌晨兩點才回到家，所以必須面對父親的憤怒。

Exercise > *Fill in the blanks.*

1. George agreed that it was _____ that the new law might not get passed.

2. Last night we were _____ a play we will perform next week.

3. The mouse's dead body had grown _____ overnight.

4. The company manager was afraid that a subordinate would _____ his position within the company.

5. All of the subjects feared the king's _____ and tried to keep him content at all times.

【解答】1. plausible   2. rehearsing   3. stiff   4. usurp   5. wrath

· List 26 · 難字分析

acrimonious 〔͵ækrə'monɪəs 〕*adj.* 尖刻的

acri + moni + ous
| | |
sharp + state + adj.

— bitter and caustic in temper, manner or speech

allegiance 〔 ə'lidʒəns 〕*n.* 忠誠

al + leg + iance
|
ad | |
|
to + law +   n.

— loyalty to a person or government

circumlocution 〔͵sɝkəmlo'kjuʃən 〕*n.* 迂迴的說法

circum + locut + ion
|
around + speak + n.

— roundabout expression

gregarious 〔 grɪ'gɛrɪəs 〕*adj.* 合群的

greg + arious
| |
collect +   adj.

— fond of the company of others

irrefutable 〔 ɪ'rɛfjutəbl͵ , ͵ɪrrɪ'fjutəbl͵ 〕*adj.* 難以反駁的

ir + re + fut + able
|
in | | |
|
not + back + pour + able to

— that cannot be disproved

juxtaposition〔͵dʒʌkstəpə'zɪʃən〕n. 並列

juxta + posit + ion | | | *beside*+ *put* + *n.*	— placing side by side

monopoly〔mə'nɑpḷɪ〕n. 壟斷

mono + poly | | *sole* + *sell*	— complete possession of trade, talk, etc.

perennial〔pə'rɛnɪəl〕adj. 長年的；不斷的

per + enn + ial | | | *through* + *year* + *adj.*	— lasting through the whole year

prerequisite〔pri'rɛkwəzɪt〕n. 先決條件；必要條件

pre + re + quisite | | | *before* + *again* + *seek*	— thing required as a condition for something else

resonant〔'rɛzn̩ənt〕adj. 共鳴的；回音的

re + son + ant | | | *back*+ *sound* + *adj.*	— resounding

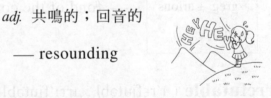

rudimentary〔͵rudə'mɛntərɪ〕adj. 基本的

rudi + ment + ary | | | *crude*+ *n.* + *adj.*	— elementary

TEST ▸ 13

請由 (A)～(D) 中選出和畫線部分意義最相近的字。

1. The two people arguing in the hallway are shouting <u>acrid</u> remarks at each other.
   (A) destructive
   (B) nominal
   (C) loud
   (D) caustic

2. Two weeks before the music festival opened, we received a <u>deluge</u> of requests for tickets.
   (A) flood
   (B) trickle
   (C) breeze
   (D) smattering

3. Not a <u>crumb</u> of cake had been left over from Tom's birthday party.
   (A) smell
   (B) recipe
   (C) bit
   (D) sound

4. What is your <u>hypothesis</u> as to how the prisoner escaped?
   (A) appetite
   (B) assurance
   (C) conjecture
   (D) wish

5. The government has pledged to give more money to centers for drug <u>rehabilitation</u>.
   (A) recovery
   (B) analysis
   (C) prosecution
   (D) intervention

6. If students score highly on an achievement test, it will <u>exempt</u> them from the beginner level English class.
   (A) require
   (B) excuse
   (C) evaluate
   (D) monitor

7. The <u>superiority</u> of Japanese and European trains to American trains is obvious.
   (A) equality
   (B) familiarity
   (C) independence
   (D) supremacy

8. He was not shot, but the bullet did <u>graze</u> his arm.
   (A) abrade
   (B) near
   (C) leave
   (D) break

9. This car's engine gets <u>optimal</u> gas mileage when driving on the highway.

    (A) best
    (B) normal
    (C) unquestioned
    (D) formal

10. The ability to swim is a <u>prerequisite</u> for learning to scuba dive.

    (A) requirement
    (B) option
    (C) nicety
    (D) motion

11. The government tried to <u>appease</u> the revolutionary peasants by guaranteeing local elections.

    (A) oppose
    (B) betray
    (C) placate
    (D) organize

12. Tattoos are often a kind of <u>badge</u> for Mafia members in Asia.

    (A) insignia
    (B) artform
    (C) hindrance
    (D) negotiation

13. Historians have long studied the <u>demise</u> of the Roman Empire.

    (A) foundation
    (B) structure
    (C) history
    (D) end

14. To people of the ancient world, it seemed an <u>irrefutable</u> fact that the earth was flat.

    (A) superstitious
    (B) undeniable
    (C) reasonable
    (D) uninteresting

15. Don is working two jobs to <u>secure</u> enough money to study abroad.

    (A) find
    (B) spend
    (C) acquire
    (D) modify

16. The large soda manufacturer's <u>monopoly</u> of the market kept other soft drink companies from forming.

    (A) exclusive possession
    (B) immediate attention
    (C) conclusive suggestion
    (D) nominal devotion

17. Huge buildings <u>crumbled</u> from the force of the earthquake.

    (A) collapsed
    (B) swayed
    (C) jittered
    (D) exploded

18. The children were exhausted but happy after their <u>frolic</u> in the ocean surf.

    (A) fun and games
    (B) trials and tribulations
    (C) ups and downs
    (D) hit and miss

19. Content people often understand the importance of balancing the <u>secular</u> and the spiritual aspects of their lives.

    (A) heavenly
    (B) scientific
    (C) earthly
    (D) busy

20. The automobile industry is hoping a <u>bilateral</u> trade agreement can be reached between Japan and the United States.

    (A) two-sided
    (B) one-party
    (C) multifaceted
    (D) polyglot

21. When spring comes, the frozen mountain streams slowly begin to <u>thaw</u>.

    (A) solidify
    (B) melt
    (C) flood
    (D) evaporate

22. This artist's <u>juxtaposition</u> of dark colors and light colors in his paintings creates an interesting effect.

    (A) omission
    (B) restriction
    (C) adjacency
    (D) interdependency

23. Farmers support that politician because of his <u>allegiance</u> to farmer's groups and support of agricultural programs.

    (A) curiosity
    (B) loyalty
    (C) investment
    (D) understanding

24. Protesters held a <u>vociferous</u> rally in front of the power company to protest against an increase in electricity rates.

    (A) delicate
    (B) clamorous
    (C) nominal
    (D) unplanned

25. There are several nice parks in the <u>vicinity</u> of the university.

    (A) neighborhood
    (B) union
    (C) presence
    (D) inside

【解答】

1. D	2. A	3. C	4. C	5. A	6. B	7. D	8. A	9. A	10. A
11. C	12. A	13. D	14. B	15. C	16. A	17. A	18. A	19. C	20. A
21. B	22. C	23. B	24. B	25. A					

LIST ▸ 27

actuate〔ˈæktʃuˌet〕*v.* 激發

——同 activate , motivate , incite , stir , arouse

The sprinkler system in this building is *actuated* by very high temperatures. 建築物裡的灑水系統因為溫度太高而啟動。

allegory〔ˈæləˌgorɪ〕*n.* 寓言 ——同 parable , fable , tale , story

Christianity and Buddhism both use *allegories* to teach followers about religious principles.

基督教和佛教都利用寓言故事，來教導信徒教義。

applaud〔əˈplɔd〕*v.* 鼓掌；稱讚 ——同 clap , praise , eulogize

The audience *applauded* the dancers' outstanding performance.

觀眾為舞者傑出的表演鼓掌喝采。

* atone〔əˈton〕*v.* 補償【常考】

——同 compensate , make up for , recompense , make amends for

To *atone* for his wrongdoing, Hugh spent his spare time helping the elderly.

為了補償自己的罪行，休將空閒時間花在幫助老人上。

brag〔bræg〕*v.* 吹噓 ——同 exaggerate , boast , crow

Everyone was tired of hearing Stephen *brag* about being accepted at Harvard.

每個人都聽膩史蒂芬吹牛說他被哈佛錄取的事。

* breach〔britʃ〕*n.* 違犯【常考】

——同 violation , infraction , contravention , disobedience

Aunt Sophie was very formal and would not tolerate the smallest *breach* of etiquette.

蘇菲姨媽非常拘泥於形式，所以不能忍受任何的失禮。

bruise 〔 bruz 〕 *v.* 打傷；瘀傷   ——同 batter , injure , contuse

My arm was ***bruised*** when I fell down the stairs.

我跌下樓梯時，手臂摔傷了。

carcass 〔'kɑrkəs〕 *n.* 屍體   ——同 corpse , dead body

Huge elephant ***carcasses*** with their tusks sawed off lay
rotting on the plain. 被鋸掉象牙的大象屍體就躺在平原上腐爛。

 ＊tusk 〔 tʌsk 〕 *n.* 長牙

clash 〔 klæʃ 〕 *v.* 撞擊   ——同 bang , crash , rattle

In a restaurant kitchen, you can always hear the ***clashing*** of
pots, pans and dishes.

在餐廳的廚房裡，你永遠可以聽到鍋盆碗盤的撞擊聲。

＊＊**constraint** 〔 kən'strent 〕 *n.* 拘束；限制【最常考】

 ——同 restraint , coercion , compulsion , confinement , limitation

The students had a three-hour time ***constraint*** for finishing
the exam. 學生的考試有三小時的時間限制。

cripple 〔'krɪpḷ 〕 *v.* 使殘廢   ——同 disable , lame , paralyze

The skiing accident ***crippled*** both of his legs.

滑雪的意外事件使他雙腿殘廢。

＊**crust** 〔 krʌst 〕 *n.* 皮；外殼【常考】   ——同 coating , rind , shell

Many children don't like to eat the bread ***crust*** on their
sandwiches.

很多小孩都不喜歡吃三明治上的麵包皮。

＊**demolish** 〔 dɪ'malɪʃ 〕 *v.* 拆除【常考】

 ——同 raze , ruin , tear down , overthrow

The old factory building was ***demolished*** so that a new
shopping center could be built.

舊的工廠被拆除，以便建造一座新的購物中心。

* **discard**〔dɪsˈkɑrd〕 v. 拋棄【常考】

—— 同 get rid of , abandon , dispense with , desert , forsake

They decided to *discard* their old sofa and buy a new, more modern-looking one.

他們決定丟掉舊沙發，並買一套新的、看起來較時髦的。

docile〔ˈdɑsḷ〕 adj. 溫順的

—— 同 obedient , gentle , tractable , amenable , tame , manageable

After the doctor gave him an injection, the unruly patient grew *docile*.

醫生給他注射一針之後，這不聽話的病人變得溫馴了。

drench〔drɛntʃ〕 v. 使浸透

—— 同 soak , douse , saturate , wet

The sudden rain storm *drenched* everyone in the tour group.

突如其來的豪雨讓旅行團的每個人都濕透了。

Exercise ⟩ *Fill in the blanks.*

1. We _____ Ms. Jamison for her achievements in creating work-training programs for the poor.

2. John is always _____ about his new car.

3. Are there any _____ on how many people we can invite to the graduation ceremony?

4. The earth's _____ is actually only a thin layer of the planet.

5. Angie's pet dog is very _____ and makes a good companion to her elderly aunt who lives with her.

【解答】1. applauded　2. bragging　3. constraints　4. crust　5. docile

* **enactment** 〔 ɪn'æktmənt 〕 *n.* 制定【常考】
——同 ordinance , proclamation , commandment , regulation
The lobby group pressed the legislature for the ***enactment*** of a
gun-control law.　國會遊說團體對立法院施壓，要求訂定槍械管制法。

* **erupt** 〔 ɪ'rʌpt 〕 *v.* 爆發【常考】　——同 burst , explode , blow up
Suddenly the volcano ***erupted***, sending local residents
fleeing for their lives.　火山突然爆發，迫使當地居民躲避逃生。

* **exonerate** 〔 ɪg'zɑnə,ret 〕 *v.* 使無罪【常考】
——同 clear , acquit , vindicate , let off , absolve
The judge ***exonerated*** her from the crime she was convicted
of five years ago.　法官免除她五年前所被判的罪。

* **extensive** 〔 ɪk'stɛnsɪv 〕 *adj.* 寬廣的【最常考】
——同 widespread , broad , extended , far-flung
There was an ***extensive*** forest surrounding the monastery on
all sides.　這修道院的四周有寬廣的森林環繞著。
＊monastery 〔'mɑnəs,tɛrɪ 〕 *n.* 修道院

filthy 〔'fɪlθɪ 〕 *adj.* 污穢的　——同 dirty , nasty , foul
The poor beggar only had ***filthy*** rags to wear as clothes.
這貧窮的乞丐只有骯髒的破布可當衣服穿。

frost 〔 frɔst , frɑst 〕 *n.* 結霜　——同 ice , freeze
The late spring ***frost*** damaged the farmer's fruit crops.
暮春結的霜損害到農夫水果的收成。

grim 〔 grɪm 〕 *adj.* 嚴肅的；恐怖的
——同 hideous , merciless , gruesome , ghastly , fierce
The ***grim*** truth was that only three of the two hundred
soldiers returned home to their families.
這恐怖的事實是兩百個士兵中，只有三人回到家中。

gusto 〔ˈɡʌsto 〕 *n.* 愛好；嗜好　——同 pleasure , zest , relish

Danny always eats his mother's Italian cooking with great *gusto*. 丹尼總是非常喜歡吃他母親做的義大利菜。

heathen 〔ˈhiðən 〕 *n.* 異教徒　——同 pagan , idolater

The missionaries felt it was their duty to convert the *heathens* to Christianity. 傳教士認爲，讓異教徒轉信基督教是他們的責任。

holocaust 〔ˈhaləˌkɔst 〕 *n.* 大破壞；屠殺

——同 disaster , conflagration , inferno , massacre , carnage

In today's world of terrorism, many people fear that a nuclear *holocaust* could occur.

在現在恐怖政治的世界裡，很多人擔心核子屠殺可能發生。

∗∗innuendo 〔ˌɪnjuˈɛndo 〕 *n.* 暗指；諷刺【最常考】

——同 insinuation , hint , overtone , implication

Everything she said about Ron seemed full of *innuendo*.

她談到朗恩的每一件事時，似乎都充滿了諷刺意味。

inverse 〔 ɪnˈvɝs , ˈɪnvɝs 〕 *n.* ; *adj.* 相反（的）　——同 (*n.*) opposition

The country's peaceful philosophy of coexistence was the *inverse* of the terrorists' ideals.

這國家的和平共存哲學和恐怖主義者的理想相反。

irreparable 〔 ɪˈrɛpərəbl̩ 〕 *adj.* 不能彌補的

——同 irrecoverable , irremediable , unfixable

The car accident had done *irreparable* damage to his left lung and it had to be removed.

車禍對他的左肺造成無法彌補的傷害，因此必須切除掉它。

loot 〔 lut 〕 *v.* 掠奪　——同 plunder , rob

The soldiers *looted* the stores and homes of the village they had just bombed. 士兵搶奪剛轟炸過的村落裡的商店和住家。

mellow 〔ˈmɛlo〕 *adj.* 成熟的 ——圓 ripe , mature

The pumpkins had grown ***mellow*** and were now ready for picking. 南瓜已經熟了，現在可以去採收。

mournful 〔ˈmornfḷ〕 *adj.* 悲傷的

——圓 tragic , woeful , grievous , sorrowful , sad

His ***mournful*** eyes told me that Heather had died.

他悲傷的眼神告訴我海德已經去世了。

oracle 〔ˈɔrəkḷ〕 *n.* 神諭

——圓 divine communication , revelation , augury , prophecy

The ancient Greeks relied heavily on ***oracles*** to help them make decisions.

古希臘人非常依賴神諭來替他們作決定。

Exercise 〉 *Fill in the blanks.*

1. They were afraid of the large gas tank _____ and sending poisonous gas throughout the area.

2. The _____ reality was that quicker international intervention could have prevented the Rwandan tragedy.

3. A number multiplied by its _____ proportion equals one.

4. Our family store was _____ by a gang of men toting guns.

5. The dog found its master dead and let out a long _____ howl.

【解答】 1. erupting   2. grim   3. inverse   4. looted   5. mournful

oral 〔ˈorəl〕 *adj.* 口頭的 ——同 verbal , spoken

Part of our Spanish class grade will be determined by an *oral* examination. 我們的西班牙文課有部分的成績以口試來決定。

plow 〔plaʊ〕 *v.* 耕作 ——同 till , cultivate , farm

After *plowing* the field, the farmer began to plant his crop.

耕過田之後，農夫開始種植穀物。

prescribe 〔prɪˈskraɪb〕 *v.* ①命令 ②開藥方

——同 1. command , impose , assign , dictate , order

Several of the political prisoners were *prescribed* to do hard labor for a period of time.

有幾個政治犯被命令去做苦工一段時間。

prosecute 〔ˈprɑsɪˌkjut〕 *v.* 起訴

——同 sue , try , bring to trial

The couple decided to *prosecute* their landlord for breaking their contract. 這對夫妻決定告他們的房東毀約。

ransom 〔ˈrænsəm〕 *n.* 贖金 ——同 redemption , release

The kidnappers demanded one million dollars for the little boy's *ransom*. 綁匪要求用一百萬元作為這個小男孩的贖金。

reimburse 〔ˌriɪmˈbɝs〕 *v.* 償還

——同 recompense , refund , pay back

If you lend me the money to buy the stereo, I will definitely *reimburse* you by next week.

如果你借我錢去買音響，我下個星期絕對會還給你。

*** rural** 〔ˈrʊrəl〕 *adj.* 鄉村的【常考】

——同 rustic , country , pastoral , agrarian

The pace of *rural* life is much slower than that of city life.

鄉村生活的步調要比城市生活慢很多。

* **segment**〔'sɛgmənt 〕 *n.* 部分【常考】

　—圓 division , portion , slice , compartment , section , wedge

Only a small ***segment*** of the student population showed interest in holding a school fair.

只有少部分學生有興趣舉辦學校義賣會。

slash〔 slæʃ 〕 *v.* 砍；削減　—圓 hack , cut , gash

The company ***slashed*** its workforce in half to keep from going bankrupt. 該公司裁撤了一半的勞工，以防止破產。

spiny〔'spaɪnɪ 〕 *adj.* 多刺的　—圓 prickly , thorny

Be careful not to touch the ***spiny*** sea urchins you see while you are swimming in the ocean. 　* urchin〔'ɝtʃɪn 〕 *n.* 海膽

當你在海邊游泳時，看到有刺的海膽小心不要碰到了。

stigma〔'stɪgmə 〕 *n.* 恥辱　—圓 disgrace , dishonor

There is not as much ***stigma*** attached to divorce as there was in the past. 現在離婚不像以前那麼丟臉。

supple〔'sʌpl̩ 〕 *adj.* 柔軟的

　—圓 limber , flexible , lithe , bending , pliable

To keep your leather belt ***supple***, you must rub this oil on it occasionally. 為了保持你的皮帶柔軟，必須偶爾在上面擦這種油。

therapeutic〔,θɛrə'pjutɪk 〕 *adj.* 治療的

　—圓 curative , healing , salutary , remedial , corrective

Jennifer does ***therapeutic*** exercises for her injured knee every morning. 每天早晨珍妮佛都為她受傷的膝蓋作復健運動。

trite〔 traɪt 〕 *adj.* 平凡的；陳腐的　—圓 banal , stale

The teacher is not going to accept the ***trite*** excuse that your dog ate your homework.

老師不會接受你的狗吃掉了作業這種陳腐的藉口。

* **utilitarian** 〔͵jutɪləˈtɛrɪən〕 *adj.* 實用的；功利的【常考】
—同 practical , pragmatic , useful , functional
The house he had designed was more ***utilitarian*** than beautiful. 他設計的房子是實用重於美觀。

* **vigilant** 〔ˈvɪdʒələnt〕 *adj.* 警戒的【常考】
—同 watchful , wary , alert
During the night, the doctor kept a ***vigilant*** watch over the patient. 在夜間，醫生仍保持警戒，看護著病人。

* **voracious** 〔voˈreʃəs〕 *adj.* 狼吞虎嚥的【常考】
—同 insatiable , gluttonous , ravenous , greedy
Tom kept eating and eating, unable to satisfy his ***voracious*** appetite. 湯姆一直不停地吃，似乎無法滿足他貪婪的食慾。

Exercise ⟩ *Fill in the blanks.*

1. The government ＿＿＿＿＿＿ that all citizens must carry ID cards with them at all times.

2. Joey still hasn't ＿＿＿＿＿＿ me the money I lent him.

3. He feared the ＿＿＿＿＿＿ of failure would haunt him for the rest of his life.

4. The dancer kept her muscles ＿＿＿＿＿＿ by stretching and practicing every day.

5. A ＿＿＿＿＿＿ watchdog is an excellent source of protection for your house.

【解答】1. prescribed　2. reimbursed　3. stigma　4. supple　5. vigilant

· List 27 · 難字分析

demolish 〔 dɪˈmɑlɪʃ 〕 *v.* 拆除

> de + mol + ish   —— to tear down
> | | |
> *down + heap + v.*

enactment 〔 ɪnˈæktmənt 〕 *n.* 制定

> en + act + ment   —— the act or practice of making (a law)
> | | |
> *in + act + n.*

exonerate 〔 ɪgˈzɑnəˌret 〕 *v.* 使無罪

> ex + oner + ate   —— to free from a charge
> | | |
> *out + burden + make*

holocaust 〔ˈhɑləˌkɔst 〕 *n.* 大破壞；屠殺

> holo + caust   —— great or total destruction of life
> | |
> *whole + burn*

irreparable 〔 ɪˈrɛpərəbl̩ 〕 *adj.* 不能彌補的

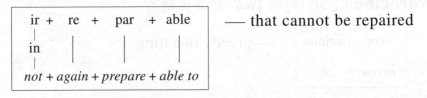

> ir + re + par + able   —— that cannot be repaired
> in
> *not + again + prepare + able to*

prescribe〔prɪˈskraɪb〕*v.* ①命令　②開藥方

> | pre | + | scribe |
> |-----|---|--------|
> | before | + | write |

— to set down or impose rules; to give something as a medicine for a sick person

prosecute〔ˈprɑsɪˌkjut〕*v.* 起訴

> | pro | + | secute |
> |-----|---|--------|
> | forth | + | follow |

— to start legal proceedings against

reimburse〔ˌriɪmˈbɝs〕*v.* 償還

> | re | + | im | + | burse |
> |----|---|----|---|-------|
> | back | + | into | + | bag |

— to pay back

utilitarian〔ˌjutɪləˈtɛrɪən〕*adj.* 實用的；功利的

> | util | + | itarian |
> |------|---|---------|
> | use | + | adj. |

— characterized by usefulness

vigilant〔ˈvɪdʒələnt〕*adj.* 警戒的

> | vig | + | il | + | ant |
> |-----|---|----|---|-----|
> | lively | + | n. | + | adj. |

— staying watchful, alert to danger or trouble

voracious〔voˈreʃəs〕*adj.* 狼吞虎嚥的

> | vor | + | acious |
> |-----|---|--------|
> | devour | + | adj. |

— greedy in eating

LIST ▶ 28

˚acumen 〔 ə'kjumɪn 〕 *n.* 明智【最常考】

—— 同 discernment , shrewdness

She was a woman of scientific ***acumen***, and won many awards in the field of physics.
她是個很有科學頭腦的女人，曾贏得許多物理方面的獎。

* **alleviate** 〔 ə'livɪˌet 〕 *v.* 使緩和【常考】

—— 同 allay , relieve , appease , assuage , moderate , mollify

This medicine should ***alleviate*** some of the pain from the operation.　這種藥應該能夠減輕一些手術所引起的疼痛。

* **anomalous** 〔 ə'nɑmələs 〕 *adj.* 異常的；不規則的【常考】

—— 同 abnormal , atypical , unusual , irregular , odd

Astronomers were baffled as to where the ***anomalous*** comet had come from.　天文學家對這顆怪異的彗星的來處，都感到不解。

appraise 〔 ə'prez 〕 *v.* 評估

—— 同 evaluate , estimate , assess , judge , rate , assay

Howard asked the jeweler to ***appraise*** the worth of the diamond.　霍華德請珠寶商評估鑽石的價值。

˚˚bizarre 〔 bɪ'zɑr 〕 *adj.* 怪異的【最常考】

—— 同 odd , eccentric , freakish

I found the artist's paintings to be ***bizarre***, but my artist friend found them inspired.　我覺得那位藝術家的畫很怪異，可是我那位也是藝術家的朋友卻覺得，那些畫非常好。

　＊inspired 〔 ɪn'spaɪrd 〕 *adj.* 有靈感的；非常好的

boost 〔 bust 〕 *v.* 提升　—— 同 promote , lift , hoist

The new commercials ***boosted*** sales of the new brand of clothes detergent.　這支新廣告提高了那種新品牌洗衣粉的銷售量。

brawl 〔 brɔl 〕 *v.* 爭吵 ——同 fight , quarrel
Teenage gangs ***brawled*** outside the video arcade until the police came. *＊video arcade* 電動玩具店
在電動玩具店外面有青少年幫派在爭吵，直到警察來才停止。

climax 〔ˊklaɪmæks 〕 *n.* 頂點；高潮
——同 apogee , acme , highlight
At the ***climax*** of the horror movie, everyone in the theater screamed. 在恐怖片的最高潮，戲院裡的觀眾都高聲尖叫。

＊**comply** 〔 kəmˊplaɪ 〕 *v.* 遵守；順從【常考】
——同 consent , conform
If you do not ***comply*** with company rules, you will be fired.
如果你不遵守公司的規定，你就會被解僱。

＊**constrict** 〔 kənˊstrɪkt 〕 *v.* 限制；壓抑【常考】
——同 contract , cramp , compress , bind , hamper
Many types of women's clothing ***constrict*** the movement of the wearer. 許多類型的女裝限制了穿著者的行動。

crisp 〔 krɪsp 〕 *adj.* 脆的 ——同 crispy , brittle , crumbly , crunchy
Laura enjoys eating a salad of ***crisp***, raw vegetables with her dinner. 蘿拉吃晚餐時，喜歡邊吃脆脆的生菜沙拉。

＊**culpable** 〔ˊkʌlpəbl̩ 〕 *adj.* 有罪的；該受譴責的【常考】
——同 guilty , blamable , liable , reprehensible , censurable
The court decided that the company was ***culpable*** for the injuries caused by their product.
法官判決這家公司有罪，因為他們的產品會造成傷害。

＊**denote** 〔 dɪˊnot 〕 *v.* 表示【常考】
——同 indicate , mean , signify , imply
In traditional Chinese opera, different color face paints ***denote*** different personality traits.
在平劇中，不同顏色的臉彩就代表不同的個性。

*discern 〔 dɪˈzɜn , -ˈsɜn 〕 *v.* 辨別【常考】

　——同 determine , distinguish , detect , discriminate

From the evidence the spy had collected, she could *discern*
where the enemy was hiding.

從那位間諜所收集的資料看來，她可以分辨出敵人藏身的地點。

doctrine 〔ˈdɑktrɪn 〕 *n.* 教義

　——同 creed , dogma , conviction , precept , teachings , belief

Each religion has its own *doctrine* which followers consider
sacred. 每一種宗教都有教徒們認為神聖的教條。

dribble 〔ˈdrɪbḷ 〕 *v.* 滴落

　——同 trickle , fall in drops , drip

As she fed the baby his lunch, he *dribbled* food on his bib,
his chair and the floor. 　＊bib 〔 bɪb 〕 *n.* 圍兜

當她餵嬰兒吃午餐的時候，他把食物滴在他的圍兜、椅子還有地板上。

Exercise ▷ *Fill in the blanks.*

1. Take time to relax to _____ the pressures of your
   daily life.

2. The boss _____ the employee's ability and decided
   how much he should get paid.

3. This book was written in an interesting style, with the
   _____ at the beginning of the story rather than the end.

4. This lettuce is deliciously _____ and fresh.

5. The ancient lettering on the coin was so faint that we
   could barely _____ the words.

【解答】1. alleviate　2. appraised　3. climax　4. crisp　5. discern

* **endeavor** 〔 ɪn'dɛvɚ 〕 *n.* 盡力【常考】　——同 effort , try
Roger felt he would succeed in his ***endeavor*** to become the first person to visit Mars.
羅傑覺得他的努力一定會成功，他將成為第一位登陸火星的人。

escalate 〔'ɛskə‚let 〕 *v.* 升高；增強　——同 intensify
Fighting between a few rival gangs ***escalated*** to a full "turf war" in only a few months.
一些敵對幫派的打鬥，在幾個月之內就演變成全面的「地盤爭奪戰」。

* **exotic** 〔 ɪg'zɑtɪk 〕 *adj.* 外來的；有異國風味的【常考】
——同 alien , foreign , imported , external , extraneous
Helen had never eaten foreign food, and the idea of eating Indian food seemed ***exotic*** and exciting to her.　海倫未曾吃過外國食物，所以想到要吃印度菜，就令她覺得充滿異國情調與興奮。

** **extract** 〔 ɪk'strækt 〕 *v.* 抽出【最常考】　——同 draw , pull , pluck out
The dentist had to ***extract*** a rotten tooth from Mr. Liu's mouth.
牙醫必須幫劉先生拔出一顆蛀牙。

* **fidelity** 〔 faɪ'dɛlətɪ 〕 *n.* 忠實；逼真【常考】
——同 faithfulness , devotion
Janet's ***fidelity*** to the cause of children's rights was admirable.
珍娜十分忠於兒童福利的運動，令人十分欽佩。
* cause 〔 kɔz 〕 *n.* 目標；運動

fitting 〔'fɪtɪŋ 〕 *adj.* 適當的；適合的　——同 appropriate , suitable
It was ***fitting*** that their wedding took place on the anniversary of the day they met.
他們的婚禮在他們相識的週年紀念日舉行是很適當的。

frothy 〔'frɔθɪ , 'frɑθɪ 〕 *adj.* 起泡沫的　——同 foamy , sudsy , spumy
The last time I saw Kelly, she was inside the restaurant sipping on a ***frothy*** milkshake.
上一次我看到凱莉時，她正在餐廳裡喝著泡沫奶昔。

grope 〔 grop 〕 *v.* 摸索 ——同 feel , fumble
After their flashlights burned out, they had to ***grope*** their way out of the cave.
在手電筒熄滅之後，他們必須摸索地走出那個洞穴。

* **homogeneous** 〔ˌhoməˈdʒɪnɪəs 〕 *adj.* 同質的【常考】
——同 uniform , identical , consistent , akin , kindred , analogous
The students at the school looked quite ***homogeneous*** wearing their school uniforms. 學校的學生穿上制服後看起來都差不多。

hubbub 〔ˈhʌbʌb 〕 *n.* 吵鬧聲 ——同 tumult , uproar
Mona loves the ***hubbub*** of big cities like New York.
夢娜喜歡嘈雜的大都市，像是紐約。

imbue 〔 ɪmˈbju 〕 *v.* 灌輸 ——同 saturate , influence thoroughly
Scott's father had ***imbued*** him with a love of learning.
史考特的父親灌輸他對學習的愛好。

* **improvise** 〔ˈɪmprəˌvaɪz , ˌɪmprəˈvaɪz 〕 *v.* 即席而作【常考】
——同 ad-lib , extemporize , play it by ear , speak off the cuff
In a live performance, if something goes wrong on stage, the actors must ***improvise***.
現場表演時，如果在舞台上出錯，演員就必須作即席的表演。

iniquity 〔 ɪˈnɪkwətɪ 〕 *n.* 邪惡 ——同 wickedness , sin , evil
After the man who had killed her brother was found not guilty, Fran hated society for its ***iniquity***.
當那位殺死她哥哥的兇手被判無罪後，法蘭就非常痛恨這邪惡的社會。

* **isolate** 〔ˈaɪsḷˌet 〕 *v.* 使孤立【常考】 ——同 segregate , insulate
Patients suffering from the strange virus were ***isolated*** in a separate wing of the hospital.
感染奇怪病毒的病人，被隔離在醫院獨立的一側。

memorandum 〔͵mɛmə'rændəm 〕 *n.* 備忘錄；便條

——同 memo , note

The company president sent a ***memorandum*** to all departments announcing the opening of a new branch.

公司總裁寄給所有部門一張便條，宣布新的分公司已開張。

muffle 〔'mʌfl̩ 〕 *v.* ①覆蓋 ②降低 (聲音)

——同 1. envelop , mask , wrap up , cloak 2. deaden , hush , quieten

She tried to ***muffle*** the ringing of her alarm clock by putting it under her pillow.

她把鬧鐘放在枕頭下，想降低它的鈴聲。

orbit 〔'ɔrbɪt 〕 *n.* 軌道　——同 course , path , track

Who was the first scientist to plot the ***orbit*** of the earth around the sun?　第一位畫出地球繞太陽的軌道的科學家是誰？

Exercise ▷ *Fill in the blanks.*

1. Donald fails in every _____ he undertakes.

2. _____ oil from the ocean floor is a very complicated and delicate operation.

3. American society is not _____, but a blend of peoples and cultures.

4. "What is all this _____ about?" asked the teacher when she entered the classroom.

5. Doctors in Africa have not yet _____ the source of the Ebola virus.

【解答】1. endeavor　2. Extracting　3. homogeneous　4. hubbub　5. isolated

peril (ˈpɛrəl) *n.* 危險 ——同 danger , hazard , insecurity

Stunt people put themselves in *peril* as a regular part of their jobs. 特技演員把置身於危險當作是日常工作的一部分。

pledge (plɛdʒ) *n.* 保證 ——同 promise , security , vow

Give me your *pledge* that you will not tell anyone else this secret. 你得向我保證不會告訴別人這個秘密。

* **preserve** (prɪˈzɝv) *v.* 保存【常考】

——同 keep , secure , maintain , retain , sustain , conserve

To *preserve* the dinosaur bones, the scientists coated them with special chemicals.

為了要保存恐龍的骨頭，科學家在骨頭上塗上特別的化學藥品。

protagonist (proˈtægənɪst) *n.* 主角

——同 central character , hero , heroine , leading character

Pauline did not like that novel because she could not identify with its *protagonist*.

寶琳不喜歡那部小說，因為她無法認同裡面的主角。

* **reiterate** (riˈɪtəˌret) *v.* 重申【常考】 ——同 repeat , iterate

Let me *reiterate* to you the importance of keeping a small fire extinguisher in your home.

我再向你重覆一次，家裡放個小型滅火器是十分重要的。

respiration (ˌrɛspəˈreʃən) *n.* 呼吸 ——同 breathing

To improve my aunt's *respiration*, the doctor suggested she move to a drier, warmer climate. 為了要改善我姑媽的呼吸情況，醫生建議她搬到氣候較乾、較溫暖的地方。

rustle (ˈrʌsḷ) *v.* 發出沙沙聲 ——同 crackle , swish

As we walked through the woods, the fallen leaves *rustled* with each step we made.

當我們走過森林時，每走一步，地上的落葉就會發出沙沙聲。

sensational 〔 sɛn'seʃən̩ 〕 *adj.* 轟動的

—同 exciting , startling , striking , amazing , dramatic , shocking

Benjamin could hardly believe the **sensational** results of the mayoral election.

班傑明幾乎無法相信市長選舉這種令人驚訝的結果。

slaughter 〔'slɔtɚ 〕 *v.* 屠殺　—同 massacre , butcher , slay

Foreign troops had viciously **slaughtered** many of the villagers. 外國部隊殘忍地屠殺許多村民。

* **spiral** 〔'spaɪrəl 〕 *adj.* 螺旋的【常考】　—同 coiled , winding

In the middle of the room was a **spiral** staircase that led to an outdoor patio. *patio 〔'patɪˌo 〕 *n.* 戶外的陽台

在房間的中間有一個螺旋形樓梯，通往戶外的陽台。

* **stimulate** 〔'stɪmjəˌlet 〕 *v.* 刺激【常考】　—同 incite , provoke

Problems of pollution have **stimulated** people to consider jobs in environmental management.

污染的問題刺激人們思考環境處理的工作。

swell 〔 swɛl 〕 *v.* 膨脹　—同 expand , dilate , bulge

The wound on Eric's arm became infected and started to **swell**.

艾瑞克手臂的傷口受到感染，而且開始腫起來了。

thoroughfare 〔'θɝoˌfɛr 〕 *n.* 街道　—同 avenue , street

Many interesting and beautiful shops line the main **thoroughfare** of the city.

許多有趣而美麗的商店，成排地位於該市的大街上。

* **trivial** 〔'trɪvɪəl 〕 *adj.* 瑣碎的【常考】　—同 trifling , insignificant

Larry was very self-important and felt that other people's problems were **trivial** compared to his own. 賴瑞總覺得自己

非常重要，認為其他人的問題和他的比起來，十分微不足道。

* **utopia** 〔 ju'topɪə 〕 *n.* 烏托邦；理想國【常考】
—— 同 bliss , heaven , ideal life , paradise , perfect place , Eden
There have been many books written about what people think
a future *utopia* might be like.
有許多書描寫人類對於未來烏托邦的看法。

vigorous 〔'vɪgərəs 〕 *adj.* 充滿活力的
—— 同 active , brisk , dynamic , energetic , lively , lusty , vital
The doctor prescribed *vigorous* exercise three times a week
for my father. 醫生指示我的父親，必須一週做三次有活力的運動。

vow 〔 vaʊ 〕 *n.* 誓約　 —— 同 promise , pledge , oath , troth
Catholic priests take *vows* of celibacy and poverty.
天主教神父立誓要獨身與貧苦。　 * celibacy 〔'sɛləbəsɪ 〕 *n.* 獨身

Exercise 〉 *Fill in the blanks.*

1. The many _____ of life in Bosnia were not enough to
   make her leave her motherland.

2. The lawyer _____ her demand that the charges against
   her client be dropped.

3. The teacher could not _____ the interest of her
   apathetic students.

4. Anne believed Gordon's interest in the _____ matters
   of other people's lives was intrusive.

5. Her _____ lifestyle keeps her feeling young and
   healthy.

【解答】 1. perils　 2. reiterated　 3. stimulate　 4. trivial　 5. vigorous

┌ List 28 ┐ 難字分析

alleviate 〔 ə'livɪ,et 〕 *v.* 使緩和

```
al + lev + iate        —— to make less hard to bear
 |     |     |
ad     |     |
 |     |     |
to + light + make
```

culpable 〔 'kʌlpəbḷ 〕 *adj.* 有罪的；該受譴責的

```
culp + able           —— deserving blame
  |     |
blame + able to
```

escalate 〔 'ɛskə,let 〕 *v.* 升高；增強

```
e + scal + ate        —— to intensify by successive stages
 |    |     |
× + ladder + v.
```

homogeneous 〔 ,homə'dʒinɪəs 〕 *adj.* 同質的

```
homo + gene + ous      —— of the same kind
  |      |     |
same + race + adj.
```

improvise 〔 'ɪmprə,vaɪz , ,ɪmprə'vaɪz 〕 *v.* 即席而作

```
im + pro + vise        —— to produce without preparation
 |    |     |
not + before + see
```

iniquity〔ɪˈnɪkwətɪ〕*n.* 邪惡

in + iqu + ity
| | |
not + equal + n. —— lack of righteousness or justice

memorandum〔ˌmɛməˈrændəm〕*n.* 備忘錄；便條

memor + and + um
| end |
remember + to be done + n. —— a short note written to help one remember something

protagonist〔proˈtægənɪst〕*n.* 主角

prot(o) + agon + ist
| | |
first + struggle + person —— chief person in a story or event

respiration〔ˌrɛspəˈreʃən〕*n.* 呼吸

re + spir + ation
| | |
again + breathe + n. —— breathing

thoroughfare〔ˈθɝoˌfɛr〕*n.* 街道

thorough + fare
| |
through + go —— a street esp. one much used by traffic and open at both ends

TEST ▶ 14

請由 (A)～(D) 中選出和畫線部分意義最相近的字。

1. Nick was lucky he was only <u>bruised</u> slightly in the car accident.
   - (A) maimed
   - (B) injured
   - (C) decapitated
   - (D) paralyzed

2. The <u>allegory</u> about the race between the turtle and the hare teaches the value of patience and persistence.
   - (A) poem
   - (B) autobiography
   - (C) fable
   - (D) dictation

3. Hunters had left the deer's <u>carcass</u> to rot after shooting it in the forest.
   - (A) antlers
   - (B) corpse
   - (C) offspring
   - (D) footprints

4. One month after the old school building was condemned, it was <u>demolished</u>.
   - (A) torn down
   - (B) build up
   - (C) thrown over
   - (D) made up

5. Environmentalists celebrated the <u>enactment</u> of a land and water protection law.
   - (A) repeal
   - (B) discussion
   - (C) passing
   - (D) possibility

6. Many people believe that the <u>holocaust</u> in Rwanda could have been stopped with international intervention.
   - (A) mission
   - (B) insurrection
   - (C) manipulation
   - (D) massacre

7. We love to go to baseball games and root for our favorite team with <u>gusto</u>.
   - (A) hatred
   - (B) purpose
   - (C) meditation
   - (D) enthusiasm

8. The air in <u>rural</u> areas surrounding the city is much cleaner than in the city itself.
   - (A) industrial
   - (B) municipal
   - (C) urban
   - (D) country

9. Due to her mechanical <u>acumen</u>, Anne had the television set fixed in no time.

   (A) cleverness
   (B) research
   (C) prominence
   (D) training

10. Peter's <u>voracious</u> appetite made him put on weight quickly.

    (A) concerned
    (B) tempered
    (C) minimal
    (D) insatiable

11. Many storekeepers are too afraid to <u>prosecute</u> the thieves because they fear Mafia retaliation.

    (A) identify
    (B) try
    (C) negotiate
    (D) accept

12. A <u>memorandum</u> on the bulletin board reminded employees of a meeting on Friday.

    (A) package
    (B) note
    (C) computer
    (D) receipt

13. The queen's guards have given their <u>pledge</u> to defend her to the death.

    (A) vow
    (B) compromise
    (C) bet
    (D) hope

14. Our company's confidence was <u>boosted</u> by winning the product excellence award.

    (A) leveled
    (B) lifted
    (C) modified
    (D) thrown

15. Students who do not <u>comply</u> with the school dress code will be sent home.

    (A) recognize
    (B) encourage
    (C) obey
    (D) protest

16. The architect proposed a <u>utilitarian</u> design for the town center in order to develop it into a public gathering place.

    (A) aesthetic
    (B) minimal
    (C) functional
    (D) legal

17. Alex looked at the travel brochures describing trips to <u>exotic</u> locations.

    (A) boring
    (B) justified
    (C) local
    (D) foreign

18. In the blackout, everyone <u>groped</u> to find candles and flashlights.

    (A) slid
    (B) jumped
    (C) fumbled
    (D) ran

19. A white cord worn around a graduate's neck <u>denotes</u> that person is graduating with honors.

   (A) indicates
   (B) ensures
   (C) preaches
   (D) foretells

20. We were very confused by the apparent lack of a <u>protagonist</u> in his novel.

   (A) main plot
   (B) central character
   (C) prevailing theme
   (D) reasonable ending

21. In fall, the apples are <u>mellow</u> and juicy.

   (A) oversized
   (B) rotten
   (C) ripe
   (D) young

22. Barry's idea of <u>utopia</u> is a small house on the shore where he can go fishing every day of the year.

   (A) boredom
   (B) heaven
   (C) sufficiency
   (D) rest

23. When the actor suddenly forgot his lines in the middle of the play, he had to <u>improvise</u> his lines.

   (A) remember
   (B) ad-lib
   (C) mime
   (D) delete

24. Our house is located on one of the city's large <u>thoroughfares</u>.

   (A) streets
   (B) parks
   (C) buildings
   (D) corners

25. The children examined the <u>spiral</u> shell of the snail.

   (A) perpendicular
   (B) triangular
   (C) coiled
   (D) oblong

【解答】

1. B	2. C	3. B	4. A	5. C	6. D	7. D	8. D	9. A	10. D
11. B	12. B	13. A	14. B	15. C	16. C	17. D	18. C	19. A	20. B
21. C	22. B	23. B	24. A	25. C					

📋 **LIST ▸ 29**

* **acute** 〔 ə'kjut 〕 *adj.* 敏銳的【常考】 ——同 shrewd , sharp , astute

Because of their ***acute*** sense of smell, dogs are often used to search for runaway criminals.

由於狗的嗅覺十分敏銳，所以常被用來尋找逃脫的罪犯。

alliance 〔 ə'laɪəns 〕 *n.* 同盟；合作

——同 connection , league , partnership , union , association

A special trade ***alliance*** was forged between the two countries.

這兩國之間訂定了一個特殊的貿易聯盟。

* forge 〔 fɔrdʒ 〕 *v.* 訂出

** **apprehensive** 〔 ˌæprɪ'hɛnsɪv 〕 *adj.* 憂慮的【最常考】

——同 afraid , anxious , fearful , uneasy , concerned

Mandy is ***apprehensive*** about skydiving for the first time.

曼蒂第一次高空跳傘時十分恐懼。

audacious 〔 ɔ'deʃəs 〕 *adj.* 大膽的；無禮的

——同 bold , daring , impudent , impertinent , insolent

It was very ***audacious*** for the reporter to criticize the Queen of England to her face. 那位記者十分大膽，竟當面批評英國女皇。

bleach 〔 blitʃ 〕 *v.* 漂白；變白

——同 blanch , whiten , wash out , lighten

The sun had ***bleached*** the red curtains to a light pink.

陽光使得紅色窗簾顏色變白，成爲淡淡的粉紅色。

* **bleak** 〔 blik 〕 *adj.* 荒涼的【常考】 ——同 desolate , barren , bare

After automobiles became popular, many small towns along railroad tracks became ***bleak*** and empty.

汽車普及之後，火車沿線的小鎮都變得十分荒涼而且空無一人。

boundless ﹝'baʊndlɪs﹞ *adj.* 無窮的 ——同 endless , infinite
A kindergarten teacher needs ***boundless*** energy to keep up with the students. 幼稚園老師需要無窮的體力，才能應付學生。

* **cling** ﹝klɪŋ﹞ *v.* 黏著【常考】 ——同 stick , hold , cleave
The small pieces of paper ***cling*** to the comb because of static electricity. 由於靜電的緣故，那些小紙片都黏在梳子上。

* **component** ﹝kəm'ponənt﹞ *n.* 成份【常考】
——同 ingredient , element , constituent , segment , unit
Excellent customer service is one ***component*** of that company's success.
該公司之所以能夠成功，良好的顧客服務是因素之一。

contagious ﹝kən'tedʒəs﹞ *adj.* 傳染性的
——同 infectious , spreading , communicable , epidemic , transmissible
The common cold is very ***contagious***, so you should try to wash your hands frequently.
一般的感冒是非常具有傳染性的，所以你應該經常洗手。

** **criterion** ﹝kraɪ'tɪrɪən﹞ *n.* 準繩【最常考】
——同 standard , principle , norm , measure , yardstick , rule
Is there any ***criterion*** students must meet to apply to this graduate program? 要申請研究生課程的學生，必須具備什麼資格嗎？

cult ﹝kʌlt﹞ *n.* 教派 ——同 sect , clique , faction
Followers of the strange ***cult*** came from all walks of life.
這個奇怪的教派，其信徒來自各行各業。

default ﹝dɪ'fɔlt﹞ *v.* 不履行 ——同 neglect , back out , disregard
George ***defaulted*** on their agreement and Laura took him to court to get her money back.
喬治不履行合約，所以蘿拉帶他上法院，要回她的錢。

**denounce 〔 dɪ'naʊns 〕 *v.* 譴責【最常考】

——同 attack , censure , condemn , declaim , stigmatize , criticize

Students ***denounced*** the college president for his racist remarks. 學生譴責大學校長，因為他說了一些含種族歧視的話。

disown 〔 dɪs'on , dɪz- 〕 *v.* 否認

——同 disavow , reject , deny , refuse to recognize

The father has told his daughter he will ***disown*** her if she marries a non-Chinese.

父親告訴自己的女兒，如果她嫁的不是中國人，就不承認她這個女兒。

*drill 〔 drɪl 〕 *v.* ; *n.* 訓練【常考】　　——同 exercise , practice , quiz

The teacher ***drilled*** the students on the English lesson they had studied the night before.

老師給學生小考，測驗他們前一天晚上所唸的英文。

Exercise 〉 *Fill in the blanks.*

1. Henry is ＿＿＿＿＿＿ about traveling to a foreign country for the first time.

2. The ＿＿＿＿＿＿ landscape of the desert has a unique kind of beauty.

3. The store did not carry any of the stereo ＿＿＿＿＿＿ I was interested in buying.

4. The bank was ＿＿＿＿＿＿ for its policy of not loaning to the poor.

5. Our class was ＿＿＿＿＿＿ by the teacher on past-tense verbs yesterday.

【解答】1. apprehensive　2. bleak　3. components　4. denounced　5. drilled

endemic 〔 ɛn'dɛmɪk 〕 *adj.* 當地的 ——同 local , native
Taiwan has several unique plants and animals *endemic* only to the island. 台灣有好幾種當地特有的動植物。

essay 〔 'ɛse 〕 *n.* 散文；論文 ——同 paper , article
Jane's *essay* is about the effects of pollution on the parks in the city. 珍的論文，是有關污染對都市公園所造成的影響。

＊expedient 〔 ɪk'spidɪənt 〕 *adj.* 方便的；有利的【最常考】
——同 convenient , utilitarian , advantageous , beneficial , helpful
We must find the most *expedient* way to distribute food to the famine victims.
我們必須找出最便利的方法，把食物分給饑荒的人。

＊extraneous 〔 ɪk'strenɪəs , ɛk- 〕 *adj.* 不相關的【常考】
——同 irrelevant , extrinsic , incidental , immaterial , inessential
We must focus on solving the problem without worrying about *extraneous* details.
我們必須專心解決問題，而不要去擔心那些無關緊要的細節。

flaw 〔 flɔ 〕 *n.* ①裂痕 ②缺點
——同 1. crack , break , cleft , rift 2. fault , defect , weakness
A *flaw* in the supporting column of the rapid transit line caused concern. 捷運線樑柱的裂痕已引起大家關切。

frugal 〔 'frugḷ 〕 *adj.* 節儉的 ——同 economical , thrifty
My grandmother is very *frugal* and throws almost nothing away. 我的祖母非常節儉，幾乎所有的東西都捨不得丟。

grotesque 〔 gro'tɛsk 〕 *adj.* 怪誕的；可笑的
——同 bizarre , absurd , freakish , odd , weird , whimsical
The townspeople believed a *grotesque* monster lived under the bridge. 鎮民相信橋下住了個怪物。

hamlet (ˈhæmlɪt) *n.* 小村 ──同 small village , burg

Our train passed through several ***hamlets*** before finally
reaching our destination.

我們的火車在抵達目的地之前行經好幾座村莊。

* **hostile** (ˈhɑstḷ , -tɪl) *adj.* 有敵意的【常考】

──同 antagonistic , opposed , contrary

Race relations have grown very ***hostile*** in the United States.

在美國，種族關係已經變得十分敵對。

imprudent (ɪmˈprudn̩t) *adj.* 不明智的 ──同 unwise

It would be ***imprudent*** to challenge the strongest kid in the
school to a fight. 向學校裡最強壯的小孩單挑打架，是不明智的。

* **initiate** (ɪˈnɪʃɪˌet) *v.* 開始【常考】 ──同 begin , commence

The university ***initiated*** a special program for foreign students
to study English.

這所大學為想學英語的外籍生開立了特殊的課程。

inveterate (ɪnˈvɛtərɪt) *adj.* 積習的；慢性的

──同 chronic , deep-rooted , long-standing , entrenched , established

It is difficult to change the ***inveterate*** sexism of our society.

要改變社會上存在已久的性別歧視的現象，是非常困難的。

* **itinerant** (aɪˈtɪnərənt , ɪˈtɪn-) *adj.* 巡迴的【常考】

──同 wandering

Itinerant theater groups come through our town every once
in a while and give a performance.

巡迴劇團偶爾會到我們的小鎮來表演。

** **lucid** (ˈlusɪd , ˈlɪu-) *adj.* ①清澈的 ②易了解的【最常考】

──同 1. transparent , limpid 2. rational , reasonable

She was tempted to drink the ***lucid*** water of the mountain
stream. 她情不自禁地喝了山川裡清澈的水。

ludicrous 〔'ludɪkrəs , 'lɪu- 〕 *adj.* 滑稽的【最常考】

——同 ridiculous , funny , farcical , absurd , laughable , amusing

Peter thought his teacher would believe his *ludicrous* story about aliens stealing his homework.
彼得認爲老師會相信他滑稽的故事，是外星人偷走他的作業。

menace 〔'mɛnɪs 〕 *v.* 威脅

——同 threaten , terrorize , frighten , browbeat , intimidate

The Ebola virus is *menacing* several countries in central Africa. 依波拉病毒正威脅中非好幾個國家。

menial 〔'minɪəl 〕 *adj.* 低賤的

——同 mean , low , servile , humble , ignoble , abject

The women in the farming community had to do the most *menial* tasks. 農業社會的婦女必須做些最低賤的工作。

Exercise　*Fill in the blanks.*

1. This type of herb is very expensive, so be very _____ when using it.

2. Many newly graduated young people find the work environment more _____ than they expected.

3. Any _____ move by the soldiers would cause the enemy to attack.

4. "You look absolutely _____ wearing that purple and orange tuxedo," Jane told Rex.

5. Foreigners were hired to do the _____ work in rich households.

【解答】 1. frugal　2. hostile　3. imprudent　4. ludicrous　5. menial

oration 〔 oˋreʃən 〕 *n.* 演說　——同 speech , address

An English ***oration*** contest was held by the English department in that university. 那所大學的英文系舉辦一場英語演講比賽。

ordeal 〔 orˋdil , ˋɔrdil 〕 *n.* 嚴格的考驗

——同 trial , experience , test , tribulation

Living through two years of war was an ***ordeal*** that Sonia would never be able to forget.

歷經兩年的戰爭，是桑妮亞永難忘懷的嚴酷考驗。

perjury 〔ˋpɝdʒərɪ 〕 *n.* 僞證罪　——同 giving false testimony

After lying in court, Edward was charged with ***perjury*** and thrown in jail. 愛德華在法庭上說謊後，被控以僞證罪而入獄。

* **pliable** 〔ˋplaɪəbl̩ 〕 *adj.* ①易彎曲的　②柔順的【常考】

——同 1. flexible , pliant　2. docile , tractable

Because plastic is ***pliable*** but strong, it is now being used to make car bodies.

因爲塑膠易彎曲而且又堅固，現在已被用來製造車身。

** **provisional** 〔 prəˋvɪʒənl̩ 〕 *adj.* 暫時的【最常考】

——同 temporary

A ***provisional*** government was set up to rule until the elections could be carried out. 在選舉實施前，成立了臨時政府來治理事務。

* **relatively** 〔ˋrɛlətɪvlɪ 〕 *adv.* 相對地【常考】

——同 comparatively , by comparison , rather , somewhat

After the elections, the city council became ***relatively*** more conservative. 選舉後，市議會變得相當地保守。

restrain 〔 rɪˋstren 〕 *v.* 限制　——同 constrain , restrict , limit

The police ***restrained*** the suspect with a pair of handcuffs.

警方用手銬限制嫌疑犯的行動。

ruthless 〔ˈruθlɪs〕 *adj.* 無情的

—— 同 merciless , pitiless , heartless , cruel , brutal

The king was ***ruthless*** in his treatment of the poor peasants.
國王對貧窮的農夫十分無情。

senseless 〔ˈsɛnslɪs〕 *adj.* ①不省人事的 ②無意義的

—— 同 1. numb, unconscious, insensible 2. absurd, illogical, irrational

Mr. Chen will not change his mind and it is ***senseless*** to
argue with him. 陳先生不會改變心意，和他爭論是毫無意義的。

slender 〔ˈslɛndɚ〕 *adj.* 苗條的 —— 同 slim , lank , tenuous , slight

After his illness, the child's frame had grown weak and
slender. 那孩子生完病之後，身體就變得十分虛弱而且削瘦。

＊frame 〔frem〕 *n.* 體格

splendor 〔ˈsplɛndɚ〕 *n.* 壯觀 —— 同 magnificence , grandeur

Everyone was captivated by the ***splendor*** of the royal
wedding. 大家都被壯觀的皇室婚禮所吸引。

＊captivate 〔ˈkæptəˌvet〕 *v.* 使著迷

suffrage 〔ˈsʌfrɪdʒ〕 *n.* 投票；同意 —— 同 vote

Women in the United States did not receive ***suffrage*** until
1920. 美國的婦女直到一九二〇年才有投票權。

＊**suppress** 〔səˈprɛs〕 *v.* 壓制【常考】

—— 同 quell , subdue , hold back , keep down , squash , squelch

The government ***suppressed*** the student demonstration by
sending in soldiers and tanks.
政府派出士兵與坦克，鎮壓學生的示威運動。

＊**thrive** 〔θraɪv〕 *v.* 興盛【常考】

—— 同 flourish , prosper , bloom , boom , burgeon , mushroom

This kind of plant ***thrives*** in a warm, rainy climate.
這種植物在溫暖多雨的氣候下會長得很茂盛。

trophy 〔'trofɪ 〕 *n.* 戰利品；獎品

——同 award , prize , laurels , memento , souvenir , remembrance

For winning the marathon, Louis was awarded a small silver *trophy*. 路易士贏了馬拉松比賽，獲頒一座小小的銀色獎盃。

virile 〔'vɪrəl , 'vaɪrəl 〕 *adj.* 男性的

——同 masculine , manly , manlike , male , macho , robust

Alice and Janet looked at the *virile* young man who had just walked into the bar.

愛麗絲和珍娜注視著那位剛剛走進酒吧，很有男子氣概的年輕人。

vulgar 〔'vʌlgɚ 〕 *adj.* 粗俗的

——同 uncouth , crude , coarse , unrefined , gross

The bathroom walls were covered with *vulgar* words and sayings. 浴室的牆壁上寫滿了粗俗的話和詞句。

Exercise *Fill in the blanks.*

1. The two sides agreed to a _____ cease-fire until a treaty could be drafted.

2. The company's _____ policy of firing less productive workers made it successful but not respected.

3. She _____ her urge to talk back to her boss and went back to her desk.

4. The children are _____ in the environment of the experimental school.

5. He was a _____ man whom we all found very disgusting.

【解答】1. provisional　2. ruthless　3. suppressed　4. thriving　5. vulgar

· List 29 · 難字分析

apprehensive 〔͵æprɪˋhɛnsɪv 〕 *adj.* 憂慮的

ap + prehens + ive
ad | |
to + seize + adj.

—— uneasy

contagious 〔 kənˋtedʒəs 〕 *adj.* 傳染性的

con + tag + ious
| | |
together + touch + adj.

—— spreading by contact

criterion 〔 kraɪˋtɪrɪən 〕 *n.* 準繩

crit + erion
| |
judge + n.

—— a standard by which something can be judged

endemic 〔 ɛnˋdɛmɪk 〕 *adj.* 當地的

en + dem + ic
| | |
in + people + adj.

—— native to a particular region

expedient 〔 ɪkˋspidɪənt 〕 *adj.* 方便的；有利的

ex + ped + ient
| | |
out + foot + adj.

—— useful or helpful for a purpose

grotesque 〔 gro'tɛsk 〕 *adj.* 怪誕的；可笑的

grot + esque
grotto + in the manner of

— strange and unnatural so as to cause fear or be laughable

initiate 〔 ɪ'nɪʃɪˌet 〕 *v.* 開始

in + it + iate
into + go + v.

— to bring into practice or use

itinerant 〔 aɪ'tɪnərənt , ɪ'tɪn- 〕 *adj.* 巡迴的

itiner + ant
journey + adj.

— traveling from place to place

perjury 〔'pɝdʒərɪ 〕 *n.* 偽證罪

per + jur + y
over + swear + n.

— the willful telling of a lie while under lawful oath

provisional 〔 prə'vɪʒənḷ 〕 *adj.* 暫時的

pro + vis + ion + al
before + see + n. + adj.

— for the present time only, with the strong probability of being changed

suffrage 〔'sʌfrɪdʒ 〕 *n.* 投票；同意

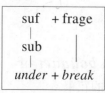

— the right to vote in national elections

LIST ▶ 30

* adept 〔 ə'dɛpt , 'ædʒpt 〕 *adj.* 熟練的【常考】

——同 skillful , proficient , masterful , expert , dexterous

Monica is a very ***adept*** swimmer, and she is considering going to the Olympics to compete.

莫妮卡很擅長游泳，並且考慮要到奧運會去比賽。

⁑ allocate 〔 'ælə,ket 〕 *v.* 分配【最常考】

——同 distribute , apportion , allot , assign , dispense

Government funds were ***allocated*** to all the schools in the district. 這地區的所有學校都分配到政府的資金。

appropriation 〔 ə,proprɪ'eʃən 〕 *n.* 撥款

——同 funding , allocation , allotment

The planned city library will not be built without an ***appropriation*** of public funds.

要是公家沒有撥款，籌畫中的市立圖書館就不會興建了。

audible 〔 'ɔdəbl̩ 〕 *adj.* 聽得見的

——同 hearable , detectable , perceptible , discernible

The music from the party was ***audible*** throughout the entire neighborhood. 鄰近地方都聽得到派對的音樂。

* blemish 〔 'blɛmɪʃ 〕 *n.* 污點【常考】 ——同 smudge , blur , spot

No one would buy the bananas because of their dark ***blemishes***. 沒有人要買香蕉，因為上面有黑點。

bouquet 〔 bu'ke , bo'ke 〕 *n.* 花束

——同 wreath , bunch of flowers , garland

In Western weddings, the bride often carries a ***bouquet*** of beautiful flowers. 在西式婚禮中，新娘常捧著漂亮的花束。

* **breeze**〔briz〕*n.* 微風【常考】　——同 zephyr , gust , whiff
A pleasant *breeze* blew in through the bedroom window.
怡人的微風從臥房的窗口吹了進來。

* **candid**〔'kændɪd〕*adj.* 坦白的【常考】
　——同 sincere , honest , guileless , impartial , unprejudiced
Randy asked to hear our *candid* opinion of the play he had
written.　關於他所寫的劇本，倫迪想聽我們坦白說出自己的看法。

* **comprise**〔kəm'praɪz〕*v.* 包括【常考】　——同 include , contain
Each team was *comprised* of ten athletes who would
compete in various events.
每個隊伍都包括了十名運動員，他們將在不同的項目裡競爭。

contaminate〔kən'tæmə,net〕*v.* 污染
　——同 pollute , defile , taint , soil , vitiate , tarnish
The city's drinking water was *contaminated* with chemicals
dumped into the water supply.
化學廢料被傾倒在供水處，污染了城市的飲用水。

* **critique**〔krɪ'tik〕*n.* 評論【常考】
　——同 appraisal , assessment , commentary , review
The magazine published a *critique* of American foreign
policy.　這雜誌刊載了一篇美國外交政策的評論。

** **cumbersome**〔'kʌmbəsəm〕*adj.* 累贅的；笨重的【最常考】
　——同 burdensome , heavy , weighty , bulky , inconvenient
Scientists wonder how the *cumbersome* stones used to build
the ancient pyramids were moved without machines.
科學家們好奇這些被用來蓋古金字塔的笨重石頭，沒有機器要怎麼移動。

* **dense**〔dɛns〕*adj.* 密集的【常考】　——同 condensed , close , thick
The population of Taipei is almost as *dense* as that of
Tokyo.　台北的人口幾乎和東京一樣稠密。

disciple 〔 dɪˈsaɪpḷ 〕 *n.* 弟子；門徒

——同 pupil , follower , believer , devotee , votary

The Greek philosopher Plato was a ***disciple*** of the famed Socrates. 希臘哲學家柏拉圖是著名的蘇格拉底的門徒。

****dominant** 〔ˈdɑmənənt 〕 *adj.* 主要的【最常考】

——同 major , principal , cardinal , chief , main

The most ***dominant*** feature of New York Harbor is the Statue of Liberty.

紐約港最主要的特色是自由女神像。

****drought** 〔 draʊt 〕 *n.* 乾旱【最常考】

——同 aridity , lack of rain , dryness , dehydration

Southern California suffers from frequent ***droughts***.

南加州遭受到經常性的乾旱。

Exercise ▷ *Fill in the blanks.*

1. An _____ gymnast, she escaped from the elevator through the elevator shaft.

2. Her voice was so quiet that it was barely _____.

3. The _____ was so strong that it knocked over the vase of flowers by the window.

4. Denise found the teacher's _____ of her paper to be helpful in rewriting it.

5. The cult leader's _____ were willing to do anything he commanded.

【解答】1. adept   2. audible   3. breeze   4. critique   5. disciples

* **exodus** 〔'ɛksədəs 〕 *n.* 離去【常考】

　── 同 going away , departure , exit , withdrawal , migration

The ***exodus*** of young people from the country to the cities left farming communities almost empty.

年輕人從鄉村外移到都市，使得農業社區幾乎空了。

** **expedite** 〔'ɛkspɪˌdaɪt 〕 *v.* 加速【最常考】

　── 同 accelerate , speed , hasten , rush , precipitate

They tried to find a way to ***expedite*** the release of the innocent people.　他們努力找尋辦法，來加速釋放那些無辜的人。

extricate 〔'ɛkstrɪˌket 〕 *v.* 解救

　── 同 release , free , emancipate

Rescue workers struggled to ***extricate*** victims trapped in the collapsed building.　救難人員拼命救出身陷在崩塌大廈裡的受難者。

forlorn 〔 fə'lɔrn 〕 *adj.* ①寂寞的　②絕望的

　── 同 1. lonely , desolate , friendless　2. hopeless , forsaken

We heard the ***forlorn*** howls of the dogs in the dogcatcher's truck.　我們聽到捕狗車中，狗兒絕望的號叫聲。

* **garish** 〔'gɛrɪʃ , 'gæ- 〕 *adj.* 俗麗的；耀眼的【常考】

　── 同 gaudy , tasteless , glaring , flaunting

Garish displays of wealth by the newly-rich are very distasteful.　暴發戶以庸俗的方式來展示財富，眞是沒水準。

grouch 〔 graʊtʃ 〕 *v.* 發牢騷　── 同 grumble , complain

Ken has been ***grouching*** all afternoon about having to mop the kitchen.　肯對於要拖廚房的地已經抱怨了一下午。

hub 〔 hʌb 〕 *n.* 中樞　── 同 center , core , nucleus

Tina's office was located in the ***hub*** of the city's financial district.　汀娜的辦公室位於城市商業區的中心。

humanitarian 〔hju͵mænə'tɛrɪən〕*adj.* 人道主義的；博愛的
——同 humane, compassionate, charitable, philanthropic
Huge shipments of *humanitarian* aid reached the site of the earthquake. 大批人道主義救災的貨物抵達地震發生的地點。

humiliate 〔hju'mɪlɪ͵et〕*v.* 使羞愧
——同 embarrass, abash, chagrin, debase, shame
Alex felt *humiliated* when his classmates teased him.
當亞歷士的同學嘲笑他時，他覺得很羞愧。

inert 〔ɪn'ɜt〕*adj.* 不活動的；惰性的
——同 inactive, motionless, slothful, idle, inanimate, passive
The poisonous gas made the victims *inert*, unable even to cry out for help. 這毒氣讓受害者無法動彈，甚至無法呼救。

innate 〔ɪ'net, ɪn'net〕*adj.* 天生的 ——同 inborn, inherent
Sam and Josephine believed their toddler's fingerpaintings showed her *innate* artistic abilities.
山姆和約瑟芬相信，他們的孩子用手指畫出來的圖顯示出她有藝術天份。
＊toddler〔'tɑdlə〕*n.* 初學走路的孩子

＊**irate**〔'aɪret, aɪ'ret〕*adj.* 生氣的【常考】
——同 enraged, furious, wrathful
Father was *irate* when I told him I had wrecked the car.
當我告訴父親我弄壞車子時，他非常生氣。

＊＊**itinerary**〔aɪ'tɪnə͵rɛrɪ, ɪ'-〕*n.* 旅程【最常考】
——同 route, course, schedule
Warren asked the travel agent to fax an *itinerary* of his trip to him. 華倫要旅行社傳真一份行程表給他。

＊**lucrative**〔'lukrətɪv, 'lɪu-〕*adj.* 可獲利的【常考】 ——同 profitable
Bert sold his *lucrative* ice cream business, so he could travel around the world.
伯特賣掉他賺錢的冰淇淋事業，如此他便可以環遊世界。

lukewarm 〔'luk'wɔrm , 'lɪuk- 〕*adj.* 微溫的；不熱心的
—— 同 indifferent , tepid
Hester's response to my suggestion to move to the city was
lukewarm. 關於我提議要搬到城市的事，海斯特的反應很冷淡。

* **merchandise** 〔'mɝtʃən,daɪz 〕*v.* 買賣；交易【常考】
—— 同 trade , deal in , buy and sell , do business
There were questions as to whether the company could
profitably ***merchandise*** such expensive goods.
關於公司銷售這麼貴的物品是否能賺錢，尚有很多疑問。

****mundane** 〔'mʌnden 〕*adj.* 日常的【最常考】
—— 同 commonplace , everyday , humdrum , ordinary , routine
Ian spent Saturday afternoon doing ***mundane*** tasks like
sweeping and dusting.
伊安星期六下午做了些像掃地、清灰塵的雜事。

| Exercise | Fill in the blanks. |

1. A letter from the company president might _____
the signing of the agreement.

2. Stop _____ about the garbage in the park and do
something about it.

3. The military defeat _____ the general, who quietly
went into retirement.

4. Ken seemed to have an _____ sense of rhythm, and
made a natural drummer.

5. We have a very full _____ for our trip to Japan.

【解答】 1. expedite   2. grouching   3. humiliated   4. innate   5. itinerary

* **organic** 〔 ɔr'gænɪk 〕 *adj.* 有機性的【常考】
　——同 biological , natural , biotic
The farmer placed all *organic* waste from the farm in a compost pile. 農夫將有機廢料從田裡放置到肥料堆中。
　＊compost 〔'kɑmpost 〕 *n.* 堆肥

* **perish** 〔'pɛrɪʃ 〕 *v.* 死亡；滅亡【常考】　——同 die , decease
Many of the apartment residents *perished* in the fire caused by the gas pipe explosion.
許多公寓居民在瓦斯管爆炸所引起的火災中喪生。

permanent 〔'pɜməmənt 〕 *adj.* 永久的；不變的
　——同 everlasting , persistent , perpetual , invariable , unchanging
The first *permanent* English settlement in America was established in 1607.
英國人在美國的第一個永久殖民地是在一六○七年建立。

* **plight** 〔 plaɪt 〕 *n.* 苦境【常考】
　——同 predicament , difficulty , dilemma
When the people trapped in the elevator realized the seriousness of their *plight*, they panicked.
當受困在電梯中的人瞭解到處境的嚴重性時，他們驚慌了起來。
　＊panic 〔'pænɪk 〕 *v.* 驚惶

* **precipitate** 〔 prɪ'sɪpə,tet 〕 *v.* 降落；凝結【常考】
　——同 fling , cast
With the arrival of a cold front, clouds *precipitate* as snow.
由於冷鋒來襲，使得雲凝結成了雪。

prevalent 〔'prɛvələnt 〕 *adj.* 盛行的
　——同 dominant , predominant
The *prevalent* feeling at the environmental conference was one of optimism. 在環境研討會中普遍感到的是一種樂觀主義。

redeem〔rɪ'dim〕*v.* 收回 ——同 regain , retrieve
She decided to go back to school to ***redeem*** her self-respect.
爲了挽回自尊，她決定重回學校。

resume〔rɪ'zum , -'zɪum〕*v.* 恢復；再繼續 ——同 continue
After the rainstorm ended, the farmers ***resumed*** planting their
crops. 豪雨停止之後，農夫就繼續種他們的農作物。

sensuous〔'sɛnʃʊəs〕*adj.* 感官的；感覺的；感官快樂的
——同 hedonistic , gratifying , sensory , lush
She enjoyed the ***sensuous*** pleasure of soaking herself in a
bubble bath after a long day.
過了漫長的一天之後，她喜歡那種將自己浸泡在泡沫浴中的感覺。

splenetic〔splɪ'nɛtɪk〕*adj.* 容易發怒的 ——同 irritable
As years went by, the lonely old man grew more and more
splenetic. 隨著時光飛逝，這孤獨的老人變得越來越容易發怒。

* **stoicism**〔'sto‧ɪˌsɪzəm〕*n.* 堅忍【常考】
——同 fortitude , calmness , forbearance , stolidity
Sarah's ***stoicism*** at the approach of the hurricane helped her
students remain calm.
當颶風來襲時，莎拉的堅忍幫助她的學生保持鎮定。

supersede〔ˌsupɚ'sid , 'sju-〕*v.* 接替
——同 replace , take over
Today's computers are constantly being ***superseded*** by newer,
faster computer models.
現今的電腦常被更新型、更快速的電腦機型所取代。

* **surge**〔sɝdʒ〕*n.* 大浪【常考】 ——同 wave , billow , flow
The devaluation of the US dollar led to a ***surge*** in US export
sales. 美元貶值導致美國出口銷售量的波動。

thrust 〔θrʌst〕 *v.* 力推　──同 shove, push, propel

The enormous rocket engines ***thrust*** the satellite into orbit around the earth. 巨大的火箭引擎將人造衛星發射到地球周圍的軌道中。

* **truculent** 〔ˊtrʌkjələnt, ˊtrukjə-〕 *adj.* 攻擊的【常考】

　　──同 bellicose, aggressive, fierce, violent, defiant

The ***truculent*** suspect refused to answer any of the police officers' questions. 這粗暴的嫌疑犯拒絕回答警察的問題。

verdant 〔ˊvɝdn̩t〕 *adj.* 翠綠的　──同 green

Thomas was homesick for the ***verdant*** meadow where he had grown up. 湯瑪斯思念他所生長的那片翠綠草原。

* **vulnerable** 〔ˊvʌlnərəbl̩〕 *adj.* 易受傷害的【常考】

　　──同 susceptible, unprotected, assailable, defenseless

Rachel was a sickly child, ***vulnerable*** to colds and various infections. 瑞秋是一個體弱多病的小孩，容易受到感冒和傳染病的感染。

Exercise ▷ *Fill in the blanks.*

1. Quite a few diseases are _____ in spring.

2. She was left with a _____ limp in her left leg after the car accident.

3. The supermarket offered to _____ coupons from any of their competitors.

4. The nervous actor was _____ onto the stage by the play's director.

5. Buildings of this kind of construction are _____ to extensive damage by fire.

【解答】 1. prevalent　2. permanent　3. redeem　4. thrust　5. vulnerable

⟨ List 30 ⟩ 難字分析

allocate〔'ælə,ket〕*v.* 分配

al +	loc +	ate
ad		
to +	*place +*	*make*

— to distribute in shares or according to a plan

appropriation〔ə,proprɪ'eʃən〕*n.* 撥款

ap+	propri	+ at(e) + ion
ad		
to +	*one's own +*	*make + n.*

— money set aside for a specific use

contaminate〔kən'tæmə,net〕*v.* 污染

con +	tamin +	ate
together +	*touch +*	*make*

— to make impure

cumbersome〔'kʌmbɚsəm〕*adj.* 累贅的；笨重的

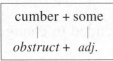

— hard to handle or deal with as because of size or weight

exodus〔'ɛksədəs〕*n.* 離去

ex +	od +	us
out +	*way +*	*n.*

— going out or away of many people

expedite 〔ˈɛkspɪˌdaɪt 〕 v. 加速

ex + ped + ite —— to speed up
| | |
out + foot + v.

extricate 〔ˈɛkstrɪˌket 〕 v. 解救

ex + tric + ate —— to set free
| | |
out + obstacle + make

humanitarian 〔 hjuˌmænəˈtɛrɪən 〕 adj. 人道主義的；博愛的

human + it(y) + arian —— concerned with promoting the
| | | welfare of humanity
man + n. + adj.

humiliate 〔 hjuˈmɪlɪˌet 〕 v. 使羞愧

hum + ili(ty) + ate —— to cause to feel ashamed
| | |
ground + n. + make

permanent 〔ˈpɝmənənt 〕 adj. 永久的；不變的

per + man + ent —— lasting; not intended to change
| | |
through + remain + adj.

vulnerable 〔ˈvʌlnərəbḷ 〕 adj. 易受傷害的

vulner + able —— that can be wounded or
| | physically injured
wound + able to

TEST ▶ 15

請由 (A)～(D) 中選出和畫線部分意義最相近的字。

1. Universal <u>suffrage</u> was recently granted to all South African citizens.

   (A) vote
   (B) election
   (C) candidate
   (D) suffering

2. An <u>alliance</u> between our two companies would make us both much stronger in the marketplace.

   (A) evaluation
   (B) partnership
   (C) negotiation
   (D) discussion

3. Barnacles <u>cling</u> to the bottoms of boats and have to be scraped off every so often.

   (A) reach
   (B) adhere
   (C) approach
   (D) swim

4. Brian was <u>disowned</u> by his father when he refused to give up his religious beliefs.

   (A) rejected
   (B) beaten
   (C) accepted
   (D) mortified

5. Rhonda sat on the beach admiring the <u>virile</u> young men playing volleyball.

   (A) insecure
   (B) angry
   (C) insensitive
   (D) manly

6. The townspeople could not believe the mayor would put such a <u>grotesque</u> statue outside of the town hall.

   (A) enormous
   (B) unbalanced
   (C) freakish
   (D) obscure

7. My mother was born in a <u>hamlet</u> located in a coal mining district.

   (A) large suburb
   (B) busy town
   (C) noisy city
   (D) small village

8. Although <u>itinerant</u> salesmen were once very common, they are rarely seen any more.

   (A) traveling
   (B) car
   (C) illegal
   (D) medicine

9. The school <u>allocates</u> a small amount of money to all of the school clubs.

   (A) demands
   (B) distributes
   (C) spends
   (D) sells

10. As Tony's airplane pulled away from the terminal, Helen suddenly felt <u>forlorn</u>.

    (A) liberated
    (B) lonely
    (C) confused
    (D) uneasy

11. Plant and animal species <u>endemic</u> to the island are protected by wildlife conservation laws.

    (A) native
    (B) imported
    (C) related
    (D) introduced

12. The <u>dominant</u> reason for the president's visit was to improve international ties.

    (A) subliminal
    (B) principal
    (C) apparent
    (D) nominal

13. Erin went to the beauty parlor to get her hair <u>bleached</u>.

    (A) lightened
    (B) cut
    (C) permed
    (D) styled

14. To apologize for being late Jack bought Lisa a <u>bouquet</u> of flowers.

    (A) few
    (B) garden
    (C) bunch
    (D) bag

15. New York City's Central Park is a <u>hub</u> of activity in the summertime.

    (A) branch
    (B) plan
    (C) center
    (D) map

16. The <u>ordeal</u> of being trapped inside an elevator with a visiting dignitary was very embarrassing for the president.

    (A) opportunity
    (B) tribulation
    (C) glorification
    (D) surprise

17. Our company <u>merchandises</u> calculators and other small electronic devices.

    (A) researches
    (B) deals in
    (C) purchases
    (D) develops

18. A <u>pliable</u> plastic joint allows the door to swing freely.

    (A) rigid
    (B) over-sized
    (C) flexible
    (D) elevated

19. Steve could not <u>extricate</u> himself from his contract with the Mafia.

   (A) release
   (B) encourage
   (C) ensure
   (D) validate

20. The <u>exodus</u> of refugees from the war-torn country was more than relief workers could handle.

   (A) fluctuation
   (B) number
   (C) speed
   (D) departure

21. Gasoline-run cars may one day be <u>superseded</u> by solar-powered automobiles.

   (A) improved
   (B) replaced
   (C) destroyed
   (D) fostered

22. Thirty buildings <u>comprise</u> the university's campus.

   (A) constitute
   (B) enclose
   (C) designate
   (D) line

23. Ella is an amazing receptionist, and is patient with even the most <u>splenetic</u> customers.

   (A) ill-bred
   (B) over-indulged
   (C) good-mannered
   (D) bad-tempered

24. People all over the world sympathized with the <u>plight</u> of the Russians whose town was destroyed by the earthquake.

   (A) difficulty
   (B) history
   (C) location
   (D) similarity

25. Being a city dweller, he never felt at home in the <u>verdant</u> countryside.

   (A) clean
   (B) empty
   (C) grassy
   (D) quiet

【解答】

1. A	2. B	3. B	4. A	5. D	6. C	7. D	8. A	9. B	10. B
11. A	12. B	13. A	14. C	15. C	16. B	17. B	18. C	19. A	20. D
21. B	22. A	23. D	24. A	25. C					

📖 英文字源對照表

PREFIX · 字首

Prefix	Meaning	Example
a , ab	away	aboriginal 96 abstruse 135
ac , ad , ag , at	to ; toward	accomplice 235 adjunct 60
ambi	both	ambivalence 96
an	without ; not	anarchy 171 anonymous 210
ante	before	anticipate 271
anti	against	antagonist 235
bene	well ; good	benefactor 171 benevolent 185
bi	two	bilateral 310
cata	down	categorize 110
com , con , col	together ; with	collaborate 110 compromise 10
de	down ; away	derivative 71 deviate 185
dis , di	apart ; not	disposition 185 disorient 121
eu	well	eulogy 85 euphonious 96
ex , e	out	elucidate 160 exacerbate 146
in , im	not	indisputable 146 integrate 160
in , im	into	inquisitive 85 insinuate 85
inter	between ; among	intermittent 211
ne	not	nefarious 61
ob	toward ; against	obsolete 247 obtrusive 147
omni	all	omnipotent 222
pan	all	panacea 61 panorama 72
per	through	perennial 322 peruse 136
post	after	posterity 186 posthumous 147
pre	before	precursor 261 predominant 272
pro	forward ; before	prognosis 122 prohibitive 136
re	again ; back	receptacle 161 renovate 136
sub	under	subsequent 186 subterranean 222

Prefix	Meaning	Example
super	above ; over	surreptitious 72
syn	together	symmetry 197 synopsis 247
trans	across ; through	transient 172 transparent 186
un	not	untenable 186

ROOT・字根

Root	Meaning	Example
ac , acr	sharp ; sour	acrimonious 321
ag , ac	do	agility 221 navigate 36
agr	field	agrarian 246
ali , alter	other	alienate 310 alternative 46
am	love	amateur 85
anim	mind ; soul	unanimous 36
ann , enn	year	millennium 86 perennial 322
anthrop	man	philanthropic 222
apt	fit	aptitude 21
auto	self	autonomous 160
brevi	short	abbreviate 46
cad , cid , cas	fall	coincide 96 cascade 110
cap , cep	take	receptacle 161
ced , cess	yield ; go	accessible 196
celer	swift	accelerate 185
cern , cret	separate	secretion 297
chrono	time	chronological 285
gnos	know	prognosis 122
corp	body	corpulent 210
cre	grow	accretion 246
cred	believe	incredulous 61
cumb	lie down	succumb 272
curs	run	precursor 261

Root	Meaning	Example
dem	people	endemic 360 epidemic 196
dic , dict	speak	jurisdiction 85 vindicate 236
domin	rule	predominant 272
dox	thought	paradoxical 86
ego	I ; self	egotistic 35
equ , equi	equal	equivalent 260 equivocal 271
fa	speak	affable 146 nefarious 61
fac	make	benefactor 171 facsimile 60
fall	deceive	infallible 211
fer	carry	vociferous 311
fid	faith	diffidence 235
flu	flow	affluent 171 fluctuate 21
fus	pour	suffuse 97
gen	produce	congenial 246 ingenuous 47
greg	collect	congregation 285 gregarious 321
here	stick	coherent 71
homo	same	homogeneous 346
hydr	water	dehydrate 235
it , itiner	go ; journey	itinerant 361 obituary 11
junct	join	adjunct 60
leg	law	allegiance 321 illegitimate 222
log , loqu	speak	analogy 160 soliloquy 297
luc , lumin	light	elucidate 160
magn	great	magnificence 11
man , manu	hand	emancipation 186 manipulate 161
mand	order	mandatory 122
mar	sea	submarine 136
meter , metry	measure	symmetry 197
mit , miss	send	commission 210 intermittent 211
mono	one	monopoly 322
nav	ship	navigate 36

Root	Meaning	Example
noc	injure	innocuous 21
nov	new	renovate 136
nom	name	nominal 136
onym	name	anonymous 210　pseudonym 222
ori	begin ; rise	aboriginal 97　disorient 121
pat	suffer	compatible 271
ped	foot	expedite 372　impediment 197
puls	drive	compulsory 21
pend , pens	hang	perpendicular 22　propensity 261
pet , petit	seek	petition 161
pli	fold	accomplice 235　duplicate 221
pos , posit	put	decompose 135　juxtaposition 322
potent	powerful	omnipotent 222
pseudo	false	pseudonym 222
prec	pray	precarious 197
put	trim ; think	indisputable 146
quis	seek	acquisition 296　inquisitive 85
rog	ask	prorogue 36
sanct	sacred	sanction 47
sat	enough	insatiable 61
scrib	write	prescribe 336
sid	sit	assiduous 260　residual 286
sent	feel	sentimental 11
sequ , secut	follow	obsequious 22　prosecute 336
son	sound	resonant 322
spect , spic	look	conspicuous 310　retrospect 61
spir	breathe	perspire 97　respiration 347
stitut	stand	destitute 121
string	tie	stringent 47
tang	touch	intangible 147

Root	Meaning	Example
ten , tin	hold	pertinent 111 sustenance 122
tens , tent	stretch	contention 35 ostensible 47
terr	land ; earth	subterranean 222
tract	draw	intractable 247
trus	thrust	abstruse 135 obtrusive 147
vac	empty	evacuate 111
vers , vert	turn	diversify 296 inadvertent 10
vi	way	deviate 185 impervious 261
vis	see	improvise 346 provisional 361
viv	live	vivacious 297
voc	avocation	avocation 46

SUFFIX · 字尾

Suffix	Meaning	Example
able , ible	able to	accessible 196 insatiable 61
ary , ate	person	candidate 46
ate	make	alternate 35 navigate 36 confiscate 185
er , or	one who	benefactor 162 precursor 261
fic	making	soporific 172
fy	to make	diversify 296
ic , ac	like ; related to	egotistic 35 eccentric 10
ile	like ; capable of	versatile 211 juvenile 97
ist	one who	protagonist 347
ity	state of being	contiguity 46 velocity 47 propensity 261
ize	to make	categorize 110 hypnotize 297
ment	result	impediment 197 predicament 236
tion	action	exaggeration 172 manifestation 147
ious	full of	infectious 236 fictitious 271
ence , ance	state ; quality	sustenance 122 diffidence 235
tude	state ; quality	aptitude 21 altitude 60

INDEX · 單字索引